For the Love of Teaching

KELSEY HODGE

Copyright © 2021 by Kelsey Hodge

All rights reserved.

No portion of this book may be reproduced in any form without written permission from the publisher or author, except as permitted by U.S. copyright law.

Contents

Epigraph		V
1.	Chapter 1—Marco	1
2.	Chapter 2—Liam	17
3.	Chapter 3—Marco	29
4.	Chapter 4—Liam	37
5.	Chapter 5—Marco	47
6.	Chapter 6—Liam	57
7.	Chapter 7—Marco	71
8.	Chapter 8—Liam	87
9.	Chapter 9—Marco	99
10.	Chapter 10—Liam	110
11.	Chapter 11—Marco	119
12.	Chapter 12—Liam	129
13.	Chapter 13—Marco	138
14.	Chapter 14—Liam	146

15. Chapter 15–Marco — 153
16. Chapter 16—Liam — 166
17. Chapter 17—Marco — 176
18. Chapter 18—Liam — 189
19. Chapter 19—Marco — 200
20. Chapter 20—Liam — 210
21. Chapter 21—Marco — 219
22. Chapter 22—Liam — 230
23. Chapter 23—Marco — 238
24. Chapter 24—Liam — 248
25. Chapter 25—Marco — 256
26. Chapter 26—Liam — 264
27. Chapter 27—Marco — 280
28. Chapter 28—Liam — 290
29. Chapter 29—Marco — 306
30. Chapter 30—Liam — 324
31. Epilogue — 335

Acknowledgments — 341
About Author — 342
Also By Kelsey Hodge — 343

"Do nothing secretly; for Time sees and hears all things, and discloses all."

Sophocles

Chapter 1—Marco

Taking a deep, cleansing breath and slowly releasing it, I realize that it is doing nothing to ease the nervous tension that is humming just under the surface of my skin, so I try again. Still nothing.

What the fuck am I doing here?

Standing on the sidewalk, I look up at the window-lined walls of an otherwise featureless block building on the opposite side of the street and think about walking away for the hundredth time. But just as I am about to turn away, the image of my brother pops into my mind, and I know I have to go inside.

You can call it sixth sense or brotherly intuition, but I know something has happened to him. I've stopped by his shop over the past two days only to find it closed, and today, there was a sign on the door saying they were closed due to ill health. Reading that sign is what forced me to come here, outside the New York Police Department Headquarters where I'm trying to calm myself enough to go inside and report my brother missing. The only thing stopping me is that voice in the back of my head—which sounds eerily like dad's—that the police shouldn't be involved in family business.

Before I have a chance to change my mind, I shake my head to clear those thoughts and walk through the revolving doors and into the building. I am oddly curious, having never been inside a police station before, so I stop the moment I'm inside to look at my surroundings. In my head, there was this vision of someplace dark and intimidating, images that had been put there by my father. Instead, I find a huge room full of light with officers in full uniform and other random people milling about.

Right in front of me, there is a large wooden panel with a colored logo carved into the front of it that reminds me of a hotel's reception desk, and I head straight for it, figuring that's the best place to start. Taking another deep breath, I keep walking forward, knowing what I have to do is important. Thankfully there isn't a line, and as soon as the thought occurs to me, it makes me chuckle. *Why the hell would there be a line at a police station?* It's not like this is the grocery store. I'm still smiling to myself when the person behind the desk looks up at me.

"Good afternoon. Can I help you?"

The stern voice that greets me is filled with authority, and the grin drops from my face as I remember where I am. I know I'm staring at the officer longer than is considered polite, but it takes a moment for my brain to catch up and I can finally find my voice.

"Yes, I need to report a missing person, please?"

"Has the person been missing for longer than twenty-four hours?" The man goes back to scribbling on whatever form he's staring at, not showing any interest in what I have to say.

"It's been a week." I can feel the shame of this statement traveling through my body. Who waits a week before reporting someone missing?

"Okay. And your relationship to this person?"

"He's my brother," I say rather quietly.

"And he's been missing a week?"

I can see the surprise and questions on his face, and I can almost hear him asking, "And you waited a week to report your own brother missing?" But he remains professional, and I avoid looking into his eyes after that, instead focusing on his shirt where his name tag is pinned with *Sergeant Williams* engraved on it.

"Yes, Sergeant. There was a family disagreement..." I have to stop myself from grimacing at this statement. Disagreement is putting it mildly. Dad had gone bat shit crazy when Lorenzo had announced last week over dinner that he was gay. But I'm guessing that explaining this to the sergeant would set off alarm bells, so I need to choose my words carefully.

"I thought it best to give him some space for a few days, but he hasn't replied to any of my texts and his shop has been closed the last two times I went there to check on him."

Pulling what appears to be some kind of form in front of him—it's hard to tell from the angle I am looking, and I don't want my curiosity to be *too* obvious—he looks up at me again. "Can you describe him, or do you have a recent photo we can use?".

Taking out my wallet, I remove one of the photos that I'd brought with me. I realized before leaving the house that a picture is something they might need and was thankful that I'd recently printed out a bunch of photos from my phone. When I hand it over, Sergeant Williams takes it, and I think I spot a look of surprise crossing his face, but it's gone before I can be sure it wasn't a trick of my mind. He goes on to ask me more questions before taking my name and contact details and asking if he can keep the photo I gave him.

"Um, yeah. Sure," I reply.

He attaches the photo to the paperwork before pointing to a line of benches that I missed on my way in and asks me to please take a seat. Making my way over to them, I note they have an uncanny resemblance to an uncomfortable church pew, but I sit down anyway—which confirms my initial observation—and keep watching the sergeant as he picks up the phone on his desk. I cannot hear him from this distance but from the glances he keeps making in my direction he is talking about me. Once he hangs up, he looks over to me and says loud enough for me to hear that someone will be with me shortly but doesn't give any more information. So, I continue to sit and wait, staring at the wall in front of me.

Not more than five minutes later, I hear the ding of an elevator bell but don't pay too much attention since I don't think anyone would've come that quickly. But when I hear a deep, husky voice begin speaking at the front desk, I automatically look over at the sound. *Holy fuck*, the man standing there is beautiful, and I watch as the Adonis walks toward me, hoping to god that my mouth isn't hanging open with drool running down my chin.

"Mr. Romano?" He asks when he steps in front of me, holding out his hand in greeting. "I'm Detective Smith. Can I ask you a few more questions?"

I'm still trying not to ogle at him as I nod my head and shake his hand, instantly feeling a jolt of electricity travel up my arm. As he sits down next to me, we both turn slightly so we're facing one another, and I catch myself staring at his lips. They are plump with a beautiful pink color, and my mind begins to wander as to what they would feel like pressed against my own. But when they start moving, I snap out of my fantasy, realizing that he's talking to me and I really should pay attention to what he is saying and not daydream about his lips on mine.

"When was the last time you saw your brother?" he asks, oblivious to the direction my mind had been wandering.

"Maybe a week ago? We were at my parents place when there was a family disagreement and he left." I'm really hoping he doesn't ask what the disagreement was about, but instead, his next question takes me completely by surprise.

"How were your parents after your brother left? Did they seem agitated?"

Why the hell is he asking about my parents? Shouldn't he be asking about Lorenzo and trying to determine *his* mental state and not that of my parents? But I answer him honestly.

"They were both very upset, and normally I would have gone after my brother, but I thought it was best for everyone if I didn't."

"When was the last time that you tried to contact him?"

"I decided to leave him alone for a couple days, then tried calling and sent some texts, but he hasn't answered. So both yesterday and today, I went to his florist shop, but it was closed and the store looks as though no one has been in for a few days." I don't bother to mention the sign on the door, worrying this will cause more questions that I can't answer. "I came straight here from there to report him missing."

"Why haven't you been to his home address?"

"I don't know where he lives," I say rather sheepishly, knowing this sounds weird, and I spot his raised eyebrow and wait for the question that I have asked myself so many times, why don't I know where he lives, but strangely, he never asks.

"Okay. I don't think I have any more questions today. If I can take a contact number, we'll look into this and get in touch with you if we find anything."

Completely confused, I take the notepad and pen that he's handing me and write down my cell number and pass it back to him. The moment he has them in his hands, he puts both the back in his pocket and stands up. Doing the same, I stand in front of him, but get distracted when I notice that we are roughly the same height and how easy kissing him would be.

Shaking my head to clear this line of thought, I notice that he's holding his hand out for me to shake, which I take, but I have to stop myself from pulling him closer so that I can finally feel those lips against mine. Instead, I give his hand a firm shake, feeling that jolt of electricity again. I catch the very slight flash of surprise in his deep brown eyes as our hands touch, making me wonder if he felt the jolt, too.

Pulling my hand free, I turn, leaving the station as quickly as possible and not even bothering to say goodbye to him. I know I have to get out of there before I think too much about Detective Smith and the reaction we both just experienced. I was there to report Lorenzo missing, nothing more.

When I'm back on the sidewalk, I take a deep breath. What the fuck had that man done to me? Hopefully he'll be able to find out what happened to Lorenzo soon and I can forget about him. I have no intention of inviting a man into my life, even if that man was as beautiful as the detective. Not unless it's someone to warm my bed just for the night. I haven't met anyone yet who I'm willing to come out of the closet for and risk my job or family over and don't see that changing in the foreseeable future.

―

Two hours later, I'm sitting back at my apartment when I hear the text tone from my cell. I can feel my heart rate increasing, just like it has all week every time my phone has gone off, hoping that it's a message from Lorenzo. That hope increases when I see that it was sent from a blocked number.

I anticipated that going to the police might cause him to get in contact with me, even though it has only been a few hours. It makes no sense for me to assume this, but I'm sure the police have more tools to locate people than I do. Well, they do in all those police dramas that are on TV, anyway.

I notice the slight shaking of my hands as I pick up the cell and open the message.

Unknown: Hi Marco, it's Lorenzo. Sorry I haven't been in touch. I'll be at The Bean coffee shop just off East 9th tomorrow at noon. If you can meet me, I'll explain everything.

Staring at the screen for what feels like hours but is probably less than a minute, I read and re-read the text, double checking what I'm seeing. Why has Lorenzo texted me from a blocked number, and what "everything" does he need to explain to me? What the shit has happened to him over the last week?

Checking my calendar app, I remember that the school where I teach is closed tomorrow for some much-needed maintenance, so I'll be free. But I know that even if I was teaching, I would've called in sick—something I've never done before but would be willing to do now in order to see my brother.

—

The following morning I make my way to The Bean, which after a quick Google search I discovered is in the East Village. This doesn't really come as much of a surprise since this is where Lorenzo's shop is located. Considering I live in the Tribeca area to be near my work, I make sure to leave with plenty of time to spare and end up arriving five minutes early. Knowing my brother, though, he'll already be there. Therefore, the moment I open the door, I'm already scanning the shop and spot him sitting in a quiet, more secluded corner toward the back. I'm so happy to see him that my face hurts from the smile that breaks out as I rush over and pull him into a bear hug. I feel him wince and hear a slight yelp as my embrace tightens, almost as if he were in pain, so I let him go, stepping back and looking him over before raising an eyebrow at him.

Apologizing, though I'm not sure what for at the moment, I pull out the chair opposite him before locking our gazes and asking, "Are you okay? Where have you been?" Although I've never been an intimidating person, he surprises me by breaking eye contact, looking off to the side before focusing on the table.

"I'm fine, Marco," he starts. "Don't worry about—"

"Don't bullshit me, Lorenzo. Not this time. I felt you stiffen when we hugged." I can always tell when my brother is lying to me, and I'm not about to let him get away with it this time. "Something's happened, and I want to know what it is."

He cringes as he looks back up at me but shakes his head when the waitress comes over to take our order.

"Please, Lorenzo, I'm worried," I whisper over to him so the waitress doesn't hear me.

Once she's taken our orders and walks away, I look back over to him and wait for some answers on what the hell has been going on.

He still looks hesitant but starts talking.

"The night I came out to Mom and Dad, I decided to walk home. Clear my head. Their reaction took me completely by surprise. Well, anyway, I was jumped and pulled into an alley, and they beat me up pretty good."

"When you say, 'beat me up pretty good,' how bad was it?"

"It was pretty bad. I ended up in the hospital with a broken collar bone, dislocated shoulder, broken ribs, and some internal bleeding that required surgery."

As he mentions each injury, my heart breaks a little bit more knowing he went through this on his own, no one there to hold his hand or be a friendly face when he woke. But as I think over the injuries, this suddenly leaves me even more confused.

"Holy shit, Lorenzo. That's more than 'beat me up pretty good.' Why the fuck didn't the hospital contact me?"

Again Lorenzo just sat there looking off into the distance before answering my question, causing my instincts to scream that something more has to be more going on. The hospital should have called Mom and Dad.

"If the hospital had called Mom and Dad, do you think they would've come?" he finally asks, looking me straight in the eye.

The question completely throws me, and I instantly desire to respond that of course they would, but something stops me. I don't think I had ever seen dad as angry as he was that night, so he probably wouldn't have. But mom, regardless of what happened, would.

"Honestly," I begin, stopping to watch as he nods before continuing. I have to find the words to convey what I want to say. "Dad, probably not. I hope Mom would have gone, but regardless of them, I would have been there in a heartbeat. You shouldn't have gone through that alone."

"I wasn't alone," he whispers back, and a smile touches the corner of his lips. "My boyfriend was there with me."

"Sorry, Lorenzo. Did you just say your *boyfriend*?"

"Yes. His name is Wyatt. We've been together for about two years. I've wanted to tell you so often but could never find the courage. I know you would've understood and been accepting. I'm sorry for keeping it a secret."

Realizing this has turned out to be the perfect opportunity to tell him my own secret, I take a deep breath. "Lorenzo, you have nothing to be sorry for. Believe me when I say I understand more than you know." Although my spirit is willing, I still can't seem to say the words out loud. "Mom and Dad were furious that night. Hell, Dad looked like he wanted to kill someone after you left."

Suddenly Lorenzo starts to choke on his coffee but tries to pass it off as his coffee "being too hot," but now I *know* there is more going on and am determined to get my answers.

I press on. "Mom has been asking me all sorts of questions about whether I knew and if I'd been keeping it a secret to protect you. Then she goes on about all the girls you dated. It's been weird. Dad hasn't really said much at all. It's almost like he's in shock."

"I am so sorry, Marco," Lorenzo starts while reaching across to take my hand. "I never meant to drag you into any of this, but I couldn't carry on with the lie. I knew I had to make a decision. My happiness or my family."

There is no way I can miss the sadness in his eyes. This had to have been one of the toughest decisions of his life.

"Was it worth it?" The words tumble from my mouth before I'm able to stop them.

"Was what worth it?" Lorenzo scrunches his brows together, seeming confused at my question and not fully catching the meaning behind it. .

"Finally deciding to come out?" I ask him.

He thinks carefully before finally answering me. "It was the right decision for me. I have no regrets, regardless of what happened afterward." He pauses. "Why do you ask?"

And in that second, I know the words are finally going to come out. My secret is going to be out in the world. So I take a deep breath before I whisper, "Because I'm gay, too."

"Sorry, Marco, you said that so quietly I'm not sure I heard you right, but it sounded like you said you were gay, too."

I find myself looking down at the table, which has suddenly become the most fascinating thing in the world, and I simply respond, "That's because I did." A silence stretches out between us as what I just told him sinks in, but slowly a smile spreads across his face.

"Holy shit. You're gay! I did *not* see that coming at all." But just as quickly, the smile vanishes. "*Fuck.* You haven't told Mom and Dad, have you?" There's a demanding edge to his voice.

Still talking to the table, I mutter a weak "no", but my head snaps up in surprise when I hear him say, "Thank god." He must have thought that once he came out, I would tell Mom and Dad, too.

"I was going to tell them and had been building up to it, but when I saw their reaction to you, I changed my mind." Because I need to know, I then add, "Does that make me a coward?"

He reaches over and grabs my hand, squeezing it. "No, you aren't a coward. Considering their reaction that night, it's completely understandable why you were staying silent. I thought they were more open minded than that."

I sit there thinking about Mom and Dad before saying, "Looks like I'm facing the same decision as you were. Do I want my family or a future where I am true to myself?"

It comes as no surprise when Lorenzo says that this isn't something he can answer for me. It took him a long time to come to his decision, but there will be one aspect that is different. Regardless of what happens with Mom and Dad, he will always be my brother.

I will never be able to express the gratitude I feel when I hear this, but I still thank him, anyway, and make sure he knows how much that means to me.

Thinking our conversation is nearing its end, I pick up my coffee to finish it when he catches me off guard.

"Okay, this is gonna sound like a strange question, but do you know what Dad does for a living?" The question comes completely out of the blue.

"You're right, that is an odd question." Instead of answering, I ask, "Why?"

"I'm just wondering."

This seems to be a completely lame answer, but just to humor him, I roll my eyes and say, "He's in the flower import business." Lorenzo already knows this. "You would know that since he supplies your wholesaler."

"True, but don't you think we're rather wealthy just from importing flowers?"

These questions are getting more bizarre, so I say, "That thought has crossed my mind before and I asked dad about it."

"Really? And what did he say?" There's a hint of surprise on his face, and for some reason, that irritates me.

"Lorenzo, what the fuck is going on? What's with all the questions? I'm the one who should be interrogating *you* after your vanishing act."

He's quick to dismiss what I've said with a wave of his hand. "It's just curiosity."

Another lie, but I decide to play along. "He said that it was because of investments he's involved in."

By the look on Lorenzo's face, he seems satisfied with this answer, and I watch as he pulls out what looks like a new cell that just keeps adding to the mystery. Lorenzo starts typing something, which I figure is a text, when his cell beeps seconds later. From the smile that transforms his face, I have a feeling he must be texting his boyfriend. I'm still wondering what's going on when he spots me staring at him and the cell in his hand.

"Are you busy this afternoon?"

The look he gives me is a hopeful one, and I don't think I've ever been so glad the school's closed before. "No, I have the day off. Why?"

"We're going back to my place. There's someone I'd like you to meet."

I can feel my face betraying both the apprehension and excitement at hearing this, and I have to stop downing the last of my coffee like it's a shot. I even make small talk about school, but the moment the last drop of coffee has hit my lips, I'm getting to my feet.

"So, can we walk, or do we need a cab to your place?" I'm trying so hard not to hop from one foot to the other in my excitement. After seeing the smile that appeared on Lorenzo's face while he was reading the text, I know that the man in his life is important, and that makes this mysterious man important to me, too, so I really can't wait to meet him. Thankfully, Lorenzo tells me his apartment is only a fifteen-minute walk away, and I'm already halfway to the front of the coffee shop before Lorenzo is even fully out of his chair.

When we get to the apartment, I know that my nervousness is showing when I go silent. He seems to look excited, too, and I burst out laughing when he says, "Remember, he's mine." This relaxes me, and I put two fingers to my temple in a mock salute of understanding and watch as he puts the key in the lock and opens the apartment door.

Following Lorenzo inside, I have to contain my surprise as I watch him kiss a man who has come to meet us in the hallway. After they're through, Lorenzo beckons me forward and finally introduces me to the man whose smile is lighting up the room just from hearing my brother say hi.

"Marco, this is my boyfriend, Detective Wyatt Johnson," he says before turning slightly towards Wyatt and saying, "Wyatt, this is my brother Marco."

Wyatt reaches out his hand, and I shake it, but Lorenzo's words finally register with me, and I have to confirm that he just called his boyfriend detective by asking him again. Lorenzo looks over to Wyatt with a smile on his face before repeating the name, and everything has suddenly become clear. No wonder Lorenzo hasn't said anything over the last two years. I can feel the laughter bubbling up in my chest, but I'm able to keep it under control somehow.

"Now I understand why you said nothing—Dad would kill you." And with that the dam breaks and I'm laughing so hard that I can feel my sides starting to hurt. But the laughs coming from Lorenzo and Wyatt seem to be fake, and it causes my laughing to cease. I know he's trying to distract me by asking if I want a tour of the apartment, but I have to admit that it works.

When we get back to the living room, I hear Wyatt ask if anyone wants a beer before I'm being steered to the couch. There is stuff that Lorenzo wants to tell me, but it appears he is going to stay quiet until Wyatt is back in the room with us. When Wyatt returns, I watch as he sits in the single chair to the left of me in front of an entire wall of windows. The silence continues even after we're all settled, so I decide I'll have to make the first move.

Looking over to Wyatt, I ask, "How long have you been a cop?"

Wyatt tells me he has been doing police work for nine years, but when I ask if he enjoys it and what division he's in, I clock him looking at Lorenzo like he's asking for permission to answer me. From the corner of my eye, I spot the slight nod of Lorenzo's head before Wyatt goes on to explain that he works in the narcotics division.

"Narcotics... I can imagine you must have to deal with some violent people at times."

I had expected Wyatt to confirm my observation, but it's Lorenzo who speaks up instead.

"Marco, that's kinda the other reason that I wanted to bring you home to meet Wyatt, especially after what you told me at the coffee shop." I watch as he takes a deep breath before continuing. "Dad is a dangerous man, and Wyatt is heading the investigation into him and his business dealings."

I'm startled at first, but as his words finally sink in, laughter bursts forth from me. I know that Dad can be intimidating at times, but a drug lord, really? That's something I just can't believe. I can feel the tears running down my face, and after a few minutes have passed and I've managed to compose myself, I look over to Lorenzo and Wyatt, only to see they aren't laughing.

"You're joking, right?" I say, looking at the pair in turn.

Wyatt gives a slow shake of his head, and the only thing I can say is, "Holy shit." Shocking me further, Lorenzo tells me there's more.

I sit and listen for the next half hour as Lorenzo tells me everything: his role in the family, what he has done on the orders given by dad. How that for the last two years he'd led a double life and kept everything a secret from Wyatt, which even I realize must not have been easy. But by the end of Lorenzo's speech, I am sick to my stomach and can feel myself shaking. It's so hard to believe that the man Lorenzo has just been talking about is actually my father, too. But I need more answers, so I turn to Wyatt and ask, "You really had no idea about Lorenzo's involvement?"

Wyatt shakes his head and then goes on to explain that it was his partner who'd figured it all out, and it was when he just confronted Lorenzo that the full truth came out. Lorenzo takes over to say that he told Wyatt everything, which caused the detective to walk out. It was this single action that made Lorenzo realize that changes in his own life needed to be made, and he had to start by telling the truth to Mom and Dad.

Everything seems to be playing on repeat in my head as I try to go over and digest all the information that has just been dumped on me, and I have to admit that relief washes over me when there is a knock on the door. The interruption will be a welcome distraction to the churning and confusion now in control.

Wyatt stands up from his chair. "I invited Liam, my partner, over for moral support. I hope that's okay."

I nod and he heads back down the hall to let in the new arrival. I can hear a voice that sounds familiar joking with Wyatt about someone not having to be killed, and then Wyatt's chuckle as he replies, "He's a nice guy." Once Wyatt says, "He knew nothing about his father," I know they must be talking about me.

I can't shake the feeling that I know this newcomer's voice from somewhere, and even though I hear him say something else, I've stopped paying attention at this point as I try to figure out who he could be. Wyatt coming into the room has me looking up to see Detective Smith from police headquarters standing in front of me now, and I can't help the smile that stretches across my face, although I'm completely confused as to why my Adonis is here…

Wait, when the fuck did I start thinking of him as my *Adonis?*

Chapter 2 — Liam

I can feel this energy humming underneath my skin, and I'm not sure if it is nerves, excitement, or a mixture of both, all because I know that in a few minutes I will be looking at the man I haven't been able to get out of my thoughts since yesterday. I've known since my teens that I was bisexual, but I always drifted more toward women, so I never bothered to tell anyone about my sexuality.

Yesterday was the first time that I've ever really felt a connection to a man, and if the hard-on I had this morning is anything to go by, it's a pretty powerful connection. When I had initially shaken his hand, I thought I felt this jolt of something but quickly passed it off as nothing. When that same jolt happened again when we said goodbye, I knew it was more than my imagination, and from how his eyes widened at our touch, I knew he felt it, too. Suddenly, Marco was a man who I wanted to get to know.

So here I am, standing outside Wyatt's apartment and trying to compose myself before knocking. I need to make sure that nothing I do gives me away. Taking a couple deep breaths, I finally knock and can hear muffled voices from the other side of the door. I'm guessing that Wyatt probably forgot that he invited me over for moral support and is explaining to Marco that it's only me. When Wyatt opens the door, I make a joke to calm my nerves about him not being dead yet. I feel even more thrilled when Wyatt confirms that Marco has no idea what activities his dad is involved in and that he is a sweet and upstanding man.

Wyatt nods his head toward the living room, and that's when I spot him wearing a smile on his face that I swear is brighter than the sun and causing me to trip over my own feet at the sight of it. Catching myself, I glance over to Wyatt to see if he spotted my little fumble, and thankfully, it doesn't look like he did because honestly, I have no idea how I would explain it. Marco is still smiling at me, and I'm fighting every instinct I possess not to copy his smile because I know the moment I do, my attraction to Marco will be clear, and I'm just not ready to go there yet. Plus, I know that in a few minutes the smile that is currently lighting up his face and my world will be gone when he's told exactly who I am.

"Detective Smith. What are you doing here?" Marco asks me, and before I have a chance to say anything, I hear Wyatt introducing me not only as his best friend but also his partner on the force, and I watch as Marco's face twists into confusion.

"But you're the detective who came to talk to me when I reported Lorenzo missing. So you're not with missing persons?" Marco states.

Seeing the confusion on Marco's face, I'm struck with the sudden feeling of guilt and pain for lying to him, and I'm sure the emotions I'm feeling inside pass over my face if the *what the hell* look Wyatt gives me is any sign to go by. I have a feeling that Wyatt's going to want to discuss my reaction at some point, so I need to start talking and get him off the scent.

"No, I'm not with the Missing Persons Unit." I almost add that I'd never said that I was, and he'd come to *that* conclusion all by himself. "Wyatt wasn't lying. I'm his partner in the narcotics division."

Marco's eyebrows stitch together, causing the skin on his forehead to wrinkle, the confusion clearly evident. It seems to only deepen as he asks why I came to take his statement, but before I can answer, Wyatt steps in to explain.

"The sergeant at the front desk recognized the photo of Lorenzo and decided Liam should take the statement since I didn't want to risk a meeting with you right then," Wyatt states.

"So my statement was never actually filed with the Missing Persons Unit?" Marco asks, looking from me to Wyatt.

"No, it wasn't. Instead, I came home and spoke with Lorenzo about your being at the station looking for him, and we then decided to send you the text," Wyatt replies.

Even as everything is being explained, the puzzlement never seems to ease on Marco's face. In fact, I think what he is being told just seems to generate *more* questions, and I'm proven right when I hear Marco ask, "But why did Lorenzo block his number?"

Wyatt goes on to tell Marco about the robbery and Lorenzo's stint in the hospital, but unfortunately, I miss the grateful look that appears on Lorenzo's face at Wyatt's explanation and interject, "You're talking about the attack, right?"

Instantly I realize my mistake when both Lorenzo's and Wyatt's heads snap in my direction, a look of both alarm and chastisement on their faces. They both turn to look over toward Marco, and I know they're hoping Marco hasn't heard me.

Luck isn't on our side, though, because Marco narrows his eyes and looks at me, saying, "You mean the robbery, right? That's what Lorenzo told me landed him in the hospital."

I consider trying to back track, but something deep inside knows that Marco needs to hear the truth about what is going on. He has to be made aware of exactly how dangerous his father is. I already feel as though I want to protect him, and in order to do that, Marco has to be told the truth.

"No, I meant attack," I say to Marco, then glance over to Wyatt and Lorenzo. "You didn't tell him?"

Marco gives a penetrating stare to each of us in turn, and when we all remain silent, I watch as the confusion on his face morphs into agitation, his lips now drawn into a thin line while his fingers fidget at his sides. It wasn't my intention to cause any problems, but I understand why my revelation does. Even I'm surprised—and a little turned on—when I hear Marco growl through gritted teeth, "Tell me what happened. The *truth* this time."

Before Lorenzo and Wyatt can try to deny anything, I start to explain everything.

"Lorenzo was attacked, but they made it look like a robbery." I pause and look over to Lorenzo, who gives a slight nod of his head letting me know I can continue. "We believe that your father organized it right after your brother came out to your parents."

As I watch the full force of what I've just said sink in and the color drain from his face, I fight the urge to rush over and gather Marco into my arms as he sinks further into his seat, but I don't move because Marco might find that a little strange after one meeting.

"Holy fucking shit. I don't believe it. How... Why would Dad *do* that? And to think I was about to come out to them, too."

It took me only a nano second to register that Marco had just confirmed he's gay. Even though I suspected, it was still amazing to hear, and I know I'll have to figure out how to spend some secret alone time with him. I'm also relieved when I hear Wyatt suggest that he stay in the closet for the time being. Although I want something to happen between Marco and myself, I'm not ready to come out, either.

Lorenzo says he's surprised that their father hasn't spoken to Marco about the business and getting him involved, then I see how scared Marco becomes when Lorenzo goes on to say that he'd agreed to work with us to bring his father down, cautioning Marco that when he's with their parents, he'll have to act like nothing's wrong. It comes to me suddenly that I now have a way in which to be alone with Marco and not raise any suspicions. I can be Marco's own personal protection detail.

****

A few hours later, I spot Marco getting up to leave and quickly follow after saying my goodbyes to Lorenzo and Wyatt, catching up with him in the hallway outside the apartment.

"Hey, Marco! Wait up," I call out and watch as he turns to me with a look of surprise on his face.

"Is everything okay, Detective?"

For a split second, I wonder why he calls me "detective" until I realize that during the entire time that we've been in Lorenzo and Wyatt's apartment, he hasn't had a chance to ask me anything directly and is probably still seeing me as Wyatt's partner.

"Yeah, everything's fine. Was just thinking we could get the elevator down together, that's all." The lie slips off my tongue so easily that I hadn't even realized I'd said it until he shrugs his shoulders and just responds, "Okay."

While we wait for the elevator, I take the opportunity to have a good look at the man standing beside me. I didn't allow myself the chance when he was at the station yesterday. He's about my height and has the same olive skin tone as Lorenzo, which leaves no doubt to their Italian heritage. His hair is black has this gorgeous wave to it, and I wonder how soft it is. Does he like it when someone runs their fingers through it? Is there enough length to grab hold of it when in the throes of passion?

I'm pulled out of these thoughts when the elevator pings its arrival, and Marco looks at me as the door opens. I can feel the blush rising to my cheeks and am hoping he can't see my thoughts on my face. He points to the elevator, inviting me to go first, and for the first time, I notice that he has beautiful dark green eyes.

"You have green eyes," I blurt out, feeling my blush deepen as Marco joins me in the elevator and pushes the button for the lobby.

"Yes, I do," he replies, a chuckle filling his voice, but I don't think he realizes that the only reason I noticed was because I was checking him out.

"How come?" *Seriously, did I just ask that out loud?* I really need to engage my brain-to-mouth filter before talking; it's just that I thought they would've been brown like his brother's.

"How come I have green eyes?" he asks, and I'm surprised to see a smile on his face after all he'd been told today. I find myself tongue-tied and can only nod in agreement at his question. "Honestly, I'm not sure. They should be brown just like Lorenzo's, but I think I'm just one of those genetic freaks of nature. But I love the fact that they're different."

I almost agree with him out loud but manage to catch myself this time, and we spend the rest of the elevator ride in silence. Before I know it, the pinging sound lets us know we've reached the lobby and the doors slide open. Marco steps out and turns to me with his hand outstretched. For a split second, I'm confused until I realize that he's saying goodbye.

Taking his hand, I hear him say, "See you around, Detective."

It isn't until he drops my hand and is walking away that I realize I'm not ready for this meeting to end, so I blurt out, "Do you want to go for a coffee?"

Marco turns back to me, and when I see the smile is back, I'm happy that my mouth decided to engage before my brain could stop the words from coming out.

"You mean like a date?"

As I make my way over to where he'd stopped, I can feel myself wanting to say yes, but I have no idea what's stopping me. There's no one in the lobby who can hear my answer, and yet I still hear myself respond, "No, not a date. Just thought it would be nice to get to know each other, especially since you're the brother of my best friend's boyfriend." I mentally kick myself for being so stupid. This would have been an ideal opportunity to say, "Yes, like a date."

It's only because I'm looking at him that I notice the light dim in his eyes, although he keeps the smile on his face. I know that Marco must have felt something for me, too, and it hurts that I caused that light to dim. It shouldn't because we hardly know each other, but it does nonetheless. I also don't miss the indecision as he weighs what to do before finally answering.

"You're right, Detective. We should get to know each other," Marco states almost matter-of-factly, his voice flat and losing most of the playfulness from the elevator.

"Is now okay? Unless you have other plans, of course. There's a coffee shop about fifteen minutes from here that's open late." I say, and I can hear a little voice in my head repeating *Please don't have plans*.

"Do you mean the Coffee Bean?"

"Yeah, that's the one." I hide my surprise that Marco has heard of the Coffee Bean since I don't know what area he lives in, but before I can ask, he explains.

"I met Lorenzo there earlier. I don't have any plans for the rest of the evening, and to be honest, I don't really want to go home yet, especially not after everything I just learned about my family. So a coffee would be nice."

"Fab." As we both turn and start walking out of the building, I glance toward the man at my side and say, "And Marco, the name's Liam. No need to keep calling me 'Detective.'" He shoots me a look and there's a small grin on his face as he nods his head.

We make our way to the coffee shop in a companionable silence, and it puts me completely at ease that he doesn't feel the need to talk the whole way there . When I have been out with other people in the past, they just seem to want to talk all the time. I always seem to find myself thinking that sometimes words aren't necessary, but then I remember that this *isn't* a date and the reason that he's not saying anything is probably to make sure there are topics left to talk about when we sit down.

We arrive at the Coffee Bean to find that it's busy, and the loud hum of voices hits us as we open the door. This is the first time I can recall that I've had to wait before two seats become available in the shop's back corner. As we sit, I notice that the spot is in a quieter section and talking will be so much easier. Marco is looking around with an odd expression on his face as if he is remembering something.

"Everything okay?" I look around myself but don't see anything unusual.

"Yeah. It's just that I think this is the same table me and Lorenzo were at earlier, and it got me thinking. If someone had told me yesterday that the meeting I was about to have with my brother would change everything I thought I knew about my family, I would have called them a liar."

"You seemed to have handled everything you've been told well. If my brother had told me what yours had, I am not sure I would have believed him."

I watch as he seems to think about what I've said and how to answer. He must be replaying everything that was discussed today.

After a few moments pass, he finally says, "If it had just been me and Lorenzo alone and he told me about the drugs, criminal activities, etc., I would have thought he was just saying it to just get back at our father. But the fact that Wyatt was there backed up what he'd told me. You being the one to mention the attack shows me that Lorenzo was still trying to protect me. Yes, he told me that dad was dangerous but in a way so as to not destroy the image I'd held of the man."

"Sorry," I say automatically, but I am not sorry, not one bit. Marco deserves to know what type of man his father is. What would have happened to Marco if he hadn't been told and came out to them, too? A shudder rolls through my body at the thought. I don't think Marco has a guardian angel like Lorenzo did.

"You have nothing to be sorry for. I'm glad you told me about the attack. I have a right to know what kind of man my father is, but that doesn't stop the truth from hurting all the same." I watch as he pauses before taking a deep breath and going on. "The hardest thing to wrap my head around is what he did to Lorenzo. That the man who is supposed to love us unconditionally could do something like that."

"A man who loves his son unconditionally wouldn't organize something like that or wish them harm in any way." I shouldn't say something like that, but it's true. Yet even as I'm speaking the words, I think about my family. *Would they still welcome you with open arms?* What would they say if I took Marco home and introduced him as my boyfriend? But those aren't questions I'm willing to find out the answers to right now and decide that it's time to steer this conversation onto a better topic.

"Lorenzo tells me you're a teacher. What grade do you teach?"

I watch as the change of subject causes Marco to relax in front of me, and his entire demeanor changes, his shoulders relaxing and a smile touching his lips as he starts talking about his job.

"I teach the sophomore English classes at a public high school." An edge of excitement fills his voice.

"You enjoy it?" I ask but think I already know the answer.

"I love it. I spent a long time studying so I could teach in high school, and it really is amazing. Don't get me wrong, there are some tough days, but I wouldn't change anything."

"How come you wanted to go into teaching? I know that I couldn't do it. Some teenagers are total punks," I say, thinking about the run-ins I've had with kids over the years.

"I always wanted to work with kids. My initial plan was to work with younger ones, but when I realized that I was gay, I thought I would go into high school instead. I figured I'd could be the cool, gay teacher that everyone could turn to. Unfortunately, I haven't been brave enough to come out just because I'm not sure how the school would react, but I still think I have become a teacher that any student could come to, anyway."

"I can totally see you as the cool, approachable teacher."

It's at this point that the waitress comes up to our table to take our order, and only when she apologizes for the delay in getting to us do I realize how long we've been talking and how much I've enjoyed my time with Marco. We both order a cappuccino, and the waitress says that she'll be back as soon as she can.

Not in any rush for the night to end, I say, "Take your time," which Marco echoes at the same moment, and we both smile at each other. Marco must be enjoying himself, too, but now it's Marco who asks the next question.

"You asked me why I became a teacher, so now it is my turn. Why did you become a cop?"

"Most of my family has been on the force at some point in their lives. My older brother went into the military, and I thought about following him, but in the end, I wanted to stay close to home and help the people here, so I decided to join the police force. And the rest, as they say, is history."

"Do you enjoy it?"

"It can be frustrating as hell some days, especially if you've spent months on a case and then something happens and you get set back. But then there are the days when everything has gone right and suddenly it's all worthwhile."

"But don't you deal with some frightening people? Surely it's dangerous, too."

"Isn't there an element of danger in any job these days?" I ask him before adding, "But we do try to take as many precautions as possible. The key priority is to stay as safe and ready as we can."

"I know I couldn't do your job. Kids are much easier."

Laughing, I turn around and tell him I would much rather face criminals than have to deal with hormonal teenagers every day. The waitress brings over our drinks at this point, and we both thank her and spend the next few hours chatting about anything and everything, from favorite films to books, and before I know it, the coffees have been drunk and Marco has asked for and paid the bill.

"I was going to pay that," I tell him

"Hey, no problem. You can get the next one."

The next one. Does that mean he wants to do this again? God, I hope so. "If you're sure."

We both get up from the table and make our way outside and hover on the sidewalk, neither of us seeming sure if we should shake hands or give a hug. In the end, Marco takes that decision out of my hands.

"Thanks for coffee. It was much needed," he says as he smiles and waves at me. "See you soon," he finishes, then turns and walks toward the subway station.

I wave at him even though he isn't looking, and although I know I shouldn't, my eyes drop to check out his ass in his jeans. I can feel myself getting hard as I take in the sight, but thankfully it isn't noticeable. I have a feeling that Marco is going to be trouble... and in the best possible way.

Chapter 3 — Marco

As I walk away from Liam, I can feel his eyes on me and hope that he's checking me out, especially my ass. It *is* one of my best features, even if I do say so myself. I have what people refer to as a bubble butt, all firm and round.

When he'd called after me as I was leaving Lorenzo's, I didn't expect him to invite me for coffee. I didn't want to think about why my heart rate increased when I asked him if it was a date or admit how deflated I felt when he said that it was just to get to know me on a professional level. But I have to say that it was the best *non*-date I've been on. Liam was so easy to talk to, and if there was any lapse in conversation, he didn't feel the need to fill the silence. If it wasn't for the waitress coming over, he might have forgotten that we were even in a coffee shop. There was a little awkwardness on how to say goodbye since I really wanted to give him a hug, but it didn't feel as though that was the right thing to do yet.

So now I'm trying to resist the urge to look back over my shoulder and see if Liam is still watching me. If I do look back and he *is* still staring, then he is one hundred percent checking me out. But if he isn't there, then this really was just a "get to know you" meeting and the attraction that I can feel is just one sided. Just as I think *fuck it* and begin to turn, I feel my cell vibrate in my pocket. Pulling it out, I see a text from my mother, and my heart sinks as I read the message.

MOM: Want to come over for dinner? Be nice to see you.

I knew that I'd have to see my parents at some point, but I was hoping I might avoid them for at least a few more days. Even though the message is phrased as a question, it's not, and I won't be able to turn it down, not without a really good reason. Like maybe getting hit by a bus, and luck is not on my side as I look up the street and see that there aren't any buses at hand, which means I will be making my way uptown to my parents.

ME: Yeah. Will be there shortly.

All too soon, I'm standing outside the house I grew up in. I always thought this was a house of love and that my parents would stand by me and Lorenzo through anything. But it's all an illusion. By the sound of it, it's only a house of love if you follow their rules. Will dad take me aside tonight and tell me what he really does for a living and say he now wants me to become the heir? How the hell do I tell him that there is no way that I will do that and not end up in the hospital like Lorenzo?

Knowing that I can't stand on the sidewalk any longer, I take a deep breath and walk up the cold stone steps, open the storm door and then the main door, and put a shaky foot over the threshold. The smell of home cooking hits me the moment I step into the foyer, making my mouth water and causing memories to assault my brain. Images of games, laughter, and love flash through my mind's eye, images that normally bring a smile but now are shrouded in darkness. Were these genuine, or were they all part of the façade?

Pushing all these feelings down, I plaster a smile on my face before calling out, "Hi, Ma."

"Marco, is that you?"

I roll my eyes at the question and have to bite my tongue before I yell back "Who the fuck did you think it was?" Instead, I wait, and sure enough, mere seconds later, she follows with, "I'm in the kitchen."

Considering Mom spends about ninety percent of her time in the kitchen, I already figured that's where she would be. While making my way down the hallway, I'm listening the whole way for sounds of my father. As I enter the kitchen, which is in the back of the house, I see Mom at the stove top stirring a large pot, and I know as soon as I lay eyes on it that it's pasta sauce. I'm reminded that the last time I had a meal here, Lorenzo had also been at the table. That night, he had sat knowing everything would change, and I never once spotted how nervous he'd been. I walk up to Mom and give her a kiss on the side of her head before making my way over to the table in the corner and sit down.

"You weren't long getting here," I hear Mom say.

"School was closed today for maintenance, so I was out and about already." I cross my fingers hoping she doesn't ask where, and luckily, just at that moment, I hear Dad coming into the kitchen muttering to himself and catching Mom's attention, so all questions about where I may have been today are forgotten.

At first I'm not sure what Dad is saying, but then I hear him repeating, "Must have been a phase," and I think it odd for a second before I realize that he must be referring to Lorenzo and that he's talking about him in the past tense. It's all very strange. Mom tells him that I've come over for dinner and points in my direction, and Dad looks up, spotting me for the first time, and only nods his head in my direction. He doesn't say hi or ask how I'm doing. Just sits in his chair at the head of the table and keeps on muttering to himself.

Ten minutes later, Mom is dishing up the food and bringing it over to us, and I watch as Dad eats his dinner without saying much, and when his plate is empty, he gets up, puts his plate in the sink, and walks out of the kitchen. That isn't like Dad, so I look over to Mom and hope that the question about his behavior is obvious on my face. She spots the question but gives a subtle shake of the head in warning not to ask. So she knows and isn't saying or doing anything about it, continuing like always. Picking up my empty plate along with hers, I take them to the sink, and for the first time, I can't wait for the evening to be over so I can go home.

―

The following afternoon, I'm still thinking about how Dad acted at dinner the night before. I'd stayed for a couple more hours after eating but didn't see him again. Mom asked how work was, asked if I was seeing anyone—the normal questions I'm asked when visiting. The only thing that was strange is that she never mentioned Lorenzo once. She would normally always ask if I'd seen him, but yesterday, there was nothing.

Shaking my head, I bring myself back to the present and am faced with a classroom full of kids just looking at me and waiting. Shit, I was in the middle of a lesson when my own thoughts overtook me.

"Sorry, what was I saying?" I ask the room, and I'm not surprised at the voice that answers me from the front of the class.

"You were talking about the book we are going to read," Noah says, always being helpful even when I can tell he isn't excited about the reading material.

"Thanks, Noah," I respond, giving him a grateful smile, too.

Before I have the chance to continue, he asks, "Everything okay, Mr. Romano? You seem a little out of it."

Noah is a good-natured young man. He's a bit of a nerd but loves reading. Although he isn't the top student in my class, I must admit that I have a soft spot for him and his eagerness to learn, and I know that he always tries his best.

"Everything's fine. Just have a few things on my mind," I reply, which has to be the understatement of the century. But it's not like I can turn around to the class and say, "Yesterday I found out that my dad is a drug lord, organized for my brother to be beaten up because he's gay, and as a result, I have put myself so far in the closet I'm amazed I can't see Narnia."

Instead, I look out over the class and continue with, "Sorry, class," and move so that my back is to them and I'm facing the whiteboard, taking a deep breath while picking up the dry erase marker and saying in a loud voice, "The book we will read is *Romeo and Juliet*." As I write out the name in capital letters on the white board, I hear the collective groan from the class and can't hide my smile.

"I can hear you groaning. This is a classic, and considering that it was written in 1594 and we are still reading it today is proof enough that it has withstood the test of time." Pausing briefly because I love saying the next part as I know that at least half the class is thinking they'll just watch the film, I grin as I stare over the room. "And no watching any of the films. This book deserves to be read in full."

I have to admit I'm delighted when I get another groan from the students, and a voice at the back of the room pipes up, "That's *so* unfair. The book isn't even written in normal English."

"That *was* normal English for the time that it was written, and I think that it adds to the drama of the story."

"But, sir, it's such a girly book," pipes up another voice.

I roll my eyes because I have been waiting for that statement. It's probably the same in every classroom across the globe, and I remember it being said when I was given this book to read back in high school.

"It is not a 'girly book,'" I say, using air quotes for emphasis. "It's a classic. There is something in this book for everyone. Love, romance, family feuds, swords, fights, murder. So, let's get started."

Once the lesson is over, I have some free time before my next class arrives, and my thoughts drift back to the dinner the previous night. I know that I have to text Lorenzo about the strange behavior from Dad, so I pull out my cell and type a quick message.

ME: Dad's acting strange. Going on about how it was a phase in your life. Why is he talking about you in the past tense?

I think it might be a while before he replies because I'm certain he said something about going back to the shop today and there will be lots of flowers to throw out, orders to sort—not to mention contacting customers—so I'm surprised when he replies just a few minutes later.

LORENZO: Remember, Dad thinks they left me for dead. Maybe he doesn't know I'm alive.

I read his reply at least five times before the words finally sink in. Of course Dad was talking about him in the past tense because he thought Lorenzo was dead, and that must be why Mom never asked after him, either. Does she think he is dead, too? Does Mom know what type of man Dad is? The questions about the whole situation are never ending, but I still have one statement on repeat in my head and text it to Lorenzo, hoping to get some answers.

ME: Still in shock that he did that.

The reply is a little longer coming back this time. I must have given Lorenzo something to think about or he's been sidetracked with stuff in the shop, but I'm just about to put my cell away when it beeps with another incoming text.

LORENZO: I couldn't believe it, either, but I just know that it's true. I know that Dad is different with you, but please don't say anything, just in case. I want you safe.

Does he really think I'll tell Mom and Dad that he's alive?

When I think more about Lorenzo's response and the part about me being safe, I realize he means about my telling our parents that I'm gay. I chuckle at this because after seeing Mom and Dad's reaction and then hearing Lorenzo explain what happened to him, there is no chance in *hell* that I am coming out.

ME: This is one gay who is very happy to stay in the closet... for now.

The rest of the day goes by in a flash, and I am thankful that I manage to keep my brain on track and there is no more drifting off during lessons. It's only as I'm packing my schoolbooks away that I decide that I might just pop over to surprise Lorenzo. I tell myself that it's because I want to check up on him, but really, it's because I hope that I might bump into Liam. Considering I live only a few blocks from the school, going to visit Lorenzo in the East Village is completely out of my way but will be so worth the time, especially if I get to spend some time with Liam....

No, not Liam. I mean Lorenzo.

Thirty minutes later, I'm at the Astor Place subway station and am so busy thinking about all the times I'd visited Lorenzo's shop and how close I was to his apartment and his whole double life that I'm not paying attention to my surroundings. Looking around to get my bearings, I notice just ahead of me the man who has been invading my thoughts so much the last few days, and I almost shout out to him until I see that he isn't alone. Next to him is a rather lovely lady. Suddenly I stop and move behind a pillar before he can spot me and then watch as they continue up exit steps up to the sidewalk, observing him place a hand at the base of her back and steer her to the right. The hand isn't there for long, but it's definitely an intimate touch and proof the attraction I was feeling was one-sided.

When we'd been at the coffee shop yesterday, we hadn't discussed our relationship status. There wasn't really much point. I had just come out to

Lorenzo and never mentioned a boyfriend, so I assumed it was a given that I was single and never thought to ask him. But I can't pull my eyes away as Liam and his girlfriend disappear before I turn around and head back down the steps for home, no longer feeling up to seeing Lorenzo. I'm also feeling rather foolish for being attracted to a straight man and thinking the attraction might actually be returned.

Chapter 4 — Liam

Staring out at the water in front of me, I'm not looking at anything in particular, just sitting and waiting in the car. It's the one part of the job I dislike, and I know Wyatt feels the same. Normally we would sit here discussing the case, maybe bouncing ideas off each other, but today, there is silence, and it's because we both know how important it is that we find something. For Wyatt, it's to make sure that Lorenzo is safe, and I'm secretly thinking the same about Marco, which is nuts considering we have only had coffee together, but I have a feeling deep in my gut that this man will be important to me. It's not something that I can shake, and my father has always said to me, "Listen to your gut, it will never let you down." But the silence is becoming too much, and I need to break it.

"Do you think we'll find anything?"

The sudden noise makes Wyatt jump, and it takes a second for the question to register but I'm not surprised by Wyatt's answer.

"God, I really hope so... *and* that we can link it back to Alfredo." Wyatt's next sentence, however, causes a chill to run down my spine. "Alfredo knows that Lorenzo survived the attack." Wyatt's voice wavers as he speaks, and I can tell there is concern there.

"How did he find out? Who told you and how reliable is the source?" There are too many questions in one go, but I'm patient while I wait for him to answer.

"Frank," Wyatt starts. "Lorenzo's driver-turned-bodyguard. He's the one who put up the signs at the shop and contacted all the customers. Frank sent the text message confirming that Alfredo somehow knows that Lorenzo is alive." There is no mistaking the worry in his voice, and it only deepens as he continues, "I just need to keep Lorenzo safe."

I almost blurt out that Marco needs to be kept safe, too, but he doesn't know about my feelings for Lorenzo's brother and that would come off as a little strange. How I don't lose it, I don't know, but even as I ask him how the fuck all that happened, I can hear the edge to my voice. He probably thinks I'm worried for Lorenzo, which I am, but damn it, Marco needs to be taken into consideration, too. I know that he's not in as much danger as Lorenzo because he hasn't been involved in the family "business," but there is no telling what Alfredo will do, especially if he finds out that Marco knows Lorenzo is helping the police.

"Don't forget Marco, too." The words tumble out before I can stop them, and I let my head fall back against the seat and snap my lips shut.

It's the wrong thing to say, I know, and I see the questions start forming on Wyatt's face. But just as he opens his mouth and takes a breath, the words "GO, GO, GO" crackle from the radio, and all other thoughts are forgotten. I heave a sigh of relief that Wyatt misses as we jump out of the car and all the teams, including the sniffer dogs, scramble into position and await the docking of the ship.

Once we are finally able to get onboard the ship, Wyatt and I can hear the captain claiming that the cargo is clean and that he randomly checks his crew for possession of any drugs or weapons on their person. As we are both standing on the deck, we're hit by a sudden blast of cold air and hear the words "temperature controlled," and I'm overwhelmed by a sinking feeling that we will come up with nothing once the search is completed. It still doesn't lessen the shock when we're told the ship is clear an hour later, after which I watch as Wyatt brings out his cell phone and starts furiously typing on the screen.

"We need to talk to Lorenzo," Wyatt says a few minutes later. "I've asked him to meet us at our place in two hours."

Just as I'm about to ask why in two hours, I remember that we still have to attend the debriefing at headquarters to discuss everything that's happened this morning and also explain how the information we were given was wrong. Both of us seem to be lost in thought about the misinformation we'd been given because the car journey back to headquarters is made in complete silence, and there is a tension surrounding us as we make our way to the conference room on the third floor.

It's only when we sit down at the front of the room and I notice Wyatt wince for what has to be the second or third time today that I ask, "Are you okay? Seen you wincing a few times."

As I watch the blush redden his cheeks, it dawns on me *why* he's wincing, and the mental image that gives me must be clear on my face considering the amused look that Wyatt now has.

"Oh God, no—don't want to know." I try to back away from the conversation as quickly as possible, but I forget that my partner is Wyatt, and he has to have the last say. What I wasn't quite expecting was his reply of, "Don't knock it till you try it," which leaves me mute.

Thankfully, it's at that moment the captain chooses to enter, and he walks straight over to Wyatt and myself. The first thing he asks is what happened today, and because I'm still mute from my partner's earlier blunt response, Wyatt is forced to answer. He goes on to explain that the information we were given was solid and that we've arranged a meeting with our source. This seems to satisfy the captain, but when he asks us if our source is reliable, I watch as Wyatt hesitates for the briefest of seconds. It's now my turn to jump in defending Lorenzo while giving Wyatt a *what the fuck* look, which seems to bring him back to the present. Wyatt then finishes by explaining that information must have been changed and that our source can no longer get any more intel.

I zone out through the rest of the debrief while my mind is playing over the words Wyatt had said—"Don't knock it, till you try it." I'd wanted the conversation to end, so why are his words still plaguing me? I realize it's because I can see him wincing whenever he sits down, meaning his behind is uncomfortable, and yet when he was joking with me and with how red his face went, it must have been a pleasurable experience.

Would it be the same for me?

Having never played with myself *there*, I'm a complete virgin when it comes to sex with men but have to admit how extremely interested it makes me as to how that would feel. Over the years, I have been with quite a few women, but it must feel different, right? An ass would feel a lot tighter, which would be amazing.

My dick chubs up at the thought, especially as I picture the ass belonging to Marco. No one notices as I shake my head to get my mind back on the debriefing before I pop an erection, and thankfully, the meeting is soon over and everyone stands to make their way out of the room. I turn to Wyatt to ask if he has any idea what we should do, and that's when I hear him call out to the captain.

My mouth drops as I hear him suggest to the captain that we should go undercover. At first I'm shocked, but that morphs into anger, and the moment the captain is out of ear shot, I turn on Wyatt.

"Are you fucking insane? Going *undercover*? With what Lorenzo said, it would take years for Alfredo to trust someone enough to hand over the business to them." And then just because Marco isn't far from my thoughts I add, "Have you forgotten that he has another son he may try to recruit?"

"I think Marco is safe," Wyatt starts, and I have to fight the eye roll at hearing this but listen as Wyatt puts a hand up before continuing. "Purely because he has been left out of it for so long. His morals are in place. There is no way that Alfredo can expect him to go from teaching school kids to killing someone."

After letting the words sink in, I admit to myself he is right and mutter, "Thank fuck." Unfortunately, it's not as quiet as I thought, and Wyatt shoots me a look before walking away while still talking. "Alfredo will need to look within his ranks, and if we can get someone in there that stands out, we might get lucky."

It's at this point I realize that he must be thinking that *he* will be the best man for the job. At that moment I want to grab hold of him and scream in his face "Hell no," but this would only make him more determined to follow through with his insane plan. All three of us will need to discuss this together before a decision is made. We also need to consider the danger this could put Marco in since he is still in contact with his father, but the one thing I do know is that Lorenzo will not like the idea of Wyatt going undercover. Hopefully, together, we will all be able to find another way.

Wyatt pulls out his cell and tells me he is letting Lorenzo know that we are on the way home, and I can't miss the concern that crosses his face when a reply is slow to be received and then again after he reads whatever has been sent.

When we finally get to their place, I'm surprised to see that we've arrived before Lorenzo, considering that his shop is within walking distance and how long ago Wyatt sent the text to say we were on our way and he needed to be here. Suddenly, I'm concerned, too.

We both sit on the couch and wait, not talking just listening, and the moment we hear a key in the lock, Wyatt shifts to the edge of the seat so he can quickly get up if needed. The moment Lorenzo comes in through the door, Wyatt is rushing over and pulling him into his arms. The pang of jealousy that rushes through me as they embrace takes me by surprise. I can feel the love and concern flow out of Wyatt as he asks what happened because Lorenzo is as white as a sheet, and beads of perspiration have broken out across his forehead. Whatever happened seems to have scared him.

I listen as Lorenzo says he wants to hear what went down today with us at the port and then with the debriefing before telling us what has him so on edge. When Wyatt looks over to me for my opinion, I just shrug my shoulders since I'm not sure what I can say. Wyatt steers Lorenzo toward the couch but never removes his arm from across Lorenzo's shoulders.

Once Lorenzo is seated, he asks Wyatt what happened. Wyatt looks over to me before looking back at Lorenzo and saying, "Okay, before I explain our morning, let me ask if you know how the flowers you sell are transported."

Holding my breath, I hope to god that he doesn't.

"They are transported in temperature-controlled cargo containers. Why?" Lorenzo confirms.

My heart sinks, and I let out my breath at the same moment Wyatt gets up from the couch. I can see he is trying hard to contain his anger, but when he snaps at Lorenzo for not telling us this vital piece of information, I jump in and, in a much calmer voice, say, "Why didn't you mention that before?" I look over to Wyatt with what I hope is a *calm the fuck down* look on my face.

"Didn't think it would matter. Did it affect today?" Lorenzo answers.

Honestly, I'm not surprised. It's not like he would know that sniffer dogs' sense of smell is compromised by the cold, and Wyatt seems happy for me to explain how this all works, probably because I'm calmer than him.

"Lorenzo, cold affects a sniffer dogs' sense of smell. They weren't able to detect anything."

As what I've just explained sinks in, I swear Lorenzo becomes even more pale before asking if I am joking, and it just confirms he had no clue about the cold affecting the dogs. I go on to explain that if the drugs were coming in in large shipments, then it wouldn't matter, but I guess Alfredo would know this, so is deliberately keeping the shipments small.

Lorenzo then asks again for us to tell him what happened today, which confuses me for a second. I thought that's what we were discussing, but then I realize he wants a play-by-play account of what went down. As I watch Wyatt come back over—this time a lot calmer—and pull Lorenzo into him, I know that it will be up to me to give the explanation.

So, I start at the beginning from when we arrived at the docks for our stakeout. When I get to the end of the account, Lorenzo asks if the captain was calm throughout the whole raid. It's then that I realize he was, and it must have dawned on Wyatt, as well, because we both say "Yes" at the same time. Just as I think back to how I wasn't surprised the ship's captain was calm because he has to be used to these kinds of raids, Lorenzo adds that if there were drugs on the ship, then surely he should have been anxious, wanting to find the evidence and bring the criminals in.

All of a sudden, it hits me. The captain must be involved. He knew which container would have the drugs, and the reason he was so calm today was because he knew that one was clean. I'm just about to tell Lorenzo that he would make a good cop when I hear Wyatt giggle and mumble something, to which Lorenzo adamantly whispers back that he wouldn't give up his flower shop for anything, but then I catch something to do with handcuffs while giving Wyatt a look. Oh god, this has nothing to do with the case and images I really don't need start dancing through my mind.

"Stop that, the pair of you!" I glare at both of them as I continue, "I don't need actual images, not after the mental ones from him earlier." I point at Wyatt, who is trying the innocent look while mouthing "What?" He must think it's because I don't want to hear the more intimate details, but it's actually because I don't want my thoughts to go in that direction again.

When I hear Wyatt explain to Lorenzo what was said before the brief started, I cringe because it causes the image of me ploughing into Marco to come rushing back, and my dick is getting hard again. This conversation needs to get back onto the case and pronto before I give myself away. I manage to pull off the "I am not amused" attitude while confirming to Lorenzo what Wyatt said, but then stating that we need to get back to the topic of the ship's captain.

As we continue to discuss the captain and the fact that Alfredo changed the schedule, I can see Wyatt is getting close to bringing up the idea of going undercover. When I see him look over to me, I know he is about to mention it, and I decide to just sit back and watch. This is something that must be hashed out between them. At first, Lorenzo is confused and thinks we're talking about Frank, but when Wyatt says this has nothing to do with Frank, Lorenzo instantly brings up Marco. Both of them are shot down fast, saving me from saying anything and drawing to light the fact that I've become very protective of Marco over the last few days.

I'm pulled from my musing when I hear an angry "No fucking way" and look up to see that Lorenzo has moved and is now towering over Wyatt, who just stares stonily up at him. I don't think I have ever seen either of them this angry. Lorenzo begins to pace and that seems to calm him for a moment, but then he stops as if a decision has hit him. Lorenzo walks back over to the couch, sits back down next to Wyatt, and takes his hand.

Thinking it would be best to leave as whatever is going on looks intimate and I'm feeling like an intruder, I quietly get up and turn to leave until I catch Lorenzo saying, "Especially as there is another option."

As I go back and sit back down, Lorenzo begins to explain that his dad came to the shop this afternoon and told Lorenzo that he wants him to return home, which leaves me in complete shock. Wyatt's face goes bright red, but then Lorenzo puts a hand on Wyatt's forearm to calm him and says, "This could be the perfect solution to our situation."

I continue watching as Wyatt turns to Lorenzo and asks him what he means. Lorenzo confirms that he is going to do what his dad asked and go back home, explaining the decision was only finalized a few minutes ago when he heard how they needed someone undercover. Wyatt looks over to me for my input. I can see the pleading in Wyatt's eyes for me to help change Lorenzo's mind, but I only nod in agreement with Lorenzo.

"You agree with Lorenzo?" Wyatt asks, the disbelief is evident in his voice.

"Yes," I say simply, but as I watch Wyatt slump in his seat, I think it best to explain my decision. "Am I happy it's come to this? No. But we need someone on the inside, and who better than Lorenzo? He will be a lot quicker gaining Alfredo's trust, meaning we will be able to close this case sooner rather than later."

Wyatt listens to what I have to say but doesn't voice any agreement or disagreement, and I don't push him. The emotions he is feeling are something only he can resolve.

I watch as the two men in front of me embrace, hearing Wyatt tell the man he loves that they've survived two years of hiding, so they can handle this. But as I see the tears roll down Lorenzo's cheeks, I know this time will be different. He won't be able to have the double life like he did before. Alfredo will have Lorenzo closely watched. Lorenzo can't risk being spotted with a man, which means he will have to let Wyatt go for a time if the plan is to succeed and everyone is to remain safe.

Wyatt is looking to me for support; he doesn't understand what's coming from Lorenzo. I know that I'll have to say something, somehow try to ease the pain lancing through Lorenzo's soul at what he knows needs to be done. Going up to Lorenzo, I place my hand on his back, which might be a little too friendly, but I don't care. He may not realize it, but he is giving everyone in this room a future.

I tell them, "Sorry that it's come to this, but this is the best option to keep everyone safe and give everyone the future they deserve."

I'm hoping it comes across that I'm talking about their future, but I'm also selfishly including mine, too. The truth is, I want to start something with Marco, even though I am not ready to come out in the open and don't want to risk Alfredo finding out and doing something like he did to Lorenzo. This way, everyone will be safe, and that can't be a bad thing—right?

Lorenzo seems to have forgotten that I'm even in the room as he confirms my earlier suspicion and explains to Wyatt that they will need to split up. That he will have to do everything by the book if he wants to gain his father's trust quickly. I shuffle away from them and cough just to draw their attention so that I can say I'm going to leave. This sounds like a private conversation, and I'm surprised when Lorenzo asks me to stay because I need to know what is going on and can be there for Wyatt.

We spend the next thirty minutes discussing what is going to happen when Lorenzo goes back, how we will get information to us, and it's agreed that Marco might be able to help. Lorenzo sends him a text to invite him over, and I can feel the excitement hum under my skin at the thought of seeing Marco again.

Chapter 5 — Marco

I'm in the middle of a lesson when my cell phone vibrates in my pocket. Since it only happens once, I know that it's a text message and leave it until I can look at it in private. Hopefully, since it is only one message, it isn't anything urgent, using the logic that if it were, someone would have kept calling me till I answered or at least sent a few messages. Thirty minutes later I finally read the text and am surprised that it's Lorenzo inviting me over. I'll admit to being a little excited that I'll get the chance to see Liam again.

LORENZO: Hi Bro. Any chance you are free this evening and can pop over?

Thankfully, I have no plans and quickly reply.

ME: Yeah, I'm free. Will make my way over once school is finished.

The rest of the day flies by, and I feel like I'm running to Lorenzo's apartment. I don't understand why I've been invited over but hope it's just an evening to get together and not to do with the case. When I knock on the door and Liam answers it, the smile on my face is instant, but as I walk into the room and see all the somber faces in front of me, I know that this isn't just a simple get together, and I try to break the tension with a joke.

"Whose cat died?"

When no one in the room laughs, Lorenzo comes up to me, pulling me into a hug, and says, "No one's, but I have had quite the day. Let me get you a beer."

"It's three o'clock in the afternoon," I state, not quite believing they are all drinking already.

"It has been that type of shitty day."

Making my way into the living room, I sit in the single chair in front of the wall of windows and watch as Liam grabs a chair from the kitchen table and places it beside me. Lorenzo comes back carrying the beers and hands one to each of us before he stops in front of Wyatt and watches as he sips his beer, looking at his throat as he swallows. It's hard to miss the desire in his eyes, and I can't help but look at Liam, suddenly understanding why the bobbing of an Adams apple is so sexy. It's only because I'm staring at Liam that I notice his lips are moving and realize that he's been talking, and I'm brought back to the present.

"Will you two stop making eyes at each other? We have to talk," I hear him say.

There is an undertone of amusement, which is confusing considering the somber faces I saw when I arrived, and so I have to ask, "Can someone please explain what's going on? Talk about what?"

At first, I thought Lorenzo was joking when he explained Dad's visit to him at the shop with an ultimatum. I demand Lorenzo tell me everything that happened from the moment our father entered the shop. As I listen, my emotions are like a roller-coaster going up and down, swinging between concern and anger. All I keep thinking about are the ways to keep Lorenzo safe until I hear him say something about going back.

"Sorry, but I must not be hearing things right because I swear I just heard you say that you are going home?"

"You did," he answers like this is nothing. Like he will be just popping home for dinner.

As the words sink in, I think I should be getting angry, but really all I feel is worry. I need to get him to change his mind. If he goes back and Dad finds out that nothing has changed, he will kill Lorenzo, making sure that it's done right this time. There won't be any second chances. I have to protect him.

"No, Lorenzo, please don't... Have you really thought this through?" Even I can hear the pleading in my voice.

"I've thought about nothing else since Dad left the shop." Lorenzo responds, but there seems to be something else that he isn't saying to me, and when I see him look over to Wyatt and Liam and say he wants to have a word with me in private, I hope that I'll get some answers.

Lorenzo leads me into their bedroom, and I sit on the edge of the bed looking at him. Not sure why, I ask if this is something that Wyatt has asked him to do and am relieved when he confirms it isn't. So Lorenzo is either being really brave or monumentally stupid, and I make sure to tell him just that. But there's still something more. When he says that he needs to tell me something and I have to hear him out before saying anything, I'm totally confused but nod my head in agreement.

"I have another plan. Yes, I will get the information that Wyatt needs, but I plan to kill Dad."

When I hear him say this, I can't help the gasp that falls from my lips. Holy shit, that is huge. Killing another person... How the hell can he even think about doing something like that?

I start to voice this, but when he raises his hand, I agree to stay quiet until he has finished and let him continue. "With Wyatt's plan, Dad would just end up in prison. But that means that he can eventually get out, and he would be a shadow over both of our lives. We would never really be free to be our true selves, and more importantly, love who we want to. This is a permanent solution, and one that frees us completely."

I want to tell him he's wrong, but deep down I know that he isn't. I just don't know how Lorenzo will be able to kill; it's not something that I can see him doing. Only monsters kill, and I need to try to find the words to ask him. I open my mouth a few times, but nothing comes out, so instead I ask if he's planning on telling Wyatt. The last thing I expected to hear is him saying that Wyatt didn't take learning about the others too well. My eyes snap to Lorenzo, and I can see that he is hoping I didn't hear what he just said.

"Others?" is the only question I manage to get out.

"Um, no, I didn't mean that. Just a slip of the tongue," Lorenzo repsonds, tripping over his words, but I know he's lying, and I can feel myself getting angry.

"That's bullshit," I rage. "Now tell me what the *fuck* you mean by' others?'"

I'm hoping that it isn't what I think it means, and I can see that he is considering what he wants to tell me. I hope to God it's the truth even if I don't really want to know. But finally, Lorenzo explains exactly how involved he was in Dad's business and that he has, in fact, killed other people on the instructions of our father. As Lorenzo continues to explain, I keep waiting to feel shocked, but part of me thought he was more involved than what he was saying. What does surprise me is when he admits he's told Wyatt about them.

Why the fuck would you tell a cop, even if you are in a relationship with said cop?

Instead of asking a hundred different questions flowing through my mind, the first being how the fuck could he kill someone, I ask why Wyatt didn't get the cases reopened by saying that there was fresh evidence.

By the look on Lorenzo's face, this is something that he must not have thought of, and he starts mumbling to himself, "Now Wyatt has my gun."

At this point, I want to reach over and shake Lorenzo and call him some not-so-pleasant names, but instead, I just ask why the hell Wyatt has his gun. Lorenzo explains that it was a present from Dad and he couldn't think of a better symbol to give Wyatt to show that he'd meant everything he'd said about leaving the family.

Unfortunately, I have to agree with him, but he has also given Wyatt the one piece of evidence that can put him behind bars for a long time. It's at this moment he asks if he should ask Wyatt why he didn't.

The strange look I give him must convey that I think he's nuts, and when he chuckles and states that we couldn't write this shit for a soap opera because no one would believe it, I end up laughing, too.

But the amusement we share doesn't last long. Lorenzo sobers and asks if he should tell Wyatt about his plan and what I am feeling about it. The first question is simple for me to answer. Yes, he needs to tell Wyatt. He must be honest with everything that he is planning to do. It might be good to have the police in our corner, but this is a thought I will keep to myself.

The second part is a lot harder—how do I feel about all this? The man I see as my dad isn't the man that Lorenzo sees, and yet I believe everything he has told me. For some strange reason, my head is saying that this is a good thing, which, considering Lorenzo is talking about murder, my heart aches. But regardless, I tell him I'm behind him one hundred percent. When he asks if I will stay while he tells Wyatt, a strange sense of pride fills me that he wants me there.

We both make our way out of the bedroom and back into the living room, and when I see that Liam isn't there, my heart drops. I had wanted to see more of him. I'm just about to ask if he left, but luckily Lorenzo beats me to it, which is probably for the best. I'm sure there would have been questions as to why I was asking after Liam, and I make sure to conceal my relief when Wyatt confirms that he's still here but had to go to the bathroom.

As Lorenzo and I take our original seats, the three of us end up staring at the hallway, waiting for Liam. When he appears and sees all eyes trained on him, he stops dead in his tracks. At this angle, I secretly appreciate the sight in front of me. He's dressed in stone-washed jeans and a plain black t-shirt, which is tight enough to show a lean and toned build, but not tight enough to show any ridges on what I guess is a very firm stomach. His look is finished off with black combat boots. Liam is literally my walking wet dream, and when he asks if there is anything on his face and runs his hand through his hair, I have to stop myself from releasing the needy groan wanting to escape my throat.

I'm so focused on Liam that I must have missed when someone responded that there is nothing on his face because Liam shakes his head and then makes his way back over to the chair beside me. Lorenzo lets them know that he needs to talk to them, and when Liam says that doesn't sound good, I want to say it isn't, but this isn't my plan to tell. Instead, I stay seated and just watch as Lorenzo explains that he wants to make a more permanent solution for Dad. From the slight rise of Wyatt's eyebrows, he seems to understand Lorenzo's meaning instantly, but by the look on Liam's face, he's completely confused.

"You agree with him?" Wyatt asks me. I think he's hoping I'll say no.

"My heart doesn't, but my head understands the logic," I respond and only continue when I've picked my next words carefully. "Honestly, Lorenzo's argument is sound. The only way that any of us can live our lives in the open and without looking over our shoulders at every moment is if our father isn't around," I tell him.

Liam is looking at all of us, still confused by what's going on, and even though he looks at Wyatt, he asks why I'm involved. Knowing the question was directed at me, I decide to answer him.

"Liam." I say his name so he has to look over to me. "I'm gay, and we're talking about my father never accepting that."

"Okay, but didn't you say that your father was different toward you?" Liam asks, but now it's Lorenzo who replies, explaining that Dad is different with me but is still too traditional to see past the fact that both his sons are gay. As Liam asks how Lorenzo's plan will change this, the look of confusion never leaves his face. I almost want to ask if he is sure he's a cop because the answer is so clear. But I can see the shock register on his face for the briefest of seconds when Wyatt cuts in and explains that Lorenzo is planning to put an end to his father.

Lorenzo is staring at Wyatt, ignoring the rest of us in the room while waiting for him to say something, and anyone can see the war that is raging within him. Wyatt knows that what Lorenzo said is true, but the cop in him knows that killing anyone in cold blood is wrong. Lorenzo is taken aback when Wyatt says this to him. Looking over to Liam, I see him nod ever so slightly, silently agreeing with me that it's best we leave. We both know that Lorenzo and Wyatt have a lot to talk about and don't need us there.

"I think it's best we leave now," we both say at the same time, and it's almost as if Lorenzo only then remembers we're still in the room and offers to walk us out. Getting to the front door first, I turn to see if Liam is following, but he seems to stay and hover by the living room entrance for a second, so I wait for him to start moving again before looking back to Lorenzo.

"Let me know when the plan will be put in motion. If I hear anything strange from Mom and Dad, I'll let you know." I then shout "goodnight" so that Wyatt can hear, too, and make my way to the elevator.

The ride down to the lobby is over in a flash because the entire evening is on repeat in my mind. When I left school all those hours ago, there was no way I could've guessed that I was about to find out that my brother had killed people because of orders that had been given by my dad, that he'd had his own gun—which he had given to a cop—and now, he was planning to kill again.

Lorenzo was right; you really couldn't make this shit up. I know that I will need to talk to someone about all this, and the best person I can think of is Liam, but I decide to wait. I don't think I can face going over everything again tonight, but I hope that he will accept my cell number and we can arrange to meet up. When I hear the ding of the elevator, I look up, hoping that it's Liam, and can feel the smile grow on my face and my pulse increases when I see that it is, indeed, my Adonis stepping out.

"What are you still doing here?" he asks with a look of surprise on his face.

"I wanted to catch you before I left," I respond, and the smile he gives me is enough to melt the ice caps. But then I remember the girl I spotted him with and remind myself that this doesn't actually mean what I want it to.

"Oh, okay. What for?"

For some reason, I think I hear a note of want in his voice but quickly dismiss it as a figment of my imagination. "I was wondering if I could have your cell number." Even before I finish asking my question, I can see Liam pulling out his cell phone, handing it over to me after unlocking the screen, and I think his smile might have gotten even bigger.

"Just put your number in, and I can text you mine," he says as I take the cell off him. "But why do you want my cell number?"

"I'd really like to talk to someone about everything I've just heard," I say as I point my finger up, hoping he realizes that I mean Lorenzo and Wyatt. "And even if I could talk to anyone else, I don't think they would believe me. This whole situation is just odd."

"Do you want to go and grab a coffee or something to eat now?" Liam asks.

"No, not tonight. I think I just need to try and process everything myself first." He looks a little disappointed at my refusal, but again I dismiss it as seeing things that just aren't there. My brain is too confused to process anything more right at the moment, and it's showing me things that aren't real. Knowing that I need to get back home, I quickly add, "But I'd like to meet up soon, and it will be handy for you to have my number, too—you know, if you need to get a hold of me for something that may be case related."

"Yes, of course," he answers and looks down at his cell.

I can see him typing and have to wonder what kind of message he will send. Hearing my cell beep, I pull it out of my pocket and can see that a message has come in with only a number, so I open it up.

LIAM: My number. Liam.

I am not sure what I was hoping for, but I'm a little disappointed that it's so straightforward and to the point. I *had* wanted a funny little joke, maybe even a kiss at the end would have been nice, but I suppose beggars can't be choosers.

"Thanks." I say once I pocket my cell again.

The silence stretches out between us, and for some reason, unlike the walk to the shop, today it feels strange and awkward, and I don't understand what's changed.

Liam shuffles his feet for a second before lifting his wrist to check the time, saying, "It's later than I thought. I'd better be going."

Liam turns to leave, and I have no idea why, but I grab his arm to stop him. The moment my hand locks around his forearm, I can feel the heat from him and electricity shoots up my arm. I hear him gasp. *Holy shit, he can feel this, too.* But just as quickly, he pulls his arm away and waits.

I want to say something. I want to know why he gasped, but instead, I say, "Thanks again for your number."

"No problem," Liam responds as he turns, and this time, I let him walk away.

Just as he opens the doors on the far side of the lobby, I call his name, "Liam." He's smiling as he looks back at me, but it's not the same one as earlier. The light doesn't reach his eyes, and I completely forget what I was going to say. The only words that tumble out of my mouth are, "Good night. Take care."

He looks like he wants to say something else but only responds, "Yeah, you, too," and then he's gone.

I stare at the spot where he was just standing and wonder what has changed. I thought that maybe we'd been building a friendship, but in the space of a few minutes, it seems to have gone up in smoke. I hope when I text him he'll still agree to meet up because not having any kind of contact with him would suck big time.

Chapter 6 — Liam

ONE MONTH LATER

It's hard to believe that a month has already passed. When the plan had originally been discussed, we believed—or maybe I'd hoped—that within a few weeks it would all be over. Or that we would at least be making some headway. As of yet, nothing has happened. The only good thing to come out of the whole situation is how things have improved with Marco. We've sent a few texts and met up a few times. We've agreed to meet up again tonight, , and I've decided that I'll finally ask Marco out on a date. The other times we've been together, we only talked about the case and how Lorenzo is doing, but this is something that I have to do for myself.

When it was decided, or I should say once Lorenzo went back, we explained to the police captain that our source was going to infiltrate the family, and the captain clarified that we were to watch him, and if he is seen to be in trouble at any point, we are to pull him out of there immediately. Wyatt didn't think he could face seeing Lorenzo every day and not be able to talk or touch him, so I agreed to watch over him. Thankfully, the only thing that I've seen so far is how unhappy Lorenzo is. He's just radiating sadness, and I know there is nothing that can be done about it. It's the one thing that has caused me the most guilt as I haven't been able to tell Wyatt. I've spoken to Marco about it, and he said maybe I should tell Wyatt, that maybe Wyatt knowing how sad Lorenzo is will somehow make Wyatt feel better. I argued with him at the time, but right now I think he may be right.

Looking at myself in the mirror because I want to look perfect for tonight, I check out my outfit for what must be the tenth time. I've decided to go with the stone-washed jeans, a black t-shirt, and my black combat boots because even though Marco might not have realized it, I had noticed that he was checking me out when I was wearing the same outfit at Lorenzo and Wyatt's, so I know it's one he likes.

We're meeting at the same coffee shop on Third Avenue, the one close to Lorenzo's apartment. Even though it is a bit out of the way for us to be meeting after work considering we're both downtown, I've started thinking of it as our place. Admittedly, that's only in my head. At one point I tried suggesting that we meet somewhere else that's closer, but he responded that it's the best coffee around and he likes it there. Honestly, it is so close to my apartment on East Sixth that I shouldn't complain.

I've lost count of the number of times I've wanted to invite him back to my place, but I always chickened out at the last moment. I'm just too frightened that he would say no because he doesn't think of me like that, and it will then destroy the friendship we've built. But watching Lorenzo and Wyatt and seeing how sad they are has made me realize that anything can happen. Life is too short.

Ten minutes later I'm sitting at our table and waiting for Marco to arrive. It's the one in the back of the coffee shop, a little out of the way, where talking is a lot easier. My palms are sweating, and I have to keep wiping them on my jeans. I can feel this nervous, excited energy rushing through my veins, making my skin tingle, and I start drumming my fingers on the table because my hands need to be doing *something*.

After a few sideways glances from the surrounding customers, I pick up the coffee menu and study it instead. That should also help stop me from staring at the door, but every time I hear the bell ding as it's opened, I can't stop myself from looking up. So far, each time it isn't Marco, and I'm beginning to get concerned. Looking at my watch, I realize I must have gotten to the coffee shop a lot earlier than I thought since he isn't due here for another ten minutes. When the waitress comes over again, I know I have been sitting there a little too long.

"You ready to order, sir?" she asks.

"I'm still waiting for someone. He's been delayed." I lie just in case she asks me to move but hoping she doesn't figure that out. "But they're due any second. When he arrives, if you want to bring over two cappuccinos, that would be perfect."

She scribbles the order down, saying, "No problem," before walking back behind the counter.

We've met so often now that I remember Marco's coffee order, even though every time he still picks up the menu and looks as if he's deciding what to have but then just orders a cappuccino. It's kinda sweet to watch.

The ding of the bell sounds again, and just like all the other times, I expect Marco to not be there, but this time, he is. He's the most gorgeous man that I've ever seen, and every time he's around, he takes my breath away. He must have come straight from work because he's wearing dark chinos, a grey button-up shirt, and a dark beige blazer. There should have been a tie, too, but he must have taken that off the moment he left the school and stuffed it in the messenger bag hanging from his shoulder. From this position I can't see his shoes, but I know they'll be his brown loafers, which are the shoes he always wears for school. To me, it's the perfect look. Just the right level of young professionalism, but he also carries this air of being approachable. I would have *loved* having a teacher like that when I'd been in school.

Even though we always sit in the same place, I watch as he scans the room looking for me. The smile that spreads across his face is breathtaking as he spots me in the corner, and I watch as a few of the surrounding women do a double take and watch as he walks towards me. All of them are appreciating the sight and checking him out, and yet he doesn't see any of it, just keeps walking toward me as if I'm the only person in the room. I know that the smile on my face is matching his. When he gets to our table, I get up and pull him into a hug as we both say hello. Not sure how we got to hugging hello, but I love it nonetheless. For a few brief seconds, I get to feel the hard planes of his chest pressed against mine. The only problem is that there are always too many clothes in the way.

"I've ordered us both a cappuccino. Hope that's okay," I say as he takes the seat opposite me.

"Damn, and here was me wanting a latte today." Looking over to him, I'm just about to apologize and say that I'll go and change it when I see the humor on his face. "I'm just kidding. That's great. Thank you."

"You know that you just gave me heart failure, right?" But I'm laughing myself and biting my lip to try and stop any sound from escaping.

"Why the hell would that give you heart failure? It's only coffee."

I realize that this could be the perfect way to let Marco know how I feel and that I want to take him on a date.

"Because I hoped that you would think it was sweet," I reply.

"Sweet," he repeats, looking confused. "It's nice of you, but not sure why I would think it's sweet."

He has no idea what is going on, so I'm quick to say before losing the nerve again, "I like you, Marco, and was wondering if you'd want to go out on a date." And I wait. When after a few minutes he still has said nothing,

I look up at him. He's staring at me while trying not to laugh, but the fact that his lips are twitching gives him away, and for a second, I'm heartbroken until he speaks.

"Sorry, Liam, but I have no idea what you just said. I never knew anyone could talk that fast."

Fucking great! Plucking up as much courage as I can muster and taking a deep breath, I try again, saying it slower so he can understand me this time.

"I like you and was wondering if you wanted to go out on a date."

Again, nothing. For several minutes there is no sound, and it starts to feel like being in my own personal hell while I watch as a myriad of emotions cross his face. First there is confusion that I'm certain turns to happiness, but it's so fleeting, I can't be sure before his face finally settles on shock and disbelief.

"When you say date, do you mean like a date, date?"

I chuckle. "Yes, I mean like a date, date. You know, dinner or the movies and then ending on a kiss kinda date".

Marco's just staring at me now, and I really have no idea why, then he says, "You're fucking serious?"

Smiling at him, I try to contain my laughter. "Of course I'm fucking serious. Why the fuck wouldn't I be?"

"Cause you're straight."

At this point, I can't hold back my laughter. "If I were straight, why the hell would I just ask you out?"

"But I saw you with a woman. You had your hand on her back, and it seemed like you knew her quite well," Marco states, just staring at me with what I can only think is sadness in his eyes.

What the hell is he talking about? I try to think about where or when he could have seen me with a woman because the only person I've been able to think about since meeting Marco, *is* Marco, in a romantic sense, anyway.

"When was this?" I ask, still unable to figure out when he could have seen me with someone else.

"Maybe just over a month ago…" He pauses as he seems to try and think about when he may have seen this. "It was probably a day or two after Lorenzo told me about Dad. I decided to pop over and see him after school let out to check on him and I was just walking out of the Astor Place station. You were up ahead of me, and I was just about to call out to you but then saw you had company."

A month ago…. Who the hell was I with a month ago? Mentally, I start going over every get-together I'd had to see if I can figure out who the hell he saw me with, but I'm drawing a blank. The case has been taking most of my focus with what was going on with Lorenzo, so most of my time was either spent at work or with Wyatt. There was that one time my sister made a surprise appearance because Mom and Dad had been worried, and they thought sending my sister would be better than arriving themselves. That's when it hits me and I burst out laughing, my entire body shaking as I try to fight to keep the tears from rolling down my face.

"What's so funny?" Marco asks, and there is an edge of annoyance in his voice.

I hold my breath, trying to compose myself. "Sorry," I manage to get out between more fits of giggles, and eventually my laughter dies down.

"Now that you've decided to stop laughing, can you please tell me what the hell was so funny?" Marco says in a flat tone, but I can tell the annoyance is still there.

Shit, I need to get my act together before I blow this completely. "The woman that you saw me with was my sister. She came to check up on me because I'd been so busy with the case and Lorenzo that I'd barely seen my family."

"Your sister," he repeats, not quite believing me.

"Yes, my sister. So, what do you say to the date?" I ask again, finding it's starting to get easier to ask Marco out.

"So, your gay?" he questions.

"No, I'm bisexual." This is the first time I've voiced that out loud, and it feels so good to say it.

"*Really?*" Marco seems to be shocked. "Wyatt and Lorenzo have never mentioned anything."

"That's 'cause they don't know. You're the first person who I've ever told."

Marco goes completely silent at that as he digests what I've just revealed. I know he will have questions, so I sit and wait.

"Oh! In that case, I'd be honored to be the first. But I have to ask, and please don't take this the wrong way, but how do you know you're bisexual?"

I can't blame him for asking; it's a fair question. "I know because I don't just find women attractive. It really doesn't matter what the person looks like or their gender. They're all attractive to me".

"It sounds like you are pansexual more than bisexual to me," Marco says.

"I'm a what?" I find myself asking, never hearing that term before.

"Pansexual," he repeats, and because I must still look confused, he explains further. "It means you're attracted to anyone regardless of their sex or gender identity".

I get so excited hearing this because that describes me to a T. "Oh my god, yes, that's so me. I didn't even know there was a name for it." But once my excitement calms, I realize that this could affect Marco's willingness to go on a date with me. "Will knowing that stop you from going out with me?"

"No. Not at all," he says.

"So, then, does that mean you will?" I ask again but add extra emphasis to 'you will.'

"I really don't know what to say. I wasn't expecting you to ever ask. Before I answer, can I ask a personal question?"

"You can ask me anything if it means that you will go out with me," I respond.

"How many guys have you gone out with?"

Oh, crap. I had a feeling this question would come up at some point, but I didn't think it would be the first thing he'd want to know. But Marco needs to be told the truth, especially after I've seen first-hand with Lorenzo and Wyatt what happens if you start off with lies. He'll probably think it's odd and may not even like it, but I still have to remain honest.

"I've never gone out with a man. In fact, I've never done anything with a man." I sit back in my chair sure he will say something about that revelation.

"Right," is all he responds, looking down at the table while picking at an imaginary spot on the top.

That's it? A one-word response?

It is at this point that the waitress comes over with our order, which I had completely forgotten about. We remain silent as she places the cups in front of us, and the quiet continues while we take the first sips.

"Okay," Marco says.

"Okay?" I have no idea why he's saying okay until it dawns on me that he's answering my question. "Does that okay mean you'll go out with me?".

"Why the hell not? It will probably blow up in my face, but let's do it." Marco says with a quick shrug of his shoulders.

That one sentence makes me want to do a fist pump, I'm so happy. "Awesome. Can you do this weekend? I can text you some details."

"Yeah, I can do this weekend," Marco replies, and this is where we leave the conversation, the rest of the time like all the others when we've gotten together. We talk and laugh, and it's just a good evening. Before I know it, we're ready to leave, wandering out through the shop. I spot the women eyeing Marco, and again, he doesn't notice.

Once we're outside, I turn to Marco for the usual hug goodbye, but he's closer than expected and I almost crash into him. It seems he had planned it as he wraps his hand around the back of my neck and pulls me toward him. Before I know it, his lips are on mine. I freeze for a second, but then I feel his tongue sweep across the seam of my lips, and I gasp. I open for him, and his tongue sweeps into my mouth, and it's the jolt I need to join in the kiss.

His lips are firmer than a woman's, and I can feel his stubble rubbing against my skin. It is the most amazing feeling. Leaning into the kiss to deepen it, I wrap my arms around Marco, pulling him to me so that our chests are touching. Our tongues continue to explore each other's months as if this will be the last kiss we will ever have, and I can feel myself getting hard. Trying to shift position so he doesn't notice, I then feel a bulge rub against my leg and realize that he's just as hard as me, and it feels so good.

All too soon we are drawing apart, panting, but I can still feel him on my lips. I quickly scan up and down the street to make sure no one who knows us has seen before looking back to find that Marco is smiling at me and adjusting himself so his erection isn't so obvious. He pulls me into a hug before stepping back, saying "Bye," and turning to walk away.

Watching as his figure goes down the street, I continue to run my fingers over my lips. That really was the best kiss that I've ever had, and I want to do it again, and soon. Taking one last look at the man who has turned my life on its head, I can't help but smile before making my own way home with a definite spring in my step.

The following morning, I'm still thinking about that kiss. I still find myself running my fingers over my lips, almost like I can somehow touch the kiss, which is completely stupid, but yet I continue, anyway. My head is still in the clouds as I walk into the shop I'm using as the look out to keep an eye on Lorenzo.

"Good morning, Liam." Hearing a voice say my name pulls me from my thoughts, and I look around to see who called, spotting Mrs. Jones, the owner of the shop, in the corner stocking some shelves.

"Sorry, what?" I ask, as I missed what she said.

Chuckling to herself, Mrs. Jones repeats, "I said, 'Good morning,'" while smiling at me.

"Sorry, Mrs. Jones. Good morning. How are you?"

Mrs. Jones is a lovely woman and friendly. She's letting me use one of the rooms upstairs where the window faces the florist's but also gives me an excellent view of the street, too. Most of the day, Mrs. Jones' shop is in the shade, so that makes it a lot harder for me to be spotted. I told her I was a PI who was hired to watch Lorenzo for cheating, and she bought it, but most mornings she's quick to defend Lorenzo as a wonderful boy who wouldn't do anything to hurt a fly—if only she knew.

"I'm good, thank you, Liam. And yourself?" she asks.

"Myself what, Mrs. Jones?" I have to ask because I'm really not paying that much attention to her this morning.

"I'm asking how you are." she states, smiling again like she knows something.

"I'm okay," I reply, not sure whether this is a half-truth.

"You sure? You seem to be off with the fairies today," she says, and the smile that was there only seconds ago vanishes and a hint of concern enters in her eyes.

"Yeah, I'm... Just a few things on my mind today. Is it okay for me to go up?" I ask.

"Yes, of course, but as I keep telling you, I really don't think he would cheat. Not that I have ever seen him with anyone, but still, Lorenzo is a nice boy."

I smile at her. "As you keep telling me, Mrs. Jones."

Making my way to the back of the shop, I go up a flight of stairs and walk down a hallway to the front of the building. Mrs. Jones provided me with a kitchen chair that I placed to the side of the window so I can look out and scan the road. Normally, I always try to make sure I get to my position early and wait for Lorenzo to arrive. Thirty minutes later, I see a car pull up outside Lorenzo's shop, and he gets out and makes his way inside.

Most of the time he gets dropped off, but sometimes when the weather is nice, he walks to the shop. His parents don't live anywhere near this area, so he has to have been somewhere before arriving, and it's those days my worry increases. I'm left wondering where he has been and what he's been up to but also hoping that wherever that is, he's getting information that will be useful for us.

Not long after Lorenzo arrives, I hear my cell beeping, letting me know that I have a text. Even without looking at it, I know who it is and what it says. It is the same message that Wyatt sends me every morning, just three little words—*How is he?* Every morning when I read those words, I want to reply that he's rough and not happy, but I don't. Instead, he gets the same reply in return. *He's okay.*

Now that Lorenzo is in the shop, it's time to leave and make my way to headquarters. When I first started watching him, I would spend all day here, but I soon realized that once he was at the shop, he tended to stay there. So it's to the point where I just stay until he arrives and then come back later in the afternoon shortly before he leaves. I know that I should be watching him more often, but I'm also trusting him to notify us if he's asked to do anything illegal or if he's gotten any information.

Walking into the office, I spy Wyatt sitting on his side of the desk looking at paperwork as I make my way to my side of the desk. Every morning since I've started coming back to the office, I've been telling him he needs to come with me to check on Lorenzo for himself even though I know it would kill him. It bothers me to see that my partner is not in a good place, but I'm starting to think Wyatt needs to see that even though Lorenzo is in a bad place, he's still working on getting the information we need to bring his dad down. Before even noticing what I'm saying, I'm telling Wyatt to suck it up and that he's coming to check on Lorenzo with me tomorrow morning. I give him a look to tell him there is no point in arguing with me, but before I can say anything else, he tells me that the captain wanted to see us.

We both walk over to the captain's office where Wyatt knocks on the door and then we wait. A voice calling out "come in" sounds almost immediately, and the captain tells us to take a seat before I've even closed the door behind me. I shoot an *oh-shit-this-isn't-good* look to Wyatt and see that he has the same expression on his face. The captain only ever asks one to sit if he doesn't have good news, and I was right as he explains to us that he received information regarding a new batch of heroin that has come into the city. It's a much stronger product and much more dangerous than the previous batches.

"Do you think it is linked to Alfredo and the drugs he brings in?" I have to ask because I would have hoped that Lorenzo would have told us of something like that.

The captain goes on to say that the batch the forensics team tested contained some of the same identification markers as Alfredo's product but also came back with new ones, but that can happen if they're trying to mask the origin of the drug. I hear Wyatt ask if the captain believes Alfredo is aware of our investigation and added the additional ingredients to throw us off his trail.

"Shit, this isn't good," I state. I hadn't realized I'd said that out loud until I hear the captain asking if there is any way for us to contact our source to get things moving faster. Surely the captain doesn't think Lorenzo knew about this and didn't say anything. Unfortunately, those very words fall from my mouth before I am able to stop them. "Do you think our source knew about this shipment and didn't tell us?"

The moment the words have left my mouth, I want to kick myself, especially with the look that Wyatt gives me. I struggle not to slap my hand over the captain's mouth when he says that he isn't sure, considering no useful information has been supplied since the source's return.

Wyatt promises the captain that we'll get in contact with our source, and that seems to satisfy the captain since he dismisses us. We make our way back to our desks, but I can see that Wyatt's head isn't in the right place and that the captain has planted some seeds of doubt about Lorenzo. I need to get him out of the office so he can talk freely.

Once we're in his car, I ask where he wants to go and am happy when he says his place. Both of us remain silent during the car ride; I'm thinking about what the captain said and the implications of it, and I can't imagine Wyatt is thinking any different. When we are finally inside Wyatt's apartment, he makes a beeline for the kitchen, and I'm really hoping he is getting us some beers. It may be the afternoon, but I think we could use them. Thankfully, my wish was granted as I see Wyatt walking back in with two beers.

With my beer in my hand, I twist off the cap and take a long swig and watch as Wyatt does the same. When he asks if I thought Lorenzo knew about the shipment, I realize this is why he has been so quiet. But what surprises me more is when he says he thinks Lorenzo never planned to give us information when he went back. That he saw his dad inviting him back as a chance to return to that life, and how he'd even given Lorenzo back his gun, the one piece of evidence we'd had.

I don't think I have *ever* been so angry at Wyatt for thinking that, but he hasn't observed Lorenzo every day and seen the struggle he is going through, all because he hasn't had the balls to check on him. So I set him straight, and even after ripping into him, he *still* asks how I can be so sure. Looking him dead in the eye, I begin to give him the reasons, but then state that the main one is because Lorenzo loves him with every fiber of his being.

Something I say must have hit home since he stays quiet for a while before finally admitting that I'm right. He's just getting frustrated. His faith in Lorenzo might have been rocked, but mine hasn't, and I reaffirm that tomorrow morning I will collect him at eight so we can go and check on Lorenzo together. Hopefully when he sees how rough Lorenzo is, it will prove how much he is struggling, too, and, keeping my fingers crossed, restore Wyatt's faith in Lorenzo.

Wyatt opens his mouth to speak when we are surprised to hear a knock at the front door. I watch as Wyatt makes his way down the hall door, and I'm already listening intently in case there is trouble. Lorenzo and Wyatt live in a secure building, so you can only get in by either a key or being let in by one of the residents, and considering no one has buzzed Wyatt's apartment, I'm on edge. I'm still not sure who it is until I hear the slightly frantic voice of Wyatt asking if everything is okay and if something has happened. There is only one person he would ask that question to, and that would be Marco.

Chapter 7 — Marco

Lorenzo made me promise to go and see Wyatt after I'd finished school for the day, and considering how miserable he'd been looking when he'd asked, it was easy for me to agree. When I turned onto their street, I was surprised to see Wyatt's car parked on the side of the road, showing that he was home. At least that means I don't have to wander around the streets waiting for him to get home.

Making my way to the front of the building and the security door, I'm about to press the buzzer but hesitate at the last second. If I can get into the building without him knowing, the look on his face would be priceless. I scan the numbers on the pad, hoping that they might have a name, but I'm out of luck, so I just push the buzzer for the one furthest away from their apartment and hope to god that because of the hours he works he isn't friendly with anyone. When an older voice comes through the speaker just saying hello, I keep my fingers crossed.

"Hi. It's Wyatt from 2B. I forgot the security key. Any chance you can buzz me in?" I'm making out that I know her and can't believe when there is a buzzing from the door, letting me know it's open. Some people are too trusting—of course she may have met Wyatt at some point and thought it was genuine, but still, it worked, and I am in the building's lobby making my way to the elevators.

It had been worth the risk if the look on Wyatt's face is anything to go by. When he closes the door and asks if everything is okay or if something has happened, I can't resist trying to wind him up a little. "What, no 'Hello, how are you? Good to see you?'" I have to stop myself from laughing out loud, especially as he repeats back my greeting but adds the word 'dick' at the end.

As I walk into the living area, I spot Liam sitting on the couch, and from the way I can see the laughter behind his eyes, I know he just heard the whole interaction between me and Wyatt. I had been hoping that Liam would be here so I could see him again even though we have plans for Saturday night. The kiss we shared yesterday has never been far from my thoughts, and, considering he'd never kissed a man before, it had been amazing. He had been a little stunned when I first kissed him, which wasn't that surprising, but he soon got into it. When I felt his dick getting hard against me, I knew he was enjoying it just as much as me. It was taking all of my restraint not to go over to him, pick him up off the couch, and redo that kiss.

It's only when Wyatt asks me how the hell I got into the building that I remember where I am and why I came over, so I start to explain. Wanting to see if I could surprise him yet again, I tell Wyatt that I pretended to be him in order to get into the building and that I have an update from Lorenzo who is getting worried that Wyatt might be starting to doubt him. Thankfully, he doesn't ask me any questions but heads towards the kitchen while stating he is getting another beer for himself and Liam and offers to get one for me, too.

Going over to Liam, I deliberately sit next to him and lean over toward his ear. "I didn't know you would be here, but I'm glad you are. I've been thinking about last night's kiss all day."

"You have? Why?" Liam whispers back.

"That kiss…" But I'm suddenly filled with doubt. If he hasn't been thinking about the kiss, then maybe he didn't enjoy it as much as I thought. Was he getting hard as an automatic reaction to being kissed?

"You enjoyed it?" he asks with what seems like surprise in his voice.

"It was amazing. I had to stop myself from pulling you back into my arms to do it again the moment I walked in."

But before he has a chance to respond, Wyatt returns with three bottles in his hands and we both shut our mouths. I'm sure he catches something if the look he gives Liam is anything to go by, but I think he has already forgotten by the time he's handed us our drinks and retaken his seat on the other end of the couch, immediately asking me how Lorenzo is. I tell him that my brother is fine but becoming very frustrated because dad was being a complete dick until Lorenzo agreed to go out on some dates, but then quickly add that the person he is going out with knows Lorenzo is gay, but so is she, and they agreed to it to get their families off their backs. Lorenzo wanted me to tell Wyatt this in case someone spotted them together and got the wrong idea.

Wyatt appears to relax after I've explained everything, and when he asks me to join him and Liam for food, I hesitate for a second only because this would be the first time that I have spent any time with Wyatt. But it would be nice to get to know him more, and so I agree. We spend the next few hours together, sharing food and beers, and it's only after me and Liam have said our goodnights to Wyatt and are in the elevator that I come to the realization that I don't want it to end.

"You interested in going for a drink?" I ask Liam.

"Sure. Would you want to come back to my place?" he answers, taking me by surprise.

Hell yes is what I want to say back to him but instead, I just respond, "You sure?" Alone time at his place where I could possibly get to kiss him again without the risk of being spotted sounds perfect—I really shouldn't have kissed him outside the shop. I got carried away...

"Yeah, of course. My place isn't far, and my beer is free," he answers back as he chuckles.

"In that case, lead the way." The smile he gives me is *so* worth the yes.

Liam lives a lot closer than I was expecting, on East Sixth Street, and it only takes us about twenty minutes to get there. From the outside, the building looks similar to Wyatt and Lorenzo's, all red brick with the metal fire escape zigzagging across the front. He tells me it was a pre-World War Two building and he fell in love with it the moment he saw it.

His apartment is on the third floor, and when he opens the front door, we're greeted by a hallway that leads to a spacious, high-ceilinged, open-concept space that is both the living room and kitchen with solid hard-wood floors. He's broken up the room by placing a couch across the middle so that each area is defined. On our side of the couch there is a large gray rug that covers most of the floor with a solid wooden coffee table in the middle and a large flat-screen tv hanging on the middle of the wall facing the couch. On the kitchen side, he just has a kitchen table with a large bowl in the middle, and to the side is an entry way that must lead to a bedroom and bathroom.

After toeing off his shoes, Liam goes over to the kitchen table and places his keys in the large bowl, takes off his coat, and hangs it on the back of one of the chairs. I manage to hold the gasp from escaping my lips as his holster and gun become visible. Sometimes, I forget that Wyatt and Liam have to carry because of the work they do.

"Go take a seat. I'm just going to put this away," he says, pointing to his gun. "Then I'll grab us some beers." With that, he turns to walk through the doorway and disappears.

Making my way over to the couch after leaving my own shoes by the front door, I drop onto the cushion, slip my shoes off, placing them by the side of the couch, and make myself comfortable in the corner. A few minutes later, I hear Liam come back into the room and turn to watch as he goes over to the fridge and grabs us the beers, seeing that he has changed into some grey sweatpants and a faded black t-shirt.

"Hope it's okay that I got changed. I needed to get out of my work clothes," he says while he walks over to me.

"It's fine," I tell him as I take the beer he's handing me.

He sits in the middle of the couch but angles himself so he is looking at me. "Is what you said earlier about the kiss true?" There is the smallest edge of doubt in his voice.

"Yep," I reply honestly, and I see that it shocks him. "You think I was lying?"

"I thought you were just being nice."

"Nothing to gain from just being nice. There would have been no point in lying. Probably wouldn't have said that you were shit, either—if it had been—but that it needed work. But for your first time kissing a man, it was amazing." The blush that tints his cheeks is so friggin' adorable.

"I have to say that it was the best kiss that I've ever had." He looks sheepish as he says, "And I'd like to do it again."

And that is the only invitation I need. Placing my beer on the coffee table, noticing that there is a coaster in each corner that causes me to smirk, I then grab his beer and place it in the opposite corner to mine, closing the small distance between us so I'm closer to him.

"Go ahead," I say when I am seated next to him, looking directly into his eyes and watching as his pupils dilate ever so slightly. He leans forward as his breathing increases even though we haven't even kissed yet, but he seems to hesitate. I have to wonder if he's concerned that it won't be as good the second time. To stop him from over thinking, I close the remaining distance and plant my lips on his, and the moment they touch, he takes over, any hesitation forgotten. He licks the seam of my lips exactly like I'd done to him, and I can taste the beer we had been drinking only moments before. He slips his tongue in and starts a duel with mine. As Liam explores every inch of my mouth, there's still the hint of uncertainty, so I lean into him, pushing him flat on the couch and straddling his legs.

His breath hitches as our chests touch. His pecs feel firm against my own, and before I even realize I am doing it, my hands are running all over him. It's only when he gasps that I remember that he's probably never had a man do this to him before. Breaking the kiss, I lean back for a moment.

"This okay?" I ask, making sure he's happy and not uncomfortable with what we are doing.

All I can see is the briefest of nods before he's leaning forward to take my mouth again as though he missed my lips in the few seconds we were apart. I oblige him and bring my lips to his. He wraps his arms around me, pulling me back down. Repositioning myself so I am lying flat over him, I can feel his rock-hard dick against me and have to forcibly stop myself from grinding mine against it.

I can't seem to move even though I know I need to stop this before it goes too far, but having his body under me is something that I've been fantasizing about for weeks. Eventually, I find the willpower to pull back and start to get off him. Suddenly, his arms tighten around me, pulling me back to him, and I can hear the faintest "please" fall from his lips.

"If I don't stop now, then I won't be able to," I state, looking him in the eye so he understands what I'm implying as I try to move again.

"Then don't stop," he whispers back.

My head snaps up to look at him, wondering if he realizes what he has just agreed to. But from the look on his face, he is being completely serious.

"Are you sure?" In response, all he does is nod his head.

Holding his gaze, I say, "You can stop anytime, okay?" I need him to know that if this gets to be too much, he can put an end to it. But desire is radiating from him, and in this moment I know he wants this, too. That's all the encouragement I need.

Leaning back, I pull his t-shirt up, getting the first look at his naked chest, and my dreams didn't do him justice. He is all sculpted abs that lead to firm pecs. His nipples are pebbled and pink, demanding to be pinched and licked. Quickly pulling his t-shirt all the way off and throwing it on the floor, I shift back to straddle him, staring at the beauty beneath me and wondering if it's too soon to take my shirt off, as well, or if he is even ready for that. But he answers that question for me. While I've been over thinking, he's managed to unbutton my shirt, and I only realize he's done this when I feel a rough hand run over the plane of my chest.

I smile down at him as I say to tease him, "Something you want to see?", and then his hand suddenly drops down. A blush touches his cheeks like a kid who's been caught stealing from the cookie jar, and he just nods his head. I decide to continue the fun, reaching for the top button of my shirt and doing it back up, watching as his face falls. "If you want to see, I need words." Again he only nods while licking his lips, so I button-up another button. His hand grabs mine with some force to stop me from doing up any more.

"No," I hear as he pulls my hand away. "Want to see you." He undoes the buttons again and slips his hands under the shirt, this time onto my shoulders, and rests them there. Playing his game, I just nod, and the smile that spreads across his face is breath-taking as he realizes what I am doing. He moves his hands to push my shirt off my shoulders, slowly exposing more of my body.

When my shirt is completely off, it joins his on the floor. I could feel the movement of his hard dick jerking next to mine through our pants, but I don't think he realizes it. He's too busy looking over every inch of my naked chest, but still not touching. He dropped his now clenched fists to his sides the moment my shirt came off like the instant my chest became fully naked, he was scared to touch it. Reaching down, I pick up his hand and place a kiss to each of the closed knuckles.

"Open your hand," I say and am thankful he does so without too much prompting.

I place his hand back on my shoulder, but instead of letting it go, I pull it down over my body, running it over my pecs and stomach. I am not as well defined as he is, but I'm still in good shape, and from the way his dick keeps twitching, he likes what he sees, too. Once I let go of his hand, I think for a second he'll drop it but instead slowly brings up his other hand and uses them to explore every inch of me, causing a moan to slip from my mouth.

Suddenly he stops his explorations, and I can feel him trying to shift, so I move off him and sit back at the end of the couch. Well, I did tell him that he could stop at any time. But instead of ending the fun we were having, he gets up from the couch and stands in front of me. His sweatpants are tenting, and I notice there is the smallest damp patch on the front as he reaches out a hand to me.

"Come with me," he says.

I reach up, letting him take my hand, and he pulls me up from the couch and starts walking us in the direction of the hallway and his bedroom, prompting me to ask, "Where are we going?"

He turns to me like I just asked the stupidest question in the world. "Well, I was thinking about the bedroom. Don't want my first time to be on the couch."

"First time!" I repeat, confused. Surely he's had sex before. There is no way that he's a virgin.

"With a man," comes his reply as he leans in, smiling at my confusion before giving me a quick kiss and tugging my arm.

Stumbling forward, I let him drag me towards his room. As we walk down the hallway, I spot two doors. Liam stops outside the one to our left, and with a nod of his head toward the door opposite, he simply says, "Bathroom."

When imagining his bedroom, I expected it would have the stereotypical masculine appearance—lots of greys and blacks with hard edges—but I'm surprised when I walk in and come face to face with walls of deep purple and a large window right in front of me. An enormous bed dominates the center of the room, made up of gray sheets and a couple of odd purple pillows and I realize that at least three men could sleep in it comfortably.

Glancing around, I take in some bedside tables whose color matches the sheets, and a dark, wooden chest of drawers against one wall, but it seems odd that there isn't a wardrobe. It's only as I feel my arm being pulled that I realize I must have stopped while taking in the room, so I start moving forward again. We walk to the foot of the bed and stop, both of us staring at one another. I know it's because he's wondering who will go where, but I need to feel him inside of me. Pushing him so he takes a step back, I move in front him, turning to face him. Slowly sitting on the edge of the bed, I open my legs and pull him to me, placing a kiss just above the waistband of his sweatpants, all the while never breaking eye contact. His eyes look almost black with desire, and he's now breathing harder. Taking a deep breath,

I grab his sweatpants, pulling them down, and *holy fuck*, he's wearing a jockstrap that is just barely containing his straining dick.

"Holy *fuck*! You're wearing a jock." And because I can't resist, I reach out and spin him around so I can get a look at his ass, and bloody hell what an ass it is. Round and firm and glorious, and my dick jerks with the thought of how amazing it would be sliding in and out of those checks, but that is for another time, not tonight.

"I thought you might like it," he says, and even from behind I can feel his blush.

"I do. Very much," I respond before I kiss his ass and then spin him back around to face me. "But I want to taste what's hidden inside your jock. Can I?"

"Oh god, yes," comes a very breathy reply, and he goes to push them off.

"Please, let me," I say as I move his hands away and run my hand up his thigh, watching as the goosebumps rise up on the skin. I want to rub my hand all over the front of his jock, but I'm desperate to get my taste. Once I reach the waistband, I pull the jock down, watching as it takes his dick with it only for it to ping back up, bobbing in front of me, and my mouth waters. I've seen a few dicks in my time, but they pale into insignificance at the sight in front of me. Liam's is both long and thick, and there is not an ounce of hair. It's beautiful.

Wrapping my hand around his thickness, I feel silky smooth skin, and when I pump it a few times, I hear a groan, and Liam pushes his cock forward in my grasp. Leaning in, I stick my nose in the crease of his groin and inhale deeply. He smells like a spicy wood, and it's so intoxicating, I take another sniff. *Heavenly.*

Turning my head, I lick the base of his dick before running my tongue up his shaft, circling it around his head and picking up a drop of precum that has appeared, feeling the bitterness burst against my taste buds. Swirling my tongue around the head for a few seconds, I feel another drop of pre-cum on my tongue, and it's then that I take his heavy cock into my mouth. I have to shift my angle to swallow him to the hilt before I start sliding back up. I do this a few more times till he gets used to me. Not for one second do I think that this is the first blow job that he's ever had, but I'm guessing that it will feel different getting one from a man. So, I want to make it good. As I speed up my pace, his moans increase, and when I reach his tip, flicking my tongue over his slit, he grabs my head, and I feel his fingers digging into my scalp.

"S-s-stop," I hear him stutter.

Letting his dick fall from my mouth, I look up at him. "You okay?"

"Yeah. But if you carried on, I would've come."

"I wouldn't have minded," I tell him honestly.

But by the look that he is giving me, I don't think he wants to come down my throat but maybe is thinking somewhere else. But is he really ready for that? Is he just going along with what I want? Maybe this is going too fast for him?

"Yeah, but I want more."

And even though we discussed this when we were on the couch, I still ask, "You're sure?" He could have changed his mind, especially after having his dick in my mouth.

"One hundred percent. I know it might seem fast, but from the moment I met you, I've wanted you." Liam looks away as he continues, appearing to be trying to hide his embarrassment. "I might have looked up some gay porn and imagined you sliding inside me. Wyatt was wincing one day, and I quickly worked out why, but the look on his face as he remembered... I want to experience that; I want to know how it feels, and you're the only man that I have ever wanted to do that with."

Wow is all I can think at hearing this. I've never felt so wanted in my life. Standing up, I cup his face with my hands and kiss him; it's the only thing I can do. I have no words. He steps in closer, pushing me backwards, taking control. He lowers me onto the bed and I lay back, waiting. Looking me up and down, he stops and stares at the bulge in my pants.

"You have way too many clothes on," he says, and he leans over and unbuttons my pants, pulling down the zipper. Raising my hips up, he pulls down my jeans and underwear in one go, then pulls my socks off so I'm lying naked on his bed, and he licks his lips when spots my hard dick lying against my stomach dripping precum. I scoot up the bed until I feel the pillows at the back of my head. Liam is still just watching me, not doing anything, and when I look at his eyes, I thought there might have been nerves but am surprised when all I see is lust and desire. He looks like he wants to eat me alive.

Kneeling at the base of the bed, he plants a kiss on my ankle and then travels up my body placing kisses on my knee, the middle of my thigh, then surprises me by kissing my balls before his tongue travels up my dick. I gasp at the sensation, and just when I think he'll continue his journey north, he slips my dick into his mouth—without an ounce of hesitation—and it feels amazing. He pumps my shaft a few times, and I have to physically stop myself pushing the head of my dick further into his mouth, but before long, he's letting go and my cock falls from his lips. I thought he would then continue his kissing up my torso, but he is full of surprises this evening and instead licks up my stomach all the way to my pecs before nipping one of my nipples with his teeth, making me yelp. Yes, I was actually fucking *yelping*.

"Thought this was your first time with a man." I hadn't realized I'd said it out loud until he answers.

"It is. This is what I like, and so thought you might, too."

"Noted," I tell him with a sly smile, but my words dry up as he moves to the other nipple and nips that one, as well.

But for the first time since we started, he pauses, and I see the first hint of hesitation.

"What do I do now?" he asks, seeming a little embarrassed. It's so adorable.

"Do you have lube? That's the most important thing."

Leaning over to one of the bedside tables, he opens a drawer and pulls out a bottle—and by the looks of it, its brand new—and a condom. Looks as if he were thinking ahead.

"Now you have to get me ready." I look down at how thick his dick is as I finish speaking, and I know that even with prep, I'm going to be feeling him tomorrow. Hopefully I won't have to explain *how* the prep is done. He said he'd watched some porn, so he should have some idea.

Liam opens the bottle and squeezes some lube into his hand and works some over his fingers, then pushes my legs open and positions his body in between them. He reaches up to kiss me, but at the same time, he grabs my cock with a lubed-up hand and strokes. With his other hand, he runs a finger down my balls and over my taint before circling my hole. Slowly he slips in a finger and my *god* does it feel good.

"Yes!" I rasp out.

He starts to ease his finger in and out of me, and I feel his confidence increase with every moan and gasp he gets out of me, and soon enough, he's adding a second finger, and then a third, stretching me out. He crooks a finger and hits my prostate, and I almost fly off the bed.

"*Oh God!*" I scream and grab the bedsheets at the same time. I'm amazed that I haven't creamed the bed, it feels so good.

Liam pulls his fingers from my hole, leaving me empty and wanting as he shifts so he is now kneeling in front of me and grabbing for the condom, tearing it open, and sliding the latex down his shaft before rubbing lube over his cock. Reaching behind me, I grab one of the pillows and gently throw it at him and lift my hips.

"Place it under me. It gives you a better angle," I explain.

Once the pillow is in place, I bend my legs so that my feet are flat on the bed. He places his hand on my knees, pushing my legs up further, and then I feel his tip at my hole right before he pushes in, taking his time. There is the slight burn as his dick stretches me, but I know that the pleasure will soon follow, and it already feels amazing.

"Holy shit, you feel amazing around my cock. You're so tight," he says, and when I look up, his head is back and eyes are closed, but pleasure is written all over his face, and a sudden wave of relief washes over me. I hadn't even been aware that I'd been concerned he wouldn't have enjoyed this.

When he's fully inside me, he stops, not moving or doing anything, and I'm just about to ask if he's okay when I feel a slight movement as he begins to slowly pull back before sliding back in, and I find myself biting my tongue not to say move faster, remembering that I need to go at his pace. He continues to move in and out slowly a few more times before increasing his pace and going a little harder. All too soon, I find myself moaning with every slide in. Grabbing my dick, I start pumping myself in time to his rhythm, but he bats my hand away and takes over.

He shifts on the bed as he's sliding out and the angle changes. The next thing I know, he's slamming into my hole and pegging my prostate. I scream "yes," and he keeps doing it, causing me to feel the telltale tingle in my balls that my orgasm isn't far off. Slamming into me one last time, I'm coming all over his hand, screaming his name and clenching my hole, which is enough to push him over, and I feel him coming, filling the condom. He leans back, the satisfied smile of a cat that got the cream on his face. Letting go of my dick, he brings his fingers to his mouth, licking off my cum, and he just giggles when he sees the shocked look on my face.

"Mmm, you taste good," he says to me.

"Holy shit," is the only reply that I can give him.

He carefully pulls out of me, making sure to hold on to the condom before removing it, tying it off, and dropping it to the floor before collapsing on top of me. Instantly, I wrap my hands around him, pulling him closer.

"Did I hurt you?" he asks.

"Nope. That was amazing," I tell him honestly because it really had been the best sex of my life, and it was with someone who had never been with a man before. What he is going to be like when he has more experience I can't wait to find out.

"Honestly, I wasn't too sure on the position, but I really wanted to see your face."

Pulling him in tighter to me, I say, "Promise. Taking me from behind might have been easier for your first time, but I loved watching you."

I feel him sigh, and if I'm not mistaken, snuggle into me slightly, and I suddenly really hope that he'll ask me to stay the night. It would mean having to get up extra early to get home and be ready for school, but it will be so worth it.

"Could you let me up... bathroom?" I hear him ask, and I instantly release my arms. "But don't move."

"Don't think I could if I wanted to," I reply but smile as I say it.

While he's in the bathroom, I look around the room again and finally spot a double wardrobe that I was wondering about earlier. No wonder I didn't spot it, considering it's almost behind the door. It's made of the same wood as the chest of drawers and makes the room even more inviting. I snuggle into the pillows, now happy and content.

A few minutes later, I feel a damp cloth being wiped over me. I hadn't heard Liam enter back into the room as I must have dozed off for a second, and I am not sure what I should do next. He hasn't mentioned me staying but also has said nothing about me going, either.

"Will you stay?" he asks, and I am beginning to think Liam can read minds.

"Thought you would never ask," I reply happily.

"In that case, you're going to have to move. Need to get under the covers."

All I do is lift myself up enough so he can just about pull the covers out from under me. Taking the opportunity to grab the pillow that had been under my hips, he puts the pillow under his head and pulls the covers up over us. We both just lie there side by side, me not saying anything, which is ridiculous considering what we've just done. Stretching out my arm, I say, "come here." He shuffles into my side so he's resting his head on my shoulder and throws his arm across my stomach. This just feels so right like he was meant to be there, and in that moment, I realize that this man is extremely dangerous for my heart.

"I have to be up early in the morning," Liam says in a very sleepy voice.

"Me too," I reply, but pull him closer to me.

"Okay. Goodnight," he answers, and just like that, he's asleep. Leaning over, I kiss his forehead and whisper, "Goodnight" before sleep takes me, too.

Chapter 8 — Liam

Waking up before my alarm, I feel too warm and for a second have no idea why. As my brain comes out of the sleep fog, I can feel a very warm body wrapped around me, and the images from last night come flooding back. *Holy fuck*, I had sex with Marco, and it had been amazing. He's spooning me at the moment, and I can feel his hard dick resting against the crack of my ass and can't help but wiggle it and hear a giggle. Turning around in his arms, I am greeted with a smiling face and sleep tousled hair. He looks gorgeous.

"Good morning," he says and leans in for a kiss.

Snapping my lips closed, I shake my head and mumble, "Morning breath."

"Don't care," comes his reply, and he kisses me, during which I feel his dick twitch, and all the blood in my brain rushes south. "I would love to stay here all day," he states while rubbing his dick against mine, "but I have to get going. School. Sorry".

"Me too," I respond, and even I can hear the hint of sadness lacing through my voice.

"What, you have school, too. How. Old. Are. You?"

"Was that *supposed* to be funny… coz it's not." I try and keep a serious face as I watch Marco smirk. "I have to meet with Wyatt. Case stuff." I was wondering if I should have told him we've been checking on Lorenzo, but then thought better of it. I'm sure he wouldn't deliberately tell him, but sometimes things do slip out.

"Please tell me you have a shower with room for two?" he asks, nodding his head in the bathroom's direction.

"I have no idea. Never shared a shower with anyone." My shower is huge with more than enough room for two, but I'm not going to tell him. I'll let it be a nice surprise.

"Really! Let's go have a look."

He slides over to the opposite side of the mattress and gets up, walking around to the foot of the bed and just stands there completely naked, holding his arm out to me in invitation and not making any attempt to get his clothes. All I can do is stare at his cock. It's thick and hard and pointing right at me, almost demanding to be taken. I loved the feeling of the weight of it in my mouth last night, and I wonder how long it would take me to get him to shoot his load down my throat.

"Ahem. Liam. My eyes are up here."

My head snaps up to see him laughing at me. "Sorry," I mumble, and I can feel the warmth travelling up my neck and over my cheeks.

"It's okay. Was kinda nice. You looked like you wanted to devour me."

"I did," I reply, pausing before I then ask, "Do we have time?"

"Unfortunately, I only have time for one or the other. Even though I would love to smell you on me all day, that may not be the best when I have to go to school." And he wiggles his fingers in the come here gesture again.

"That's too bad," I say as I get out of bed and link my hand with his.

"Maybe next time, though."

"Next time…" I repeat, and I stumble over the words as I say them.

"Well, I hope there would be a next time. Do you not want to?" I spot a flash of disappointment go across his face before he could school his feelings.

"Of course I want to do it again. Just wasn't a hundred percent sure *you* would." The sex had been mind blowing for me, but I wasn't sure what he thought.

He tugs me towards him and drops my hand only to cup my face, placing the softest of kisses on my lips before saying, "Last night was amazing, and I can't wait till we do it again. Okay?"

All I can do is nod my head since I'm at a total loss for words. He retakes my hand and leads me to the bathroom.

―

Dead on eight, I'm pushing the button for Wyatt's apartment and waiting for the buzzing sound to let me know that the door is open. I'm not surprised when it happens without his voice coming over the intercom, so I make my way inside, riding up in the elevator to his floor while all I can think about is Marco. We'd ended up wanking each off in the shower before washing each other, and I loved that he did, in fact, leave my place smelling like me—even if it was just him smelling like my shower gel.

There's a huge fucking grin on my face, and I hope Wyatt doesn't make a big deal out of it, but of course, he doesn't miss a trick and just has to mention it. He stands there and says I look like the cat that got the cream, and even as he says it, I can feel myself blush, so I kinda tell him a half-truth that I did have a good morning when really I'd had a wonderful night, too.

We decide to walk to Mrs. Jones' shop because it's what I would normally do. It also lowers the risk of Lorenzo spotting Wyatt's car. As we turn onto the street, Wyatt asks where I normally watch him from, and I point to the shop opposite Lorenzo's, explaining that the woman who runs the store thinks I am a PI investigating Lorenzo for cheating. Wyatt shoots me a look at this, and I want to say "What? I had to think of something," but instead just remain silent.

Walking into the shop, I call my customary greeting over to Mrs. Jones and, thinking fast on my feet as to why Wyatt would be there, tell her that he's a newbie, hoping that will be enough for her. I then have to stop myself from bursting out laughing when she goes on to defend Lorenzo—*again*—only this time to Wyatt.

We make our way upstairs and position ourselves by the window, and as I'm looking down toward the other end of the street, I hear Wyatt almost shout at me, "I thought you said he was okay," and realize Wyatt has spotted Lorenzo right before he bolts from the room. I try to grab him in order to stop him, but he's just too fast.

Turning back to the window, I spot him walking across the road to Lorenzo's shop, thankful that he's not running and possibly drawing attention to himself, but I do catch a movement out of the corner of my eye. When I look, I can't see anything and think it must have been a bird or something and go back to observing the shop. From this angle, I can't see Wyatt. Shit, that means I'm going to have to go over and drag him out somehow. I'm just praying that he's acting like a customer. We've spent too long on this case to lose it now.

I make my way over to Lorenzo's shop window, peering around the corner so I can see Lorenzo, also observing that Wyatt is trying to act indifferent, but there is nothing but happiness in his eyes. I know I won't be going in and dragging him out. Instead, I retrace my steps to watch from the window back at Mrs. Jones's store. A few minutes later, Wyatt leaves Lorenzo's shop holding a bunch of flowers, and if anybody else was looking, they would have thought he was just a normal customer. But I've known Wyatt for a long time, and I can tell just by the look on his face he's up to something.

Rushing out from my position, I glance up the street hoping to spot Wyatt so I can talk him out of whatever he has planned, but he's vanished. Normally I would have walked up the street to see if I could spot him, but I can't risk Lorenzo seeing me, too. Wyatt going in there was bad enough; knowing that I have been here, too, might cause Lorenzo to do something reckless and put himself in even more danger. After a moment's hesitation, I decide it's probably best to make my way to headquarters and wait for Wyatt to contact me, hoping that it's not too long.

The moment my butt hits my chair, the captain is walking over to me. *Oh shit.*

"Morning, Detective. Where's Detective Johnson?"

"Morning, sir. He's checking up with the source and then chasing up a lead." It's about as close to the truth that I can give at the moment. "I have a feeling that he may be out for the rest of the day."

"How come you're not with him?"

Shit, I hadn't thought of that when trying to think on my feet. "Detective Johnson thought it might look suspicious, the two of us turning up. We don't want to break the source's cover."

For some reason, the captain seems to believe this. "Good, good. We *must* remember that the source has put himself in great danger and keeping him safe is a priority."

"Yes, sir," I reply, trying not to show my sigh of relief.

"Keep me updated on any developments."

"Yes, sir," I reply, and it's only when he's walking away from me and his back is turned that I finally let go of my breath.

Looking at my watch, I see that it's still only mid-morning. So much has happened that it feels much later, and it's got me thinking… I wonder what

Marco is doing right now? Is he thinking of me or is he so engrossed in teaching a class that he hasn't had a chance?

Picking up my cell, I decide to send him a text.

Liam: Thank you for a wonderful morning.

I'm surprised when the reply is almost immediate.

Marco: You're welcome. I enjoyed myself, too.

When my cell beeps a few minutes later, I'm again shocked to see that it's *another* text from Marco.

Marco: Can't wait to see you again.

As I read his words, I can feel the smile on my face, and it gets me thinking about what he said this morning about staying in bed all day, and suddenly I have an idea for our date and quickly reply before I get a chance to change my mind.

Liam: You still up for our date, coz I was thinking you could come over for food and maybe bring an overnight bag.

I'm spending way too long looking at my cell waiting for a reply. Will he think I'm being way too forward? Just as I am about to give up, my cell finally beeps.

Marco: Think we're way past dating lol. But I would love to do that.

Laughter bubbles up out of me at his reply, resulting in a few strange looks from the other detectives because he is right, of course. In all honesty, it's kinda felt like we have been dating over the last few weeks without either one of us realizing that was happening. Needing to text him back to confirm a time but having no idea what to say, I start typing four or five openings. *Okay* seems so indifferent, *Cool* just sounds lame. In the end, I just send a basic message.,

Liam: Great. My place at 7. Looking forward to it.

Putting my cell down and pulling the file on my desk toward me, I try to get on with some work. When it beeps a little while later, I think it may be a text from Wyatt to explain what the hell is going on, but my heart rate increases when I see it's Marco.

Marco: Me too.

Two words have never looked so good to me, and they leave me with a wide grin on my face for the rest of the afternoon until I finally receive a text from Wyatt saying that there has been a family emergency and he won't be in for the rest of the day. I'm tempted to text him back and say that I had thought he wouldn't be back and cleared it with the captain but decide against it.

The following morning, the first thing I do the moment I'm awake is check my cell to see if I have any messages from Wyatt. When I see there is nothing, I start to get worried. Just as I'm wondering if I should send him a message, my cell beeps. Lo and behold, it's Wyatt.

Wyatt: Can you get to my place? Need to talk.

Oh, shit, that's not good. I *really* hope that he hasn't done something stupid and jeopardized the case. He might not fully realize it, but it's not only Lorenzo we have to protect.

Liam: Was just about to text. Yeah, I can get to your place. Give me thirty.

I can make it to Wyatt's a lot quicker than that, but I'm guessing that Lorenzo is involved somehow and think Marco should be there, too. It will take him that long to get there if he can get out of school, so I shoot him a quick text.

Liam: Do you think you can get to Wyatt's? Something's going on and I think it involves Lorenzo.

Lying in bed, I do nothing but wait for his reply and slightly berate myself for feeling excited that I might be seeing him again when I should be more concerned about Wyatt and Lorenzo. Even so, my heart still jumps when I hear my cell beep.

Marco: See you there in half an hour.

Twenty-five minutes later, I'm standing outside Wyatt's apartment waiting for Marco. I wanted to spend a few minutes with him before we went up. When I see him walking down the street a few minutes later, my breath catches. *Wow, he is gorgeous.* He's wearing dark navy pants with what looks like a white shirt and a dark grey cardigan, finished with dark brown loafers.

When he finally reaches me, I almost reach out to kiss him but then catch myself just in time. We are out in the open and have no idea who could be watching. So I just smile and nod my head in greeting. Turning, I push the button for Wyatt's place and wait. Soon enough, the door buzzes and we go inside.

"Wyatt didn't ask who it was," Marco points out as we walk across the lobby.

"He knew it would be me," I explain. "He'll leave the apartment door unlocked, too."

"Do you know what this is about?" he asks while we wait for the elevator.

"Nope." I should tell him he went to see Lorenzo yesterday, but I don't. "How did you get out of school?" is what I ask instead.

"I told them there was a family emergency and needed a day to handle it."

Just then the elevator pings and the doors open, so we walk in. The moment the door closes and it's just us in there, Marco pushes me against the wall and kisses me.

"I've wanted to do that the moment I saw you outside," he says when he breaks the kiss.

Just as I am about to reply, we arrive on Wyatt's floor, but as we get to his door, I pull Marco to me and kiss him back.

"I had to stop myself from kissing you outside, too," I say before quickly giving him another peck. "And that one is because I have no idea when I will be able to do it again today."

Pushing open the door to the apartment, we make our way inside and spot Wyatt coming out of the kitchen. When he raises an eyebrow at me and gives a quick look to Marco, I know he's asking the silent question, "Why the hell Marco is here?" Debating whether or not to lie, I decide the truth is the better option, so I explain that I contacted Marco when I received his text as I guessed that Lorenzo was involved.

Thinking that would be enough for Wyatt, I go to move, but of course, it's not. When I hear him say that he didn't know that me and Marco were in contact with one another, I have no idea what to say. But while I have stood there trying to think, Marco comes to my rescue and says that he got my number in case he couldn't get in touch with Wyatt and it's an emergency—which is absolutely perfect. Wyatt seems to buy it, which is even better, and as he turns back into the kitchen, I give Marco a quick smile in thanks. When Wyatt asks how Marco likes his coffee, I pay close attention since I know how he likes it from the coffee shop, but not when he's home. So I make a mental note when he says that he likes the French vanilla creamer and plan to get some for the weekend.

Wyatt suggests sitting at the kitchen table to talk, and I know that means it's serious. I try to steel myself, but what I'm not expecting is the reaction from Marco when he hears that Wyatt went to see Lorenzo yesterday. He's trying his best to stay calm, but when he talks, you can hear the anger lacing through his voice.

"You let him go talk to Lorenzo? Are you fucking *insane*? What if someone saw them?"

"I didn't have a chance to stop him," I reply to defend myself from Marco's irritation that is now bubbling to the surface. Then, trying to lighten the situation, I add, "He's fast when he wants to be." But Marco's having none of it.

"You should have been faster!" comes his brittle retort.

Oh shit, this isn't good, and I have no idea what to say. How long is he going to be angry with me? Will this be the end of us? And before we've even started... All I want to do is climb onto his lap and wrap my arms around his neck and kiss him till it's okay again.

Instead, I say, "I'd planned to go into the shop and drag him out, but Lorenzo looked so happy at seeing him, so I stood back and let them have five minutes. I kept a lookout but didn't see anyone, so I think we're safe."

Marco looks like he is about to calm down after my little speech, but then Wyatt throws in, "We were seen."

Fuck! Marco becomes furious, and it's a scary as shit sight, especially with the daggers he is currently shooting toward me and Wyatt. When he asks, "By whom?" through gritted teeth, I'm not sure I want to hear in case Marco gets worse, but I'm pleasantly surprised when he actually seems to calm down when Wyatt says, "Frank."

Watching Marco closely, he goes on to explain that Frank is actually a good man and has been looking out for Lorenzo. I'm relieved until we hear Wyatt say that Frank didn't seem like a good guy when they were talking earlier, and now I need to know what's going on. Wyatt's text came through really early, so what the fuck had happened from then to now? When I ask, Wyatt goes on to say that after he spoke with Lorenzo, he booked a hotel room for them. On hearing this, both me and Marco look at him and at the same time say, "You did *what*?"

Wyatt tries to say that he wasn't sure if Lorenzo would turn up, and I'm still annoyed. "So that was the family emergency yesterday afternoon? I should totally kick your ass."

Wyatt says that he wasn't lying and that Lorenzo is family, but he did turn up and they had an amazing evening, but when he woke up this morning, Lorenzo was gone. He pulls out what looks like a crumpled piece of paper and proceeds to flatten it out on the kitchen table, explaining that it is a note that Lorenzo left for him. Marco and I lean over and read the note. Basically, Lorenzo is telling him to stay away and they cannot do that again. Wyatt also says that this is the same thing Frank said when he was cornered by the man earlier in the morning.

After Wyatt is finished, Marco comments that must be why Lorenzo looked so sad this morning, and my instant thought is how he saw his brother this morning. It means Marco must have stayed at his parents' home last night. I don't want Marco anywhere near his dad, but it's not something I can stop. It's only when I hear Wyatt ask what happened that I remember we are there to discuss Lorenzo, and I listen as Marco explains Lorenzo's quick thinking at explaining it away, but Wyatt then says that he wants to get Lorenzo out.

Looking over to Marco, I try to gauge his reaction and can see that getting Lorenzo out isn't going to happen. Wyatt deflates in front of us as I say, "Not going to happen." It breaks my heart to hear him ask, "Why?"

"Because this was Lorenzo's plan, and we have to trust him to know what he is doing." I don't add if he wanted to get out, he would have said so yesterday instead of telling Wyatt to stay away. I don't think Wyatt would want to hear that again, especially when he just heard Lorenzo is unhappy. But Wyatt is adamant there has to be a way to bring Alfredo down without Lorenzo hurting anymore.

I hate that the rest of the conversation causes Wyatt pain, but the initial plan needs to keep going as it is. When I reiterate again that he *has* to stay away from Lorenzo, the pain on Wyatt's face is heart-breaking. Marco spots it, too, and says that he'll try to update us more often.

Suddenly, Marco looks at his watch and says that he has to get going, and I have to stop myself from asking where. After we had finished with Wyatt, I thought he could spend the day with us, and even though we couldn't touch, I was looking forward to just being in his presence. It kinda annoys me, which only gets worse when Wyatt calls after him asking if he has a second. *What the hell?* I give Wyatt a look that clearly states I want to know what is going on, but he just ignores me and goes to talk with Marco.

When Wyatt walks back in a few minutes later, he looks a lot happier than when he went out.

"What the fuck was that about?" I ask as Wyatt sits back at the table.

"Nothing. Just something I needed to ask Marco."

"It's not nothing if it's something to do with the case," I say, trying to reel in my aggravation.

"It's personal. So drop it." By the look on his face, I know that he's not going to say anything more. Reluctantly, I drop it but decide I'll ask Marco later what the hell is going on, that's for sure.

Chapter 9 — Marco

2 Months Later

When I arrived at Wyatt's two months ago, I'd thought I'd end up spending the day there, and I couldn't wait. But that was mainly because I knew that Liam was going to be there, too. After finally kissing him in the elevator, my heart jumped into my throat when he'd said that he had wanted to do that outside. I'd thought I'd seen a slight movement and was glad he'd done nothing. I think we made up for it on the way to the apartment. Then everything changed. The moment I heard that Wyatt had gone to see Lorenzo, to say it pissed me off was an understatement. All I could think about was the danger they had put Lorenzo in, and I knew I had to go and check on Lorenzo myself and decided to make my way to Mom and Dad's and wait for him.

There was no mistaking the look on Liam's face. When I said that I had to get going, he wasn't happy. You could tell he wanted to ask me where I was headed to, but then Wyatt would have wanted to know why Liam was asking such a personal question, so he kept quiet. When Wyatt asked to talk to me privately, the annoyance on Liam's face went up a level. He must have thought it was something to do with the case and that we should have involved him. Little did he know it was because Wyatt wanted to ask my permission to marry Lorenzo. I have no idea why he did it, but I felt so proud that he'd asked me, and I have kept a very close eye on Lorenzo since, determined to make sure he gets back to Wyatt safe and in one piece.

When I'd arrived at my parents, my Mom had been surprised to see me, especially with it being a school day, but because we never lied to them, Mom easily believed me when I said that I had a free day and thought I would come visit her and Dad. It turned out to be a lovely day; I helped Mom get everything ready for dinner, and when Lorenzo finally came home, I saw a resolve in his eyes that hadn't been there before. I knew that he would be returning, but I didn't think even then that two months later he would still be there.

That night, I ended up staying at my parents', which isn't something I'd done in a long time, but I'd hated the look on Mom's face the following morning when I said that I had to get going because I was meeting a friend later that night. Her eyes lit up, and even though I said a friend and never mentioned if they were male or female, she automatically assumed female, and I could hear the wedding bells that started ringing in her mind.

It had been mine and Liam's 'first date,' even though both of us knew it wasn't, and I can't help smiling when I think about it, even now, two months later.

When I got to Liam's, I'd wondered how long it would take for him to ask about what Wyatt had said, and he actually lasted longer than I thought he would. We'd eaten our dinner and moved to the couch to watch a movie. Initially we'd sat at opposite sides, which I wasn't happy about, and when he didn't seem to be moving, I pulled him over to me so he had no option but to swing his legs up onto the cushions and lean into my side.

"So, what did Wyatt say to you yesterday?" he asked, trying to be all nonchalant about it, but I found myself smiling at the question.

"*How long have you been wanting to ask that?*" *I responded, leaning in to kiss his head, which caused him to sigh. I'll need to remember in the future that he likes that.*

"*Oh, from the moment you walked in the door.*"

There was no way to stop myself from laughing when I heard this. Fair play to him. It took some patience, and I wonder if I could tease him for a little bit longer.

"*Nothing of importance,*" *I replied, and he shifted positions so he was straddling my legs. I decided that teasing him had turned out to be a* very *good idea.*

"*It wasn't 'nothing.' Wyatt looked a lot happier when he came back in.*"

"*In that case, maybe you should ask him.*" *I was enjoying myself too much to tell him the truth, especially as he hadn't moved from my lap.*

"*I did, but he wouldn't say,*" *he replied and went to move off my lap, but I quickly grabbed him by the hips, holding him in place. He settled back onto my lap but had this pouty look on his face, and I was lost.*

"*He asked my permission to marry Lorenzo, but swear you won't say anything. I probably shouldn't have told you, but you look too cute when you pout.*"

"*I wasn't pouting,*" *he said with some indignation, but he wasn't making any move to get off my lap this time, so I didn't say anything more but waited for when the rest of my sentence would filter through. And then his eyes widen.* Bingo! "*Did you just say permission to marry Lorenzo?*"

"*Yep.*"

"*Holy shit.*"

"*That's what I thought when he asked, but I kinda love the fact that he did.*" *What I don't mention is the pang of jealousy that I felt. I wanted what Wyatt has with Lorenzo, and if I am being truly honest with myself, I want* it with the man who was currently straddling my legs. *My feelings for him have grown so much in such a short time, and it's frightening.*

"Hey, you okay?" Liam asked, pulling me from my thoughts.

"Sorry, I was just thinking that a cop is going to be my brother-in-law," I lied, not wanting to reveal where my thoughts had really gone. "Dad always told us not to trust them, and one is going to be family."

Something flashed over his face, but before I was able to figure out what, it's gone, and then he kissed me, causing all my thoughts to flee. Before I knew it, we're both grinding our hard dicks against each other.

We never ended up watching that movie. Instead, we'd stumbled to his bedroom where we stayed until late the following morning. If I thought the sex had been amazing the first time around, I had been wrong, so very, *very* wrong. That second time with the extra confidence... Liam had blown my mind. The proud face he wore for the rest of the night after telling him about Wyatt's question had been heart-warming, and it's only gotten better over the last couple months. It's gotten to the point where I'm thinking about asking him to get tested. Seeing if he wants to go bareback. But I haven't had the courage to bring it up. That's not something that simply rolls off the tongue.

When I hear my cell beep and see that it's a text from him, I swear that he can hear my thoughts or knows when I'm thinking about him.

Liam: How's your day going?

Marco: Good, but it's better now. Was just thinking of you.

Liam: Good thoughts, I hope.

Marco: Always good when you're involved.

Liam:

It always makes my day when he sends silly texts, like the kiss emoji. Hell, I love it when he sends me any kind of text message. In fact, I think I love everything about Liam. I really need to talk to someone since I've never felt like this about anyone before and wonder if I can talk to Lorenzo without giving anything away. I decide that maybe I'll go see him after work when I receive another text, and it already has me smiling, thinking that Liam has added to the last text, but I'm surprised to see it's a message from my brother.

Lorenzo: Think tonight is the night. Keep phone close.

For a few seconds, I'm confused about the message. Tonight is the night for what? And then I realize that he means tonight is the night he plans to kill our father. When I thought about this moment, I'd always envisioned myself feeling sad, but it's relief that washes over me. Tomorrow could be the start of a new future for Lorenzo and me if I ever decide to come out the closet, and it leaves me feeling almost excited.

For the next few hours, I keep my cell close by, and when it finally rings late in the evening and I see it's my mom, I know that Lorenzo has completed his plan.

"Mom, is everything okay? You're calling kinda late," I ask, trying to sound sleepy so she thinks she woke me up.

All I can hear is hysterical crying, and it takes her some minutes before she is able to say, "L-Lorenzo... H-he kill... he killed y-your fa-father," she sobbed through the phone.

"What?" I'm trying to sound shocked but don't think she is paying that much attention, anyway. "I will be there as soon as I can," I respond with no real intention of getting there till the morning.

When I wake up the following morning, I expect the weight of Dad's death to finally hit, but it doesn't. All I still feel is relief. Wondering if there is something wrong with me, I go about changing the plans for my day. First thing to do is call the school and tell them that my dad died suddenly in the night. They, of course, say how sorry they are and ask what happened, but all I respond is that I'm not sure of the details yet, but the death was unexpected. This seems to stop any further questions, and they let me know that I can take as many days as needed.

I arrive at my parents' house at the same time the undertakers are removing my father's body from the house. Mom is at the top of the steps crying, and when she spots me, she comes running down them and crashes into my arms.

"Marco, where have you been? I thought you would be here hours ago," she cries into my shoulder.

I don't say anything to this but wrap my arm around her, leading her back inside the house and into the kitchen. There is no sign of Lorenzo, which is good. I'm guessing he's probably staying out of Mom's way, and if I know him, packing to go home. Deciding that we both need coffee, I go about making some for me and Mom, taking a cup over to her. She jumps when I place the cup in front of her on the table, probably forgetting that I was even there.

"You have to do something about Lorenzo," she says, looking up at me.

"Do what, Ma?"

"He killed your father. Call the police, or better yet, call one of dad's friends. They would know what to do."

For a split second, I'm taken back by what Mom just asked, forgetting the police bit, but did she really want me to call some of Dad's "friends?" Does this mean she may know more about Dad's business than we all thought?

"No. I'm not calling the police and *definitely* not calling any of Dad's 'friends.'" I snap back.

"But Lorenzo needs to be punished! He shot your father. Don't you understand that?" It's at this moment I realize that my mom is probably never going to talk to me again, and it's this thought that finally makes me sad. That today the actions of one man have caused this woman to lose both her sons.

"Oh, I understand, Mom. But Lorenzo has been punished enough. He did what he had to do to stay alive."

The sheer horror that passes over her face as she realizes that I am on Lorenzo's side will haunt me for a lifetime.

"Really?" There is actually a hint of sarcasm in her voice as she says this.

"Dad was a dangerous man, and the world is a much better place without him in it."

She presses her lips together so tightly that they turn white, and I can see she is getting angrier by the second, but I'm not going to let up.

"How can you *say* that? He's your *father*."

"Very easily, Mom. Did you know that Lorenzo was recently in the hospital? Got beaten up on the night he told us he was gay," I tell her frankly.

"What?" I'm pleased she is at least shocked at hearing this. "Why didn't they call us?"

"Because they were told not to, and for God only knows what reasons, the hospital listened."

"But that's wrong. We should have been there."

"No, Mom. You shouldn't have." I watch as she flinches when I say this. "You may have been welcomed, but Dad wouldn't have been."

"I don't understand any of this," she says, the confusion ringing clear in her voice. "We're his parents."

"Who do you think organized for Lorenzo to get attacked?" I ask, but she doesn't understand the implication.

"I don't know. I guess he was in the wrong place. Right?" But she has to be wondering why I'm asking such an odd question and just not saying anything.

"Nope." Anger is now coursing through my veins at this point. I never thought I'd ever feel such fury toward my mother, but she can't see the monster behind the man that was her husband. I'm hoping the next statement opens her eyes. "Do you remember Dad making a call on his cell just after Lorenzo left?" She nods her head in agreement, and so I continue. "That was Dad calling his people to organize the attack on Lorenzo, and Mom, he wasn't supposed to survive."

"No!" she screams. "Your father wouldn't do that. He loved him, loved *both* of you." I don't miss that she's already referring to Dad in the past tense. "This is *Lorenzo* poisoning your mind. *He's* the monster here." She stands from her chair, but I grab her hand, stopping her.

"Sit down! We are *not* finished." The edge in my voice is clear and Mom must catch it, too, as she pales but slowly sits back down. "No, Lorenzo is *not* poisoning my mind. He just made me see the truth. Dad was the monster." All Mom is doing is shaking her head, refusing to believe what I am saying. "Think about it, Mom... Dad was acting so strange after Lorenzo left that night, then suddenly Lorenzo is moving back home. Like nothing happened. Did you ever question that?"

"Of course I did. Your father explained that he went and spoke with Lorenzo, who confessed to making a mistake and didn't mean anything that he'd said. Your father told him to come home for a while and that everything would be okay."

At this I burst out laughing, and it turns into a full-on body shake, and I can feel the tears starting to run down my face. Eventually, I compose myself enough to tell her the truth.

"No, Mom. Dad threatened Lorenzo to make him come home. Told him that if he didn't, the next 'accident' he had would be permanent. And before you tell me again that Dad wouldn't do that, think. Did Lorenzo look happy to be home?"

I'm not sure what I said in the last statement that Mom finally believes, but I watch as her shoulders slump. "I knew he wasn't happy. You just had to look at him. But I honestly thought it was because of everything that had happened. That he was embarrassed."

"He didn't want to be here, Mom," I say gently. "He came home to finally put a stop to Dad, and he walked away from the man he loves in order to do that. *That* is why he's been so sad. Imagine if you had been separated from Dad for that length of time with no contact. How would you feel?"

"Man," is the only word that Mom seems to register out of all that I'd said as she repeats it back to me.

"Yes, Mom. Man. Lorenzo is gay, and you will have to accept that if you want to see him again."

The look that Mom gives me after hearing this sends ice through my veins, causing me to shiver and goosebumps to rise on my skin. "No! Love between two men is *wrong*. I will *never* accept that. And he still shot your father. I never want to see him again."

"Even after everything I told you?" I ask, not really believing what she is saying.

"Maybe you're right. Maybe your father was a monster, but he was still *my husband,* and I loved him. He was always kind to me. The moment Lorenzo shot him, he shot me, too. So yes, even after everything, Lorenzo is dead to me."

"In that case mom, you have a decision to make. I do not plan to lose my brother. So, are you prepared to give up both your sons today? Because there is no way I can be in your life if you aren't prepared to believe and accept Lorenzo." I also know that if she can't accept Lorenzo being gay, she will never accept me. Now, I could come out to her right at this moment, but it would cause her even more pain and just seems a fruitless gesture, so I just sit, watching as I wait for her reply.

"If you are on Lorenzo's side, then you are making the choice for me." Her voice is completely devoid of any emotion now, and she turns her face from me, no longer wanting to look at me.

"I wish I could make you understand, but it looks like there is no point." I get up from the table and walk to the kitchen doorway.

"Marco." Her voice has me turning to face my mom once more. "Before you leave. Can I ask you something?"

"What is it, Mom?"

"Did you know what Lorenzo was going to do?"

I consider lying to her, but what's the point? From the look in her eyes, I know she is never going to talk to Lorenzo again, and even if there had been the smallest seed of hope that maybe one day she would come round, I didn't honestly think it would happen. So may as well make her hate me, too.

"Yeah, Mom. I knew what he was going to do and was behind him one hundred percent."

For that split second, she appears shocked, but it quickly morphs into white, fiery anger. *"Get out!"* She screams, physically shaking with rage. "You and your brother aren't welcome here any longer." Her rage is fucking scary to see, but I'm determined that she won't be having the last word.

"Happily," I reply and turn before she has time to say anything else.

When I get into the hallway, Lorenzo is standing at the bottom of the stairs, staring in the direction of the kitchen.

"You know it's rude to eavesdrop." I state, pulling him into a hug.

"What the fuck did you just do?" Lorenzo says while pushing me back, and he sounds almost angry.

"Stood up for you. That's what I did." This seems to make him angrier, if that's possible.

"You weren't supposed to do that! You aren't supposed to lose Mom. Only I was."

"Lorenzo, listen to me. I stand by everything I said. I don't know how much you actually heard, but Mom was never going to accept that Dad was a monster or that you're gay, so there is no way she would accept me, either. We both don't need that type of person in our lives. At the end of the day, I still have you and Wyatt. You two are my family. So, I haven't lost anything."

Once I finish my speech, there are tears running down my face, and Lorenzo pulls me to him in a fierce hug, and I can't help the yelp that escapes me.

"Sorry," he says before stepping back. "Thank you, and I promise, I'll be there for you always. You'll never regret this."

"I know. Now go get your stuff and text Wyatt. He should be up by now. It's over, Lorenzo. You're finally going home."

Watching the smile spread over his face makes everything that happened worthwhile, and as he turns and runs up the stairs, I watch as he pulls his cell out of his pocket.

Chapter 10 — Liam

When I heard Wyatt's cell beep a couple of hours ago, I never once thought it would be Lorenzo sending us information that was invaluable to the case, but it was, and here we are, watching as the *Fiore Rosso* docks. Warrant and customs are ready, and something in my gut is telling me this is it; we will finally be able to get everything we need to bring down Alfredo. I had almost texted Marco to tell him but didn't. I'd decided that there wasn't any point, and the suspicious side of me didn't want to jinx it.

The moment the gangplank is in place, I watch as Wyatt gets out of the car and goes over to the customs team, showing them the information that Lorenzo sent, and I know that he must be explaining that we believe the sequence of numbers are linked to the containers and crates. Watching as they go around the ship and pick out certain containers, I know we were right about the numbers.

Getting out of the car, I join Wyatt, and we both walk up to the captain. He's still as calm as last time even though we have the containers marked out, so he must still think we aren't going to find anything. But once he spots the crates being moved away from the cold refrigeration, he gets more and more agitated. He knows the drugs are going to be found, and soon enough, the customs officers signal to Wyatt that they've found something, and Wyatt arrests the captain, reading him his rights.

As we walk him down to the car, I hear him asking about making a deal. Wyatt explains that any deal is going to be up to the district attorney and based on the information he supplies. Still pleading, he says that he can give us the name of the boss, the one behind everything, and even agrees to stand up in court and give evidence. That is one ballsy thing to say, considering he would be getting up in front of Alfredo and, no doubt, signing his death warrant.

Once we have the captain at headquarters, Wyatt takes him into the interrogation room to get his statement. I go into an adjacent room that has the two-way mirror along with the recording equipment so the interview can be observed. The first thing I do is make sure the equipment is turned on and recording everything the captain has to say so we don't miss a single word.

The moment Wyatt begins to question him, the captain is singing like a canary, and I know we have him and almost dance around the room. *Lorenzo and Marco are going to be free!* I'm so glad I don't do my victory dance, otherwise, I might have missed the slightest nod of Wyatt's head. Shit, I have no idea where the thought comes from, but I know the captain's going to drop Lorenzo's name, and Wyatt's picked up on it, too, hence the signal.

I hit the stop button on the recording just as the captain says that Alfredo was grooming his son to take over the business. The smug look on the captain's face while saying this makes him look as though he has a trump card that not only can we get the current boss but the future one, as well. The look on Wyatt's face is pure enjoyment as he leans over and states,

"Who do you think gave us the information we needed to search the ship?" and I watch as the captain's face pales. *Priceless*.

Wyatt stays with the captain as he gets him to write out his statement, making sure he signs it so that it's a legally binding document, and then gets up to leave. Waiting for the door to close behind Wyatt before leaving the room I'm in, I meet up with my partner outside, and he's already asking if I stopped the recording before Lorenzo's name was mentioned. I confirm I did, and then we make our way back to our desks using the ship captain's statement to get a warrant to go and arrest Alfredo, and I'm suddenly itching to leave. I need to go find my Marco, and I know that Wyatt wants to get Lorenzo.

We'd just risen from our chairs when my cell beeps, and when I see a text from Marco, I somehow know that we won't be making the arrest, and even though I'm shocked, relief is the overwhelming feeling. I know that it must be written all over my face when Wyatt asks me "What is it?" and when I say that I got a text from Marco, I can tell that he thinks it's to say that Alfredo has found out and is possibly making a run for it. Not sure if I can actually say the words that are in front of me, I hand over my cell, and watch as he reads the message.

Marco: Father died last night.

The realization is instant. It's finally over. And when I hear his cell beep, I know that Lorenzo has just sent a text, too. I have no idea what he's written, but by the joy that fills my best friend's face, I know that it's something good.

"Come on, Wyatt. Let's go get Lorenzo., I say and have to stop myself from adding, "and Marco." Even though the major threat to Marco is now gone, I don't feel ready for my relationship to be out in the open.

"Can you believe this is over?" Wyatt asks, still looking at his phone.

"I wish we could have arrested the bastard and seen him behind bars, but somehow, this feels better." And it's only as I say this that I realize we won't be able to leave, that we are going to have to tell the captain what's happened. I'm just about to say this to Wyatt when I spot the captain making his way over to us.

"Detectives, could I see you for a moment in my office, please?" Before either of us has a chance to answer, he turns and walks back to his office, leaving us no option but to follow. Once in his office, he indicates for us to close the door and take the seats in front of his desk. *Oh fuck, this isn't good.* From the look Wyatt shoots me, he must be thinking the same.

"Sorry to be rude, sir," I hear Wyatt state, "but we were just about to leave to go and arrest Alfredo. Will this take long? We don't want him to get wind of it and make a run for it."

"That's why I called you in here. I have some news on your case, and I don't think you're going to like it."

Fuck, the captain already knows that Alfredo is dead. How the hell can he get this information so quickly? Hopefully Wyatt's and my acting skills are still in top form, or we'll give ourselves away instantly.

"What is it, Captain?" I hear myself ask, and even to my own ears, I sound normal.

"They pronounced Alfredo Romano dead this morning."

"Your fucking joking, right, Captain?" Wyatt asks, and I can't help but think okay, he *is* a good actor.

"I wish I were, detective. The news just came through from the coroner's office. They're stating that it's a heart attack, mostly likely caused by stress. Personally, I think it's bullshit, but anyway, for now, the case is on the back burner. We need to wait and see who takes over his operation."

"Do you think that someone will?" I ask. It never occurred to me that someone would because of Lorenzo being groomed to take over. But that doesn't mean someone else in the organization wouldn't have a go. We're going to have to talk to Lorenzo and see if he can somehow shut it down completely.

"Yes, Detective Smith. I *do* think someone is going to take over. They'll want to lie low for a while, keep up the pretense of Alfredo dying suddenly, and then they'll jump right in, and it will all start again. Just keep your ears to the ground, and the moment that you hear something, let me know, and we will get you back on the case ASAP."

"Yes, sir," we say in unison because there really isn't a lot else that we can say.

"Good," he replies, dismissing us with a look. We get up from the chairs, and all I can think is how the hell are we going to be able to get out of the office now. I'd been planning on using the arrest of Alfredo as an excuse.

"Detectives." Both of us turn to the captain. "You guys have been busting your balls over this case. You were at the docks early this morning only to get this outcome. Must be a real kick in the teeth. Go home. You'll get the next one, okay?"

"Yes, sir" we both say, again at the same time, and leave the captain's office. We don't actually say anything to each other until we're in the car and driving out of the headquarters.

"Can't believe that the captain told us to go home. I was wondering how we could get out of there." I say to break the silence.

"Tell me about it."

"You heard anything more from Lorenzo?" I ask because I know that he would have quickly put his cell on silent the moment the captain had called us into his office.

"Yeah. He says he's home. I guess he didn't want to stay in his parents' house longer than he needed to."

"Did he mention Marco at all?" I regret the question the moment it's out of my mouth.

"No, he didn't. But now that you mention it, I've been meaning to ask. What the fuck is going on with you guys?"

"What the hell, Wyatt? Nothing's going on with us." God, I hope he can't tell I'm lying. "He's just become a good friend over the past few months. I don't want to see him hurt, that's all."

"You sure that's all it is?" he presses, shooting me a skeptical look.

"Yes, I'm sure." And I roll my eyes for good measure.

"Sorry. Just ignore me. I have no idea what I'm saying. You're as straight as they come. Don't know why I thought it was something more." Wyatt chuckles and shakes his head once he finishes speaking.

"It's fine. Don't worry about it." I hate myself at the moment for lying. This would have been the perfect time to tell him the truth. I know he wouldn't have said anything, and yet the words wouldn't come out. I'll have to talk to Marco and see what he wants to do, but I can't help but pray that he wants to keep it quiet for now, too.

We stay silent for the rest of the trip to Wyatt's place, both of us lost in our own worlds. Wyatt is probably thinking about his future with Lorenzo and wondering when he is going to propose. Will it be soon now that the shadow over them is gone, or will he wait a while? It suddenly seems strange that I'm thinking about Wyatt and Lorenzo when me and Marco should be free, too, yet I still feel this shadow over me. It might not be as dark and suffocating as it was when I was always wondering if Marco was safe, but it's still there nonetheless.

The lingering thought in the back of my mind is that nobody will understand if I suddenly appear with a man on my arm instead of a woman. My family is pretty forward thinking, but with my brother being ex-military and my dad retired from the police force, I'm not sure if they would accept that. But what do I do if Marco wants to come out? Am I prepared to lose him because of my own insecurities? The only way I'll find out what he wants us to do is to talk to him.

Before I know it, we've parked and are almost to Wyatt's front door. As he opens it, we hear voices from inside, and my heart rate increases. I have to stop myself from running in, grabbing Marco, pulling him into my arms, and kissing every inch of his face. Instead, I calmly walk in and watch as Wyatt and Lorenzo do exactly what I was just thinking. The pure joy on their faces is intoxicating, and I can't help but smile. Marco looks over to me from the other side of the room and smiles, giving me a wink, and I know he is sending me a kiss, too.

But when the kiss between Wyatt and Lorenzo seems to be getting hotter, I know it's time to leave.

"Hem." I try clearing my throat but am ignored as they continue kissing. "I think it's time to leave," I say to Marco, "before they start stripping each other's clothes off. That's not something I want to see."

From the laughter that is showing on Marco's face, he agrees. "I think you might be right." He walks around the kissing couple, slaps Lorenzo on the back, and says, "See you soon, bro." Without breaking the kiss, all Lorenzo does is wave, but at least he acknowledges him.

We leave the apartment, making sure that door closes behind us. When we are both in the hallway, I look up and down, ensuring that we are alone before I pull Marco into my arms, kissing him just as passionately as the one we were just witness to.

"Wanted to do that the moment I saw you," Marco says when we finally came up for air.

"Me, too. How are you doing? I know that I should say sorry about your Dad, but I'm not."

"I'm doing okay, actually. When Mom called, I thought I was going to feel sad, upset, maybe even devastated, but all I felt was relief. Is that wrong? Dad never did anything to me." He looks a little guilty when he finishes speaking.

"No, it's not wrong. You know what he did to Lorenzo, and I'm sure that you were scared the same could happen to you. You, Lorenzo, and the world are much better off without Alfredo in it." As I say this, I look at the door. "Shit, we were supposed to talk to Lorenzo. Oh well. Suppose that will have to wait."

"Talk to him about what?" he asks, concern in his tone.

"Our captain is concerned about who is going to take over the organization. We are off the case at the moment, but it hasn't been closed. He wants us to keep an ear out, and the moment we hear something, the investigation is going to start again."

"Don't worry about it. There is no way Lorenzo is going to let someone take over the Alfredo empire. As far as anyone is concerned, Lorenzo is the heir, and knowing that he was trained by Alfredo will keep people from doing anything stupid until he can shut everything down. And he *will* close everything down."

"Well, that, at least, is good to know." I don't add that evidence will be needed to get the case closed completely since the captain is not going to just take our word for it, so I change the subject. "You have any plans for this evening?"

"Well, I was thinking of going home to wash my hair," he replies with deadpan seriousness.

"Always the bloody comedian," I retort.

"It's just one of my many charms that you lo—" He catches himself before saying what I guess is the word love. "That you adore," he finishes after clearing his throat. From the way his eyes meet mine, he must be hoping that I haven't caught his slip up.

"If you say so," I reply, smiling to make it seem that I hadn't heard anything. "Want to come back to my place and celebrate? You can stay over, too, if you want."

"Now *that* sounds like a celebration. Especially as I don't have to go to work tomorrow." When he sees the confusion on my face, he goes on to explain that he called the school this morning to let them know of Alfredo's death, and they told him to take as long as was needed.

We walk down the hallway holding hands, safe in the knowledge that no one is going to see us, but the moment we are on the sidewalk, we drop them. For the first time, I feel the pang of regret that we aren't out in the open, and I know it's because Marco was going to say that I loved his charms. If I look at my feelings closely, I will see that I did love his charm, but not only that… I love all of him, and that realization scares the shit out of me.

Chapter 11 — Marco

6 Months Later

It's hard to believe that six months have already passed since Lorenzo killed Dad, and even though I normally just think of it as when dad died, so much has changed. Lorenzo tore the organization apart, closed everything down, and even changed the name of his shop. I would love to say that it's been smooth sailing, but sadly, that's not the case. Mom was true to her word and hasn't spoken to Lorenzo since that fateful moment, although I must admit I'd tried to reach her a few times, hoping that it was simply grief that was making Mom talk so harshly that night. Unfortunately, that wasn't the case.

But what surprised us both was when some of our aunts and uncles heard about Lorenzo and Wyatt being a couple and disowned him, as well. I'd hoped that our family would be more open minded than they were proving themselves to be. We have some cousins who don't care, but that's about all. I asked Lorenzo if he would've changed anything if he knew that he was going to lose the entire family, and he looked me dead in the eye and said that he wouldn't change a thing. He has me, Wyatt, Liam, and Wyatt's family, and we're all the best family that anyone could ever wish for.

I never say anything, but I'm jealous of the family Lorenzo had made for himself. I've tried to ignore it, but I miss Mom. The family dinners or just popping home when I was having a bad day and getting a mom hug—because they are seriously the best. I know I can call Lorenzo, but it's not the same. If Lorenzo ever found out I am feeling this way, he would end up feeling guilty. He never planned on Mom walking out of my life, too, but as I have said to him a thousand times, the moment she found out I was gay, she was likely to walk away, anyway, so he just brought forward the inevitable—but that still didn't stop me missing her.

After having had a crappy day at school, I didn't really want to go back to my place. Liam was working late, so he wasn't available, but that also meant that Wyatt would be working late, as well, so I figured if Lorenzo were free, I could spend a few alone hours with my brother, and that sounded nice. So, the moment the school day had finished, I sent a text asking if I could come over for a few hours. His reply had been immediate, saying that he was about to send me a text asking the same, and that is how I now find myself standing outside of Lorenzo's apartment.

When Lorenzo opens the door to let me in, the smile on his face is infectious, and he pulls me into a breath-stealing hug, squeezing me hard.

"What's with you?" I ask when he finally lets go.

"Nothing," he replies, but I know it's a lie.

"Bullshit!" comes my reply even though I'm still smiling as I say it.

"Wyatt is working late. So let's order a pizza and we can talk, okay?"

When he says that Wyatt is working late, I almost slip up and say, "I know," but catch myself just in time. If I had, he'd have asked how I knew, and if I said it was because I knew that Liam was working, too, there would have been more questions, and these were answers that both me and Liam had decided to keep quiet.

Once all the business with dad's death had been settled, we sat down and discussed us coming out. Liam had said that he wasn't ready because he wasn't sure how his family or other members on the force would react, but considering that Wyatt was out and proud, he thought it would be more of a surprise. But he still didn't want to risk it yet. And honestly, I'd been so relieved he'd felt that way because even though Liam was the best thing to happen to me in maybe forever, the world was changing slower than I'd hoped, and I wasn't prepared to come out, either. It may be the twenty-first century, but I didn't know how the school board would react or how the student's parents would take that news, and I loved my job. There were just too many narrow-minded people for me to feel comfortable, even in a diverse city such as New York. I even grabbed a copy of the code of ethics for the school, and it made no mention that a teacher can't be gay.

When I had told Lorenzo I was gay, it had been such a freeing feeling that I thought I might just risk it and tell the school, thinking it might help so many students who were gay or confused about what they were feeling. To know they had a teacher they could turn to. But that changed the moment Lorenzo told me about his attack and that dad had organized it. If your own father—who seemed like a down-to-earth person—could do that, it made me think of what other people could be hiding, and so I took the step back into the closet.

"Marco." I stand there blinking a few times as I look at my brother and realize that he must have been talking to me and I'd missed everything that he'd said.

"Sorry, what?" I ask

"You okay? You seem a little out of it."

"I'm okay. It was just a crappy day in school today, " I lie.

"You sure?" Nodding my head, he continues. "What pizza toppings do you want?"

I just look at him with my *Really?* expression since he knows that when it comes to pizza, there is only one. "Seriously?"

"What? You might have had a change of heart since last time," comes his reply, but I know that he's just trying to be funny, so I decide to play along.

Putting my finger to my mouth and tapping it a few times to make out as if I'm thinking, I finally say, "You're right! I think I'll have ham and pineapple this time."

Lorenzo must think I'm serious when he looks at me as if I've grown another head.

"You're joking, right? Please say you are joking because pineapple should *never* be put on pizza."

I pretend to protest before finally bursting out laughing. "Of course I'm joking. You're such an idiot at times. I want the best pizza topping in the world ever—double pepperoni."

"Git," is the only comeback he throws at me.

I'm still giggling to myself while I go and sit down on Liam's couch as he places the order for delivery. Once he's done, he wanders into the kitchen where I hear the telltale sound of bottles clinking together. Looks like we're having a couple beers, too.

"So, how come you had a crappy day?" he asks as he comes over to me, handing me a beer.

"Couple of boys were fighting, but neither would say why. So the pair got suspended for a few days."

"They're teenage boys. I bet it involves a girl," he states as if that's the only explanation needed.

"I'm not so sure. It just wasn't like one of the boys. He's never been in trouble before and has always had good grades."

"So he got beat up for being a nerd. Probably happens in every school across the world."

"Maybe..." But I know that there is more to the fight that happened today. I'm really hoping the fact they were suspended will put a stop to it, but there's this feeling in the pit of my stomach that it isn't over. "Let's change the subject. What did you want to talk about?"

And all of a sudden, that smile is back.

"Well," he starts and holds up his left hand, showing off a ring on the fourth finger.

"About damn time," I say and stand up to pull Lorenzo in for a hug. "I am so happy for you. Wyatt is an amazing guy."

"Thanks." Lorenzo looks at the ring and appears to be about to say something else but stops. "Wait! What do you mean, 'About damn time?'"

I smile and say, "Nothing. Just that this should have happened a long time ago."

"You fucking knew, didn't you?" There is no anger behind his words, maybe a hint of shock, and I wonder how long I can string him along for.

"I might have," I say with a wink

"How long ago? Does Liam know, too?"

I'm sure he has more questions, but these two are the most important. My initial thought is why would he ask me if Liam knows? "How the hell would I know if Liam knows?" Considering it was me who told Liam that Wyatt was going to propose... but it's all about keeping up the act.

"I don't know! It just seems the two of you have become good friends, that's all."

He's right. Liam has become a good friend, but he just has no idea how close we have become, so instead of confirming *that* statement, I go back to the other two questions.

"I've known about it for a while."

"How long is 'a while?'" Lorenzo demands, staring at me.

Damn, I'd been hoping he wouldn't ask this. "Um…" I look down at my hands but can still feel Lorenzo's eyes burning holes into me.

"Don't 'Um' me. How long?" He's getting frustrated, but I'm having so much fun.

"Well, I can't remember the exact date." Biting my lip, I pretend to be thinking.

"Bullshit. Just fucking *tell me*. You're having *way* too much fun at my expense," Lorenzo states in a raised voice, throwing his hands up in the air.

"Sorry, but you're right, this is just too much fun." The glare he gives me just makes me laugh. "If you want me to tell you, stop glaring at me."

"Well I wouldn't be glaring at you if you just told me."

"Okay, okay," I say through my laughter and then take a few deep breaths to calm myself. "He might have said something the day after you spent the night together. When you were still getting the information on Dad."

"That was eight fucking months ago, for fuck's sake. And you didn't think to warn me. What did he say?"

"Um, no, I wasn't going to fucking warn you. It was meant to be a surprise. There was no *way* I was going to spoil anything for Wyatt—he's a cop, you know. He could make me disappear." And I click my fingers together to show just like that.

"And you called *me* the idiot," he snarks back.

"You better not say anything to Wyatt, okay?" He nods his head in agreement. "But he asked my permission to marry you."

"He did *what*? Holy fuck." But he can't hide from me how happy that makes him, his eyes widen and a hint of a smile plays across his lips.

"That was my thought, too. But I also think he did it to make sure I kept you safe. It was his way of telling me you were his everything, and it worked. I would have pulled you out of that house in a flash if anything had happened. It was so sweet."

Lately I've been thinking about that night a lot. The love that I felt coming off Wyatt was something I thought I'd never experience, but Liam, he changed all that, and I wonder if he will ask Lorenzo for his blessing if it ever comes to it. The thought always makes me smile because I can only guess how much Lorenzo will make him suffer before granting it, *especially* if he knows how happy I am.

"Wow," he says, his voice bringing me out of my little daydream.

The sound of the buzzer surprises the pair of us. We had forgotten about the pizza. He lets the delivery guy in and waits for the knock-on door. Once the guy has been paid, Lorenzo is walking back with the pizza box in his hands, placing it in front of us, opening it up, and taking out a slice. I put my beer on the table and follow his lead, and it's just as I am biting into my slice when Lorenzo says.

"So, will you be my best man?"

I know he waited for me to take that bite before asking as payback for winding him up, and I almost choke. I'm about to retaliate but then decided not to this time.

"Oh my god. Of course I will." I say because nothing would make me prouder than being his best man.

"But remember, no making out with Liam. He's straight!" he says just as I am taking another bite of pizza, and this time I choke for real. Lorenzo leans over and slaps my back hard and dislodges the bite. I pick up my beer and take a swig to help. "You okay? What happened?"

"Why the hell would you say that about Liam?" That slips out before I can stop it, but I need to watch what I say and how I react. I don't need Lorenzo thinking something is up.

"'Cause Wyatt's going to ask him to be a best man, too—you know, his side. And normally the bridesmaid gets off with the best man, which is kinda you."

At least my laughing is genuine. "I have gone from being the best man to a bridesmaid in ten seconds flat. Thanks. But I promise to stay away from Liam," I deadpan and pull the two-finger, scout salute. "Scouts honor."

He's laughing at me this time. "You were never a Boy Scout, so you can't pull that bullshit."

"True," I say back, laughing with him. Crisis thankfully averted.

We end up spending the next few hours catching up on everything that has been happening in our lives and eventually put a movie on, and it's only when Wyatt comes home that I realize how late it's gotten. It's been so good to spend the time with Lorenzo, but I don't feel like making the long trek home yet, so I pull out my cell and text Liam, hoping he's awake.

Marco: Hey. You still up? I've been at Lorenzo's and was wondering if you wanted some company.

The reply is almost instant.

Liam: Of course I want your company.

Marco: OK. Will be there in five.

If anyone had seen the hug Liam gave me the moment I entered his apartment, they would think it had been months or maybe even years and not just mere days since I had last seen him.

"God, I missed you," Liam whispers in my ear. "Please tell me that you can stay over."

Smiling back at him, I reply, "It's only been a few days. You can't have missed me *that* much. Plus, I was hoping to stay over, but I'll need to get up early so I can pop home to change before school."

"Of course I can miss you that much. And yes, you can stay anytime. I wouldn't have asked otherwise." He stops talking for a second, and I can see that he is trying to choose the words he wants to say next. "I've been thinking. How about you leave some of your stuff here?"

"What stuff?" I know what he's trying to imply, but I want to hear him say the words.

"You know, clothes and stuff. For when you stay over during the week. You wouldn't have to get up so early and can go straight to school from here."

"Clothes and stuff…" I grin back at him.

"You're enjoying this, aren't you?" he says, but he's still smiling.

"Yep! And I think that would be great for two reasons." I hold up two fingers to emphasize my point.

"And those are?" he asks, wonder written all over his face.

"One, it would be a lot easier just going straight to school from here." I can't help but grin. "And two, I hate having to get up so early in the morning." I quickly turn my head so he can't see the grin on my face and get the desired reaction out of him.

"Charming! So nothing to do with staying longer with me. No. It's because you hate mornings." Liam says, pursing his lips together and pretending to be annoyed.

At this point, I'm already starting to laugh, and the look he gives me just makes me laugh even harder.

"Sorry," I say when I can control myself. "Of course it's because I get to spend longer in bed with you. Cuddling up to you is my second favorite thing we do. I'm just messing with you."

"You're a git at times, you know that, right?" he says back at me, but he's smiling now, too, so I know I'm not in *that* much trouble.

"Yep. It's just one of my many charms," I reply and pull him into my arms for a kiss, nipping at his lips so I can draw him deeper into me. Suddenly, he pushes me back.

"Wait, you said it was your second favorite thing. So what's your first?"

Giving him a quick peck, I then start to trail kisses along his jaw, making my way to his ear where I whisper, "Feeling your rock-hard cock pounding into me." And with that, I lick the shell of his ear.

I can feel the shiver that runs through him and see the goosebumps rise on his skin. I run my hand down his chest and abs until I reach his groin and cup his dick. I feel it getting harder in my grasp as I gently caress it, all while continuing to kiss his jaw and finally his lips again before I start making my way down his throat.

Between kisses I ask, "Bedroom?"

He doesn't even answer me, just grabs my hand and leads me to his room.

When the alarm on my cell goes off the following morning, I quickly silence it so as not to disturb the man that is currently tucked up next to me. I've deliberately set the alarm for thirty minutes before I needed to get up just to have this cuddle time. I then set a second alarm because I know me and am betting that I'll end up dozing again.

Pulling Liam closer to me, I gently brush the hair back from his face. He looks so relaxed and peaceful. This is something I want more and more of—waking up with Liam in my arms—and since he made mention about leaving some of my stuff here last night, I've been thinking about just how much stuff does he really mean? Could I persuade him to allow *all of* my stuff here or even maybe all his belongings at my place? Coming home to him every night and being with him every morning sounds amazing. I have no idea how that would work, but if Lorenzo managed to keep quiet about living with Wyatt for two years, then so can I.

There is just one problem—I need to find the courage to ask Liam to move in with me.

Chapter 12 — Liam

Wyatt's been acting strange all day. He keeps opening his mouth like he wants to say something but then closes it before anything comes out. I would swear he is nervous, but it makes no sense to me. I could push him and get him to talk but decide to let him do this in his own time. We're just coming to the end of the shift when the captain calls us into his office.

"Detectives," he says with a nod, pointing to the chairs in front of him as we step in, and we sit. "I know your shift is almost over, and I'm sorry for calling you both in, but this is important." He slides over a file to us. "We think someone is trying to take over where Alfredo Romano left off. Some drugs have come into the city that look to be of the same strength and quality as Alfredo's, if not stronger. We need you to investigate. See if there's any link to the Romano family."

"What type of link, sir?" Wyatt asks.

"We're not sure. We're wondering if someone in the family has started up the production again." the captain replies.

"After all this time? Seems a little strange. Wouldn't they have just taken over the moment Alfredo died?" is the response from Wyatt. I seem to have become a mute due to shock at the revelation.

"We think that whoever it is has waited for the heat to die down. Are you still in contact with your source?" the captain asks, looking at Wyatt. "Do you think he would be able to get any information? Maybe you should check the shipping records again, too."

"My source?" Wyatt fumbles before regaining his composure. "Yes, I can still get in touch with them, sir. I'll try to contact him tonight."

"Good. Keep me informed. Dismissed." With that, the captain waves his hand in the door's direction, telling us we can leave, so I lean over and pick up the file as we go.

Wyatt and I don't say anything as we walk back to our desks. I'm holding the file so tightly I'm surprised my fingers haven't gone straight through it.

"Want to go grab a beer? I was going to suggest we go to a bar, but maybe we can go to your place."

"Yeah. This isn't good, is it?" I finally say, finding my voice.

"Shit, no, this isn't good. But let's not talk here."

Once we're back at my place, I point Wyatt towards the couch while I turn towards the kitchen, and that's when I spot Marco's coat hanging on the back of one of the kitchen chairs. *Shit*, I'd forgotten that was there. Marco left it the last time he was here. It had been so nice outside when he'd left that he hadn't needed it, so I had just told him to leave it here. Hopefully, Wyatt won't spot it.

"Is that Marco's coat?" *Seriously?* Wyatt doesn't miss a trick. Sometimes I do wonder how Lorenzo had kept his true identity a secret for so long.

"Um..." I need to think of something, "He popped over the other night for a beer and forgot it. Haven't had a chance to get it back to him."

That sounds believable, right? Just two friends getting together. I don't say anything more and wait to see if Wyatt's going to try and dig deeper.

"You two really have become good friends," Wyatt says, quirking an eyebrow at me.

Managing to stop myself from sighing with relief, I sat down. "Suppose," I reply with a shrug, trying to be nonchalant about it—if only he knew what good friends we've become.

"He's a good guy, and it's nice knowing that he has another good guy in his corner," Wyatt states, and that is one statement I cannot argue with. Marco *is* a good guy and probably way too good for me.

"I'll grab us some beers, you go and take a seat," I tell him and point to the couch again, hoping to end this conversation. Thankfully, he listens this time and turns to the couch while I make my way to the fridge and pull out a couple beers and then head back over to Wyatt. After handing him a beer, I twist the cap off my own and throw it on the coffee table before sitting on the couch, turning so I'm facing him.

"What do you think about what the captain said?" I ask him.

"Not sure. As far as Lorenzo is concerned, everything was closed down. But I have no idea how. We'll have to ask if anyone in the Romano family could be trying to pick up where Alfredo left off. I think he destroyed all the paperwork that was in the house, but that doesn't mean Alfredo didn't have some stashed elsewhere. He was a crafty fucker like that."

"Yep, but I do think that the captain is wrong. If it's someone taking up the Alfredo throne, there's no way they will keep using a ship. They may have laid low for six months, but it's still way too soon. They would know the shipyard would be watched more closely than before." I'm hoping that Wyatt has had the same thoughts on the subject as me. From the moment that the captain mentioned the shipping records, I'd thought it was wrong.

"Yeah. I'd been thinking the same. We're just going to have to figure out how they are getting the drugs into the country, and that's going to be a complete pain in the ass because we're going to need to check all the transport options available to whoever is doing the smuggling."

Shit, I hadn't thought about that, but then I realize something. "Not necessarily all of them. Think about it. If they are following in Alfredo's footsteps, then they are going to use something that looks run of the mill but isn't. We need to start looking at the road and maybe the rail links."

"That's brilliant. You take the road, and I'll take the rail. We can start tomorrow."

I'm about to say okay when I realize how many vehicles travel across the southern border of the United States. "How the fuck do I get road and you get rail? Do you know how many vehicles are on that road?" From the smile on his face, he knows exactly how many. "Right. We're flipping for it. You got a coin on you?"

Laughing, Wyatt stands and pulls a coin from his pocket and flips it, catching it and slapping it onto the back of his hand. "Call it?"

"Tails," I say, keeping my fingers crossed.

Wyatt lifts his hand, revealing the head on the coin. I sit there groaning while Wyatt fist pumps the air while shouting, "Yes!"

"Lucky bastard," is the only response he gets from me.

Laughing at my misfortune but not disagreeing with me, he picks up his beer and tilts it at me in a salute before taking a big swig.

"There's something else I wanted to talk to you about," he suddenly says. "I've been trying to say it all day, but the office didn't quite seem the right place—hence the beer after work."

"Okay, this doesn't sound good. I don't have anything stronger than beer in the apartment. Just saying."

"Nah, beer is good. It's just, I asked Lorenzo to marry me."

If I had beer in my mouth, I'm sure I would have spat it all over the coffee table. Leaning over, I pull him into a hug. "About fucking time. Congratulations." But then I decide to have my payback over the whole rail/road outcome. "Oh fuck, he said no, didn't he? He finally came to his senses."

But apparently he's only heard the first part of the conversation. "What you mean 'About fucking time?'" But then, as the rest of what I said registers, he adds, "He said yes, you fucking cockwomble. You really are a twat at times." But he knows that I'm being playful so there is no venom in his voice.

"Cockwomble, really! Gonna have to try and remember that one. Being serious, I'm genuinely happy for you guys. Lorenzo is a great guy." And because I'm me, I add, "Well now, anyway."

"You have me there. But I still want to know what you meant when you said, 'About fucking time.'"

Of course he has no idea that Marco told me all those months ago about Wyatt asking him for permission, and I wonder if I should lie about it, but I'm already lying about so much in my life that this is something that I can at least be honest about.

"I might have known that you asked for Marco's permission all those months ago. But I can't believe you waited eight months."

"I'm going to kill Marco when I see him," Wyatt states.

"It's not his fault. I kinda dragged it out of him. I thought you had spoken to him about the case, and I wanted to know why I hadn't been involved. In the end, he told me."

"You know I would never keep anything to do with a case from you," he tells me and looks a little hurt.

"Yeah, I know, but the case with Lorenzo was different. Sorry." I hate that this one statement hurts him—even if it's only a little.

"Well, I was going to ask you to be my best man, but considering you're being a dick, I think I'll just go ahead and ask my brother," he says, but I can see the smile he is trying to hold back crinkling the skin at the corner of his eyes.

"Best man?" He was going to ask me to be his best man? Why the fuck would he be doing that? I would have thought his brother would be his first choice—he has to be joking, hence the laughing.

"Yep, best man."

"You're joking, right? You were going to ask your brother all along, right?" I ask him.

"Nope." And he just continues to smile before adding, "I want you to be my best man. You were there for me through everything that's happened with Lorenzo, and my bro understood—he actually said that he was happy not to be the best man because it meant he didn't have to organize my bachelor party."

"Shit, I hadn't thought of that—in that case... Nope. There is no *way* I want that responsibility. If something happened to you at a bachelor party organized by me, Lorenzo would kill me. Literally."

Wyatt opens and closes his mouth once, then twice, and still no words come out. I'd been doing so well to contain my own bubbling laughter, but after looking at his codfish expression, I lose it. "Oh, for god's sake Wyatt, I would love to be your best man."

I don't think I've ever seen Wyatt so happy. The last time I saw him like this was probably after his first date with Lorenzo all those years ago. It's nice to see. But as I sit there thinking about a wedding, I realize that I will probably have to find a date unless I can think of a way to take Marco. There's no way that I'll be able to take a fake date. I couldn't pretend like that all day, and it sure as hell wouldn't be fair to Marco. Having him watch while I pretended to like someone else.

"Cool. Plus, it's good that you and Marco are friends. Will make everything a lot easier." Wyatt says.

"Why's that?" I ask, wondering why he's bringing up Marco again.

"Well, he's going to be Lorenzo's best man. So, you'll both end up spending more time together, and if you guys hated each other, you know, it could be awkward."

"Nah, it wouldn't. Lorenzo would put his foot down, and neither of us would want to cross him. But as we're friends, it's not an issue. When did Lorenzo ask him?"

"Um, last night, I think. Why?" But now he's looking at me with a confused look.

"Being nosey." I'm wondering why Marco never mentioned anything last night. I would've thought he'd want to share something big like that.

"Right!" he replies, but I don't think he believes me. He then changes the topic slightly. "I know Lorenzo will ask me the moment I walk in the front door, but will you want to bring someone?"

Shit, could he tell that I was just thinking that? What the fuck am I going to say? "Um…" I need to say something else, but I also need to talk to Marco first about what we plan to do. I need to think of an excuse that will give me a little time. "Not sure. I'm not really seeing anyone at the moment." The instant the lie is out of my mouth, I hate myself, and yet it falls from my lips so easily. I should have been saying, "I don't need a date. I'm with Marco, and as he's already going, so that's already taken care of." But no, that didn't happen.

"Really?" Wyatt asks, looking surprised.

"Really, what?" I'm hoping he doesn't say he thought I had been seeing anyone.

"It's just I thought that you might have been seeing someone," he replies, almost like he can hear my thoughts and is just repeating them back to me.

"Why?" I need him to forget this conversation, and quickly.

"Don't know. You seem different recently. Happy. I thought it had to have been from having someone in your life."

Okay, I can work with that. "Nope. Being happy doesn't automatically mean dating, and you know that if I were seeing someone, you'd be the first to know." *When the hell did I become such a good liar?* God, I hope that Wyatt understands why when the truth comes out.

I hardly hear Wyatt when he goes on to say, "That's what I told Lorenzo." He laughs but looks at his watch. "Shit, I didn't realize the time. I've to get going. Thanks for the beer."

"What?" My brain is currently going into overdrive, not really paying attention to anything he's just said, but he's already getting up from the couch and walking toward the front door. "You sure you cannot stay for another beer?" I ask, trying to deflect the turmoil my brain is in while following him to the door.

"Better not, but thanks."

"Oh, right, okay. Say hi to Lorenzo for me. See you tomorrow." That's the normal thing to say, right?

"You okay?"

"What! Sorry, think I drank my beer too quickly. Better go get some food." I might be a good liar, but it's obvious that my acting skills are shit.

"Good idea. See you tomorrow."

I don't even have the chance to say anything else before Wyatt is gone, and I'm left just standing there staring at a closed door. Eventually I make my way over to the fridge and grab some beers before making my way back to the couch, wishing I had something stronger in the apartment because of all the lies that I've spewed this evening. All the times I dismissed what me and Marco have. I just hope Wyatt doesn't hate me when the truth comes out—but what scares me the most is when in the hell did I decide that this would be coming out into the open and then how happy that thought makes me.

Chapter 13—Marco

Liam had been quiet for days, and there had been very few texts exchanged between us. On the few times I'd tried to call him, it had gone straight to voicemail, and honestly, I was starting to get worried. Has something happened? Has he changed his mind about us? Maybe me agreeing to move some of my stuff into his place became too much for him to cope with, which means my idea of asking him to move in with *me* isn't going to happen. But at the moment, I'm too concerned to be hurt. I just need to know what's going on.

I've just finished school for the day when my cell beeps, letting me know I have a text. I'm not really expecting it to be Liam, but when I see his name, I swear my heart misses a beat and butterflies take up residence in my stomach. Taking a deep breath to steel myself, I open the message.

Liam: Want to come over tonight?

Five words. That's *it*. Five words that give no indication of what the hell has been going on or what he is thinking, and now I am starting to get annoyed. I decide to leave it a while before answering him. Maybe it will make him sweat if he even realizes that something is wrong. But I only manage an hour before I'm replying to him—*so much for making him sweat*.

Marco: Sure. What time?

His reply is almost instant, and I can't help but feel some satisfaction that he might have had the cell close by waiting for my reply.

Liam: Whenever you're ready. At home.

I hadn't been expecting him to say come over right away. He's normally not home this early. *God, I'm overthinking everything.* I just need to get over there and sort this out; otherwise, I'm going to drive myself insane.

Marco: Be there soon.

Once in my apartment, I stare at the duffle bag that I'd packed some of my clothes in. It's been in the same spot for days, tormenting me like it knows it should be at Liam's and not here. Now as I keep staring at it, an internal debate starts. Should I take it or not? But this only annoys me more. *Oh, for Christ's sake.* I've never been like this before. Never second guessed myself so much… ever. But then again, I've never been so head over heels before. There's no point taking anything if Liam will end things, so I quickly dress in some jeans and a t-shirt, pulling on my boat shoes because getting socks, putting them on, and getting another pair of shoes seems to be a complete waste of time.

Not sure how, but I've made it to Liam's in record time. I can feel my heart pounding in my chest when I knock on his door, and my palms are sweating. Then, the door opens and he's standing there looking sexy as hell dressed in his sweats, t-shirt, and nothing on his feet—which I had never even thought of as being sexy until this point. But it's his smile that's causing me to have trouble breathing. He grabs my hand and pulls me into the apartment and into his arms, crushing me.

"God, I've missed you," he breathes into my ear.

"You have?" I say, surprise ringing clear in my tone.

Leaning back, he looks at me. "Of course, I have." He must have seen something relax on my face because he's pointing me towards the couch and saying that he will get us some water—even though I fancy something a lot stronger at the moment.

The moment we are both on the couch, he's staring at me "Now. Do you want to tell me why the hell I wouldn't have missed you?"

Shit. "Well, um…" I lick my lips to moisten them, and when I see that he's watching my tongue, I do it again before answering just to watch his reaction. "You've just been really quiet and distant the last few days."

"Really! Oh my god. I've been busy with a fresh case. That's the reason I'm home so early. Wyatt and I had to get up at some god-awful hour this morning to go check on a lead, which annoyingly was a dead end."

A fresh case? It's the one thing that I'd never considered. Everything else, yes, but not the fact that he had been busy at work. Sometimes I really was an idiot. When I look over to him, he's looking around my feet and then over to the hallway by the front door, and I see the smile drop from his face.

"I thought you would have brought some stuff with you," Liam says to me once he's finished looking around.

Okay, this is where I am going to look stupid, but here goes. "I wasn't sure if I should," I reply

Liam just stares at me, and I think he's waiting for me to say more, but when he releases my gaze, nothing else is forthcoming. He starts laughing, and I have no idea why. Eventually, he manages to get himself under control.

"Come here," Liam says and opens his arm to me so I can cuddle into his side. Moving over to him, he wraps his arm around my shoulders and pulls me into him, then kisses the top of my head. "You thought I was calling it off, didn't you?"

"Might've." It's the only reply that I can think of as I turn around to look at Liam.

"You're an idiot. Do you know that?"

"Might've," I say again, and we both chuckle at my response.

"I didn't think. In the future, I'll let you know if I'll be busy at work—okay?" As he finishes speaking, Liam leans down, kissing the tip of my nose.

"I should've just asked instead of overthinking everything. Sorry."

I feel him pulling me tighter before he takes a deep breath. "I can understand why you would jump there. You're my first relationship with a man, and I'm sure that you're worried that I'd second guess everything. But I wouldn't say for you to bring your stuff over and then break up with you—that would be mean, and I'm not like that."

"I know you're not mean. I'd just gotten used to you being in contact all the time," I tell him while rubbing my hand up and down his arm. I'm not even sure how long I've been doing it, but I don't stop.

"But there was another reason why I asked you over."

Wiggling my ass, I reply, "Now that we've established I'm an idiot, I thought that would be in the cards, anyway."

"Not that!" But then he stops speaking and his mouth hangs open, appearing to think for a second. "But hmm... now you mention it. Maybe later." I just wiggle my ass some more. "What I wanted to talk to you about is Wyatt and Lorenzo." This causes me to shift around and look at him. "Wyatt asked me to be his best man"

"Really? Lorenzo asked me to be his."

"I know. Wyatt told me. Why didn't you say anything?" Liam asks and sounds almost hurt.

"When Lorenzo asked me, he said that Wyatt was going to ask you. When you didn't mention anything, I'd guessed he hadn't asked yet, so I didn't want to say in case it spoiled the surprise."

"Honestly, I would've thought he'd ask his brother. I was so surprised when he asked me, but then he asked if I wanted to bring someone, like a date—hence the talk with you."

"Shit, I hadn't thought of that. What do we do?"

"At the moment, I have no idea. I'd thought about maybe getting a fake date, but then if you got one, too, the thought of seeing you with someone else, even pretending, would kill me. So I quickly squashed *that* idea."

"Let me think a second." When Lorenzo had asked me to be his best man, I never even thought I might need a date. As far as I'd been concerned, me and Liam were going to be there together and nothing else was needed. But nobody would know that we're together and they would expect us to have dates. Unless we put a spin on the best man duties.

"Maybe we can use the fact that we're the best men to get out of this." I continue, thinking as I am talking. "Every wedding I've been to, either the best man or bridesmaids have been busy all day. We can pull the 'didn't seem fair to bring one, so we decided to have fun and just be each other's date.' That way, it stops the questions and will still feel like we're going there together."

"Brilliant. That could so work. Why in hell didn't I think of that?"

"Because your boyfriend is the genius one here." I feel him tense ever so slightly before pulling me in closer, if that's at all possible.

"That's the first time you have called me your boyfriend," he states.

"We've been together for at least six months; I'm sure I've called you my boyfriend hundreds of times."

"Nope, and we've been together for eight months. Well, as far as I am concerned, it's only been you since the night you first stayed over." I can feel his breath on my ear as he whispers, "And I like being called your boyfriend."

Eight months! He's thought of me as his boyfriend for eight months? Wow. I'd thought it was just me that felt this way, but it's so good to hear that he feels the same, and if I ' ever going to ask him to move in with me, then this will be time.

"Listen, when you asked me to leave some of my stuff here, it got me thinking. Instead of moving some of my stuff, how about *all of* my stuff? And instead of at your place, you come to my place or a place we chose together?"

"That sounds like you are asking to move in together," he replies, but there's an unsure edge to his voice. Maybe moving in completely was too much for him, but no point turning back now.

"Because I am."

He spins me around so quickly I'm amazed I don't get dizzy. "You're joking, right?" He's staring right at me, but I can't figure out if he is happy, excited, scared, or dumbfounded. But he's waiting on my answer.

"No. I want to be here when you get home from work. Be the first person you see in the morning."

Suddenly he's getting up from the couch and starts pacing on the other side of the coffee table. I don't say anything more. It appears he needs time to think about what I've just said, so I leave him to pace. He stops a few times and looks over at me before continuing to pace some more. Eventually, he must have arrived at a decision and stops, coming over to the coffee table and sitting on the edge, taking my hand in his—oh fuck, that's not good, is it?

"Look, I want that, too. I always sleep better when you stay over, but…"

"I don't like the sound of that 'but,'" I interrupt him.

"Let me finish." Liam gives me a pointed look, and I nod, and only then does he continue. "But think about it. How the hell do we explain moving in together? Right out of the blue. I know that I shouldn't say this, but I'm still not ready to tell the world about us."

"Well, I thought about that, too." Because I had. In fact, I had thought about nothing else since realizing that I was going to ask him to move in. "Rent." When the idea came to me, it had seemed perfect.

"Rent?" he repeats, confused.

"Think about it. New York isn't the cheapest place to live. I was thinking of saying that maybe your rent had gone up, and I said that you could stay at my apartment till you got yourself another place. When a few weeks or months have passed, we decided to make it permanent because it was working so well."

"You've really have thought about this."

"I have. If Lorenzo can keep Wyatt a secret for two years, then I am sure we can do the same. It will probably be easier for us because they already know we are friends."

"Can I think about it?" There was a slight hesitation before he asked. It worried him what my reaction was going to be.

"Of course. Tell me when you're ready." And with that, I lift his hand that's still clutching mine to my lips and kiss each knuckle. It's my way of telling him I understand he has to think about it and that nothing has changed, even if he were to say no, but just to make sure, I say, "Let's go to bed."

"But it's the middle of the afternoon!"

"Did I say anything about sleeping?"

And it's all the encouragement he needs. I can see the outline of his dick as it gets hard in his sweats. I love that he is so responsive to me and can't help but run my hand over his dick, causing a small whine to escape from him. He pulls me to my feet and into his arms, trying to kiss me.

His dick's rubbing against mine, so before all my blood runs south, I whisper to him, "Before you overthink things, even if you say no to moving in, nothing changes. You're still my *boyfriend.*" I emphasize the last word, and it has the desired effect because he doesn't say anything back to me but drags me to his bed, me laughing the whole way.

Chapter 14 — Liam

While sitting at my desk with files spread out in front of me, all I can think about is last night. When I invited Marco over, never in my wildest dreams did I think it would result in him asking me to move in with him. I'm not sure why I thought he was joking, but when I saw how serious he was, I didn't know how to take it. But I do now fully understand why Wyatt paces when he needs to think. With every pass back and forth, it made me realize I wanted what he asked for so much. The thought of being the first thing he saw every day, knowing he would be there when I got from work, it sounded so good. But sometimes things are too good to be true, right?

Wyatt's noticed that my head hasn't been in the game but hasn't said anything to me yet. I really wish I could talk to him about all this, but it was my decision to keep everything quiet, and now, I'm too scared. But it's at times like this I really need the advice of my best friend. Is there a way that I can talk to him without giving the game away? So far, the words have failed me.

"You okay? Your head doesn't seem to be with us today." Wyatt says, his voice invading my thoughts. I'm seriously beginning to think he's telepathic.

"Yeah, just a few things on my mind." It's the honest answer, at least.

"Anything I can help with?" There's genuine concern on his face when he asks.

God, how I wish I could say yes to that question. "Nah. It's something I have to figure out for myself." This, too, is an honest answer, but it would be nice to have that help.

"If ya sure." Wyatt's next question distracts me from my musings. "How's it going with the road investigation?" But I also don't miss the smirk while he says it.

"Do you have any idea how many vehicles pass through the border daily?" He's still smiling as he shakes his head. "No? Didn't think so. Around fifty thousand. That's how many." The ass is full-on laughing at this point.

"Sorry," he manages to rasp out.

"No, you're not. You're enjoying my misery."

"Okay, maybe I am a little. But I looked into the train network, and it was a bust. The infrastructure just isn't there. It *has* to be coming in on the road. If we both look, we might find a link quicker."

"What did Lor... I mean the *source* say about the Romano operation?" Shit, I look around the office hoping that nobody heard me slip up, but there is no one nearby.

"They confirmed that as far as they're concerned, it was closed down, but they no longer have contact with most of the family, so no idea if someone else might have set up anything. They will try to speak to some relatives who are still willing to talk to them and see if they can find anything out, but it really isn't that hopeful."

"Let's keep our fingers crossed they get something."

For the next few hours, I try to concentrate on my work, but the more I try, the more the words and figures in front of me blur, and I know the case should be getting my undivided attention. Maybe some fresh air will help, a change of scenery and all that. Or maybe I just need to get out of the office for a few minutes.

"I'm gonna pop out and go grab some decent coffee. You want one?" I say to Wyatt as I get out my desk chair. Don't think I have ever been so thankful that there's a coffee shop just a few minutes' walk away.

"I'll come with you. Need to walk away myself. Everything is starting to blur," he replies, rubbing his eyes.

Damn, I really wanted some time to myself, but if I tell him not to bother, it'll just make him suspicious and ask questions I can't answer—or I can but don't want to. We walk in silence over to the shop, and, lucky for us, there's only a small line. I had thought once we got to the shop Wyatt might have said something, but he remains quiet. I'm thankful he isn't pressing me to find out where my mind is at. We order our drinks and move down the counter to wait for them to be prepared.

"Do you think this case will be linked to the Romano family?" Wyatt quietly asks, looking around to make sure no one can hear us.

"Honestly? No. But I do think they are using the same production facility, which is why there is a similarity. It has to be someone who knows what was made there. This is someone aspiring to be the next Alfredo, and if they're new, they'll slip up, and we'll catch them."

Just then, our drinks orders are called, we collect our coffee, and begin our walk to make our way back to the office and our desks. Wyatt goes silent again, and from the way something crinkles his brow, he's thinking over what I've said. No doubt by the time we get back to our desks, he'll have an alternative route for us to look into, which will probably mean that we'll be spending the rest of the day looking at more figures—*great*.

As I reach my desk, I see an envelope propped up against my computer monitor. For some reason, my skin prickles and an unease fills me, my gut instinct telling me that something is wrong. Looking closer, I can see that my name hasn't been handwritten on the front but printed onto a white label that has been stuck on. Wyatt spots it, too.

"Who's that from?" he asks while pointing at the letter.

"No idea. Must have been delivered while we were out?"

"Put some gloves on before opening it. Just to be on the safe side, okay?" Wyatt suggests, looking over to me.

"Okay…" I open my desk drawer and grab some gloves, quickly pulling them on. Picking up the envelope and looking a little more closely, I can see there are no postmarks, so that means it must have been hand delivered, and my unease lessens. "Looks like it's been hand delivered. Probably from one of the other departments."

"But why isn't it in with the internal mail?" Wyatt asks, always the cop.

"Again, no idea." I try to pull the flap on the envelope to open it, but it's stuck hard. This can only mean that someone has glued it down, and just like that, the unease is back. The only reason someone would glue down the flap is to make sure there's no saliva that could be used to get trace DNA. Opening my desk drawer again, I pull out some scissors and carefully cut a slit open across the top and pull out the letter. Unfolding the paper, I read the words a few times before fully taking them in.

WE'VE BEEN WATCHING YOU.
WE KNOW YOUR SECRET.
YOU'RE ON A NEW CASE.
STOP INVESTIGATING NOW.
YOU'VE BEEN WARNED.

Wyatt moves behind me and reads the letter over my shoulder, and I am glad that he can't see my face. He'd spot the concern immediately and want to know why.

"Someone is pranking you," Wyatt says as he walks back to his side of the desk. "You're a crap liar, so there's no way that you could be hiding anything."

"Yeah, you're probably right." I make a show of folding the letter back up and putting it in my desk when in reality, I slide it into my messenger bag. When Wyatt isn't looking, I'll sneak in some gloves, too. I need to show this to Marco and get his take on it. This isn't a prank. Someone has taken their time doing this. The paper is ordinary printer paper, and if I were a betting man and the ink were to be tested, it would be the kind that could be purchased in any computer shop, rendering it completely untraceable. If they do know my secret, what exactly are their intentions? Do they just plan to out us and hope there are repercussions, or are they planning something more physical?

For the rest of the afternoon, the words on that piece of paper play on a reel in my brain, along with what Wyatt had said, and by the afternoon, I've changed my mind and decided Wyatt is right and I've jumped to conclusions. We've only had our fresh case for a few days, and there is no way that anyone would know what we're investigating. It's probably one of the guys on the force hoping that I go into full panic mode, so I decide to just act like nothing's happened and hope by *not* getting a reaction out of me, it bursts their bubble. But I still don't take the letter out of my bag and still secretly put the gloves in there with it.

"That's me done for the day. You need a lift?" Wyatt asks as he turns off his computer monitor. I hadn't even noticed it was that time of day.

"I'm good, thanks. Not quite finished and gonna stop for some groceries on the way home. See you tomorrow."

"Okay. You want a lift in the morning?"

"Um..." I'm thinking of going over to Marco's straight from here and hopefully will be spending the night. "Nah, it's okay. Thinking of going to visit the folks once I'm done with grocery shopping, so I'll make my own way in. Thanks for the offer, though."

"Hey, no problem. Have a good night. See you tomorrow."

Watching Wyatt's retreating back, I wait till he's left the office and is out of sight before picking up my messenger bag and pulling out my cell, causing a piece of paper to fall out at the same time. I thought it was the letter at first and was just about to put the gloves back on when I see it's smaller and then remember exactly what it is. Seeing it causes me to smile for the first time all day before I stuff it back into my bag. But with Marco's question of moving in and then the letter this afternoon, it completely slipped my mind; I'd got myself tested a few days ago, and it's my results. I'd been excited to tell Marco so that maybe he could get tested, too, and we could go bareback for the first time. Maybe once I've shown Marco the letter and we both agree it's nothing, I'll show him this. Suddenly I'm very eager to get to his place, so I send him a quick text.

Liam: Just finished for the day. Can I come to your place?

While waiting for him to respond, I shut down my computer and make sure there are no documents left on my desks and that I've locked my draws. I'm just getting to my feet when my cell beeps.

Marco: Just walked in myself. Come over when you're ready.

I wonder for a moment if I should reply and tell him I'm on my way, but then decide not to bother and just make my way there. He only lives a few blocks from headquarters. I could take the subway and get there quicker, but I'm in the mood for the walk. It's a nice day, and it gives me some time to think, but I've only walked about two blocks when the hairs on the back of my neck start to stand on end. Turning around, all I see are crowded sidewalks. If someone were watching me, there's no way I would be able to spot them. Walking a few more blocks, I turn again, that same feeling of being watched coming over me, but again, nothing. Nobody looks familiar, either. That damn letter has made me completely paranoid. Shaking my head, I turn around and continue to Marco's, but I'm walking a little faster now.

Chapter 15 – Marco

Just as I'm getting out of the shower, I hear the apartment phone ringing. Quickly wrapping a towel around my waist, I rush out of the bathroom and cross my bedroom to the extension which is on my bedside table.

"Hello?" I blurt out, short of breath after rushing to the phone.

"Mr. Romano, this is Roy at the front desk. Wanted to let you know that Mr. Smith is on the way up to you."

"Thanks, Roy."

Shit, I know he said that he wanted to come over to my place, but I didn't think he would be *that* quick. I've just dropped the phone receiver back into the cradle when there is a knock at the front door. Moving quickly through the apartment—which isn't the easiest while trying to hold a towel around your waist—I whip open the front door.

"Is this how you greet all your guests or just me?" Liam asks while looking me up and down before stepping into the apartment.

"Shut up. I just got out of the shower. You arrived earlier than expected." Although I have to admit I don't mind one bit when he checks me out.

"Damn, I knew I should have been quicker. I could have joined you." He pulls me into his arms and all thoughts on holding my towel up are forgotten, and it promptly falls to the floor. His lips are on mine, and I can feel his hand travel down my back, grabbing my butt and massaging it. Being naked in his arms as his tongue duels with mine is making both of us hard, and I can feel the zipper on his jeans pressing against my skin, but before I can take this any further, he's breaking us apart, turning me around so I am facing my bedroom door and pushing me forward with a swat on the ass.

"Go get changed. Need to show you something."

Wiggling my ass in his direction, I reply, "You sure you don't want a bit of this first?"

"Yes, I do, and you're a bad influence on me, but later. Now go get changed." And with that, Liam swats my ass again.

"God, you're sexy when you're bossy."

The stern look he gives me just leaves me laughing as I walk into my bedroom. I had just reached my bed when I'm hit in the back of the head with a wet towel and the words "laundry basket" are called out as Liam continues down the hallway toward my open-plan living room and kitchen.

Pulling on my sweatpants after deciding to go commando and then a t-shirt, I'm soon following Liam's footsteps into the living room. He's sitting in the corner of my couch, and as the afternoon sunlight shines through the windows behind him, he looks as though he is surrounded by a halo, and my breath catches in my throat. For a few seconds, I can't help but watch him, hoping he doesn't spot me.

"Stop staring. It's creepy." Damn, he caught me.

"Sorry. I couldn't help it. You just look beautiful in the afternoon light." The blush that creeps up his cheeks definitely doesn't take away from him looking beautiful. "You want something to drink?" I ask, trying to distract myself from the scene in front of me.

"Yeah, please."

"Water okay?" I check in case maybe he wants something stronger.

"Perfect. Thanks."

Turning, I head over to the fridge and pull out two bottles of water, then make my way to the couch, sitting down next to him. He has a strange look on his face and is glancing around the apartment like he's seeing it for the first time.

"Everything okay?" I ask him, confused at the expression considering he's been here a few times now.

"Yeah, it just dawned on me that this is a really nice apartment for a teacher."

"Ah, yes, it is." I'd been waiting for this moment since the first time I'd invited him over. From the outside, it just looks like any other apartment complex on a busy street. But I live in the Tribeca area, so the moment you walk through the front door, it stops being ordinary and becomes a lot more than I can afford on a teacher's salary. Hopefully, he'll drop it and just accept that I live here.

"So, how can you afford it?" So much for dropping it.

"Please don't hold this against me, okay?" I start while he continues to look at me, not even nodding his head, but I continue anyway. "Dad gave it to me. He had bought it years ago and had been renting it. Then, when I had graduated and started teaching, he called it a graduation congratulations present. When I found out how earned his money, I wanted to sell it, but honestly, I love it here. I probably could never afford somewhere like this. What I pay in fees is basically what I would pay in rent for something half this size. Is that wrong of me?" I'm worried he'll think badly of me for keeping it.

"Of course not. This was your home for a lot longer than you knew what your father did."

"But could you be happy living here knowing who bought it." From the look on his face, he hadn't thought about that. He looks around the place again and finally looks back at me.

"If, and that is still a big *if*, I decide to move in, I will always think of this place as yours."

"If this makes it any easier, I spoke to Lorenzo, and considering Dad helped him get his place, too, he said we should think of it as a payment for all the shit we had to put up with—I didn't mention that Dad had always been fine with me; I just agreed with him."

Laughing, Liam states, "That works, but you could say that if your Dad had found out you're gay, he wouldn't have been impressed, and as this place is legally yours, he could never have taken it away from you, and that would have pissed him off more."

"I hadn't thought of that, but I like it." I take a sip of water before asking, "Now, you wanted to show me something?"

Liam shifts and pulls out some gloves from his messenger bag that I had noticed was on the floor at his feet and passes me a pair. If we have to put gloves on, then this isn't good. Once his are on, he pulls out what looks like a letter.

"I received this at work today. Wyatt thinks it's a prank. I wasn't sure to begin with, but the more I thought about it, the more I figured that he was right."

He's passing the envelope over to me, and I'm just about to take it from him when he pulls his hand back and looks at the gloves in my other hand. I shrug and say, "If you think it's a prank, why the gloves?"

"Just in case it isn't," is all the reply he gives, and that makes me think that maybe he doesn't whole-heartedly believe his last statement as much as he thinks.

Quickly pulling on the gloves, I take the envelope from him and pull the letter out, carefully unfolding and reading it. In fact, I read it twice. I don't understand how, but I know that this isn't a prank.

"When did you get this?"

"It was left on my desk earlier today. Why?"

"Someone handed it to you?" I'm trying my best to stay calm, but I think I'm failing completely.

"No. Wyatt and I popped out to get some coffee. We were gone about ten minutes, and it was on my desk when we came back. I'm sure it's nothing to worry about. Just wanted to show you."

"Nothing to worry about... When someone you love gets a letter like this, of course you would worry." I'd been so concerned about making him realize that this was real, I didn't know what I was saying until the words were out. Hopefully he hasn't picked up on that bit. This is not how I planned to say, "I love you."

"So, you actually think it's real?" he says, looking at the letter in my hands.

"Yes, I do." I know it's wrong, but at the moment, relief fills me that he seems to have missed the confession of love I just made. That is, until his head snaps back to look at me, his eyes brimming with shock.

"Did you just say, 'when someone you love?'"

Oh shit. Do I try to blow it off, or do I just tell him? Looking at him, the words just seem to find their own voice. "I love you. Have for a while. But this was not how I intended to tell you."

When I thought he'd looked beautiful when the sun was shining behind him, I was mistaken, because the smile that has now covered his face has transformed him from beautiful to outstanding.

"You love me?" I hear him say, sounding amazed.

"Yep. I know that it's probably too early for you, and I am not expecting you to say it back..."

Before I have a chance to finish my sentence, Liam is pulling the letter from my hand, throwing it onto the table, and jumping into my lap. My arms wrap around him to stop him falling back and keep him secure on my lap. He places his gloved hands on each side of my face, and only then he remembers he has them on and is quickly pulling them off, placing his bare hands back on my face. He leans in and gives me one of the sweetest kisses I have ever had, and I can't help but close my eyes, letting the sensation wash through me.

"I love you, too, Marco."

The minute I hear these words, my eyes fly open, and I'm faced with Liam's gorgeous brown eyes staring back at me. They are just so full of love and sincerity, and maybe a little hesitation at my response. But there are no words to be said at that moment. To repeat an old cliché, actions speak louder than words.

Closing the distance, I capture his lips with mine and kiss him like he is the last man on earth. The kiss deepens, our tongues dueling and exploring each other's mouths, and I can feel Liam's hard dick through my sweats, and my dick soon follows. Liam begins grinding his dick into mine. Keeping one arm secure on his back, I move a hand forward, rubbing it over his dick through his jeans before popping open the button and sliding down the zipper. Slipping my hand inside, I can feel the damp spot on the front of his underwear and run my thumb over the spot, massaging the head of his dick and causing the spot to get wetter as Liam moans into my mouth.

Removing my hand from his jeans, I move it so it's resting just under his ass and shift to the edge of the couch before standing up. The movement causes Liam to jump, tightening his legs around my waist and wrapping his arms around my neck, finally breaking the kiss. Turning, I start to walk towards my bedroom. That gorgeous dick of his needs to be in my mouth.

"Stop!" Liam shouts. "Put me down."

Liam loosens his legs, and I let him slide down my body, making sure that he feels my hard dick as I do. When his feet are firmly planted on the floor, I watch as he strides back over to his messenger bag and pulls out *another* piece of paper. He hands me the paper, and as I look at him in confusion, I see the blush pink up his checks. Opening the paper, it takes me a second to realize that it's test results.

"Thought maybe, if you wanted to get tested... we could... you know..."

As I look at the paper, I can feel the smile growing on my face. When I'd thought about getting tested, I'd gone out and done it straight away but hadn't had the courage to mention it, so the paper with my results had remained in the kitchen drawer. Without saying anything, I turn and walk to the kitchen to retrieve my results, returning and handing the paper to him. The smile never leaves my face. He carefully opens the paper and looks at one almost identical to his.

"I got tested a while ago," I say a little bashfully. "I'd been wanting to mention it but couldn't seem to find the right words."

"So, do you want to?" I can't believe the hint of uncertainty in his voice.

"Have you bareback in me... oh my god, yes," I rush out in reply, and from the way my dick is twitching, he likes the idea, too. It had deflated a little while this conversation had been taking place but was now standing at full attention again. The thought of feeling Liam's bare dick in me, marking me as his, seems to make me even more desperate for that to happen, and from the bulge pushing through his open zipper, Liam is feeling the same. Grabbing his hand, I turn and pull him toward my bedroom, but the next words that come from his mouth almost cause me to trip over my own feet as I come to a grinding halt.

"Well, I was thinking about you... maybe in me?" The hesitation is heavy in his voice

Holy fuck. Did he just say that he wanted to bottom for me? He squeezes my hand, and I turn to look at him. The smile and nod of his head confirms what he just said, but I still ask, "You sure?"

"Yep. I want to feel you. Have for a while."

There is nothing more to be said. We're both virtually running to my bedroom, only slowing as we enter and both breathing heavily as we stand in front of the bed just looking at each other and trying to comprehend what is about to happen. It's Liam who makes the first move by standing in front of me, and I take a step back to give him room. He pulls my t-shirt off and runs his hand down my chest and over my abs, then unbuttons the cuffs of his shirt and the top buttons and pulls it over his head, dropping it onto the floor with my shirt.

I thought he would step into my space, but instead, he takes hold of my hand and pulls me to him while moving backward at the same time. Once he's lying flat on the bed, he pulls me so I fall onto the bed with him, our bare chests crashing together. Raising up onto my forearms, I kiss Liam's lips and look at him, triple checking that he is okay with this, and when he nods, I begin kissing my way down his body.

Starting at his Adam's apple, I continue to his collarbone, then the space between his pecs before moving off to the left and taking his nipple into my mouth, sucking it gently until it pebbles. I nip the hard bud with my teeth while tweaking his right nipple with my fingers, causing Liam to buck up from the bed and moan at the sensations. Letting go of his nipples, I blow on the now damp left bud and watch as the goosebumps rise on his skin. Sliding down his body, I place kisses every few inches. When I get to his groin, I pull apart his open zipper and lean my face in, taking a deep breath and smelling the musky scent of his precum. I had wanted to tease him, but one smell of him and all I want now is to taste him.

Getting up from the bed, I take hold of his jeans and tug them off his body, his underwear quickly following, and I take a second to appreciate the sight in front of me; Liam in all his nakedness is a glorious sight. Pushing down my sweats, his eyes widen when he sees that I haven't been wearing any underwear and then the surprise leaves as desire fills them. When he licks his lips, I know he wants to taste me, too—unfortunately that won't happen.

Kneeling on the edge of the bed, I open his legs wider and move so I'm right between his legs and run my tongue up his length, lapping up the pearl of precum that appears at the head, the bitter taste exploding in my mouth. I run my tongue over the sensitive head, pressing it into the slit before leaning back and blowing on it, causing it to bob. He moans loudly as I take him fully into my mouth, not moving but enjoying the feel of him against my tongue. When I feel him relax, I move up and down his length, teasing the head each time I get to the tip, and I keep going till I see him fisting the sheets and arching his back to get his dick further into my mouth, trying to get more friction.

Letting his dick fall from my lips, I move off him and open a drawer on the bedside table and pull out a bottle of lube, placing it on the bed.

"Roll on to your front," I tell him. Taking him from behind will be a lot easier for him.

"I want to be able to see you."

"It will be easier on you this way," I try to explain.

"Please," is all Liam pleads back, and I nod. The look of want on his face drives me to do anything he asks of me at the moment, but first, I need to be sure he's well prepped.

As I'm reaching for one of the pillows, I'm about to tell Liam to lift his hips when I notice he already has—I can't help smiling at how eager he is. After placing the pillow under him, he shuffles till he is comfy, keeping his feet flat on the bed before he spreads his legs open. Crawling into the space and going into a kneeling position, I then part his ass checks, taking a moment to just stare at his sweet virgin hole, a thrill rushing through me at knowing I will be the first person to breach it.

Moving down, I run my tongue over his hole, getting the desired yelp from him. Smiling, I start exploring his hole in earnest, twirling my tongue around before slipping it inside. As Liam gets used to the sensation, his muscles relax, and he begins to moan and writhe on the bed with each insertion of my tongue. When I can feel he's fully relaxed, I get back up onto my knees and grab the bottle of lube, flipping it open and covering one of my fingers.

Watching him closely, I begin to massage his hole, teasing the rim and gently applying pressure, taking my time to loosen and ease the muscle. When he relaxes, I slowly slip the tip of my finger inside before pulling it back out. I keep doing this until I'm able to insert the digit all the way down to the last knuckle. He winces slightly and clenches, so I stop pushing and give him time to get used to the sensation.

"Relax," I whisper to him and shift my body so I can wrap my fingers around his dick with my other hand and pump him to take his mind off the sting. When his clenching eases, I start pushing again while stroking his dick so the pleasure overrules any discomfort he may be feeling. With his mind now distracted, I slide my finger in and out of him a few more times before letting go of his dick. Easing the finger out of him, I lube up a second finger and begin to push two digits inside to stretch him. But I know that I'll need to get at least three fingers in before even thinking about using my dick. Going slower this time, I can get my fingers in him all the way to the bottom knuckle and am soon easing them in and out of him comfortably. When I crook my finger and find his prostate, massaging it, his howls of pleasure that fills the bedroom are so good to hear.

"Like that?" I ask, smiling at the reaction

"Oh... *hell*... yes," he says between deep breaths.

"Can't wait to be inside you. You are going to feel amazing."

He is so lost in the pleasure of my fingers he doesn't answer me, and so I pump into him a few more times. When I remove my fingers, he moans in protest, so I quickly lube up a third finger. He winces and automatically clenches his sphincter as my fingers breach him, but within seconds, he's relaxing, and I continue pushing until all three are fully in him. Stopping briefly so he can get used to the size, I then begin to slide them in and out, hitting his prostate with each pass, and it doesn't take long for the moans to start again.

Removing my fingers, I pick up the lube bottle and cover my dick. Lifting up his legs and placing them on my shoulders so his ass is higher, I stop to look down at him. I thought I might have seen apprehension but am surprised when all I see is desire, love, and maybe even a little excitement.

"Ready?" I ask, and he just nods and takes a deep breath.

Lining my dick up to his hole, I start to enter him. "Remember to relax," I say when he clenches again. He leans his head back and tries to hide the flinch as I push past the tight ring of muscle. I caress his leg with my hand, hoping to convey that it won't be painful for long. He stops clenching around me, and I move again, taking my time until my dick is fully seated, and I pause to allow Liam to get used to the feeling. It's then I start thrusting, slowly at first, hardly moving out of him at all. But when I feel his channel relax around my shaft and he pushes his ass tighter against me, I begin pumping in and out and increasing my speed, pulling out to the tip and quickly gliding back in.

"You feel amazing," I gasp. He's so tight around me and the skin-on-skin contact means I'm not going to last long, but I am determined he will come before me. Shifting my angle, I thrust in and hit my target.

"Oh *god*," he yells out, head falling back, hands fisting into the bedsheet and his breathing becoming faster.

Taking hold of his dick, I begin pumping him in time with my thrusts, making sure to hit his prostate on each inward push, and it doesn't take long before he shouts my name and long ropes of creamy cum are shooting over his chest. The sight pushes me over the edge, and my orgasm courses through me, my cum pumping out deep inside his channel, marking him as mine. Dropping his legs, I collapse on top of him, not caring that I'm smearing his cum between us. He instantly wraps his arms around me. Once I become aware that all my weight is on him and I need to get a cloth to clean us up, I try to move, but he just grips me harder and whispers, "Stay."

Giving him a quick peck on the lips, I respond, "Need to clean us up." He reluctantly lets me go, and I gently pull my softening dick out of him, trying to ignore the flinch he gives as I do. Walking into the bathroom turns out to be harder than I expected as my legs feel like jelly. I hadn't realized how much control I was exerting, but it was so worth it. I dampen a washcloth and pick up a clean towel and head back into the bedroom. Liam hasn't moved, but as I study him on my way over, he has a happy, content look on his face.

Kneeling by his side, I remove the bottle of lube, placing it on the end table before running the damp cloth over his chest, hole, and then my own dick before drying us and dropping the towel and cloth on the floor. Standing at the edge of the bed, I pull the covers back, and Liam must feel them move because he lifts up his hips. Getting back into bed, I roll over onto my back and hold my arm out, inviting Liam over. He shifts into me so that his head is on my shoulder and his arm is resting across my stomach, and then I pull the covers over us.

"Did I hurt you?" I ask, hoping that he isn't too sore.

"It *was* uncomfortable at first. Thank you for taking your time." I don't say anything back to him at this but just pull him into me harder.

A few minutes later, I feel him wiggle his body and soon he is giggling into my side.

"Should I be more concerned that you're laughing?" I ask.

"I am laughing at something Wyatt said," Liam explains

"Should I be concerned that you're thinking about Wyatt after what we just did?" The question just falls from my mouth.

Liam moves so he's now looking down at me. "No. But do you remember me telling you about him wincing in the office? Anyway, what I didn't tell you is that I commented on it, and he told me not to knock it till I tried it. He was trying to embarrass me. Well, my ass is delightfully sore, and I now understand what he meant."

I burst out laughing. "I cannot believe Wyatt said that to you."

"That was when I started to think about bottoming. Never forgot the look on his face every time he winced. And he was right. Totally worth it." What can only be a contented sigh then escapes from him.

He places his head back on my shoulder, and it's not long before his breathing evens out. Thinking he has fallen asleep, I kiss the top of his head and whisper, "Love you," and I'm surprised when his exhausted voice whispers back, "Love you, too." The smile is still on my face when the darkness of sleep pulls me under a few minutes later.

Chapter 16 — Liam

A few days later and I can still feel Marco. Every twinge reminds me of that night. Each time I think about it, I can't help but smile. When I headed over to Marco's that night, it never entered my mind that I would end up having some of the best sex of my life. I really shouldn't have been surprised because every experience I've had with Marco up to this point has blown my mind.

But what shocked me the most was the fact that Marco had told me he loved me, and how the moment he said those words, I knew that I wanted to say them back to him. There wasn't a shadow of doubt in my mind that I loved him, and I needed him to hear it, too. Waking up the following morning, I knew something had shifted within me. There was no longer any apprehension. I wanted to live with this man, and I wanted us to be open to the world, and I couldn't wait to tell him.

"Liam, have a look at this." Looking up from the pile of folders on my desk in front of me, I see Wyatt holding a folder out to me. Thankfully he hasn't seemed to notice my daydreaming so far. Leaning over, I grab the folder, sitting back down harder than intended and wincing when my ass hits the seat.

"Hey, you okay? Meant to ask earlier," Wyatt asks with a look of concern on his face.

"Yeah, I'm good. Why do you ask?" I'm praying he doesn't mention that he's seen me wincing. I'd been trying to hide it and thought I'd been doing a pretty good job, too, by sitting down more carefully.

"Just seen you wince a few times." *Crap.* He *had* seen me. Shit. And in that moment, I'm hit with a strange sense of déjà vu, but there is no way that he'll guess it's for the same reason. And there's no way that I'll tell him till I've spoken to Marco first.

"Pushed myself too hard at the gym," I lie, "and stupidly pulled a muscle."

"I thought you might have finally taken my advice and come over to the fun side." Wyatt wiggles his eyebrows and keeps a straight face for about ten seconds before laughing at his own joke.

"You think you're so funny," I say, pretending to laugh along with him.

"Yep, but only *you* can pull a muscle at the gym, considering how often you go now."

I just nod back at him. The gym has been my go-to recently when I've wanted to get together with Marco, and considering how often we've been meeting, I should be the size of a small house, but that fact seems to be lost on him.

Remembering the folder that Wyatt passed over to me, I look at the information. It looks like it could be a list of companies and dates, but it's hard to tell. Wyatt's handwriting is completely unique to him, in that it's normally only *him* who can read it.

"What am I looking at?" I finally give in and ask.

"I looked at all the companies that frequently cross the border to see if I could find anything that might be of interest. Most seem to be transport companies who wouldn't take the risk of smuggling drugs. I was looking for something that wouldn't stand out, and then it hit me. Fuel tankers. They travel all over the place and blend into the traffic."

Looking down the list, I see they are all the companies transporting fuel, and I think he might be on to something. But when I look at where the companies are located, I see a problem.

"Good idea, but there is only one slight issue. All these companies are in Mexico, and the last time I checked, most of the drugs come from further south. Shouldn't we be looking for companies that are headquartered in Colombia?" I ask, thinking about normal trade routes

"Yeah, I thought that, too. But what if one of those companies was the distribution link? And yeah, before you ask, I have no idea how the drugs would get to Mexico." Wyatt confirms.

"Basically, you're telling me that you're about to double our workload." I deadpan.

Smiling at me, Wyatt just shrugs. "Maybe, but what do you think?"

I might have been teasing about the double workload, but as I think about what he's just said, I can see the possibilities behind it. Using a company that is registered in Mexico wouldn't be seen as suspicious and would be a great way to get drugs into the country, even if it's unconventional.

"Honestly?" I ask, and Wyatt nods. "I think you may be on to something. We'll have to look at how the drugs are getting to Mexico in the first place and then how they are being transported from there."

"Maybe we need to go and talk to someone at the Department of Transportation and see if there might be a way they could use fuel tankers. There's no point looking into it if it's not possible," Wyatt replies and nods toward the captain's office. "I'm gonna have a word with the captain and see if he has any contacts that we can use."

I watch as Wyatt strides across the space to the captain's office, weaving around desks. The more I think about it, the more I believe that Wyatt might have hit on something. The only thing that's worrying me is how we are going to be able to trace how the drugs are getting into Mexico. Without that link, there is no way we will be able to close this case down.

A few minutes later, Wyatt is back. "Cap thinks we could be on to something and called a contact he has. We can go see them now, so grab your coat."

The meeting turned out to be highly informative. We discovered fuel tankers are only allowed to transport liquids and that the body of the tanker is comprised of six separate compartments that must conform to certain specifications, from the size of the compartments to the thickness of the steel used. We also learned that, at the moment, more fuel was being transported from the US into Mexico because of a shortage. Hearing this news had felt like a kick in the gut. We had been so certain that they had been using the fuel to mask any smell from the drugs.

We're just walking back into the office when Wyatt turns to me. "Looks like we are back to the beginning."

"No. I still think you are on to something…." But I lose all my words when I look over to my desk and see another white envelope propped up against my computer monitor. It looks exactly the same as the one that was delivered the other day, and a cold shiver travels down my spine. I can't be sure if Wyatt is saying anything to me since I've stopped paying attention.

Sitting down in my desk chair, I pull out some gloves from the drawer. Picking up the envelope, I don't even bother trying to open the flap but reach for my scissors. Carefully, I pull out the paper and see the same typing as the last letter.

YOU'RE NOT LISTENING!
YOU'VE ALREADY BEEN WARNED.
IF YOU DON'T FOLLOW MY ORDERS

YOU WON'T LIKE THE CONSEQUENCES.

What the fuck! I read the letter three, four, five times and can't think of what they mean by "my orders," but then I remember the first letter. Reaching into my desk drawer again, I pull out the original letter, which I had placed in there after my night with Marco, wanting to keep it safe. Originally, I'd planned to throw it away, but when Marco thought it was genuine, I kept it, and am glad that I did. Re-reading the first letter, I see what order they are talking about—whoever this is wants us to stop investigating the case. I lay the letter on my desk, and when both letters are side by side, I can see that, other than the wording, the letters are identical. Same typeface and paper, so they must be from the same person.

Feeling a hand on my shoulder, I turn my head and see Wyatt standing there with a concerned look on his face,

"I don't think this is a prank anymore."

"I think you might be right. Was there anything on your desk?" I ask, wondering why I'm the only one being targeted when he is investigating this case, too.

"No, there was nothing on my desk, why?"

"They're telling me to stop investigating the case, but what about you? You're investigating it, as well."

Lowering his voice so only I can hear, he replies, "Maybe my connections."

Lorenzo. Of course. He might not be the man that his father was, and he might have walked away from it all, but the name still stands. He was the best marksman in his father's organization. There's no way that they would risk getting on Lorenzo's bad side. But surely Marco would come with the same protection. They're brothers, for Christ's sake. I quickly think back to every conversation I've had with Lorenzo and Marco about their father and remember one thing—it was only Lorenzo being groomed. Maybe they aren't aware that Marco is his brother.

"Fuck! What the hell am I supposed to do?" I don't realize I've said this out loud till I hear Wyatt reply.

"First, you'll have to show these to the captain. Then we will have to work out what he means by secret and what the consequences could be. Do you have any idea?"

Yes, I want to scream, but the words dry up in my throat and my mouth stays shut. The only secret that I have is Marco, and the only consequence that would kill me is if he were to get hurt in some way, and this thought finally helps me find some words. "I think they plan to hurt someone I care about," I whisper.

"I had a feeling you would say that. Look, call your mom and check that everyone is okay and then we are going to the captain's office."

Picking up my cell, I do as Wyatt instructed if only to keep the deceit and lies going even though I know it isn't my family who is the target. My mom confirms that everyone is okay and that they haven't seen any suspicious looking people hanging around. Then, like all mothers, she proceeds to berate me for not staying in contact more often and says that I need to come home for a meal soon. I promise her I will do just that and will call her again soon and hang up before she can add anything else to the list.

Looking up, Wyatt nods his head in a silent acknowledgment, and now we must talk to the captain. Picking up the letters, we make our way over to the captain's office. Wyatt knocks on the door, and when we hear "Enter," we walk in, and I close the door behind us.

"Sorry to bother you, sir, but there's something you need to see," Wyatt says to him.

"Is it important? I'm up to my eyeballs in paperwork," the captain replies, sighing and waving a hand over his desk.

"Yeah, it is. Liam?" Wyatt looks over to me, and I walk over to the captain and place the letters on the desk in front of him.

Pointing to the first letter, I say, "I got this a few days ago." Then I move my finger to point to the second letter. "And I got this one today. Both have been hand delivered while I was out of the office."

The captain immediately gets up from his desk, walks to the door, opens it, and hollers across the office floor, "Did anyone see somebody deliver an envelope to Detective Smith's desk today?"

One of the other detectives from the back of the office shouts that they saw a uniformed officer leave something on the desk but figured it must have been information requested from one of the other departments. That person was only here for a few minutes, if that, before they were gone, and they didn't get a good look at his face.

Hearing the other detective, I realize that whoever is behind this has done their homework. They knew how to blend in, what desk is mine so they wouldn't have to ask, and they know to be quick. Hearing the stern voice of the captain brings me out of my thoughts.

"Until further notice, anybody leaving *anything* on anyone's desks is to be stopped. Is that understood?"

A chorus of "Yes, sir," comes from around the office.

Closing the door, the captain makes his way to his desk, sits down, and looks at the letters again.

"Why didn't you come to me when the first letter was received?"

I'm about to answer when Wyatt beats me to it. "That was my fault, sir. I thought it was a prank. You know, one of the guys trying to be funny."

"You still should have come to me." The harshness and censure in the captain's voice can't be missed.

"That was on me, captain," I say. "I thought if it was a prank, that coming to you was exactly what they wanted, so I didn't."

He's not impressed with my answer, either, by the grimace he gives me but doesn't say anything more, just looks down at the letters again. "Do you think it's linked to the fresh case you both are investigating?"

"Yes, sir, I think they are." *They must be. The letters only appeared once me and Wyatt started on it.*

"Right, in that case, I'm pulling you off the investigation."

"No!" I snap. The words are out of my mouth before I have time to think.

"Excuse me?" the captain states, not taking too kindly to my outburst.

"Sorry, sir," I respond quickly. "I didn't mean to snap. But please don't take me off this case. We're onto something."

"And?" He doesn't need to say anything more; I know what he's implying. He doesn't care that we might be onto something. There's no way that he will let one of his officers get hurt.

"And at the moment, they are just threats, sir." Thinking fast, I add, "Let me send them to the crime lab for processing. When we have the results, we can decide on the next course of action."

"Are you sure?" There's a wariness on the captain's face as he asks this.

"Yes, sir, one hundred percent."

"Fine. But let me know the moment the results are back." He hands me back the letters before dismissing us from his office.

Once back at our desks, I look over to Wyatt, who's staring at me, and he isn't happy, but I ignore him and continue to tell him my thoughts from earlier.

"I tried to tell you this earlier but got a little distracted. I've been thinking about the fuel tankers. Once we were told that the fuel was being delivered to Mexico, you thought, like me, that it was a dead end. But what if it isn't?" I had thought Wyatt might have said *something* at this point, but he's still just looking at me with the same unhappy expression on his face, which I continue to ignore. "What if that is the legit side of it, but once they deliver the fuel, the tankers don't come back empty? If they are seen going in full, it's presumed that when they're coming back, they're empty."

Leaning back in my chair, I wait for Wyatt to get over himself and tell me I am onto something and that we need to look at the companies that are following the same routes all the time. What I don't expect are the angry words he throws my way.

"Do you honestly think I give a flying fuck about the case at the moment?" Wyatt slams his hand on the desk, causing me to jump and several heads to turn our way.

I'm about to answer him, but he holds up his hand to stop me and continues his tirade. "What the fuck are you doing?"

"What do you mean?" I literally have no idea what the issue is.

"I mean, why the fuck did you stop the captain from taking you off this case?"

Okay, that explains the unhappy look on his face. He must have realized that me sending the letters to the crime lab is a load of bullshit, and he's right. I already know what the results will be. There is no doubt I should have taken the opportunity to get off the case. That would be a way to protect Marco, keep him safe, but my determination to find this person overruled everything else.

"Will you fucking *answer* me?" Wyatt's harsh words bring me out of my reflections.

"Everything is linked," I tell him. "I want to get the bastard who thinks it's okay to threaten me."

"And your willing to risk you or your family for that?" he snarls back

Shit, I don't think I have ever seen Wyatt this angry with me before, and I know that it stems from concern for me and my family.

"My family can handle themselves. They are a tough bunch. You know that," I reply, trying to appease him.

"That's not the point, and you know it." He stops, and I can see that he is thinking. "Until this is over, you're staying with me and Lorenzo."

"Wyatt, don't be ridiculous." I say, thinking he *has* to be joking

"No, I'm not." Wyatt's glaring at me, his eyes narrowed and lips pinched in a thin line.

Oh fuck, he means it.

"Shouldn't you check with Lorenzo?" That's a stupid question, but I need to try and get him to rethink this.

"No. He'll understand. And this isn't up for discussion." The finality in his voice tells me there will be no arguing with him.

Shit. I hadn't planned for Wyatt to react like this, and there is no way I'll be able to change his mind now, and this alters everything. While I was sitting in the captain's office, another plan had formed. Getting the captain to agree to the crime lab meant that I had a few extra days to investigate the case, hopefully giving us enough time to start getting some answers. In the meantime, I had thought of another way to protect Marco. Quite simply, he needs to be removed from the equation. If he's no longer a secret, then there is no way that they would hurt him, and the only way I think of doing that is to remove him from my life.

Pain lances through my heart just thinking about it, but this is nothing compared to the pain I would feel if someone were to hurt him because of me. With my heart breaking, I know what I must do. The moment that I can get away from Wyatt and Lorenzo, I'll let Marco go and pray to god that one day he understands that I did it to save him and, when he realizes that, he'll forgive me.

Chapter 17 — Marco

Everything seemed to be fine. Everything felt good, but then suddenly, it all changed. For the first few days after the 'I love you' and Liam bottoming, it felt as though something had shifted. There was an ease between us that hadn't been there before. I'd convinced myself that Liam would say he was going to move in, but then I got a text to say that the fresh case was getting complicated and he would be busy. I thought nothing of it, just that maybe it would mean he would have some late nights and that we wouldn't be meeting. But then came the radio silence. Nothing. He never bothered to answer the last few texts, and the times I called his cell, it either went straight to voicemail or the call wasn't answered. In the end, I gave up leaving any voicemails when the calls weren't returned.

A week had now passed since I'd seen him last. This is the longest we'd been apart since our first night together, and I was getting worried, and when I worry, I overthink. I've looked back over that night a thousand times and nothing stands out. Everything was amazing from the moment we admitted our feelings—so what changed?

"Mr. Romano?" My name being said brings me out of my thoughts.

Shit. I'd been daydreaming in class again, and this hadn't been the first time that a student noticed. I need to get my act together and find out what hell is going on. Maybe I should pop over to Lorenzo's and see if I can get some information from him without giving too much away.

"Sorry, Noah. Where was I?"

"Romeo and Juliet. You know, star-crossed lovers." He's giving me a smirk as he says it. What the hell had I been saying? I look at some notes and still can't remember, but then the bell rings.

"Looks like we've been saved by the bell," I say, and the whole class is giggling before they are closing their textbooks and rising to make a dash for the door. "Hold it." Thankfully, they listen. "I want you to read to the end of the next chapter so we can discuss it in the next class." The collective groan from the entire class makes me smile.

Moving back to my desk, I try to work out my notes for the next class and am so engrossed that I haven't noticed Noah was slow in leaving the room until he's standing next to my desk with a nervous look on his face.

"Everything okay, Noah?"

He bites his lip before answering. "Um, I was wondering if I could talk to you, but it's kinda personal."

"Of course," I reply, checking the time on my watch. "My next class starts in a few minutes. But why don't you come by at the end of the day. We can talk then, okay?"

"Okay. Thanks, sir," Noah replies and virtually runs out the room.

Watching his retreating back, I wonder what it's all about. Noah's a good kid with good grades, but he is one of the ones who was involved in the fighting the other day, which isn't like him at all. Hopefully, whatever he needs to talk about will clear up what's going on with him. Just then, the next lot of students start to enter my classroom, so I quickly pull out my cell to send a quick text to Lorenzo asking if it's okay for me to come over after work before slipping it back into my pocket. The phone vibrates a few minutes later with his reply, but all the students have arrived and are waiting on me, so that leaves me no option but to check it later.

The rest of the day seems to go by in a flash, and I manage to keep my head in the game for the rest of my classes, thankfully. Liam really does have a lot to answer for. Before him, I never got distracted in class, but then I never had a reason before, either. Luckily for me, my students find it amusing and haven't said anything to the other teachers.

Because I've been so focused on my classes, I completely forget that Noah is coming back to see me until he's knocking on my classroom door at the end of the day, looking decidedly nervous.

"Come in, Noah, take a seat." I watch as he comes in, closes the door behind him, and takes his normal seat at the front of the class. He's still biting his lip, but now he's tapping his foot against the leg of the table, and I don't think he even realizes he's doing it. What on earth could make him this nervous? "Everything okay?"

"Can this stay between us, sir?" he asks, clearly worried

"Of course, but if it's illegal, I have no option but to have to report it," I respond, trying to reassure him.

"No, it's nothing like that. It's just that I need to talk to someone, and I can't talk to my parents."

"But you feel that you can talk to me?"

"Yes, sir. You're one of the coolest teachers at the school."

I can't help but smile at this, feeling rather proud of myself. "Well, thank you, Noah. Now, what's on your mind?"

"It's just..." He stops. "Um, I'm..." And Noah stops again and looks down at the floor before picking up his bag and getting up from the seat. "Doesn't matter. Sorry to have bothered you."

"Noah, stop!" I say, which he does and then he turns around to face me. "Sit," I add softly, and thankfully, he sits back down, dropping his bag back on the floor. "This isn't like you. Not to mention the fight you got into. Talk to me."

He shifts in his chair, bites his lips, and the foot tapping starts again, but he doesn't look like he'll try to leave again. So, I just sit there and wait. Give him time to find the words. Finally, he talks.

"It's just... I'm so confused," he starts.

"Confused about what?" I ask, but I'm beginning to think I know where he's going with this. I was about his age when I discovered that I was gay, but I'll let him find his own words.

"Boys," he whispers.

Bingo! I just need to figure out what to say so that he can admit it. "What about boys?" I ask as gently as I can.

"It's...." he starts but stops, and I can see he's considering his words. Whatever he decides, a new determination settles over him. He sits a little straighter in his chair and looks at me before saying, "I think I'm gay."

"You think your gay?" I'd thought he would say that he was.

"Yeah. All my friends keep talking about all the girls they want to bone, but I just don't see the attraction. But some boys on the football team..." He gets this dreamy look on his face, and I have to try not to laugh. Then just as quickly as the dreamy look appears, it's gone and now replaced with worry. "But being gay is a sin, right?"

For a second, I think he's joking, but from the look on his face, I can see that he's being deadly serious. Then I remembered that his parents are more than just a little religious, which would explain why he wouldn't be able to talk to them. What the fuck do I say to that?

"What do you think?" He's old enough to be able to think for himself. Know what right and wrong is. It's his opinion and feelings here that are the main things.

"Me?" He looks at me like he's never been asked his thoughts on it before. "Me," he repeats. "It's hard not to believe something you've been told all your life. But I believe that God made me and so that means that He made me this way. How can that be a sin?"

That is some deep reasoning and shows this is something he's thought long and hard about. "Noah, I can't tell you what is right or wrong, or what you should or shouldn't believe in. Only you can do that. But I will say that I believe that there is nothing wrong with being gay because"—and this is where I should say "because I am" since it would show understanding from where he is coming from, but I don't and instead just say—"my brother is gay, and I only recently found out, and it changed nothing. He's still my brother."

"Is he younger than you?"

"No. He's older. Why?"

"If he's older, why did it take him so long for him to come out?"

Should I tell him my family doesn't approve, show him I know what it's like to have parents who disapprove? In the end, I go with, "Everyone's coming out story is their own. They do it when they are ready and not before. You'll be the same."

He finally looks relieved, and all the nervous ticks have stopped. He picks up his bag and walks to the door.

"Noah?" He stops and turns. "The fight you were in, was it because someone said something?" He just nods, and I know that he isn't going to say what was said. He isn't going to rat them out. "If they say or do anything again, report it, okay? There is a zero tolerance at this school. You know that."

"Yes, sir," he replies, but I remember being his age and know that he won't say anything.

As I make my way over to Lorenzo's, the conversation with Noah plays on repeat. I'd checked my cell earlier in the day between classes and was pleased to see there was no issue with going over, but what pleased me more was Lorenzo saying that Wyatt was working late, which backed up what Liam had said about being caught up in the case and actually made me feel a lot better. I just needed to let Liam do his thing. I just wish he weren't so quiet. But after talking to Noah, I needed to talk to Liam more than ever.

Today could have been such a different conversation if Noah had known I was gay. Having a teacher who understands what he is going through could be so beneficial for him or anyone in the school who is maybe confused over their sexuality. It's made me think that it's time I come out of the closet for my students—I just hope he understands and that the school is behind me, too. Before I have a chance to change my mind, I pull out my cell and make a call to the principal and ask for a meeting before school tomorrow.

By the time that I arrive at Lorenzo's, my mind is made up that regardless of what Liam says, I will come out, and I'm excited to share this news with Lorenzo. I know that he'll be right by my side, and I know deep down he wants me to live my true, authentic self, especially since dad died and he's been confused as to why I haven't. But I'm still not going to tell him about Liam. That's something we must do together, but I have a feeling it will happen soon, and that's good enough for me.

Lorenzo opens his apartment door and pulls me into a hug even before saying hi and then is walking me over to the couch.

"I was so pleased when you sent that text earlier. I hate it when Wyatt has to work late."

"Aww, do you get lonely?" Lorenzo, for some reason, always seems to bring out my teasing side.

"Of course. Sex on your own is boring." He smiles as he says it because he knows how I'm going to react.

"No, no, no. I do not need that image," I say, putting my fists to my eyes and faking horror.

"You started it," he chuckles.

Holding up both my hands in defeat, I reply, "Okay, I'll stop. Has he been working late a lot recently?" I can't quite believe my luck that Lorenzo has given me an in to find out what Liam has been up to without having to ask him directly.

"Not really, but I know the fresh case is getting to them, and with Liam staying here at the moment, the apartment feels emptier when they aren't around."

Wait, did he just say that Liam was staying here? "Did you say that Liam is staying here?" I'm hoping that I've misheard him.

"Yeah. He got some threatening letters and Wyatt got concerned, so he told him to stay here."

And just like that, my stomach drops. Why didn't he tell me about staying with them? Then the rest of what Lorenzo said registers and pain pulses through when I realize he got more letters and yet said nothing to me. He needed to take them seriously, which I told him, and by the looks of things, I was right.

"Threatening letters?" I hadn't meant to say it out loud, but it just slipped out.

"Yeah. Telling him to stop investigating the case." This isn't news to me. I saw that first letter, but Lorenzo hasn't finished. "Then he got another to say that he wasn't listening and that there would be consequences if he didn't."

Shit, that is definitely an increase from the letter he got last week, but before I start jumping to conclusions, I need to find out when he got the second letter.

"When did he get them?" I make sure to ask about them so as not to give away that I knew about the first one.

"Wyatt said he got the first one about a week ago and then the second, maybe three or four days ago."

Well, four days would tie in to when I got the text from Liam telling me about the case, but that also means he had no intention of telling me about the other letter he got.

"The captain isn't happy about it all," Lorenzo continues, not realizing the inner turmoil I'm in. "He wanted to remove Liam from the case, but Liam said no and that he wanted to get the chance to continue investigating. Wyatt was furious and said Liam wasn't staying alone until they sorted this, which is why he is staying with us."

The more I listen, the sicker I feel, getting more confused by the whole situation. Whatever I am feeling must be written all over my face because I feel Lorenzo's hand on my leg.

"You okay? You've gone as white as a sheet."

"What? Yeah, sorry. Just worried about Liam." At least that is truthful.

"Yeah, Wyatt told me you two had become good friends." I just nod, as Liam goes on. "He'll be okay; you know."

"Yeah, I know…" That's how a friend would respond, right? "Still, it's a worrying time."

As I sit there and digest everything and think about the fact that Liam has been lying to me, something we agreed never to do after seeing the fall out that happened with Lorenzo and Wyatt, I wonder if this will change everything. The feeling in the pit of my stomach says it does and I won't like it. But if I let myself think too much about it, I'll go insane. The question

I find myself asking now is, does this change the fact that I wanted to come out? As I think back over the day, I know it doesn't.

Looking over to Lorenzo, who still has a worried expression on his face, I know that I should change the subject, and asking his advice about coming out seems the best way to do it.

"I wanted to ask your advice," I say and see that his interest is piqued.

"You want my advice? That's an interesting turn of events."

"Jackass!" It's been a long time since I asked for his advice. "Well, I think it's time for me to come out."

"Holy shit!" He's not able to contain his surprise. "When did you decide this?".

"Today. Do you remember me telling you about the kid who got into a fight?"

"Yeah. Didn't you say it was unusual for him?" Seriously, the things my brother remembers are astounding at times.

"Well, he asked to see me after school, and it turns out he thinks he might be gay. He needed someone to talk to, and it made me realize that if I'd been open about my sexuality, he might have come to me sooner, stopping him from getting into the fight in the first place. Maybe having a gay teacher will be helpful for other students who are struggling. Having that someone they can talk to who understands."

I almost miss the smile that appears on Lorenzo's face before he pulls me into one of his bear hugs.

"That's wonderful, Marco. When are you thinking of doing it?" He pushes me back so he can see my face.

"I called the principal on the way over and will be seeing him before classes tomorrow."

"Wow, you aren't holding back. So, what advice do you need? You seem to have everything planned."

"Actually, I have no idea what to say. This probably should've happened a long time ago. But what do I say if they ask why I haven't told them sooner?" I should have come out once Dad was gone, but then Liam happened, and I was happy staying in the closet. But in hindsight, maybe we should have only kept the relationship secret.

"When Dad was around, you had your reasons, so just say that. I don't think they will ask why you haven't said anything till now, but I must admit I have wondered why you hadn't come out myself."

"Looking back now, me, too. I just got comfortable being in the closet."

"Which is totally fine, but I am so excited that you're planning to come out. This will be the start of a new adventure. Next thing will be to get you a man." And then he starts wiggling his eyebrows and making a strange sound. "Ooo, we can go clubbing. Me and Wyatt could be your wingmen. Oh my god, it would be so much fun."

His enthusiasm is making me laugh, and the wiggling eyebrows has morphed into a strange wiggle-jump thing in his seat, and I almost get caught up in it all and almost agree, but then remember I have a man and don't need to go out clubbing.

"Let me get the meeting over with in school before we do anything, okay?" But I'm still chuckling with him.

"Fine! But I want to go out soon. I haven't been out to a club in ages." He's stopped his odd movements on the couch but is now wearing his determined face, and no matter what I say, he won't change his mind.

"All right, all right. We can go out clubbing," I say, and then he starts his wiggly jumping thing again. "But," I say firmly, "I'm not talking like tomorrow. Maybe in a few days when everything has settled down."

"That works for me. Gives me time to work on Wyatt. He's not a fan of clubs." Lorenzo chuckles.

"I suddenly feel sorry for Wyatt," I tease back.

"Oh, I'm sure I can think of something to change his mind." Lorenzo gives a wiggle of his eyebrows again, but this time, it means something different.

"Oh my god, again. *No!* I do *not* need to know about that." I can't believe that he went there again.

He's laughing at me, but there's a mischievous look in his eye. "I can give you some tips if you'd like, ready for when you have a man of your own."

"Really! Um, no. I don't need tips from my brother on my sex life. That's just too weird." And I pretend a shiver of disgust, causing the pair of us to fall about laughing.

Once we stop, Lorenzo looks over to me, and his face is suddenly serious. "I love this," he tells me.

"Love what?" I'm really confused by the sudden change in conversation.

"This," he replies, waving a pointed finger at him, then me. "Us, laughing about men. I really wish we would have been able to do it sooner."

"With Dad alive, you know that it wasn't possible. But you're right, and I love it, too," I respond, but now I want to see if I can get us back to the laughter. "But that doesn't mean that," I start, holding up one finger, "one, I need to know about your sex life, and"—I raise a second finger—"two, need tips on my sex life. There have never been any complaints. I do this thing with my tongue…"

Before I can finish my sentence, Lorenzo's clapping his hands against his ears. "No, no, no. I don't need to know that. Eww."

"Payback's a bitch, right?" I laugh at him.

"Suppose. Probably deserved that." He chuckles.

"Yep." And we both crack up laughing.

"Do you want to stay for food? Wyatt and Liam should be home soon."

Part of me wants to say yes just to see Liam's face as he walks in and sees me sitting there and for him to realize that I know he's avoiding me, but the other part of me can't see that, either.

"Nah, it's okay. I have some homework I need to grade, so really I need to get going."

"Are you sure?"

"Yep, the papers don't grade themselves."

"Give them all B- and stay," Lorenzo says, determined to try to get me to stay.

"Sorry, it would be nice if I could, but I can't. We'll get together in a few days, okay?" With that, I get up from the couch and make my way out.

"Good luck tomorrow. Let me know how it goes," Lorenzo states before pulling me into a hug and wishing me good night.

Making my way home, I find that thinking about Liam's letters has gotten me paranoid. It feels like I'm being watched all the way back to my apartment. I even stop a few times to have a look around, which is stupid. Yet as I walk through the front door of my building and see Roy sitting behind his desk in the lobby, I have to ask, "Evening, Roy. You haven't seen anyone suspicious hanging about?"

He chuckles at this. "Sir, this is New York. There's *always* someone suspicious looking hanging around, but nothing out of the ordinary."

"Thanks, Roy. Good night."

"Good night, Mr. Romano."

Did I really just wonder if someone was watching me? Why on earth would someone be watching me? I really *am* just a nobody, but I still sigh with relief as I walk into my apartment. Heading straight to my fridge, I pull out a beer. Normally I don't have a drink when I have grading to do, but tonight, I need it. Within a few mouthfuls, the beer is gone, and I am jumping in the shower, letting the water relax my muscles, and I feel the tension of the last few hours wash away. Liam might be avoiding me, and I can't force him to talk to me. I just need to wait and hope he comes back to me.

Chapter 18 — Liam

A week. That's how long I have been avoiding Marco. Every one of those seven days I've wanted to reach out to him, talk to him, see him, and then I remember the words in those letters and my imagination goes wild. Images of a broken, hurt, and bloody Marco flash through my brain, and it stops me. But it hasn't stopped me from doing the right thing to keep him safe. No, I've been a complete coward when it comes to that. I've lost count on the amount of times I pulled my cell from my pocket to text him to meet up, only to put it away with no text sent because each and every time I think about it, another crack appears in my heart, and I know that it will shatter into a million pieces. But what scares me most is what if he doesn't come back to me once this sicko is caught?

Wyatt knows that something is wrong, too. I've been far too quiet and throwing myself into the case. He hasn't said anything, but I hope he thinks it's just the situation with the letters keeping me silent. We haven't received any more, and I've been trying to tell him it was fine for me to go home, but he's having none of it. As far as he's concerned, until we have caught the blackmailer, I will be their houseguest.

We've just walked through the apartment door when Lorenzo appears from the kitchen.

"You guys should've called to say you were on the way home," he says, smiling at the pair of us.

Wyatt walks straight over to him and pulls him into an embrace before kissing him, and my heart squeezes at the sight and a pang of jealousy that races through me.

"Sorry, I didn't think," Wyatt replies.

"Oh, there's no issue. It's just that you just missed Marco. If I'd known you'd be home so soon, I would've tried harder to get him to stay, but he said he had grading to do," Lorenzo says, shrugging before adding, "So I guess it doesn't really matter."

When Lorenzo said that Marco had been there, I stumble. Neither of them saw it, thank god, but just hearing his name made me forget about the whole secret thing, and I'm standing next to Lorenzo, firing questions at him,

"How long was he here? How was he? Did he look okay? Does he know that I am staying here? Did he ask about me?"

The moment the last question is out of my mouth, I know I fucked up. Wyatt looks over to me, cocking an eyebrow, and I really should be back peddling and trying to think of a way out of it, but I want the answers more.

"Um, okay…" Even Lorenzo looks confused and glances over to Wyatt, who shrugs his shoulders. "He was here for a couple hours, maybe? He seemed normal, perhaps a little preoccupied, but considering what he's planning, that's understandable."

"Why? What's he planning?" I fire off, interrupting him.

"Apparently a kid came out to him at school today, and I think he felt ashamed that he couldn't say he understood, so he's decided to come out."

Holy crap, that is a *huge* step for Marco to make, and I should have been there to encourage him. To tell him how proud I am of him even though I have no idea how it would affect our relationship. Instead, I've been hiding. Staring back at Lorenzo, I wait for the answers to the other questions, but they never come, so I prompt him again.

"And! How did he look? Did he ask about me? Does he know I am staying here?"

"He looked a little tired, but I wouldn't say any more than normal. He didn't ask about you, but he knows that you're staying here."

Shit, shit, and double shit. If he knows that I've been staying here, then he knows I've been avoiding him. And I've made the whole situation a hundred times worse. Before Lorenzo or Wyatt have the chance to question my odd behavior, I dash by them, mumble something about wanting a shower, and get to my room as quickly as I can.

The moment the door closes, I lean against it and pull out my cell, open the contacts, and scroll to Marco's name, but find that I *still* can't push the send button. Instead, I do what I've done every time I've been alone this week and hit the button to connect to my voicemail, put the cell up to my ear, and listen to Marco's voice.

"I know you said that you're busy with work, but I miss you. Call me when you have the chance. Just want to hear your voice."

The message ends and I hit replay, just needing to hear the voice again, and feel a lone tear slides down my cheek. Wiping it away angrily, I straighten up, walk over to the bed, throw my cell on it, grab my shower stuff, and hurry into the bathroom and get the shower going. When the temperature of the water is hot enough to make my skin tingle, I step in facing the wall and lean forward, feeling the water hit my back. I push forward, bracing my hands against the wall to stop me falling over and tilt my head so the water can wash over my face, and it's only then that I let the tears flow, mixing with the water. I try to imagine the water taking the pain away, but it's still there. It's just I'm getting used to it, so when the time comes, I hope I'll be able to cope.

Every time I look up from my desk, I see Wyatt staring at me. He seems as though he wants to ask me something but apparently can't form the words. Normally I'd ask him to spit it out, but not today. Last night, I ended up staying in my room, needing some space. Lorenzo, being the sweetheart he is, brought me some food, but then left me alone, and this morning they mentioned nothing about my weird behavior. Apologizing, I said it was because I was concerned about the letters and dragging friends into the situation. Lorenzo might have bought it, but I wasn't too sure about Wyatt.

"I think you are right on the tankers," I say to him and watch as he blinks a few times.

"What you got?" he asks, but I don't think he is one hundred percent interested in what I have to say on the case at the moment.

Leaning over, I hand him a file. Once he opens it, I explain. "We know that tankers are coming from the US into Mexico, so I tried to see if I could figure out how often, and most companies deliver about every two weeks, *except* one who is coming in once a week. When I looked up the company, I noticed all the tankers are completely white or have a small logo, so they could belong to anyone. I haven't been able to get a list of the stops, but they would hold that information at the company headquarters.

"I believe that once the tanker has emptied the delivery, they make one final stop where they pick up the drugs and come across the border. From there, they are then distributed around the US. The only thing that I can't figure out is how the drugs get to Mexico."

"So we need to try and get access to the company records. It might be worth contacting some of our colleagues in Texas. That's the only logical state to go through."

"I'll have a word with the captain and see if he knows anyone we can talk to so we don't step on any toes or screw with jurisdictions, but you do seem to be forgetting something… we need to try to figure out how the drugs are getting to Mexico so the letter agencies can help put a stop to this at the source."

"Well, I might have an answer," Wyatt replies but then pauses. He must think his answer will sound strange. "Submarines."

When I look over and see he is being serious, I burst out laughing. "Oh for god's sake, where the hell did you get that idea from?"

"I googled it." He straightens his shoulders and sits taller, and he looks so damn proud of himself.

"You googled it…" Now I'm laughing even harder. "Seriously?"

"Well, I just couldn't figure it out and thought, 'why not?'" Wyatt's acting like this is the most normal thing to do, which I supposed it might be in the outside world.

"We'll need something more than Google, but we can use it as a start. But I wouldn't mention *that* to the captain just yet."

Wyatt nods in agreement before pointing to an internal envelope on the edge of my desk that I hadn't spotted.

"That for you?" he asks.

"No idea."

Reaching over, I pick up the manila envelope, not really paying too much attention to it, and open it, pulling out the contents. It's only then that I look at what's in my hand, and I drop the envelope so quickly you would have thought it had burnt me. Now, lying on the desk is another letter, the white envelope with its typed name label screaming out to me.

"Liam, are you all right? You look like you have seen a ghost," Wyatt asks, concern in his voice over my sudden change in behavior.

"Got another letter," I manage to whisper back.

"Oh *fuck*. But how? We haven't left the office today."

"It came in the internal mail," I choke out.

"He's changed up how you get the letters. What does the letter say?"

"I had hoped they'd stopped." I say out loud before picking up the white envelope and look at it, turning it around in my hand. "Haven't opened it yet."

"For fuck's sake, Liam, *gloves*. Your prints are all over it now."

"I pulled it out the manila envelope, so my prints are all over it already." But I still get some gloves out of my desk, anyway, so I can open it up. Once open, I pull out the paper and lay it flat on my desk and spot from the corner of my eye Wyatt getting up from his chair and making his way over so he is standing behind me to read the letter over my shoulder.

YOU'RE NOT TAKING ME SERIOUSLY.
YOU HAVE TWENTY-FOUR HOURS TO DESTROY
THE EVIDENCE
OR SOMEONE YOU LOVE WILL PAY.
THE CHOICE IS YOURS.

"Liam, you have to show this to the captain... Now!"

Wyatt is right, I know he is, but the moment I show the captain this letter, he'll ask about the forensics on the first letters, and even though I got the results, I haven't mentioned anything. As expected, they came back clean. Standard paper, standard ink, no DNA or prints. Add in this letter today, and he *will* pull me from the case. Hell, he might even stop me from coming into the office—god, I hope that doesn't happen.

Wyatt squeezes my shoulder. "Come on. Let's get this over with. Then I think you need to call your family, and this time, tell them what is going on so they can keep a lookout."

"Probably," I respond, but I don't think this message has anything to do with my family. It's Marco who's in the greatest need of protection, which means I must end it tonight. There is no avoiding the situation now. Hopefully, the fact that I haven't seen him in a week may deter whoever this is.

Picking up the letter, we make our way over to the captain's office, knocking on the door. The moment the captain looks up at us entering, he spots the paper in my hand.

"You got another one, haven't you?" he asks bluntly.

"Yes, sir. Just now."

"Just now. But you haven't left the office." Sometimes I'm shocked at just how observant the captain can be, even when he looks busy at his desk.

"It came in the internal mail."

"What's the letter say?" Walking over to the desk, I place the letter in front of him and watch as he reads it. "This is what I don't understand. How the hell do they know what case you're working on? Plus, they changed up how you get these letters. They're getting information from somewhere. I really hope it doesn't turn out to be someone on the team."

"Do you really think there is a mole in the department, sir?" That thought never once occurred to me until the captain said it out loud.

"I'm not ruling anything out now. Did forensics get back to you in regard to the other letters?" the captain asks, looking from the letter to me.

"Yes, sir," I answer and deliberately don't mention when. "Nothing of use. Whoever this is knows what they are doing."

"I had a feeling that you would say that. Sorry, Liam, but you're off the case. Your safety is a priority."

My heart sinks at this even though I knew it was coming, but I keep my fingers crossed that he doesn't tell me to stay home.

"Not sure if I should make you stay home, too," he adds as if he's just read my thoughts.

I'm just about to jump in and plead my case to stay in the office when Wyatt comes to my defense.

"Sir, Liam has been staying with me since the second letter arrived. If he agrees to only come in and leave with me, would he still be able to come into the office?"

Holding my breath and keeping my fingers crossed, I wait to see what the captain says. "Only you?" he asks Wyatt, who confirms. "Fine. But you aren't to leave the office once you are here. Is that clear?"

"Yes, sir." Being stuck in the office all the time gives me an idea. "I know you said that I'm off the case, but I wonder…" I pause for a brief second to get my nerve. "If I'm desk bound, maybe I could still work on the case. Nobody would have to know. Just call it desk duty. It's just that I've already worked my butt off on this case."

The captain looks over to Wyatt. "What do you think, Detective Johnson? I personally want him completely off, but if you can vouch for his safety, I'm willing to give that a trial run."

"If he promises to stay in the office and let me do the leg work, I think it should be okay. But I think Liam's right to say that we need to tell the office that he's been assigned to desk work in case there is a mole."

From the look on the captain's face, he isn't happy, but he also knows that if he puts someone else on the case, there would be a delay in bringing them up to speed on what we've found so far.

"Okay. But if any more letters come in, then you are off and on house arrest. Do I make myself clear? And make sure this letter is put into an evidence bag," the captain states as he hands the letter back.

"Yes, sir," we say in unison. Leaning over, I pick up the letter and we make our way out of the office before he changes his mind but stop when he calls out to Wyatt.

"Detective Johnson. Please be extra careful. I don't want him to switch focus to you or start threatening you. One is enough. Report any suspicious activity at once."

"Of course, sir." Thankfully Wyatt keeps the smile off his face till we get back to our desk, and I can't resist.

"I wonder what the captain would say if he knew the whole truth about Lorenzo."

"Shut up! And keep your voice down." Wyatt looks around the office to see if anyone heard before smiling. "Having the protection of the Romano name has its perks. Just wish I could figure out how to get it for you, too."

"Me, too." I'm pretending to think about it, as well, but now I'm wondering why Marco hasn't got it if he is the target. Thinking about Marco reminds me I need to organize a meeting with him tonight. Looking over to Wyatt, I say, "If I'll be staying with you guys longer, I need to pop home tonight, pick up some more things, and check the place over."

"Yeah, of course. I'll stay with you."

Fuck, I was planning to sneak out and get to Marco's. How the hell do I stop him, then think of Lorenzo. "Why don't you use the alone time and spend it with Lorenzo. Drop me off, and when I'm done, I'll text. You can come get me or I can walk. Give you guys a couple hours. I bet it's not fun having a houseguest."

For a second, I thought he would argue, but the thought of spending a couple hours with Lorenzo wins out. "Fine. I'll drop you off and pick you up. You aren't to wander about the streets. Just text when you're ready."

"Deal."

The rest of the day drags, and every time I check my watch and hope that another hour has passed, the hand has only moved five minutes, but I don't remember what I did during the day, either. I think I stared at the same pieces of paper on my desk pretending to cross reference them with something.

"You ready to go?" Wyatt's voice makes me jump.

"Yeah." It's what I've been waiting for all day, but suddenly I don't want to leave the office. My legs manage to get me up from my chair and walk me to Wyatt's car, and when he drops me off at my apartment, they manage to get me inside and to my couch. As I sit down, I pull out my cell and quickly type a text to Marco.

Liam: Can I pop over to see you?

And I wait for his reply. I presumed that it would be instant. He should have just been getting home from school, but when I haven't heard from him ten minutes later, I decide to get some clothes together to make this rouse believable to Wyatt when he picks me up later. When twenty minutes have gone by and still nothing, I go to pick up my cell so I can send another message. Time is getting away from me, and it will take me at least twenty-five minutes to get there, but hopefully the conversation won't take long and I can get back before Wyatt wonders what's taking so long. As I pick up my cell, it beeps, and a reply from Marco finally comes through.

Marco: Home. Come over whenever.

The text message is so straight forward that it surprises me. I had thought he might have put *Of course. I've missed you.* The starkness tells me he knows something is going on. He may not realize the full extent, but he knows.

I don't reply but head straight out. It's only as I'm on the street making my way to the subway station that I get the feeling that I am being watched, and it just spurs me on, telling me I am doing the right thing. But it doesn't stop the relief washing over me as I step through the front doors of Marco's apartment building and see Roy in his usual place behind the desk.

"Good afternoon, Mr. Smith."

"Good afternoon, Roy." I used to ask if it was okay for me to go up but don't really have to anymore, so I make my way to the elevators, knowing that Roy will let Marco know I am on my way. A few minutes later, Marco opens his door, a huge smile on his face, and my heart breaks because the moment he looks at me, the smile vanishes and his eyes flash with pain.

Chapter 19 — Marco

When I woke up this morning, the day had been full of so many promises, I never imagined that by the end of the day, everything would change. Going to school I had been so nervous. I'd read the school code of ethics so many times it was etched in my brain, and I could probably recite it by heart. Yet my meeting turned out to be better than expected. In fact, it might have been the best day in school ever.

Standing outside the principal's office, I could feel the sweat on my hands, and I'd rubbed them quickly on my pants so they aren't damp when I shake his hand. Taking a deep breath and patting my bag that contains the code of ethics for reassurance, I knocked on the door and waited.

"Come in," announced a friendly voice.

Walking in, the principal rose from his chair, stretching out his arm. Shaking his hand, I said, "Good morning, Principal Parry."

"Good morning, Mr. Romano. Please, take a seat. I have to say I'm a little surprised that you asked for a meeting this morning. Is everything okay?" I've always loved that when on school grounds, the principal uses a more formal way of addressing me, making me feel as though I'm respected and being taken more seriously.

"I need to talk to you about something." I deliberately did not answer the question because I didn't know if everything is okay. "It's regarding a personal matter."

"Well, that doesn't sound good. You aren't planning on leaving us, are you? I know a lot of the kids are fond of and respect you."

"No, I'm not planning on going anywhere," I replied as I collected my thoughts. Figuring it was for the best, I dove right in. "Yesterday, a student came to see me in confidence and spoke to me about his sexuality. I think he needed to talk to someone who wasn't going to judge him. When he left, it got me thinking about how many other students I could help if they knew a teacher understood what they're going through."

Before I had a chance to complete what I was saying, I heard him ask, "Understand what?"

"The confusion you feel when you realize that you might be gay." I'd thought he would look surprised, but his expression remained blank.

"Is that what you're telling me, Mr. Romano? That you're gay?"

"Yes, sir," I responded, and before he could say anything more, I continued with, "Before coming to see you, I read the code of ethics, and it mentions nothing regarding the orientation of a member of staff."

"And if it did, would you have stayed silent?" Principal Parry asked, leaning back in his chair and resting his elbows on the arms before steepling his fingers in front of his face.

Last night, I'd gone over all the questions I thought he might ask, and this one never occurred to me. And I was taken aback. I'd stayed silent this long, so would I have continued? The answer: probably.

"Honestly," I started, and when I looked over to the principal, he nodded. "Probably. But this is something I couldn't stay silent about forever, so eventually I would've looked for a new school." He had been expecting this answer by the look on his face.

"Well, lucky for us, this school is completely inclusive. In fact, a few students have approached me to start an LGBTQ club. I had been thinking about which teacher to ask, and it looks like you might be perfect. Are you up for it?"

"Yes, sir," I said in response, and there is no hiding the enthusiasm in my voice.

"Good. I'll get the kids to come and see you to discuss the best day for the first meeting."

"Okay. Sounds great."

"Is there anything else I can help you with today?"

I'm shocked that he had taken this so well. I'd been expecting to fight for my position and the right to teach here. "Um. No. That's it, really."

"In that case, just two things before you go. One, who was the student that came to talk to you? Is he in any trouble? And secondly, how come it took you so long to say something?"

"If it's okay with you, sir, the student spoke to me in confidence, and I don't want to betray that. And the reason it took so long for me to say anything is due to my family. My dad wouldn't have approved," I told him honestly.

"Oh! You recently lost your dad, is that right?" Principal Parry asked.

"Six months ago," I confirmed, but to my ears, it sounded so emotionless. I stared at the principal trying to gage his reaction.

"Losing a parent is always tough." The principal's face was somber for a second, and I guess that he was thinking about a beloved parent he'd lost. I wondered what he would think if he knew what kind of man that was my father. He shook his head, bringing himself back to the moment. "And you're sure about the student?"

"Yes, sir. But I promise that if I see any signs of trouble, I'll come to you directly."

Principal Parry looked at his watch, then up at me. "You'd better get to class. The hordes will arrive soon."

Getting up, I made my way to the door and was just about to walk out when the principal called my name again.

"Mr. Romano, thank you for coming to see me. That took a lot of courage, and I want you to know that my door is always open."

"Thank you, Principal Parry."

Walking back to my classroom, I felt like I was walking on air. That meeting really couldn't have gone any better, and it looked like I'd be helping students straight away with this club. I can't wait to tell Liam; I'm so excited for the future. Hopefully, he'll understand and realize it was something I needed to do. I had just gotten to my classroom when I spotted Noah walking down the hall.

"Good morning, Noah. You're here early."

"Morning, Mr. Romano. Thought I'd get some studying in before class."

There wasn't going to be a parade or assembly with the big announcement of 'Today we celebrate Mr. Romano being gay.' I think there was an understanding that it would probably just come out over time, and if I would be looking after the club, it would be sooner rather than later. But as I looked at Noah, I knew there is one kid in this school who needs to hear it from me, and the sooner the better.

"That's good. Can you come to see me after school? It's regarding what you spoke to me about yesterday and will only take five minutes."

For a second, he looked concerned. "Is there anything wrong?"

"No, not at all. I just wanted to talk to you about something."

I could see the relief on his face as he nodded and replied, "Okay."

"Have a good day and try not to get into any more fights."

"I'll try," *he said as he walked away, chuckling to himself.*

The morning flew by, and by lunch, I thought at least one of the kids the principal mentioned might have come to see me regarding the club. The fact that nobody did was a relief as I really wanted to talk to Noah before anything got out. Then, before I knew it, the afternoon was over and Noah was at my classroom door, knocking to come in.

"Come in, Noah. Take a seat."

He closed the door and walked over to his normal seat and sat down, just looking at me. "Listen, there's something I wanted to say to you. First, thank you for feeling that you could talk to me yesterday. I know that must have taken a lot to trust someone with your secret. And second is that I understand what you're going through because I've been there myself. I was probably about your age when I discovered I was gay, and it was so confusing. I would've loved to be able to talk to someone about it. You coming to me with your story gave me the courage to talk to the principal this morning. Something I should've done a long time ago."

The only part that he picked up appeared to be the principal bit, and it took a second for alarm to cross his face. "You spoke to the principal? About *me?*"

"No, Noah. I mentioned a student, and that's it. No names. I promise. I wouldn't do that."

He instantly relaxes, and then I see him register the rest of my words.

"Wait. Did you just say that your gay? I thought you said your brother was?"

"Yep, I did, and so is my brother." The look of shock on his face is priceless.

"Wow, your parents must be over the moon." I couldn't help but hear the sarcasm in his voice.

"My dad died six months ago, and I don't really talk to my mom anymore." I probably didn't need to say this, but if he ever comes out, then I have a feeling that his parents aren't going to embrace him, so I wanted him to know that there is someone that will be in his corner. Someone he can turn to. Someone he can trust.

"Oh." I saw his eyebrows raise in surprise. "I'm sorry about your dad. But did you stop seeing your mom cause you're gay?"

"It's not the main reason, but it was a factor."

"That must be tough. Not having your parents around." He was trying to be sympathetic, but I know there is a hidden agenda beneath that question, and so I answered truthfully.

"To begin with, it wasn't easy, but I have a great relationship with my brother and his fiancé and also have some great friends. It took me a while, but it's my mom who's missing out and not the other way round." I could see that he was thinking over this and absorbing what I'd said, and I really hope that he remembers it and it helps him in his future decisions. "I'm not sure if this would be an interest for when or if you're ever ready, but there will also be an LGBTQ club here at the school."

"There is!" And for a split second, happiness flashed across his face as he must have realized that there are other people in the school like him, but it's gone before it has a chance to settle. "That's not something that I'll be able to attend."

I wondered why he couldn't and am about to ask him when I remembered him mentioning his family was religious. There is no way that they would allow him to attend, and he wouldn't be able to lie to them, either.

"Okay, just remember that I'm here for you. Now, off you go." I smiled at Noah before turning to collect the papers from my desk.

He got up from his chair and walked over in the direction of the door, but before I heard the telltale sound of it opening, he must have turned back to me. "Mr. Romano?" I looked up from my papers and over to him, and the smile on his face told me everything, but he still said, "Thank you for telling me."

"You're welcome, Noah. Have a good evening."

"You, too, sir."

When Noah had said that earlier, I had agreed, thinking my evening would be amazing. Yet here I am, looking at the man I love more than anything, and my heart is breaking before he's even said a word. When Noah left, I'd been so excited that I'd pulled out my cell to text Lorenzo, and that's when I spotted the text from Liam, and all thoughts of telling Lorenzo vanished. I would finally see Liam, and I could tell him everything that had happened. It had felt so good, but that probably wasn't something that would be happening now.

When I open the door wider to let him in, he just strolls past me. No hug, no kiss, nothing. His face hasn't changed from the serious expression he's had since I opened the door. I watch as he walks into the living room and makes his way over to the couch and sits right on the edge, letting me know he isn't planning on staying long.

"Want something to drink?" I ask as I walk toward him.

"You got any beer?"

"Yep." Grabbing two bottles from the fridge, I pass one to him and deliberately sit away from him. Normally we would've been sitting next to each other, or more likely climbing all over each other.

"Lorenzo told me you came out at school. How did it go?"

I had thought he may have been hurt that I hadn't spoken to him about it first, but he's talking to me like he would Lorenzo. "Yeah, it went better than I thought it would. Sorry I didn't talk to you about it first."

"It's okay. I don't mind. Lorenzo said it was something to do with a student."

He doesn't mind? What the... He should've minded, and even though I don't want to, I can feel the anger beginning to boil in my veins.

"Well, it looks like Lorenzo's told you everything, anyway," I snap, my earlier happiness from the day slipping further and further away from me.

Either he hasn't noticed how angry I'm getting or he isn't bothered in the least. I thought he still might have asked why I didn't talk to him first, but instead, I'm getting this air of indifference.

"Yeah. We'd just missed you when we got home yesterday, and Lorenzo was explaining why you'd stopped over."

Now even more infuriated, I decide to try and demand some answers. "Were you ever going to tell me you were staying with Lorenzo? Or maybe tell me what the *fuck* is going on?" I'm not sure what's happened over the last week, but the man that is sitting on the couch with me is not the man I fell in love with. This man is devoid of anything that made Liam, well, Liam.

He must decide to completely ignore my question and instead looks at his watch and takes a swig of his beer before saying, "I really don't have much time. Tell me about your day first."

No, I want to shout at him. *Tell me now.* But something deep down is telling me he needs to hear me talk for a while, either just to hear my voice or he needs the time to muster the courage to say or do whatever he plans to do. So to humor him, or maybe just to keep him at my side a little longer, I begin to tell him.

"Well, Lorenzo is right; a student came out to me yesterday, and it was the catalyst I needed to cause me to come out at school. I saw the principal this morning, who was amazing when I told him, and he even explained that kids had approached him to set up a LGBTQ club and then asked me to head it. Which I, of course, jumped at."

"Aww, Marco, that's great. It'll be good for students to be able to talk to a teacher and have them know they understand." He seems genuinely pleased for a second.

"Yeah, but it also got me thinking. If the school can be this cool, maybe the guys at the precinct will be, too. After all, Wyatt's gay and they accept him. I'm not saying that our relationship has to come out, but it could be a start."

Throughout my entire speech, I watched him carefully, and it's only when I started talking about him coming out that I see him flinch, and I know then he's not even going to entertain the thought. I'm not surprised, though it shocks me the realization hurts like it does. I had hoped that him knowing I'd found the courage would be enough for him, but by the looks of things, that isn't the case.

"No!" I hear, and there is both a determination and harshness to his voice. "I'm not ready to do that. Wyatt's been out since the moment he started. The guys think I've always been straight. It's *completely* different."

He looks at his watch again and takes another swig of his beer, then another, and just when I think he's going to put the bottle down, he looks at his watch again and drinks the rest of the beer in one. Looks like he's finally gearing up to tell me the real reason he's here, and instead of letting him start, I try to distract him. Suddenly he's not the only one that wants to prolong this.

"You want another beer? How long can you stay?"

"Yeah, another beer'd be nice."

Finishing my own within a few swigs, I go grab each of us another before sitting back down next to him.

"I wish I could have told you about school and that you didn't have to hear that from Lorenzo," I say again, hoping to get a better reaction this time.

"Like I said, I don't mind. It's not like we've been in contact with each other much this week."

"That fresh case must really be busting your balls. We haven't spent this much time apart since we got together."

"Yeah, the case has been difficult," he replies, but it feels as if there is something else hidden behind these words.

Considering how much beer he chugs from the bottle, I guess that whatever he has to say is somehow linked to the case, and I'm beginning to get worried. Our conversations have never been this strained or labored before.

"Whoa, slow down. You'll be hammered." When I see he's drank almost half of the second bottle, I'm certain I hear him say something like, "I wish. Be so much easier then," but he mumbles it, so I can't be sure. He seems to listen to me and slows down with the drinking but says nothing more.

A few minutes later, he looks up at me and his expression has finally changed, except I want the serious one from earlier back. Not the scared, hurt man that is looking at me. There are already tears in his eyes, and I watch as he closes his lids and takes a deep breath. When he opens his eyes again, the tears are gone and there is now a steely resolution in them, a stark coldness that sends shivers down my spine.

The only words that come out of his mouth, flat and without emotion, are, "We need to talk."

And just like that, my world drops. I've never hated four words more in my life. It must read all over my expression because Liam visibly sinks back in his seat, and where just a few moments ago I wanted to prolong my time with Liam, I now want this over and done with.

Looking him straight in the eye, the only words I can muster are, "So, talk."

Chapter 20 — Liam

My heart has been breaking from the moment Marco had opened his door and I saw his face fall. I had done nothing but try to avoid this conversation, even knowing we needed to have it. He thinks I didn't notice how angry he got when I said it was fine that Lorenzo told me about his coming out at school, but really, it had hurt. This was something we should've discussed and celebrated together.

He probably didn't realize it, but the moment that he started talking about what happened in school, his demeanor changed. There was a lightness about him. He was so happy that everything had turned out okay, and the fact that he would head up the LGBTQ club was exactly what he wanted, and I couldn't have been prouder of him. Now, I'm fighting every instinct to pull him into my arms and tell him that—but I can't, and time is running away from me.

Every time I look at my watch, more time has gone, and I know that I can't put this off any longer. I think he knows what's coming but keeps trying to talk to me to put it off. He noticed the tears I'd tried to hide and failed, but when he mentioned about my coming out at work, I took that as my chance, steeled myself, and said the four words I'd never thought I'd utter to him.

I'll never forget the look on his face when I said, "We need to talk." The pain that contorted his features was quickly followed by anger, and I felt the knife stab through my heart when he simply said, "So talk." At the end of all of this, I hope he understands why I am doing this and knows I wouldn't have done it if there'd been any other way to keep him safe.

Taking one last look at my watch and seeing that I have fifteen minutes to get this over with, I finally start. "Did Lorenzo explain why I am staying with them?"

"He mentioned something about the case and threatening letters, and that the captain wanted to take you off the case."

"Okay, so he told you most of what's going on. I've gotten another letter, and they're threatening to hurt the people I care about. Wyatt refused to let me stay on my own, and the captain only agreed to let me stay on the case if I only came in and left with Wyatt."

"So how come you're here now?"

"Because we needed to talk. I told Wyatt that I need to get some stuff from my place. He dropped me off and is picking me up. Once he left, I hightailed it down here, and I'll have to leave soon."

"You better start talking then. So far, everything you said, I knew. You could have called me and explained. I could've come and seen you at Lorenzo's place."

"Seriously? You're fucking joking, right?" I can't believe that he just said that and am instantly out of my seat, pacing to get my thoughts together. "We struggle to keep our hands off each other when we're on our own, and you would've expected me to sit there and pretend that you're only my best bud when all I would've wanted to do was climb you like a pole? Yeah, that would *not* happen."

"So, you decided that lying to me would have been better. You should have told me, and *we* could have discussed the options." Marco's becoming more animated as he speaks, and I notice when he emphasizes the "we."

There is a hint of bitterness in his voice, and it takes me aback. I hadn't thought he would get angry. But then, what the hell did I think would happen?

"Did Lorenzo give you advice on how to lie?" he spits back at me, and I look over to him, surprised at the venom behind the words and that he could even say something against Lorenzo. This isn't like Marco and shows me that he is already hurting.

"No! They still have no idea about us. And don't you think that's a little unfair to Lorenzo?" He just shakes his head. Honestly, I can fully understand why Lorenzo kept his life with Wyatt a secret for so long. It was virtually for the same reason that I am doing this today.

"Just tell me what's happening?" Marco states, his voice lowering as he sinks back against the couch in defeat.

Walking back over to the couch, I sit back down on the edge again, ready to make my escape as quickly as I can once this is over.

"My family are tough sons of bitches, so I'm not worried about them even if Wyatt is under the impression that I am, but you... You mean everything to me, and I need to keep you safe."

"You remember that I'm Alfredo Romano's son, right? There's no way that someone would come after me."

"I haven't forgotten who you are. Wyatt and I thought this is why they are targeting just me and not both of us. It wouldn't have taken long for Alfredo's associates to learn about Lorenzo dating a cop, but Wyatt has the protection of Lorenzo's name. His reputation means that no one would want to cross him. But you're different, Marco."

"How the *fuck* did you come to that conclusion? I am *still* Lorenzo's brother."

"Yes, that's true. But while no one knows about us, you're safe. You don't need the protection of your brother."

"So are you saying that we need to keep our distance from one another until this is over?"

"No, what I'm saying is that we"—and I point between us for emphasis—"are over." And the moment the words leave my mouth, the tears I'd been fighting finally win the battle and spill down my cheeks. I should wipe them away, but I'm trying to be strong. Trying to pretend that this isn't killing me as much as it is. I need to compose myself and think of what I can say that will drive that final wedge between us and keep him away.

"Oh, so you mean until this is over?" There's no mistaking the note of hope that comes through in his voice.

"No. I mean like permanently. There's no way that I can put your life at risk, and if we stay together, then that will always happen."

"So what? Are you planning to stay single forever?"

That's one question that I've been going over and over in my head since I decided to end this. If I feel this now, then is it going to be the same with every relationship I have. But I can't think about the future at the moment, only what is happening in the here and now.

"I can't answer that. I don't know what the future holds." I tell him, saying the only honest thing at that moment.

"Right. So, what you're saying is that there is something wrong with me."

"All I am thinking about is the best way to keep you safe and alive now. I have no idea about future relationships or even what the future will hold."

"Future relationships!" And this time there is no mistaking the devastation lacing his voice, and I see the first sign of tears brimming his eyes.

"I'm sorry." I clear my throat, turning away from Marco, getting up from the couch, and making my way to the front door.

"You're *sorry*? You don't seem very sorry." There is now anger clear in his voice as he goes through so many emotions. This is good. It means everything I've been saying has been working, but there needs to be more. He has to despise me when I walk out that door at the end of this.

I stop walking and turn to him, saying the one thing that I know will destroy him. Composing myself to make sure what I am feeling inside isn't showing on my face, I look straight into his eyes and say, "You know something. You're right. I'm not sorry. Not in the smallest way. This was a mistake. This isn't me or who I am, after all. Probably should have done this a while ago."

I can hear the sobs coming from him as I turn once more to leave, hearing him stutter out, "Y-you said y-you l-l-loved me. You j-just said I m-mean every-everything t-to you."

"I lied." My voice is callous, cold, and empty of any feeling. I know I'm being deliberately and purposefully mean, but with each word that falls from my mouth, with each step I take away from him, the more my world crumbles around me. In my head, I thought this would hurt less now that I had allowed myself to get used to the pain. I was wrong.

"*Get out!*" Marco screams behind me, his voice raw and watery. The rage in his voice breaks what's left of me, but I somehow manage to keep going. Just as I get to the door, he calls my name. I stop but don't turn to look at him. I can't. "I'm not Lorenzo," he says, his voice flat and devoid of emotion. "There are no second chances with me. You walk out that door, then don't bother ever coming back."

Opening the door, I take one step over the threshold before saying, "Wasn't planning to." And then the door closes, officially ending things.

Taking one last look at Marco's door, I whisper, "I love you and always will," and then run to the stairwell.

Normally I would've waited for the elevator, but I don't want to risk Marco chasing after me. Honestly, I don't think he will, not after what I'd just said. Once through the stairwell door, I chance a look at the time once more and see that I'll have to get going if I don't want any questions as to why I was gone so long. So I run as fast as I can down the stairs, but the moment I reach the lobby and see Roy sitting there, I know there is one last thing I can do.

"Roy," I call out, and he jumps when he hears my voice, probably not expecting anyone to come from the stairway, and he turns to look at me.

"Mr. Smith. You scared the life out of me."

Knowing that I don't have time for chitchat, I acknowledge his comment with nothing more than a "sorry" and say, "Can you do something for me? Don't let anybody up to Marco's apartment unless you know them and they've been here before, regardless of what they say. It's important."

"Of course. Is everything okay?" Roy responds with a nod, turning to grab a clipboard to make a note of my request.

"No," I respond but don't say anything more. "Bye, Roy," I close and leave the lobby as fast as I can. Once out on the street, I decide to flag down a cab, not wanting to wait on the subway with everyone's eyes on me, and it will be quicker—just.

Sticking my hand out to flag one down, I'm pleased that one stops almost immediately. Sliding into the back seat, I give the man my address and pray the driver isn't a talker, but I must be giving off "don't talk to me" vibes because as we pull into traffic, he remains silent.

I'm not sure how I'm holding it together, but I am, and as the city rolls past me, all I can think about is the gaping hole that has appeared in my heart that is Marco shaped. Pain is radiating through my body, and I can feel it pulsing through my veins with every aching pump of my heart. Even when I witnessed Wyatt going through the same thing with Lorenzo, I thought there was no way losing a boyfriend could hurt that badly and Wyatt was just being a drama queen. I was wrong, so very wrong. This has to be some of the worst pain I've experienced in my life, and all I want to do is crawl under a rock and never come out, but there is no way that I can break down in the back of a cab. I just need to hold it together till I'm back at Wyatt's and I can be on my own.

Before I know it, the cab is pulling up outside my apartment. After paying the driver, I rush inside and to my place. The moment I close the door behind me, I pull out my cell and text Wyatt.

Liam: Ready when you are.

His reply comes back instantly, and I can see why. I've taken longer than the two hours I promised I would be, but only by about fifteen minutes.

Wyatt: Be there in ten minutes. Stay in the apartment.

Exactly ten minutes later, Wyatt is there, and, taking one look at me, he knows something is wrong. I might have been able to fool Marco, but Wyatt can see straight through me. I was expecting a hard time for being longer than intended, but instead, he looks at the bag on the floor before looking at me.

"You got everything?" Wyatt asks, his eyes not moving from me.

"Yeah. Got enough for a few weeks." I confirm, refusing to meet his stare.

"All that time and just that one bag?" he deadpans, then snorts before shaking his head and saying, "Let's get going then."

Ah. There's the jab over the time.

He picks up my bag and I follow him out of the apartment, making sure the door closes behind me. Once outside, I spot that he's parked a little way down the street. As we walk to his car, I see Wyatt looking around him, and I know that he's checking for anything out of place. I should do the same;

I might spot someone. But I just want to get in the car and to Wyatt's. We remain silent on the drive home, and we still haven't said anything to each other as we enter the apartment.

"Hey, Liam," I hear Lorenzo say, and when I look at him, I can see a red flush to his cheeks that only could have happened from having sex, and I'm filled with jealousy.

It's rude, I know, but I can't talk. The moment my mouth opens, I'll break. Taking my bag from Wyatt, I walk over to my bedroom, and just as I'm closing the door, I hear Lorenzo speaking to Wyatt.

"Is he okay?"

"Nope," Wyatt replies.

"What's up?" I don't miss the concern in Lorenzo's voice.

"No idea. He's been quiet since I picked him up. Let's give him some time."

Closing my door, I don't hear if Lorenzo replies, but sink to the floor and let the emotions finally escape. The tears roll freely down my cheeks, and I feel the last piece of my heart collapse. As the sobs rack my body, I bury my face in my arms to muffle the sound.

I'm not sure how long I stay seated on the floor, but eventually the tears dry and my sobs ease. Getting up, I make my way over to the bed, sit on the edge, kick off my shoes, and swing my legs up and then pull my cell out of my pocket. I shouldn't do it, I know, but I open my pictures and look through them. We don't have many, most of them taken when we were just joking about. But there is one I took in secret. One morning, I woke before Marco, and he looked mesmerizing, the sun highlighting his face all peaceful in sleep. I had to take a picture, and it's become my favorite one of him.

It's only when I feel a drip on my arm that I realize the tears have started again, and because I must be some kind of sadist, I go into my voicemail and listen to the last message Marco left me. Then I do it again, and on the third time, I say to myself, *tonight*. I am giving myself tonight to wallow in what I have done.

Curling in on myself, I hit replay one more time before opening the picture again. Hugging the phone to my chest, I whisper into the empty bedroom, "Please forgive me," and close my eyes, completely exhausted. As sleep takes me, I welcome the empty darkness.

Chapter 21 — Marco

The sound of the door slamming rings in my ears, and all I can do at that moment is stare at the spot where Liam had been standing just seconds before. Suddenly I'm on my feet, running for the door. He must be joking... He loves me. The last few months *must* have meant something. When I open the door, he'll be standing there, I'll call him a twat and pull him into my arms and tell him everything will be okay, and we will get through this.

Flinging the door open, I'm met with silence and an empty space. He isn't there. Looking up and down the hallway, I find no evidence that anyone had even been out there. Slowly closing the door, I make my way back over to the couch and sit down. He wasn't there. He *left*. And that's when I break down. Curling into the fetal position, I hold myself because it feels like if I don't, I'll smash into a million pieces. Sobs wrack my body, and I can feel the couch cushion getting damp from my tears.

My brain is going over everything that was said, trying to figure out where it went wrong, but my heart keeps telling me *You knew this was coming, why are you surprised?* But it doesn't make me feel any better. Until he walked away, I had thought he was acting. His voice, when he said this was a mistake, was so cold and unfeeling. It had hurt so much that I lashed out, shouting that if he walked out the door, that was it. I was hoping the words would make him think about what he was losing. It backfired, and all it did was cause more pain. When he replied that he wasn't planning to, it was as if someone were carving the words into my very soul with a hot knife. Each letter becoming more and more painful.

At some point, I must have fallen asleep, because the next time I open my eyes, the apartment is in total darkness. Confused for a second and wondering why I'm sleeping on the couch, I suddenly remember the events from earlier. *Liam left me.*

And the pain slams into me again. I need to get out of the apartment. There are just too many memories in here now, plus I need something stronger than the beer in my fridge. Walking into my bedroom, I quickly change out of my work clothes, grabbing some black jeans and a black T, and then throw on my biker boots. The black outfit fits my mood, and I decide to visit a local bar that's within walking distance.

Just as I leave my building, my cell starts buzzing in my pocket. I quickly pull it out, hoping to see Liam's name, but it's Lorenzo's lighting up the screen. I want to ignore the call, but I know if I do, Lorenzo will probably just keep calling.

"Hello," I answer, trying to make my voice sound as normal as possible.

"Hey. What are you up to? I was wondering if you could pop over." He sounds worried.

"Why, what's up?" There's no way I'll be able to go over to Lorenzo's till I know that Liam isn't going to be there. This is why you shouldn't get involved with friends. It'll be a *long* time before I'll be able to stay in the same room as Liam.

"Something happened with Liam. We thought that maybe the three of us might be able to find out what—"

"Nope. Sorry, can't," I interrupt, and it comes out harsher than I intend.

"Oh…"

I can hear the surprise in his voice at my curt response, but if I don't say something more, he'll find it strange that I'm not going over there straight away to help a friend.

"I'm actually on the way out to meet a friend that I haven't seen in ages." I say the first thing that comes to mind and change my tone to make it sound friendlier.

"Well, do you have any ideas as to what we can do?" Lorenzo asks, the desperation lacing through his voice.

I roll my eyes before saying, "Just leave him. He's probably processing something and will tell you when he's ready."

"Okay. But if there is no improvement tomorrow, can you come over?"

Shit! "Yeah, of course," I lie, because I can't think of anything to get out of it right then. "Keep me updated."

"Will do. Have a good evening." And with that, Lorenzo hangs up the phone.

Hearing the concern in his voice makes me wonder if Liam was more cut up by what happened, but that wouldn't make sense after what he'd said and done. But I'm not going to think about it anymore tonight. Opening the door to the bar, I'm pleased to see it's quiet and make my way to the end of the bar, perching myself on one of the stools.

"What can I get you?" the bartender asks once I am settled.

"Bottled beer and a vodka soda, please?"

"Are you waiting for someone? If so, I'll hold off getting them till they arrive." The bartender must think I'm ordering for two people.

"No. It's just me."

"Well, shit, you must have had a bad day." He leans his hip against the bartop and gives me a sympathetic smile.

"You could say that."

Without another word to me, he walks down the bar, but he's left me confused since he hasn't asked what type of beer I want. I watch as he opens a fridge and grabs a bottle before bringing it back to me.

"That's the strongest beer in a bottle we have. I guessed that if you're also asking for a vodka chaser, you need something stronger than normal."

I laugh at that. "Yeah, you're right. Thanks."

"You want ice in the vodka?"

"Please."

While I'm sipping my beer, the bartender goes and makes my vodka. Then, when he brings it back over to me, he doesn't walk away, just leans against the side of the bar, but I can see he's watching the other customers, ready to move and get their orders when needed.

"So, fired or dumped?" he asks

"What?"

"It's early evening. You came in and ordered a beer and vodka. That means one of two things. You were either fired and don't want to go home or you were dumped and don't want to go home."

"Maybe I just had a bad day at work."

He chuckles at this. "Nope! If it was a bad day, then you might have asked for the beer or vodka, not both. So, what is it, fired or dumped?"

"Dumped." I admit.

"Knew it. You or her?"

"Excuse me? Me or her?" I'm completely lost by his statement but have to admit that the bartender is taking my mind off everything. I look for a name badge and see a silver tag pinned to his shirt with the name *Trip* in bold, black letters. The name makes me smile. It strangely suits him, but he catches me looking.

"Before you ask, yes, it is my real name. My mom is a raging hippie, and she told me I was conceived on this epic trip... hence the name."

I almost spit out the beer I'd taken a sip off. "Your mom *told* you that?"

"Yep. She's *quite* proud of the fact but quit changing the subject. You or her?"

Still confused, I'm about to ask him to explain again when he spots a customer at the other end of the bar and makes his way over to serve them. *Me or her?* It's then I realize he thinks it was a girlfriend and he's trying to figure out if it was me or her that did the dumping. I burst out laughing so loud that some of the other customers look over. Apologizing, I go back to my beer, finishing what was left before I take a sip of the vodka that is now ice cold and enjoy the feeling of coolness and burn as the liquid travels down my throat.

Once the customer has been served, Trip makes his way back up to me, and I have a feeling that until the place gets busy, I'll have company—which is the opposite of what I wanted. But there is just something about Trip... He's approachable, which is a good trait to have as a bartender.

"So, come on, spill. Who dumped whom?"

"He dumped me."

His face registers shock for the briefest of moments. Looks like he wasn't expecting me to say that.

"You're gay?"

"Well, considering I just said that my boyfriend dumped me, that's a pretty good sign."

"You don't look gay." I don't think he meant to say that out loud if the horrified look on his face is anything to go by, and an apology quickly follows. "Shit. Look, I'm sorry. I didn't mean to say that out loud."

"It's fine." And I chuckle, guessing I may have to get used to statements like that. "I only just came out. Told my family a few months ago and my work today."

Trip just stares at me before deciding something. He turns and walks away. There are no customers demanding his attention, so he must have decided that he doesn't want to spend the evening with this sad case sitting at the end of the bar, but a few minutes later he's walking back up to me with another drink in his hand and gives it to me.

"You came out and got dumped on the same day. That's on me," he states, giving me a smile

I sniff the drink and take another sip, tasting the vodka and soda. "Thank you."

We don't say anything more for a few minutes, but he continues to stare at me. Trip has something on his mind and is trying to work out how I'll react. In the end, his curiosity wins out.

"Okay. I still can't see it."

"See what?"

"The gay thing," he replies, waving a hand over the part of me that is visible above the bartop and then looking me up and down once more.

"How does gay look then?"

"Well, the ones that come in here are... they're what you might call 'fabulous.'"

"We come in all shapes and sizes, you know." He laughs at this, and if I'm not mistaken, a blush tints his cheeks.

"Yeah, I know, but you seem to be... oh, I don't know, so straight, like a teacher or something."

The laugh that comes out of me causes my entire body to shake, and within minutes, there's a tear rolling down my cheek.

When I finally manage to compose myself, I look at Trip, who's staring at me like I've lost it and asks, "What the hell was so funny?"

"Well," I start and wipe my eyes with a finger. "I *am* a teacher."

"Well, blow me." And his eyebrows shoot up when he realizes what he said.

"You're cute, but I don't think so with just being dumped and all."

The red starts below his shirt and travels up his neck and face, and I can't help laughing again. That was mean of me, but Trip has made me feel better. It's been nice laughing and joking with him, but the place will start to get busy soon enough, and any chance of a conversation will be over.

"Sorry," I say to him, "that was mean of me. I didn't mean to embarrass you."

"Nah, it's okay. Just wasn't expecting it."

"Surely you've heard worse."

"Yeah, of course. Women flirt with me all the time; it goes with being a bartender. But I've never heard it from a man."

Never heard it from a man? Really? Taking a closer look at Trip, I see he is younger than I thought, maybe early twenties. He has a slim build with dusty blond hair and a tan glow to his skin.

"You're not a native New Yorker, are you?" I ask him.

"Is it really that obvious?"

"Not really in the looks since the city is a melting pot of people and cultures, but your accent and air of innocence definitely gives you away."

"I moved to New York a few months ago. I lived in a small town and couldn't stay there anymore."

There's more to that statement than what he's saying, but it isn't the right time to pry. But maybe he could use a friend.

"You got a piece of paper?" I ask and watch as Trip walks to the cash register and picks up a notepad, pulls off a sheet of paper, and picks up a pen, too, bringing them over to me. Trip watches as I write down my name and cell number, folding the paper in half as I hand it to him. But he doesn't take it from me, just stares at it.

"Look, I'm not hitting on you or anything. But you seem like a good guy, and you've made me laugh tonight. It was just what I needed. You're new to the city and probably could use some friends. So, take it. You never have to use it, but I want you to have it."

Finally, he takes it out of my hand and puts it into the back pocket of his pants. "Thanks."

Soon after, the rush starts, and I watch as more and more customers enter the bar. But the busier it gets, the more hairs on the back of my neck stand up. I feel as though there is someone watching me. I keep looking around, but no one is standing out, and it's putting me more on edge. Trip notices.

"Hey, everything okay?" It's kinda sweet, he's already concerned about me.

"Yeah. Just got this feeling that someone's watching me."

"Of course someone would be watching you. You're the hottest guy here."

Okay, there is definitely something more going on with Trip if he is saying that I'm the hottest guy here. A few more visits to this bar are in order. I want to get to know Trip better.

"Well, thank you."

He must not have realized what he'd said until then and that delightful blush is back on his cheeks and he tries to back track.

"You just have to look at all the women who keep staring in your direction, drooling, to know you're hot."

"I don't really look at women," I say with a smile.

He laughs. "Oh, yeah, right."

He pauses for a second, and he has that look on his face again where he seems to want to ask me something but is not sure it will be well received.

"Okay. Have to ask. You seem like a nice guy. Why the hell were you dumped?"

And just like that, everything comes rushing back, and my breath catches at the pain lancing through me.

"He said this wasn't for him. Basically, didn't want to be with me." I say out loud.

"Ouch, harsh. But why weren't you right for him? You seem like a pretty solid guy to me and have a good job, to boot." The surprise is evident by how far he raises his eyebrows.

"Well," I start, wondering if it's right to tell Trip that I was the first man that Liam had ever been with. Will Trip think I brought it on myself and that I shouldn't have gotten together with him in the first place? But it will be nice to finally talk to someone, though I still won't mention any names. "I was the first man he'd been with."

"Wow. But you seem to be more cut for someone experimenting. How long were you together?" Trip asks.

"About eight months," I tell him honestly.

"Eight months?" he asks, making sure he heard me right, and I just nod my head in agreement. "In that case, I'm calling bullshit on the 'it wasn't for him' line. There is no *way* you test the waters for that long."

"That's what he said." I confirm.

"Still calling bullshit. There is more to this." Trips says, unconsciously wiping the bar top.

"I don't think so, but it was nice of you to say." I say giving him a slight smile.

Trips looks up the bar, and I follow his gaze and notice it's even busier now and there is more than one customer waiting.

"Wow, it got busy fast. Sorry, but I better get going."

Trip turns to go and serve the other customer, but before he's too far, I call out to him. "Hey, Trip!" He stops and looks at me over his shoulder. "Thanks for the chat, and the name's Marco."

"I know. You wrote it with your number. And you're welcome," Trips says as he smiles over at me.

Not quite ready to leave, I stay at the bar nursing my drink for a while, and I'm just about to take the last mouthful when Trip comes up to me holding another glass.

"You've already got me one."

"Nah, this is from a customer," he says and turns to point them out to me, but he seems to be scanning the crowd before lowering his hand. "Oh, he's gone."

Normally I wouldn't take a drink from a stranger, but considering this has been made and brought to me by Trip, nothing could have been slipped into it, so I accept it from him and settle back into my seat. Five minutes later and the world is getting fuzzy around the edges of my vision, and I know I need to get home while I still can.

Picking up my glass, I down the last of my drink. Standing up makes me feel dizzy, and I have to grab the bar to steady myself, feeling more drunk than I realized. By taking my time I thought it would be okay, but it looks like I was wrong. I keep hold of the bar until the dizziness passes, but the edge of my vision remains fuzzy. *Once I'm outside, the fresh air will help.*

When I'm finally feeling steady on my feet, I make my way to the door, waving over to Trip as I open it, but he doesn't see me since he now has a barrage of customers. The cool night air hits me the moment I step out, and I take a few deep breaths, but my vision remains blurred. *Bed is what I need.*

I turn towards my apartment and start walking, but I have only taken a few steps when my vision gets worse, and I feel myself stumbling and grab hold of a lamppost to stop myself from falling over. *Shit, those must have been some strong drinks.* If I just take my time, I'll be able to make it home.

Pushing myself away from the lamppost, I try to walk again, but it's becoming more of a stumble and it's getting harder to keep my eyes open. I'm so preoccupied with trying to stay upright that I don't hear the hurried footsteps of someone coming up behind me. I'm just passing an alley when I'm grabbed from behind, causing me to fall backward, and then am dragged down the alley. A bag is forcefully yanked over my head, and I find myself being stuffed into the back of what must be a vehicle.

No longer able to even sit up, I lay back on the cold metal beneath me and hear a deep, gravelly voice as cold as steel say, "I have him."

I have one thought before the darkness finally takes me: *What the hell do they want me for?*

Chapter 22 — Liam

When I woke up this morning, I'd hoped I would feel better, that my brain would have told my heart in my sleep that we did the right thing, that we were keeping Marco safe. But I was wrong. The hole that appeared in my soul yesterday is still there and still feels like it's bleeding. My eyes are still sore and slightly red rimmed, but I don't think they look like I've been crying. There's no way I can avoid breakfast with Lorenzo and Wyatt after blowing them off last night, so I make my way to the kitchen and join them. When they both look at me, I wonder who will break first.

"You look like shit." Wyatt states, not pulling any punches.

"Thanks. Just what I needed to hear." And then I give a weak smile, trying to distract them. It fails.

"Wyatt!" Lorenzo berates before turning to me, asking, "You okay?"

"Yeah. Just feeling like shit." *Well, it is the truth.* I'm just going to try and make it seem that I just don't feel well.

"We have to go to work today. You gonna be okay going in?" Wyatt asks, and I'm thankful that they believe the lie.

"Yeah, I should be fine." But I would have said pretty much anything to make sure I'd be at the office today just to try to keep myself busy. To forget about the pain. Because if I stop long enough to think about Marco, the tears will start again even though I am not sure there are any left.

"You want anything to eat?" Lorenzo asks, and there is no mistaking the concern in his voice.

"I think I'd like to leave in a bit," I reply just to try and make the lie more convincing and then look over to Wyatt

"Ready to go in five?" Wyatt asks.

"Yeah. I'll just go grab my cell and wallet." Leaving the table, I head back to my bedroom. As I walk back to join them in the kitchen, I can hear Wyatt and Lorenzo talking, and it's obviously about me, so I slow down to listen.

"Do you believe he's unwell?" Lorenzo asks Wyatt.

"Hell no. But whatever it is, he'll tell us when he's ready."

"But he looks so unhappy," Lorenzo comes back with.

"I know."

"You ready to go," I say as I walk back into the room, pretending to stuff my cell in my pocket so it doesn't look like I was eavesdropping.

"Yep," is all Wyatt says as he gets up from his seat and leans over and kisses Lorenzo, saying, "Have a good day, baby." It's an interaction I've seen them do so often, and yet today, it makes my heart hurt, and I look away.

On the car ride to the station, I thought Wyatt would make some small talk, but he remains quiet, and it's almost unnerving. We normally use the journey time to bounce ideas off each other, but I have no clue what to say to get us back to normal. All I can think about is the look on Marco's face yesterday. The pain I caused is haunting my every waking moment, and it's causing me to second guess everything. If I don't talk to someone, I'll go insane, so it may as well be Wyatt. I just need to be careful on how I word what's on my mind.

"Hey, can I ask you something?"

Wyatt jumps at hearing my voice, apparently as deep in thought as myself. "Of course. Is it something to do with the case?"

"Um, not really." In reality, it has everything to do with the case.

"Is it something to do with you looking like shit and brooding?"

"I'm not brooding," I whine.

"Sorry, but that's bullshit. What the fuck is going on with you? Lorenzo is really concerned."

"Yeah, I know."

Wyatt shoots me a look, and I know that he's waiting for more, but I've lost my words. I don't want to mention Marco by name, but I wonder if I can make out that there was someone special in my life and just not mention for how long or the gender.

"Look, we're just about to pull into the garage. Let's park and you can tell me what's going on and what the fuck you did," he says.

"What the fuck? What makes you think I did something?"

"'Cause." He smirks. "I fucking know you."

I huff at this but don't say anything more because I know he ' fucking right, but I don't want *him* to know that. A few minutes later, he's pulling into a parking space.

The moment the engine is turned off, he turns to me. "We have about five minutes, so spill."

"What would you say if I told you that there might have been someone special?" I thought he would be surprised, but he didn't miss the fact that I'm talking in the past tense.

"Might have been?"

"Yeah, when I got the last letter, I might've called it quits." I cringe when I see his eyes widen in shock and then he smacks the palm of his hand against the steering wheel.

"You did what?" His raised voice reverberates through the car, and he closes his eyes to rein in whatever he's feeling. "Why the *fuck* did you do that?"

"Hang on a second. Why the fuck aren't you surprised by all this?" I ask in shock.

"Seriously? You're not that good of an actor. I knew you were seeing someone. Don't know why you've been so hush hush about it and then outright lied when I asked you to be my best man. Guess that's your business," Wyatt replies.

"How?" I had been trying to be *so* careful.

"Really? You're asking how I noticed?"

"Yeah. I thought I was doing a good job at keeping it under wraps. Especially when I basically told you I wasn't seeing anyone," I mutter.

"Liam, you've been happy. Anyone could spot it," Wyatt tells me.

"Oh."

"So, explain. Tell me what you did so we can fix this," he urges.

"Can't be fixed. I said some really hurtful shit, and I don't want it to be fixed, anyway. By letting them go, I'm keeping them safe."

"Safe from who?" Wyatt asks, not getting the link to the letters.

"From nutters who like to send letters," I answer.

I watch as the realization dawns on him. "Shit." But then he stops to think before raising an index finger in the air and wagging it, saying, "We can help."

"What do you mean by 'we?'" I ask.

"Us." He says it like I should instantly know what he's talking about. "Me and Lorenzo. I'm sure if we explain it to Lorenzo, he'll know someone who could watch her."

"Like whom?" I ask, ignoring the fact he instantly thought I was seeing a woman. At least the rest of my acting paid off.

"I don't know. Frank, maybe? He would have been able to watch her, and she would never know. Look, when we get home tonight, let's talk to Lorenzo and see what we can do. I'm sure he would make a bouquet so big that she would forgive you instantly."

"Trust me, this isn't fixable," I state again.

"Bullshit. Anything is fixable. Just look at me and Lorenzo."

I know that Wyatt won't let this drop, and so I just nod my head in agreement, and he finally looks pleased. I now have an entire day to try to figure out how I get them to let this be without telling them the whole truth.

But the problem with getting advice is that it can also plant seeds of hope. For the rest of the morning, I keep thinking over Wyatt's words, and I wonder if he's right and we could think of a way of protecting Marco. All we'd need to do is let a few people know that he's Lorenzo's brother, that he's just as much of a bad ass as his brother, and have him watched. If I grovel at his feet, tell him I lied, that I was only thinking of him, he might take me back. It's wrong, I know, but I start to feel excited until I look up and see that Wyatt is staring at me, and I realize that no matter how much I grovel, until I can move back home, then there is no way I can start something back up with Marco unless I come out. We could be like Lorenzo and Wyatt, but the thought of coming out no longer scares me like it did before. Losing Marco permanently is scarier.

Knowing that solving the case will also help with the situation with Marco, I pull a file toward me that contains information on the transportation routes. I'm soon engrossed in figures and journey times, and it's only when I hear Wyatt say 'Hello' that I look up, thinking he's talking to me but then realize that he's talking on his cell.

"No, I haven't heard from him. Hang on, let me check with Liam." He pulls the cell away from his ear and looks over to me. "It's Lorenzo. You haven't heard from Marco today, have you?"

Out of nowhere, a coldness washes over me. Something's wrong. "No. Why?" I reply, but I think I can guess.

"Lorenzo's tried to call him a few times and there's been no answer."

Fuck, fuck, *fuck* this isn't good. "Does he want me to try?" Lorenzo must have heard me since Wyatt just nods. Pulling out my cell, I call Marco, but it goes straight to his voicemail. "Straight to voicemail," I let Wyatt know.

This must cause Lorenzo to panic because Wyatt's telling him to calm down and then asking when the last time he'd spoken to Marco, but I can't hear the reply.

"Wyatt," I snap. "What did he say?"

"Hang on," he says to Lorenzo and then looks over to me. "He said that he called him last night to come over, but Marco said he couldn't because he was going out with a friend for drinks."

Relief, pure unadulterated relief, rushes through me. "He's probably hung over and his phone died. Give him a few more hours, and he'll be in contact," I say after releasing a breath I wasn't aware I'd been holding.

"No, Lorenzo, I'm not reporting him as missing," Wyatt says and looks over to me, rolling his eyes. "You know that someone has to be missing for twenty-four hours before we can report it. Look, Liam is right, he's probably just hungover. We can start to worry in a few hours, okay?" Lorenzo must ignore him, and I hate that I am only hearing one side of the conversation. I wish I could demand that he put the speaker on, but that would look a little strange. "Yes, I agree it's not like Marco, but remember he came out to the school principal yesterday, and maybe he wanted to celebrate. Just wait a few hours."

Wyatt hangs up the phone and sighs deeply.

"How much was he panicking?" I ask.

"A lot," Wyatt states, running his hand over his face. "Thanks for the common sense about the hangover. Lorenzo instantly jumps to the bad. Hopefully, Marco calls him soon. If not, we'll have a frantic Lorenzo when we get home. He'll demand we all go to his place to check on him."

"Oh no, you can forget about me joining for that." There's no way in *hell* I am going there. "I don't want to watch Lorenzo tear Marco apart for not calling him."

"What happened to moral support and all that?" he asks, pretending to whine.

"It's null and void when it comes to getting in between brothers," I tell him.

"You shit."

We both laugh, but I can tell that Wyatt is worried. Over the next two hours, I spot him checking his phone every couple minutes just to make sure he hasn't missed anything, and honestly, I'm beginning to worry myself. There's no way that Marco would've waited this long to call Lorenzo, and I might have even tried his number myself when Wyatt wasn't looking, and it was still going to voicemail.

When it becomes obvious that neither of us are concentrating on work, we decide to call it quits for the day. We're just shutting down our computers when the internal mail delivery arrives, which seems really strange, considering how late it is on a Saturday and the fact I haven't requested anything. But before I can question the officer who dropped the manila envelope off, he's gone. Something about this just doesn't feel right. I don't miss the confusion on Wyatt's face as I pull out some gloves, putting them on before opening the internal envelope. Looking inside, I see a single white envelope that looks remarkably familiar. When I pull it out, I watch as the color vanishes from Wyatt's face as he recognizes it, too.

Dropping the internal envelope on my desk, I notice from the corner of my eye that Wyatt is out of his seat and walking to stand behind me as he did the last time so he can read the letter over my shoulder. Carefully I cut the white envelope open and pull out the paper, unfolding it and laying it flat on the desk.

YOU FAILED TO HEED MY WARNING.
NOW YOU MUST LIVE WITH THE CONSEQUENCES.

The moment I read the words, I know why Marco isn't answering any of our calls. It's because they have him.

Chapter 23 — Marco

Something doesn't feel right. I'm not lying down in my bed like I should be, so I try to move and realize I can't and I'm not able to figure out why. Opening my eyes, I immediately regret it, suddenly aware of the pounding in my head. *What the fuck is going on?* I shift my legs again in an attempt to lift them, but still nothing happens. It's at this moment it slowly dawns on me that I'm sitting in a chair and not in a bed at all.

Carefully opening my eyes even though the pounding hasn't stopped, I look down and see that my wrists are tied to the arms of a chair. As I become more aware of my body, it feels like my legs are, too, but nothing seems painful, so I guess nothing is broken. Not making any sudden movements, I look around, wondering where I am. By the look of things, I'm in the middle of a room. It might be a disused office, but why the fuck am I here and why am I tied up? The pounding in my head intensifies, and before I can think too much about my situation, the darkness pulls me under once more.

I have no idea how long I was out for, so it takes me a while to figure out that someone is slapping my check, pulling me out of the darkness.

"Hello," I rasp, my lips and throat so dry.

"Well, look who's finally ready to join us." A gravelly voice fills the room.

"Water," I say but hear nothing in reply and carefully open my eyes. The pounding has eased but is still there. Looking around the room, I try to find the person who was slapping my face. I spot him in the corner, lurking in the shadows, and look over to him and repeat my plea. "Water, please?"

I thought he would move—he must see how desperate I am—but he doesn't, nor does he say anything more to me, just keeps looking in my direction, staring at me. *What the fuck is going on?*

I'm so confused and my head is hurting so much that I can't think straight. I need to try to figure out why I've been taken. It must be a case of mistaken identity. The man finally pushes himself off the wall he's been leaning against and comes out of the shadows. Hope rises in me that I'll finally get some water, but instead, he walks behind me, and I'm not able to get a good look at his face.

Next thing I feel is a sharp scratch like he has plunged a needle into the base of my neck, and a voice in my ear says, "Night, night," and it's one of the most menacing voices I've ever heard, but the darkness descends before I can react.

The next time I open my eyes again, the room is darker, so I'm guessing that it must be nighttime. The dimness of the room is a lot gentler on my eyes, so the pain in my head eases and I can get a better look at my surroundings. I'm definitely in some kind of disused office, maybe in a warehouse somewhere. There is an eerie silence, telling me we aren't in the city anymore.

"Welcome back."

The voice comes from the shadows, and I look around trying to locate the person but can't find him. I try to lick my lips, but there is no saliva to moisten them, and my throat is so dry that swallowing is almost painful.

"Water," I croak into thin air.

There is a shuffling sound, and the man comes out of the shadows. For the first time, I get a look at his face. I had thought that maybe he would look familiar to me so I could work out why he'd taken me—stupid I know, especially since looking at the man in front of me shows he is a complete stranger and looks completely out of place. Looking him up and down, I take in the dark gray three-piece suit, black shirt and tie, and matching high gloss black shoes, all of which scream expensive. But the look reminds me of the suits my dad used to wear, and suddenly I get an idea of why I'm here. I bet they want something from Lorenzo and are using me as leverage. They must have worked out my connection to Lorenzo, but they probably think since Dad died, Lorenzo has gone soft. They'll be in for a shock.

"Water," I try again and add a "please," but it's more like a squeak.

The man takes a step toward me, brings his hand up, and I unconsciously flinch, making him laugh.

"Scared?"

But he's not waiting for me to answer. Instead, the man brings a bottle up to my mouth, tipping it so I can feel the liquid against my lips. I open my mouth to take a drink, but the man pulls the bottle away. I suck on my lips, trying to get the moisture. More laughter erupts from the man, and he places the bottle back against my lips. This time, he lets me drink the smallest amount before pulling the bottle away. He knows it's been hours since I've drank anything and is enjoying this game he's playing, the torture of providing tiny sips when all I want is to drink down the entire bottle. When I have just got used to the tiny sips, he changes up the game, and the next time that he brings the bottle to my lips, he keeps pouring. At first, I'm gratefully take the larger amount, but he just keeps pouring, and soon I am struggling to breathe and am spitting the water everywhere, resulting in more menacing laughter and the removal of the bottle.

Once I have stopped coughing, I manage to splutter out, "Who *are* you?"

"Who am I..." he repeats while walking around me in circles. "I am many things, most of which don't concern you except for one." And he stops dead in front of me, leans down hard on my hands, pushing them into the arms of the chair, and whispers, "I'm the one who decides if you live or die."

He goes back to walking around me, and I'm trying my best not to let him see how much those words have affected me. He will grasp onto any sign of weakness and use it against me. I need to somehow make him think I'm tougher than I really am, scare him before he can fully break me.

"Do you know who I am?" I ask and put as much force behind those words as I can muster.

"Oh, I know who you are," he says, not once breaking his steps, not offering anything more.

"So, who am I?" I have no idea why I ask. I'm still kind of hoping that he has the wrong person.

"You're Marco," he says matter-of-factly and walks around so he's standing right in front of me before adding, "Marco Romano."

My head snaps up to meet his gaze and there is nothing but hatred coming from him. It takes all my strength not to show the cold shiver that runs down my spine, and I hope he doesn't spot the goosebumps that have risen up on my skin. He fucking knows who I am and doesn't care. This is bad, so fucking bad, but I somehow need to keep him talking and walking. As long as he's doing that, I'm safe.

"So, you do know who I am. So that means you know who my father is." I try to sound threatening when I feel anything but.

"Your father's been dead for six months."

And just when I think he will start walking again, he doesn't, but goes and leans on the wall directly in front of me, never taking his eyes off me.

He's worked out that I'm braver when I don't see his face. Digging deep, I try to find my hidden Romano.

"He has been, but that doesn't stop me from being his son. That comes with certain protections."

The laugh that comes from him is pure evil. "You? Do you really think you have protection?" The laughter cuts as he leans forward and stares straight into my eyes, continuing in an icy voice, "You don't. You're the throwaway son. A nobody to your father."

Fuck, this shithead has done his homework. So, if my connection to my dad isn't enough to scare him, maybe I need to try using Lorenzo.

"Maybe so, but my brother wasn't."

"Ah yes, Lorenzo. He was one scary son of bitch... six months ago." He shifts his stance but never once takes his eyes off me. "But then daddy died, and that changed, didn't it?"

"Your so fucking wrong," I spit back. "Lorenzo will come after me, and it's *you* who will pay the price."

"Aww, it's sweet that you would think that, but"—he pauses for more effect—"I think you're mistaking about how badass your brother is. He's gone soft since, which is a shame. He was exceptionally good at his job."

I'm about to ask him what he means by "his job," but considering what we are talking about, I'm guessing he means the jobs Lorenzo did for Dad. But just maybe I can use this to my advantage, try to scare him into thinking Lorenzo is still just as bad.

"That's where you're wrong. My brother still knows people, still has connections."

"Do you mean Wyatt, his cop fiancé?"

Fuck, if he knows Wyatt and knows that he's engaged to Lorenzo, then he really does know that Lorenzo walked away from our father's business. Which then brings up the question of exactly how long has this fucker been watching us? But if he wants something from Lorenzo, why the fuck didn't he go after Wyatt?

"You're asking yourself why we didn't go after Wyatt, aren't you?"

He'll demand that I answer his questions, but I really don't want to. I don't want to give him the satisfaction of knowing what I am thinking. Pain suddenly radiates through my face and my cheek stings as the sound of a slap echoes through the room.

"When I ask you a question, you *will* answer me... Now, were you thinking about why I didn't go after Wyatt?"

"Yes," I respond, trying to sound as sarcastic as possible, but it really has no effect on him. He just smiles, enjoying my discomfort.

"At first I was going to, but then I discovered *you*. Your dad was a clever bastard, and I'm still not sure how he hid who you were, but once we found out, we really couldn't believe our luck."

"I still don't understand. Why me?"

He pushes himself off the wall and walks over to me. Quickly grabbing my hair and pulling it backwards, snapping my head back as he says through gritted teeth, "Why you? You turned out to be a much better prize."

"A better prize. How? As you said, I'm a nobody."

Letting go of my hair, he goes back to leaning on the wall. "You are more than a nobody. You are my key to everything."

"Key to everything?"

What on earth is he going on about, and why? All the questions and riddles are making my head hurt, and I can feel the darkness trying to take me. All I want to do is sleep, but it looks like he has other ideas. He must have spotted me losing consciousness because he is suddenly walking back over to me. and I can feel the bottle back against my lips.

"Drink, or I'll make you."

I try to resist at first, wanting the darkness to consume me, but the man wants me awake and grabs my face as he pushes my cheeks together, forcing my mouth open and pouring the liquid between my lips. At first, he pours it slowly, but soon he's forcing it down my throat, choking me. He's telling me that he has all the power by doing this, no matter how hard I try to stop him.

"Good boy. We haven't finished our little talk. I'll tell you when you can sleep."

"Fuck you." The moment the word leaves my mouth, I regret them. You can't miss the anger that flares in his eyes, and I don't see the punch coming until it's too late. He connects with the side of my face, slamming my head to the side. When I straighten my head, there's the metallic taste of blood on my tongue. I guess the blow split my lip.

"You need to watch your fucking tongue," he spits at me.

When Lorenzo had first explained our father to me, it had terrified me. Even though he had never done anything to me, knowing what he was capable of was enough. I never thought I'd be afraid of a man like that again until today. The man standing in front of me is more terrifying. My father probably could have only dreamt of being like this. This man is hands on; he doesn't care if he dirties his own hands, something that Dad never did. He always got someone else to do that. That makes this man so much more dangerous.

"Cat got your tongue? Maybe you need another drink," he sneers at me.

"*No,*" I scream back, and he takes the opportunity to put the bottle to my lips and pour. The liquid flows so fast that it takes only seconds before I'm choking again. Laughing at my discomfort, he stops after a few seconds and pours the rest of the bottle over my head. Thankfully there wasn't a lot left and it just wets my hair, but I can feel the drops running onto my shoulders and down my neck.

"I have a feeling that you will be more fun than I expected."

I almost tell him to fuck off again, but the stinging of my lip reminds me of what happened last time I answered back to him. Instead, I try to give him my best death stare, and that just causes him to laugh harder at me.

"I'm not scared of you. You can look at me like that all you want if it makes you feel better."

How the fuck am I going to get out of this? I need to try to figure out what he wants with me, and I need to get him to talk, try to get information that might be useful.

"Where the fuck are we?" I'm hoping to throw him off by the simple question.

"Wouldn't you like to know?"

"How long have I been here?" Maybe knowing that will give me the hope that maybe help is coming soon.

He looks at his watch. "Well look at that. It's almost twenty-four hours. Looks like I miscalculated the dosage.

Twenty-four hours? What the fuck? Lorenzo must have figured out that I'm missing by now. *Hang on, did he say dosage?* I don't realize that I've said that out loud till I hear him answer me.

"Well, you know you should never accept a drink from strangers."

Drink from strangers? The fucking vodka last night. Shit, did that mean that Trip was in on this, too? He seemed so nice.

"The vodka," I say

"Ding, ding, ding. And we have a winner!"

"Trip?"

"Who the fuck is Trip?" he asks, so I'm guessing that means Trip isn't involved, after all.

"Bartender," I say.

More fucking laughter. I have a feeling that I'll hear that laugh in my nightmares for a while. God, I hope Lorenzo digs out the badass he was with Dad and wipes the smug smile off his face.

"Ah, yes, the bartender," the man snaps, seeming to lose his patience for a moment. He takes a deep breath before continuing, that sadistic smile returning to his face. "He'd taken quite the shine to you, I do believe."

"But he brought me the drink." I'm trying to figure out how someone could slip something into the drink without Trip knowing. But I wasn't really asking him the question, more talking and thinking out loud. He must have assumed I was asking him, though, because he goes on to explain.

"He did indeed. But he's new and turned his back on the drink, and I took my chance, leaned over the bar, and added a little something extra to your drink when he wasn't looking."

"That's why he couldn't spot who had bought the drink for me."

"You're getting good at this. Then I just needed to sit back and wait for the drug to take effect. Unfortunately, I might have added a little too much, but it got the job done quicker, I suppose."

"You could have *killed* me!" I scream at him.

"And?" He's just so blasé about it all. How can someone have so little regard for human life? But I'm starting to understand now why Lorenzo kept everything quiet if this was the type of man he dealt with daily. *Did Lorenzo have to put on an act like this to do Dad's dirty work?*

"*And?* Until you get what you want, surely it's better I'm alive more than dead."

"Maybe. Either way, the message gets across, so I win."

"Someone must have seen you dragging me off a busy street. Why the fuck didn't they stop you?"

He looks at me to see if I'm joking, and when he sees I am being serious, he cackles again.

"Because this is fucking New York, that's why. You were just another drunk. By the time the hired muscle had you down the alley, you were out of sight, out of mind. Nobody noticed him stuffing you into the van."

"You're fucking nuts." *Oh fuck, did I say that out loud?* Considering how fast his head snaps in my direction, I'm thinking that's a yes.

He's up on his feet again and walking towards me, and I hate to admit that he's scaring the crap out of me. I hope he can't see that on my face, but as he gets closer, I observe the evil sneer on his lips and panic grips me. Pulling on my restraints, which is fruitless but an instant reaction, I try to get away from the man stalking towards me. When he's in front of me, his sneer morphs into a smile at how petrified I am.

He raises his hand, and I thought he would hit me, but instead, he goes into the pocket of his suit jacket and pulls out a syringe, flashing it in front of my face so I can clearly see what it is.

"You are talking way too much."

"No." It's barely a whisper, but he still hears it and smiles.

He walks to the side of me, and I feel the pain as he plunges a needle into my neck, the cold liquid entering my body. I then feel his breath against my ear.

"Hope your boyfriend comes through. Now, night night."

At first, I'm completely confused when he said "boyfriend." Whose boyfriend? But then as the darkness pulls me under, I realize... *Liam.*

Chapter 24 — Liam

Fuck, fuck, fuck. They have Marco. I *know* they do. I sit there, frozen, just looking at the words in front of me and panicking. What the fuck do I do now? Getting up from my chair and pushing Wyatt out of the way, I know I have to get out of the office. I need to go find Marco, and I need to make sure he is safe.

"Hey, where are you going?" Wyatt asks, grabbing my arm and stopping me in my tracks.

"Out," I snap back while trying to tug my arm back, but Wyatt just tightens his grip.

"Don't be fucking stupid."

"Let go of me," I hiss and don't miss the look of shock on Wyatt's face when he hears the anger in my voice. I've never spoken to him like this before, but he still won't let me go.

"Not happening! Now sit the fuck down, or I'll make you." He's not angry, but from the look of determination and the commanding tone in his voice, I know not to try to disagree with him.

Reluctantly I sit back down at my desk, and Wyatt makes his way back round to his, watching me the entire time. When he's happy that I'm not going anywhere, the barrage of questions starts.

"Do you want to explain what the fuck that was about? You know that the captain would have had a shit fit if you left, and you'd be off the case." He points to the letter on my desk. "That wouldn't be a good idea."

Staring at the letter again, I re-read the words even though they're already ingrained in my brain. *Live with the consequences...* Does that mean they are planning to hurt Marco, or worse? There is no way I'll be able to live with myself if they do. To keep him safe, I broke up with him, but it appears I failed and have ended up causing him more pain than I ever imagined. My thoughts are making me restless, and I can't sit still anymore. I need to do something. But Wyatt is right, there's no way that I can leave the office, so I do the next best thing and start pacing.

Wyatt is watching me, waiting for an answer, and I know I'll have to tell him something, but what? It would be easy to explain that they've taken someone that I care about since he'll instantly think they have someone from my family or the mysterious girlfriend he thinks I have. But that's not good enough now—no, I need to tell him the truth but have no idea how.

I stop pacing and look at him. He doesn't say anything but keeps waiting. I open my mouth, but instead of words, a giggle comes out. Suddenly, I remember Wyatt doing this all those months ago, and for some reason, I'm finding the whole role reversal funny. The whole situation isn't funny, and Wyatt's looking at me as if I've lost my mind.

"Really?" he deadpans.

"Sorry, just a major case of déjà vu," I reply, but he has no idea what I'm going on about, so I decide to explain. Plus it's a way to put off the conversation that even my sub-conscience wants me to avoid.

"Me pacing while you're sitting there watching reminded me of a few months back when I was the one watching you pace, waiting for you to tell me something, and it just seemed hilarious."

"Yeah, but that was different. I was trying to find the words to tell you about Lorenzo."

Okay, I need to sit down for this, yet the moment I am back in the chair, I can't admit it. Wyatt has just given me an in to explain everything, but I know he'll lose it. Getting out of the chair, I start to pace again, looking at Wyatt on every turn. Each time opening my mouth only to close it and pace some more before deciding there is no avoiding it anymore. Realizing I will need to explain everything and will need to be sitting while I do it, I make my way back to my chair and look over to Wyatt.

"You wanted to tell me something important, right?" I ask, trying to help me get started.

"Yeah, but I couldn't figure out where to start," he confirms.

"You were pacing trying to find the words, right?" Wyatt nods in agreement. "So, yeah, this is exactly the same." When he doesn't get my meaning straight away, I look down at the letter.

"Holy shit, you know something."

Taking a deep breath, I answer, "Yeah. I think they followed up on the threat and have taken someone I care about."

Before I can explain who, Wyatt is out of his chair and coming round to me and pulling me out of mine, crushing me in a hug.

"Fuck, Liam. I'm so sorry. That's why you needed to get out of the office."

Nodding into his shoulder, I try and pull away so I can tell him that there's more. Before I can do that, he's pushing me back into my chair and rushing back round to his own. He pulls out a notepad and pen, and then more questions fly at me.

"When was the last time you saw her? Have you tried calling her? What does she look like? Fuck, the first question I should have asked is what's her name?"

Wyatt looks up at me, waiting for me to answer all the questions, and I will, but with the right content.

"Okay, I'll answer everything, but I need you to promise me something. Don't freak out, okay?"

"You're confusing the fuck out of me. Just get talking so we can find her."

"Him," I say, and when I am met with nothing but confusion, I repeat, "It's a him, not a her."

Silence. All I get is silence. I thought he might have said "you're joking" or "yeah right," but he knows that there would be no joking in this situation. But the silence is still unnerving and, in the end, I break first.

"Say something!" I demand.

"You better fucking tell me everything... and now."

Holy shit, he's pissed at me, and it's probably only going to get worse. But I start answering his questions, anyway.

"The last time I saw him was yesterday. Of course, I've tried to call him several times, but it keeps going to voicemail. He's about six-foot tall, dark hair, and the most gorgeous green eyes..." I pause before I answer his last question, watching as he's been making notes as I've been talking and then looks up expectantly when he notices that I've stopped. "And his name is Marco."

He writes the name down, then looks up at me and opens his mouth as if he is about to ask another question, but then he closes it and snaps his eyes down to the paper. I can see he's reading over the name he just wrote, probably checking to see if he's heard right.

"Marco? As in Lorenzo's *brother*, Marco?"

All I can do is nod in agreement and wait for the fireworks to start, but all I'm getting is silence again, and his face has gone completely blank. I can't tell if he's surprised, angry, pissed, worried, or if it's a mixture of all of the above.

"You're joking, right?" He knows I would never joke about something like this. This is a knee jerk reaction.

I shake my head and simply reply, "No."

"How long?" He's eyes are burning into me, and I know I should answer, but the words are failing me. "For fuck's sake, Liam! *How long?*"

The answer is on the tip of my tongue, but I'm so scared of what his next reaction will be. Once everything is out, will we still have a friendship, still have a partnership? I don't know, but at the moment, all that matters is Marco, and the only way we will find him is if Wyatt knows the truth.

"About eight months," I whisper back.

And Wyatt loses it. "Eight *months? Eight fucking months!*" He's so loud that some of the other detectives who are in the office look our way.

"Keep your fucking voice down, Wyatt. I don't need the entire force knowing my business."

Wyatt glances around and spots some guys looking, shrugs, and shouts over, "Making me look at eight months' worth of files." There are only looks of pity in response, and some even mutter, "Harsh."

Lowering his voice, he says, "Explain and quickly. We need to tell the captain, and then we have to get home where I will watch while you tell Lorenzo."

"Cliff notes version. I was attracted, went for coffee a few times, and it went on from there."

"But you're straight."

"The fact I have been going out with Marco surely shows that I'm not."

"Not in the mood for your smart mouth. So what is it? Did you meet Marco and suddenly decide that you like dick?"

Wow, I don't think Wyatt has ever been that brutal with me. I understand that he's probably feeling betrayed, but I'm not going to let words like that slide.

"No. I've always 'liked dick,' as you so nicely put it," I snap back. "But I was always too scared to act on it till Marco."

He has the good grace to flinch when I repeat his words, but I know that he's still confused by it all.

"So, are you gay now or what?"

"No, I'm not gay. Marco said I'm pansexual. I had thought I was bi. Never even realized that there were other definitions out there."

"Oh." He isn't sure what else to say to that, and considering I will have to go through all of this with Lorenzo, I really hope that he changes the topic. "We need to go show this letter to the captain, but at the moment, I think it's best we say we have no idea what's going on and you are trying to contact members of your family. Hopefully, he'll send you home. You know that you aren't going to be able to investigate this anymore. You're too close."

"Yeah, I know," I say, glancing over to the office. "Come on, let's get to the captain. The sooner this is over with, the sooner I get to tell Lorenzo." Wyatt tried to hide it, but I saw the smirk on his face when I mentioned Lorenzo.

We get up at the same time, and after I grab the letter from my desk, we make our way over to the captain's office. I find it odd that the door is open today, something that's unusual. We knock on the door frame, and the captain's head pops up. The moment he sees us, he beckons us in. It's only as we get closer that he spots the glove on my hands.

"You got another one, didn't you, Detective?" He bypasses the pleasantries, knowing how important this is, and points to the chairs in front of his desk to sit down.

"Yes, sir. Just arrived in the internal mail again." I place the letter on the desk in front of him and wait.

"This is taking things to another level. Do you know if he has taken anyone?"

"I don't, sir. We brought the letter straight to you. I will need to contact my family and find out."

"Shit, Liam." Oh fuck, if the captain is calling me by my Christian name, that isn't good. He must seriously be concerned to do that. "Sorry, but you're off the case, and I think it's best for you to stay home while the investigation takes place for your own safety."

"Yes, sir."

"You need to tell us the moment you hear if anyone is missing. Detective Johnson will keep you updated on the investigation from our end."

I had considered fighting the captain like I did after receiving the third letter, but I know it would be best for me to stay out of it. One needs to stay levelheaded, and that just wouldn't happen for me now.

"Yes, of course, sir. We were just leaving for the evening when the letter arrived."

"Are you still staying at Detective Johnson's?"

Before I can confirm that I am, Wyatt answers for me. "He is, sir. I've refused to let him return home until we've caught the perpetrator."

"Good, let's keep it that way. Now get home."

In unison we reply, "Yes, sir," before getting up to leave.

As we reach the door, the captain shouts over to me, "We *will* get him; I promise Detective Smith."

"I know, sir."

With a nod, the captain dismisses us, and we make our way back to our desks. Once we're back in our seats, I look over to see that Wyatt has this enormous smile on his face and is making no attempt to hide it.

"Why are you smiling like a Cheshire cat?" I ask, but already figure it involves Lorenzo.

"Oh, I'm looking forward to getting home, that's all," Wyatt replies, his voice pure innocence. *Bastard.*

"Why?"

"Cause I can't wait to watch you tell Lorenzo about you and Marco. I'm just glad he hasn't got his gun anymore." The smile never leaves his face. In fact, he seems positively giddy about the upcoming reveal.

So I was right and Lorenzo *is* the reason behind the smile. "You're enjoying this too damn much."

"Fucking right I am. You should have told us, and payment for that is watching Lorenzo as he rips you apart."

"Do you really think he will?"

"No idea," Wyatt says, shrugging, "but he will be pissed."

"Great. Will you at least help defuse him?"

"Not a fucking chance in hell. You've made your bed, now lie in it." He looks at his watch to check the time. "And he should be home now. So come on. Time to face the music." And if possible, the smile on his face gets bigger, his enjoyment of the situation growing.

I try to think of anything to delay that, but Wyatt's already out of the office and I have to rush to catch up with him. Hopefully the journey back to his place is over quickly. The nervous butterflies in my stomach are now doing a full dance, and I've never wanted something to be over with as much as this.

Chapter 25—Marco

Slowly I open my eyes, but the brightness causes pain to flash through my head, so I close them again, hoping to ease it. It doesn't work. I feel fuzzy and confused, and I'm not sure where I am, but it doesn't feel like home. Opening my eyes again, I give them time to focus on the room around me, and everything that happened slams back to me. I was kidnapped and tied to a chair, and it has something to do with Liam. Snippets of conversation come back to me. He'd been following me for some time , knew that me and Liam were together, and he's using me to get some kind of information. I try to think back to how long I've been in this chair and realize that it must be close to thirty-six hours.

"Well, good morning, sunshine. Glad to have you back with us."

That voice... I remember hearing it in my dreams. I thought it wasn't real, but it's here. It's like waking up in your own nightmare, except this one is very, very real.

"Water," I whisper, my throat so dry again I can barely swallow.

He walks over to me, bottle in hand, and once he gets closer, I flinch slightly, visions from the last time he gave me water crashing over me. He spots my reaction and a pleased, smug smile crosses his face. I take a few deep breaths getting ready for the onslaught of water that is about to happen but am surprised when he gently places the bottle against my lips and carefully tips the bottle so I can drink slowly. I'm also surprised when I manage to drink about half the bottle before he takes it away.

"I'm really going to have to lower the dosage. Don't want there to be an accident before you are useful to me."

And the riddles have started again. But then I hear what sounds like a photo being taken, and I look up and see he is holding a cell phone towards me.

"Smile for the camera," he sing-songs.

I don't move, not going to give him the satisfaction of moving on commend.

"Come on now, we need your boyfriend to be able to see your pretty face."

"Fuck you." The words fall from my mouth before I realize what I've said, and I tense, waiting for retribution, but it never comes. Instead, all I hear is his laugh.

"Getting bold, aren't we? Come on now, your boyfriend wants to see that smile," the man taunts.

If I plan on getting out of here, then I need to convince him I don't have a boyfriend, that whatever he thinks we are is nothing, but I have no idea how. When Liam had been sitting in my apartment saying I was in danger, I'd thought he'd been overreaching, but now, all this proves he had been right. Now it's my turn to protect him, or at least try.

"What boyfriend?" I ask, trying to sound confused.

"Don't play dumb with me. You know what I am talking about."

"Honestly, I really have no idea. I only just came out publicly, anyway, so how the hell would I have a boyfriend already?"

He throws his head back and laughs, the sound vibrating over me. It feels like a thousand insects crawling all over my skin, but I manage to hide the shiver it causes.

"So, it's the hard way that you want," is his only response.

"I don't have a boyfriend," I repeat trying to make him understand.

This finally gets a reaction out of him, and he storms across the room, slapping me hard across my face, which causes pain to shoot through my cheek and the metallic iron taste of blood is back in my mouth as he reopens my split lip.

He then starts circling my chair, and when I look up at him, I see the cell is pointed at me. I don't hear the telltale sound of a shutter going, so I'm guessing he must be making a video of me.

"Look at me. Let your boyfriend see that pretty face."

Looking up before I'm forced to, I observe the action causes him to smile at me.

"I told you I don't have a boyfriend."

How he manages it, I have no idea, but the slap comes from the other direction, and he gets the whole thing on video. It must be something he wanted, because the moment the action is over, he's turning off the cell and putting it in his pocket.

"You're lying to me. It's not going to help you."

"I'm not lying," I plead with him.

"I've been watching you for months, saw you kiss outside the coffee shop months ago. But I must admit you had us fooled for a while. But I took my time. I knew to wait for more, and then you went over to his apartment and didn't come out till the following morning. At first, I wondered if it was a one-off occurrence, but then it happened more and more. So, there really is no point in lying.

"We're just friends."

"Bullshit. I know that Liam's place is a one-bedroom apartment."

"And there is such a thing as a couch. You know you can sit *and* sleep on them."

For a split second, I see him waver, and I think he finally believes me, but something on my face must give me away, and his features brighten as he remembers something.

"You almost had me there. But you *did* kiss."

Shit, that kiss. I remember looking around and not seeing anyone that looked familiar, but of course, I wouldn't. I didn't think anyone was watching me. But how can I get him to forget about that kiss?

"That kiss was nothing. Misunderstanding. I thought he was gay, and I was trying my luck. It's always the cute guys that are straight. Luckily, he didn't hold it against me, and we stayed friends."

"That is a fetching little tale, but you didn't see the smile on his face as you walked away. That kiss meant something even then. And I've been watching him, too. He's been different since you came into his life."

Oh fuck. I've thought of everything I can to try to persuade this nut case that there is nothing between Liam and me, but he has been watching way too closely for that to happen. I need to try to figure out what he wants, what his demands will be, and then what he will do with me. If I can somehow keep myself safe and alive, it gives Liam more time to find me.

"What are you planning to do with me?" I ask, trying to change the direction of the conversation while still not confirming that Liam is my boyfriend.

"Trying to change the subject, I see. Do I take that as confirmation that we were right?"

This man is sharp. Do I still try to deny it or tell him the truth? But if I do that, am I then putting Liam or even Wyatt and Lorenzo in danger, too? I know that Lorenzo can handle himself, but I really don't want to put him in a position where he has to, especially if it means doing something like killing the nutter in front of me. He's worked too hard to get past that. So, I decide to try to go with indifference.

"I'm not confirming anything. You've already decided what the truth should be."

"You're right, I have." And I have never wanted to wipe the smug look off someone's face as much as I do this jackass.

He walks back to the wall and leans against it, pulling out his cell, pointing it in my direction, and taking a few more pictures. My guess is he'll use these pictures to get his point across. That he is serious so he gets whatever demands he makes.

"You never answered my question. What are you planning to do with me?" I say, breaking the silence. He must have known that by staying silent it would get me thinking. He must be aware that I'm going over all the likely scenarios, trying to figure everything out.

"Again, you're right. You really are cleverer than you look. Someone like you would have been useful in my team. It's just a shame you aren't more like your dad."

"I will never be anything like my dad," I spit back at him.

I had been expecting him to lash out at me for answering him back, but it seems to do the opposite, and he takes on a sad countenance.

"True, and that's why it's a shame. I could've made you wealthy beyond your wildest dreams."

So is that what this is all about? He wants money? But then why would he target Liam? Surely Lorenzo would've been the better option if that's what he's looking for. I'm not sure what he did with any of the money that was left over from Dad. I know that he gave some to Mom and some to me, but I never wanted to know where the rest went.

"Is that what you want, money?"

He laughs at this. Everything I say seems to be funny to him. It's almost as if he thinks I should know what's going on or I should know who he is. But to me, he's just the nut case who's using people to get his own way.

"Oh, I have money. More money than you could make in a lifetime now that daddy's gone."

"Then what in the hell do you want with me?" I'll keep asking this question until he gives me an answer.

"You are my leverage."

"Leverage for what?" Confusion laces my voice. *Leverage? What the hell?*

"Leverage to become bigger than Alfredo ever was," he explains as though talking to a child who should already know the answer when he hears my confusion.

"You want to become bigger than my dad? So, what has that got to do with me?"

"They feared Alfredo. You knew that if you messed with him, you'd end up dead. I want that, but the difference between me and Alfredo is that I don't worry about someone else doing my dirty work."

"So, you want to be bigger than Alfredo. Good for you. You'll just end up being on the most wanted list."

"Oh, but this is where you come in. You see, I don't just want to be feared. I want his empire."

"His empire?"

It feels like he's talking in riddles, and I really have no idea what on earth he's going on about. Dad's empire... What empire? But then reality starts to sink in. He wants to be bigger than my dad in the drug world, and someone who is prepared to do his own dirty work would be so much worse than Dad. Looking at my kidnapper, I see that he's waiting for me to realize what he means, and he spots the moment I work it out.

I still give the thought voice all the same. "You want to take over his drug empire?"

Instead of answering me, he gets up from the wall and walks over to me, and I find myself praying to god he doesn't start walking around my chair again. Not being able to see what he's doing is what freaks me out the most. But then he surprises me by stopping in front of the chair and crouching down so we are at eye level with each other.

"There is no want. I've already started."

"If you plan to use the same methods as Alfredo, they *will* catch you soon enough," I respond, trying to keep as much venom from my voice as I can. The less I provoke him, the safer I will be.

"Do you think I'm stupid?"

I'm not sure what to say. Is he genuinely asking me a question or is he being rhetorical? I decide that the best thing to do is remain silent, which turns out to be the wrong thing, anyway. He stands up so quickly that I don't realize he's moved until I feel his hand around my throat, applying just enough pressure to imply his intention but not enough to block my airway.

"I've told you before. When I ask you a question, you fucking answer it. Do you *understand* me?"

Taken back by the sudden violence, I am completely mute with fear, and it's only as he squeezes my throat tighter that I manage to whisper out a simple "yes" with a nod of my head. Happy with my answer, he lets go of my neck and walks back to his position against the wall.

"Glad we understand each other. So, I'll ask again. Do you think I'm stupid?"

"No," I say back.

"Then why ask such a stupid question? It doesn't take a genius to know not to follow the same plan as the last person. They would be watched, and I've figured out a *new* way."

His smug look is back, which tells me he feels rather proud of himself for figuring out a new way to get the drugs into the city. That can only mean it has to be something never thought of before, possibly not even by my father.

"So, you want to be this badass leader of a drug empire. I still don't understand why I'm important," I say, hoping he will finally give me some answers.

"Well, we need to get the police off my ass, and that's where you come in."

"I don't understand. How do I get the police off your ass? Taking me is only going to make them want to find you more."

"That's true. But I plan to be long gone by the time that happens, hopefully with everything I need."

My head is starting to hurt with all the confusion and riddles being thrown at me. "I still don't understand what this has to do with me?"

"As I said before, you're my leverage. I'm using you to get all the information your boyfriend has on their fresh case, aka me. And if they listen, you're safe. But I'm hoping they mess up." He pauses here, and I look up at him. He did it so he has my full attention. "Killing the son of Alfredo, even the unknown one, would send such a perfect message to those out there who would try to overthrow me."

By the tone of his voice, I know he isn't lying, and I'm suddenly scared that by the end of this, I'll end up dead instead of going home like I'd hoped.

Chapter 26 — Liam

The smile never leaves Wyatt's face on the journey back to the apartment. He's enjoying my suffering way too much. Maybe it's deserved, but it's not putting me at ease for what is about to happen.

"Do you think Lorenzo will be really pissed?" I ask when the silence in the car is getting too much for me to handle.

"I have no idea. I've never been there when someone has told him they have been dating his brother in secret." Wyatt shrugs without even glancing my way.

"Any advice?"

"Tell him everything. Don't try to bullshit your way out of it"

"Thanks. So helpful." I didn't mean for it to happen, but I can hear the sarcasm in my voice.

"You brought this on yourself." Wyatt deadpans.

He's right, of course, but I'm also hoping that by explaining everything to Lorenzo, he'll understand the reasons behind everything we did and try not to kill me. Silence returns to the car, but before I can think too much about it, we're turning onto their street. I'd been hoping that the parking spaces would all be full, but luck is not on my side today. Wyatt pulls up and parks right out front of the building and is already getting out of the car, waiting for me on the sidewalk. Taking a very deep breath, I open the door and get out, then we walk together to the front door. My nerves increase as I watch Wyatt unlock the security door so we can enter the apartment building.

Again neither of us talk as we travel up in the elevator. When it finally pings to let us know we've arrived at Wyatt's floor, I discover my feet are glued to the elevator floor and don't want to move. Wyatt steps out and looks back at me still frozen in place and starts laughing. Just as the door closes, he leans in, causing the doors to slide back open, then grabs my shirt and pulls me with more force than is necessary, and I stumble out.

"You can't avoid this," he says as he pushes me down the hallway toward the apartment of doom.

He's still pushing me through the front door once he's unlocked it, and I have to move out the way as Lorenzo comes barreling out of the living room and down the hall into Wyatt's arms.

"Have you heard from Marco? I'm seriously getting worried," Lorenzo hurries out in a watery voice, and before Wyatt has a chance to answer, Lorenzo is looking over to me. "What about you? Have you heard from him?"

I open my mouth to say something but spot the quick shake of Wyatt's head. This isn't a conversation that should be taking place by the open front door. Wyatt gives Lorenzo a kiss before saying, "Let's go into the living room. Liam has something he's just *dying* to tell you."

"What?" Lorenzo asks, and you can hear both the worry and curiosity in his voice.

"Let's just go sit, okay?" Wyatt then places his arm around Lorenzo's shoulders and steers him toward the couch.

Lorenzo and Wyatt sit on the couch next to each other, and I take my place in the single chair that faces the couch by the front window. The moment my ass hits the cushion, Lorenzo is looking at me, demanding answers without having to say a word, but I don't know where to start.

I look over to Wyatt for help, and for reasons beyond me, he takes pity on me and says, "Lorenzo, Liam needs to tell you something about Marco, but promise to just listen to all he has to say before reacting."

Lorenzo doesn't agree or disagree, just looks over to me and takes another deep breath. I decided to try to defuse the situation first by explaining what has happened to Marco.

"We believe that Marco has been kidnapped," I start but can't say any more before Lorenzo is up off the couch and pacing frantically, throwing his arms into the air.

"What do you mean you 'believe' Marco's been kidnapped? Either he has or he hasn't. There's no in-between." Taking a steadying breath, he throws out a volley of questions, "Do you know where he is? Has someone hurt him? Why in god's *name* do you think he's been *kidnapped*?" All the while he's pacing, getting louder and more animated with each sentence.

Wyatt gets up from the couch and walks over to Lorenzo, embracing him to stop his pacing, and then brings Lorenzo back over to the couch.

"Liam will be able to answer those questions," Wyatt says as they both settle back down and look over to me.

I pause for a split second to compose myself, then start.

"I received another letter stating that I had to face the consequences of my decisions. That someone I love has been taken, and the reason we believe that Marco has been kidnapped is because he is that someone special. We've been seeing each other, and I have no idea where he is or if they've hurt him."

I blow out a breath and look down at my feet, but when there is no response to what I've just revealed, I look back up. At first, I'm not sure if Lorenzo actually heard what was said. He's just remaining silent, staring at me, and there is an awkwardness building around me. I start to wonder if I should say anything, ask if he needs me to repeat something, but then I notice his breathing speeding up, and the look he gives me causes my blood to run cold.

"Did you just say that you've been seeing Marco?" he says, eyes narrowed at me as he leans forward on the couch as if he will spring off and attack me if I give the wrong answer.

"Yes," I whisper back, unable to tear my gaze from Lorenzo's.

"How fucking long?" comes the stony response, and there is no mistaking the anger now in his tone.

"Eight months," I tell him, my voice barely above a whisper, and I'm now avoiding all eye contact.

And that is when he explodes. I flinch, and when I look over to Wyatt, it appears he's holding Lorenzo back to stop him from rushing over and attacking me.

"Eight months!" he rages. *"You've been seeing each other for eight. Fucking. Months. And never said* anything?" Lorenzo is panting now and his hand, white knuckled, is digging into the arm of the couch. "You'd better explain yourself and do it *now*. You have thirty seconds, Liam, or I'll come and rip the answers I want from you."

Oh *shit*, no wonder he had the reputation of being a badass. This man is fucking scary as shit when he's angry. It also explains why he was able to pull answers from those who had crossed Alfredo.

"When he came in to report you as missing, I was instantly attracted to him. There was just something about him, and I found it was still there when we saw each other again. We met for coffee a few times, and it went from there." I explain, unable to hide the emotion in my voice. Lorenzo seems to relax as he listens, and I watch as Wyatt wraps him in his arms, which I hope will do two things: relax Lorenzo even more and also restrain him if I say anything that sets him off again.

"Why didn't you tell us?" The hurt is now evident in Lorenzo's voice, and his eyes show the mixture of emotions the man must be feeling.

"When it first happened, your dad was still alive, and I didn't want to risk Marco's safety. Then, when Alfredo died, I wasn't ready to come out, and Marco was worried about the school, so we remained quiet. We thought we were being careful, but it looks like we may have been being watched for a while."

"Well, that does explain why Marco has been so happy lately and why he wasn't too thrilled when I said that you were staying here with us." Lorenzo stops and thinks about something for a second. "Care to explain why that is," Lorenzo asks, pinning me with that hard stare yet again.

"Well, I kinda ignored him for a whole week," I say, embarrassment filling me as I finally look over to Lorenzo. "We'd just got the second letter, and I worked out that Marco could be in the limelight and knew that I needed to end things with him to keep him safe but just didn't have the guts to do it, so I ghosted him."

"Did you break up with him?" Lorenzo asks, disbelief and irritation tingeing his voice.

"Yes. I was trying to keep him safe," I confirm.

"When?" Lorenzo demands, squirming in Wyatt arms, whether to come at me again or out of worry for his brother, I'm not sure.

"When what?" I asked, needing clarification because I'm confused at what he's asking.

"When did you break up with him?" Lorenzo demands.

"Yesterday," I respond, giving an involuntary flinch as the word leaves my mouth. "I didn't go home just to get some stuff. I used that time to sneak over and see him."

"You broke up with him on the day he came out to his school? The day Marco felt everything would change for him." Every syllable on each word is heavy with both anger and shock.

Lorenzo's words cut deep, but I deserve every single one of them. "I was trying to keep him safe. I had no idea they would take him. I thought by doing that I would be taking him out of the equation," I state.

"Do you love him?" Lorenzo asks suddenly.

The question completely throws me. I thought he would say something about the kidnapper and how we are going to find Marco, but it looks like this is something that he needs to know.

"Yes," I say defiantly, "more than I ever thought possible."

His whole demeanor changes, almost softens when he hears this. I'm not sure if it's because he knows that I never meant to get Marco in trouble or because he likes the fact that there is another person in the world who loves Marco as much as he does. But then something seems to dawn on him, and his head snaps back to look at Wyatt and then back to me.

"Hang on... You're *straight*!" Lorenzo blurts out.

Both Wyatt and I burst out laughing, and I hear Wyatt state, "I'll explain it all later, but it looks like he's not as straight as we thought."

As soon as the laughter starts, though, it stops, the three of us remember why we're talking in the first place.

"So, they took Marco. Has anyone been in contact since he was taken?" Lorenzo asks, looking between Wyatt and myself.

"No, there's been nothing. His cell is still going straight to voicemail, and if it is turned off, we can't use the location app on it. If they even let him keep the cell," I say before Wyatt has a chance to.

"Can you think of anyone who would want to take him?" Wyatt asks Lorenzo, and the question throws me for a second. If the kidnapper wants me to destroy the evidence we have collected so far, why would Lorenzo know who they may be?

"No idea. I made sure we cut all ties to Dad. Made sure that everyone knew that I was getting out of the business for good, too, but also let them know that if anyone came after me or my family, there would be hell to pay, and I would sing like a canary. The last thing these people want is the cops sniffing around," Lorenzo says.

"This is more to do with the fresh case and the new drugs that are coming into the city," I say before looking over to Lorenzo and asking, "I know you said you'd cut all ties, but is there anyone you can contact who might be able to get us some answers?"

"No one will talk to me," Lorenzo replies sadly, "but I think I know someone who might be able to help."

"Who?" I find myself confused. If there isn't anyone Lorenzo can talk to to get answers, then who does he think will help?

Lorenzo turns to Wyatt, who nods his head, and the pair of them look back at me and at the same time say, "Frank."

"Frank. As in your driver Frank?" I'm completely confused why anyone would still talk to Frank. Surely everyone knows that he still works for Lorenzo, and any information given to him would get straight back to Lorenzo. Who in their right mind would give him anything useful?

"Yep. I'm sure he still has connections or at least people that will talk to him." Lorenzo says, and there is an edge of hope in his voice.

Looking at Lorenzo, I decide to voice my concerns. "I'm sure he does, but how useful would that information be? Everyone knows he'd come straight back to you."

"The thing is, Liam, Frank is still one scary motherfucker when he wants to be. So I'm fairly certain he would get something useful."

I want to disagree with him, but there's something in his tone that is telling me not to. He's not going to listen to my argument, anyway, and what other options do we have anyhow? We currently know nothing, only that Marco is missing and presumed kidnapped. Anything to start with at this point will be good, so I nod my head and then watch as Lorenzo takes out his cell, pushes a few buttons, and puts it to his ear.

"Frank, can you come up to the apartment? We need to talk to you," he says before pocketing the cell again. I'm not sure what their relationship is like now that Alfredo is gone, but I'm surprised at how formal he sounded. There was no hello or goodbye, just a blunt statement. You could say there was a friendly undertone, but still, I was under the impression they were closer now. My thoughts have to be showing or he caught me staring at him

"Did I say something wrong?" Lorenzo asks.

"Sorry, didn't mean to stare. It just surprised me how direct you were with Frank." I explain, a little stunned that Lorenzo picked up on my shock.

Thankfully he doesn't seem to take offence to what I've said but instead seems quite amused by it.

"To be honest, we still fall into old habits when dealing with each other. Kinda direct and to the point."

"Suppose you were like that for a long time," I reason out loud.

"Yeah, we were, but we're getting better," Lorenzo replies.

Lorenzo smiles when he talks about Frank, and I take that to mean that he has grown fond of the man. I think it all started when he found out that Frank knew about Wyatt and didn't say anything. Let's hope he's just as cool when he learns about me and Marco.

Five minutes later there's a knock on the apartment door, and I look over to Lorenzo as he gets up from the couch. "It's Frank. He has a key to the place for emergencies, but when I'm home, he still likes to knock. Not that he's been to the apartment that often," he explains before walking to the front door and letting Frank in.

When the pair of them walk into the room, Frank spots me and his look changes. He's instantly on guard, and if I am not mistaken, the worry lines on his face deepen. He goes and grabs a chair from the kitchen table, bringing it over to the edge of the couch so he can see us all.

"Okay, wanna tell me what is going on?" Frank asks, getting straight to the point much like Lorenzo.

"We believe that Marco has been kidnapped," Lorenzo replies, and for a brief second, I think I see Frank flinch, but it happens so quickly that I can't be one hundred percent sure.

"When?" Now there is no mistaking the concern in Frank's voice.

"The last contact any of us had with him was last night," Lorenzo explains.

"What time?" Frank now has an edge to his voice.

"We aren't sure on the time. I called him last night at maybe seven o'clock, and he told me he was going to a bar to meet a friend. There's been no contact since then."

"Did he give you a name of who he was meeting?" While he's asking Lorenzo the questions, he keeps shooting looks at me, and I really have no idea why.

"No, just said that he was meeting a friend, but to be honest, he sounded off." The moment that Lorenzo says this, Frank *definitely* gives me a look. He knows more than he's letting on.

Still looking at me, Frank asks, "How do you mean 'sounded off?'"

Lorenzo spots Frank staring at me but doesn't question it and goes on to explain, "Not himself. I invited him over and he quickly shot me down, which isn't like him."

"Do you know what caused this behavior?" But he directs this at me and not Lorenzo.

"Yeah. I went over to his place yesterday and broke up with him. Was trying to keep him safe." God, I'm beginning to sound like a parrot with the number of times I'm having to repeat this.

Strangely, Frank doesn't look surprised, but he does avoid looking at us, his eyes darting around the room as though he's dealing with guilt. There is something that he's not telling us, and by the way he glances at Lorenzo, Franks gauging his mood and worried about what his reaction will be. But his lack of reaction has now been picked up by Lorenzo.

"Frank, you don't seem overly surprised. What do you know?" The dangerous edge is back to his voice, the one that demands answers and no bullshit.

"Well..." Frank starts, "I've kinda been watching over Marco since your dad died. Just wanted to make sure that no one was going after him. I spotted him with Liam a few times. They looked like you two." He stops and points to Lorenzo and Wyatt. "It was cute, and honestly, if I hadn't seen you acting the same way, I would've thought they were just friends."

"Hang on! If you have been watching him, does that mean you saw him Friday night?" Lorenzo asks, shifting to the edge of the couch.

Frank goes quiet, and if I am not mistaken, a blush is beginning to stain his checks. *Holy fuck, he did see him.* So why the hell didn't he jump in and protect him, stop Marco from being taken. Anger bubbles up in my veins, and I have to forcibly restrain myself from lashing out.

"Oh shit, you did. What the fuck happened?" I snarl.

Frank glances over to Lorenzo for moral support, but from the thunderous look on his face, it isn't going to happen.

"You better explain what happened, Frank." Lorenzo says in a much calmer tone than expected, and one that certainly doesn't match his face.

Frank takes a deep breath and states, "When he left his place on Friday, I could tell something was wrong and decided to follow him. I was relieved when he went into the bar, thinking that being surrounded by people would keep him safe. There was a seat in the corner where I was able to watch him from, but it was dark enough that if he looked around, it would be hard for him to see me. He just sat there talking to the bartender.

"After a few hours, the bar started to get busier, and just as I thought he was about to leave, he got another drink. It was then everything changed. That last drink hit him hard, and I spotted him swaying. Thinking it best to go over to him, I started to get out of my chair, but before I could walk over there, I got a call on my cell. Normally I wouldn't have taken it, but when I looked up, he was still sitting on the bar stool, so I answered. I wasn't on the call for longer than a minute, but when I looked up, he was gone. I am so sorry, Lorenzo."

"Frank, I know you. There was no way you would have answered unless it was an emergency, but they still took Marco. When you noticed he wasn't on the bar stool, was he still in the bar?" Lorenzo asks, and I see the understanding in his eyes, but all I can think of is that he let Marco get taken because of a damn cell call, and I'm so angry it's making me nauseous. But as Frank continues his story, I use all the energy I have to listen in case it contains anything useful.

"I spotted him again just as he was just walking out the door, but someone must have seen me watching him, because the moment I tried to get to him, there was always someone in my way. It took a lot longer to get through the crowd than it should have. By the time I got onto the street, he was gone. It was wrong of me to think it, but I assumed he'd just gone home."

"Did you recognize anyone in the bar?" I suddenly voice, hoping to get a lead.

"No one. Whoever took Marco is new but has done their research."

"So, what do we do now?" I ask, looking at the three of them in the hopes of getting some answers. It's Frank who speaks first.

"Give me twelve hours. I still have some contacts."

With that, he gets up from the couch and walks out the apartment without a goodbye or explanation where he was going. He's just gone.

"He'll be riddled with guilt. I almost feel sorry for whoever he'll talk to." Lorenzo voices.

"He should feel guilty," I snap. "He was there and could have protected him."

"Liam, calm down." Wyatt's voice rings out. "Whatever the reason, they were Frank's. You know if you were in his shoes and it was an emergency, you would've answered the call, too."

When I open my mouth to object, nothing comes out, because no matter what I feel, Wyatt is right. I would do the same, especially if it was family calling me. I consider the reaction from Lorenzo and Wyatt and realize that this isn't normal behavior for Frank, so I'm going to have to try to let it go even if I don't want to.

"So, what do we do now?" I ask, looking at the pair of them.

"We wait," comes Lorenzo's reply as if this is the simplest thing in the world.

"Wait. Just like that," I state.

"Yeah, just like that," Lorenzo confirms.

I want to argue, but Wyatt stops me in my tracks. "I know that you want to go out there and find him, but you can't. The risk is too great. Both of us"—he points to himself and then Lorenzo—"want to find him, too, but in a city this big, I have no idea where to start. It's gonna be a tough few hours, but we have to wait for Frank."

"It's just…" I start, but I don't have to finish the sentence for them to understand. They're feeling it, as well. That need to find him, make sure he is safe. But for me, there is the added need to hold him in my arms again and feel his body against mine. If he forgives me after all of this, I sure as hell am *not* going to let him go again.

———

Those twelve hours were the longest of my life. All of us tried to keep busy, keep our minds occupied, but you could tell we were all watching the clock until finally Frank came back this morning. We're now all sitting in the same positions as yesterday, waiting with bated breath to find out what he has discovered.

"So?" Lorenzo asks, and you can hear how desperate he is.

"It took me some time, but I did find something, a name. Antonio Valentini," Franks explains.

Lorenzo and Wyatt look confused, but I've heard that name before, or maybe seen it before, and I start trying to mentally figure it all out, but Frank talking takes away my concentration.

"It looks like he's new. He's picking up where Alfredo ended." Frank pauses here, and it's long enough that all three of us look over to him.

"What? There's something you're not saying." And it's my voice asking the question.

"Yeah. So, here's the thing. It took me a long time to get this guy's name. We thought Alfredo was a mean mother fucker, but from what I've heard, this guy makes Alfredo look like a kitten," Frank says.

There is a resounding "Fuck" from the three of us.

"How bad are we talking?" Lorenzo asks.

"Bad enough that most of my contacts, whom I have known for years, didn't want to talk in fear they ended up missing—if you know what I mean." Frank's nodding his head slightly.

"But Dad was the same. You talked; you went missing," Lorenzo says, shaking his head.

"The difference is that Alfredo would always get someone else to do the dirty work. This guy likes to be involved, and it can be painful. Whatever he does, it's already put the fear of God into people."

"Did they give you any clues at all on where Marco could be?" I hear Wyatt ask. Lorenzo has gone as white as a sheet. The shock of hearing there is someone out there who is potentially worse than Alfredo must be overwhelming him, and it's the same person who has Marco.

"Someone mentioned a dockyard. One that you might have been familiar with," Frank states while looking over to Lorenzo. "But they wouldn't one hundred percent confirm."

"Really? That would make sense. It's not a small area, and there are abandoned warehouses dotted all over. It's the perfect place to hide someone. That will be a total pain in the ass trying to figure out which one he could be using," Lorenzo says

Looking over to Wyatt, I see that he looks just as confused as me. Both of us have no idea what area they're talking about, and yet Lorenzo and Frank seem to be going over all these probable locations.

"Hang on," I interrupt. "Can you please explain where you're talking about and how you know about it?"

"Um," Lorenzo starts and looks a little ashamed. "Well, there was this disused warehouse in the Brooklyn dockyards that I used when I needed to have a little chat with someone."

It takes me a few seconds to realize what he means by "a little chat," and the only response I could mutter was, "Oh."

"Do you think this Antonio could be using the same place?" Wyatt asks, and if he is as surprised at the revelation as I am, he's doing a damn good job not showing it.

"No, I don't think he is," Frank states. "This guy knows that this is the first place we'd look. But one of the other nearby warehouses could be a possibility."

Looking over to Wyatt, I'm just about to tell him the area has to be investigated when we all jump at the sound of the intercom ringing. I watch as Lorenzo slowly gets up and answers the phone. Picking up the receiver, he quietly says, "Hello," and then nothing for a few seconds before saying, "Thanks, we'll be right down,"

"What the hell was that about?" Wyatt asks as he gets up from the seat to join him.

"Package downstairs for Liam." Lorenzo says, giving me a puzzled look.

"Have you ordered anything?" Wyatt asks, glancing at me, and I shake my head.

"I'll go down for it," Lorenzo replies.

"No. Liam will have to collect it. They might not give it to anyone else. I'll go down with him and keep an eye out," Frank says, getting to his feet and coming to stand by my chair.

Nodding my head and standing, the pair of us leave the apartment before Lorenzo and Wyatt can respond. We travel down to the front lobby in silence, both of us understanding that this isn't the best situation. Once we're off the elevator and at the front of the lobby, Frank moves to the side so as not to be seen but making sure I'm still in the line of sight. I open the door but don't step out, looking around, at first, for some suit-clad mobster, but instead, all I see is a normal bike courier.

"Liam Smith?" the courier asks.

"Yes," I confirm.

"Sign here, please," he says as he hands me what looks like a phone and stylus. Signing my name as quickly as I can and handing back the device, he passes me a brown padded envelope.

I nod and then quickly turn, heading back to Lorenzo's place with Frank hot on my heels, not wanting to open the envelope in the middle of the lobby. It feels like forever before we're back up in the apartment. Once we are sitting in our respective chairs with the envelope laying on my lap, a feeling like a lead weight comes over me, weighing me down.

"Have you opened it yet?" Lorenzo asks, staring at the package in my hand

"No," is all I respond. I haven't because I don't want to see what is inside. I know that it is going to be important, but my gut is telling me I'm not going to like what I find.

"Do you want me to?" Lorenzo's voice comes again.

"No. I'll do it." Turning the envelope over, I slowly slip my finger under the flap and open it, then tip the envelope upside down so that the contents can fall onto my lap. A cell tumbles out, and I'm just about to pick it up when I hear Wyatt mention gloves, to which I say, "The other stuff was clean, so I'm guessing this is, too, plus it looks like it's a touch screen. Won't be able to open it with gloves on."

Waking up the cell and watching it come to life, I then carefully swipe across the screen. An image lights up the background, and I can't help but allow a gasp to escape. The cell is being snatched from my hands before I can react, and more gasps come from around the room. That image has already been burnt into my memory, and the nauseous feeling returns, only this time it's stronger. I rush from the room and just about make it to the bathroom before vomiting up what little food I had in my stomach. I close my eyes, hoping to get some relief, but all I can see is the image of a bruised and bloody Marco tied to a chair.

Chapter 27—Marco

The slamming of a door startles me out of my sleep. Disoriented, I look around the room, trying to move my arms but find that I can't. Then I remember the kidnapping. It's always the same; I forget and then the memories come flooding back. Taking a deep breath, I glance around again trying to locate the person who slammed the door and brought me out of my dark dreams. I don't see anything, but then a voice comes out of the dark shadows.

"Aww, did I wake you?"

"Nope, been awake for hours. Just decided to have a sit for a while," I respond, trying to be as sarcastic as possible, but all it does is cause laughter to echo around the room.

"You have to be the comedian, don't you?"

He saunters out of the shadows and over to me, and I can see that he's holding a brown paper bag in one hand and carrying a chair in the other. I wonder how long I have been out for this time. I don't remember him leaving, so it must have been a while. He places the chair in front of me and unwraps the bag, pulling out a sandwich, and my stomach growls loudly.

"Looks like someone is hungry," he sneers before eating the sandwich in front of me. The smell of the bread and meat hits me, my mouth filling with saliva, and my stomach makes another sound of protest, betraying how hungry I am. I watch as he removes another sandwich from the bag and just holds it in front of me, and I wonder how long he'll torment me with it.

"*Eat!*" he screeches as he waves the food around my face.

"W... what?" I'd thought he'd eat this one, too, not offer it to me.

"I said *eat*! You have to keep your strength up. Can't have you collapsing on me."

I don't argue this time and lean my head forward to take a bite of the sandwich. It tastes as good as it smells. The meat is tender and melts in my mouth, and the bread fluffy. It might be the best sandwich I've ever had, and I almost contemplate asking him where he got it, but I don't want to give him the satisfaction of knowing I'm enjoying something he gave me.

When the sandwich is gone, I look around the room and attempt to figure out the time of day, hoping to work out how long I was asleep for.

"What time is it?" I ask in the hopes he'll give me an honest answer.

"Mid-morning. I didn't let you sleep long. Today the fun starts!" A sadistic smile crosses his mouth.

If he's being truthful, then I was only sleeping for an hour, maybe two, and my heart sinks. I'd been hoping that I'd somehow been asleep for longer. The more I sleep, the less I have to deal with. *What the hell does he mean by "today the fun starts?"*

"What the fuck does that mean?" I snap at him.

He makes a tsk sound as he lightly slaps my cheek, then says, "Language. Language. No need to be rude."

I'm fighting the urge to lash out and say something more, but my cheek is still hurting from the last time, and I wouldn't be surprised if I have a black eye, too. I have no desire to get hit again. So I bite my tongue and try to find a way to ask him, politely this time, what is going on. My thoughts are interrupted when his cell goes off, and he appears annoyed by the interruption, but when he looks and sees who's calling, his entire demeanor changes.

Getting up from his chair, he answers, "Hello."

He's moved far enough away from me so I can't hear the other voice, but I watch the guy in front of me closely, hoping to see a sign for what the call is about. He gives nothing away until he looks over and I spot a flash of something in his eyes.

"How interesting," he says and then hangs up the phone. He makes his way back to the chair, never taking his eyes off me. Once he's seated and settled, he remains silent. His actions are designed to let me stew and overthink, but eventually, he starts talking,

"Who's Frank?"

"Frank?" Honestly, I have no idea. For a second, I'm completely confused. "I don't know anyone called Frank."

Lashing out, he grabs my fingers and starts squeezing them together. "Don't fucking lie to me. Someone called Frank was snooping." He tightens his grip and pain radiates up my fingers from my knuckles. "Now, who the *fuck* is Frank?"

Not able to think of anything but the shooting pain and knowing he won't stop till I give him an answer, I do my best to block everything out while trying to figure out who this Frank person is. *Come on, think.* Frank. Then it hits me. There *is* a Frank I kinda know, but he works for Lorenzo, and before that, he was on Dad's payroll. He's never really ever spoken to me.

"A Frank works for my brother," I say, knowing I might have just put Frank in danger as I say this, but needing the pain in my hand to stop is more important to me at the moment.

"That would explain the questions he was asking and confirm that your brother *is* looking for you."

I bite my bottom lip, forgetting about the spilt as pain tingles across it, but it helps to stop the smile from spreading across my face. If Lorenzo has Frank asking questions, then it's only a matter of time before they find me, and god, I hope that the fucker sitting in front of me gets his rewards.

"If you're hoping this means your brother will find you," the man starts and then leans over to whisper, "you're wrong." He sits back with a smug, a satisfied look on his face. He's wrong, and I want to scream back at him that he's underestimated Lorenzo, but I don't.

Instead, all I respond with is, "Maybe."

"Frank doesn't have the connections he thinks he does. No one will tell him anything. I pay well, and people already know what the consequences are if they're found out. All he may have discovered is my name."

"Which is?"

He stops and thinks about my question, the corner of his mouth quirking up as he looks at the ceiling, probably debating on whether to tell me. He must be aware that if I manage to escape, I'll know who he is and have seen his face, but if he kills me, no one will know it was him, and in his world, reputation is everything.

"My name is Antonio Valentini."

By the look of things, reputation wins out. Valentini isn't a name I'd heard my parents mention, and they knew everyone, so he really is new to the area. If he's already gotten everyone quiet, then he really is one sick mother fucker.

"Nice name," I say with obvious fake pleasantries.

Before he says anything else to me, his cell phone beeps. He looks at his watch and a smile spreads across his face even before he checks his cell. Looks like this is one interruption he's been waiting for as his eyes flicker over the message.

"Well, it looks like they've delivered my package."

"What package? What's going on?" I can hear the panic in my voice. I need to know what he's planning and what this all has to do with me.

"Sent your boyfriend a little gift just to make sure he knows I am serious."

"I'm sure he knows you're serious."

"Yes, but now he has pictures, too."

Oh my fucking god. The pictures he took... he sent them to Liam. My stomach rolls at the thought, but thankfully, my sandwich stays put. Poor Liam, he must be so worried and not able to say anything to Lorenzo and Wyatt about why must be killing him. He's probably using the "my friend's been kidnapped" lie when his behavior is being questioned.

Antonio swipes the screen of the cell, and I can see his fingers moving like he's typing—must be text message to someone.

"Let's see just how much the boyfriend loves you." Valentini smirks as he finishes with the phone.

"He'll never give you what you want, regardless of what he feels for me."

"Let's just see about that, shall we?"

The slap that lands on my face echoes around the room, and I can feel warmth as blood trickles down my chin from the re-opened lip. Then, the next thing I know, my head is being pulled back and his cell is hovering above my face and yet another photo is being taken. Antonio sits back down and starts typing again.

"That should give him some extra incentive." That smug look returned to his face.

"You really are one sick motherfucker, aren't you?" I mumble out through my swelling lips.

It was meant to be an insult, at this point I'm not caring what the repercussions might be, but he just smiles at me like I have given him some kind of compliment.

"Why, thank you. I do try my best."

I am completely at a loss for words at his statement. There really is nothing more one can say, so I just remain silent and watch him. He doesn't move from his chair, doesn't walk around me like he normally does, just stays silent, eyes locked on his cell. The silence is somehow worse than the pacing. The sound of the steps echoing through the room gives me something to focus on, stopping my brain from thinking too much about the situation I'm in. But this silence only allows me to think. Staring at Antonio in front of me, I go over everything that we've talked about so far, and in the pit of my stomach, I get this feeling. He'll never let me go, regardless of what he's said before.

"You aren't going to let me go, are you?" I say, breaking the silence in the room.

"Of course I am. If your boyfriend plays ball." But he's lying. For the first time, he's not looking at me, instead still busy looking at his cell.

"And when he doesn't?" I ask the one question that gives me the most fear, but I need to hear him say it.

"Then you will be made to suffer and pay the ultimate price."

Suffer? I expected that Antonio would basically say, "Yes, you will die," but suffer sounds worse, and *that* terrifies me. Suffer means pain. Pain for both me and Liam. But isn't it better for me to suffer than have Antonio on the streets doing even more harm and possibly hurting innocent people? It's that thought I hold on to, letting a calmness wash over me. If I die,

Liam can use the pain I experience to catch this bastard, and it might end up saving hundreds of people. That can only be a good thing.

"What? Nothing to say to that?" Antonio asks.

"Nope." He wanted a reaction that I can no longer give. A kind of peace has settled over my mind, and I just need to talk when he wants and await my fate.

When his cells beep again and he reads the message, he gives me a look that screams, "I was right."

"Looks like your boyfriend is coming through."

No, Liam would never give away information like that. There must be a mistake. He must have a plan, something to try to fool Antonio. There's no way the police would let him give away the case like that. So what the hell is he up to? With the satisfied look still on his face, Antonio gets up from his chair and walks out of the room, leaving me in solitude and to my own thoughts.

My mind drifts between Lorenzo and Liam, the two most important people in my life. Since Dad's death, Lorenzo and I have gotten a lot closer, if that was at all possible, and I keep imagining what his reaction would be when he found out about me and Liam. The color would have gone from his face, to be sure, and I laugh at the thought. He would've gotten over it, eventually, but he sure as hell wouldn't have let me forget. Then there's Liam. He is special. What we have is special. I'd always sniggered when I saw people on the television who said their partner was their best friend. Always thought it was ridiculous until it happened to me. Because without even realizing it, Liam had become my best friend as well as my lover.

Closing my eyes, I do something I haven't done in an awfully long time. Pray.

Dear God, I know it's been awhile, but if you're there and listening, please keep Liam, Lorenzo, and Wyatt safe, and if possible, give me the chance to see them again.

A single tear falling down my cheek is the only sign that the joy I'd just been feeling over Lorenzo has morphed into sadness. My thoughts settle on the fact that I might not get the chance to see any of them again. Anger surges through me, and I want to wipe away the tear, though I know I can't. The sense of calm I had when Antonio was talking to me, I want that back. I want to have my mind at peace. Instead, I shake my head; crying won't change anything. I need to find my inner strength again. And I am not sure if it's because my eyes are still closed or because my emotions are all over the place, but an image of Liam appears in front of me and he's waving, beckoning me forward, and I soon drift off to sleep, running into Liam's arms.

"Wake up!" The sound instantly jars me awake.

Antonio is back and sitting in front of me, a brown file resting on his lap. Behind him, there seems to be a tripod holding a cell phone pointing in my direction. Antonio catches me looking at the tripod and sniggers—and the bad feeling in the pit of my stomach returns.

Picking up the file, he opens it and looks at it like it was the best novel in the world.

"I need you to look at this and confirm that the handwriting is Liam's."

Nodding, he places the file on my lap and opens it once more. Looking at it as best I can, I recognize the handwriting immediately and somehow manage to hide my shock. He gave them the information. Why? Why has he risked everything he has worked so hard for?

"Yes, that Liam's" I say, and there is no mistaking the disappointment in my voice.

"You sound disappointed. Did you think he wouldn't fight for you?"

How on earth do you answer a question like that? If I say yes, he will know I am lying, but then if I say no and that I was hoping he wouldn't, he will know my spirit is broken and he won't get any enjoyment out of my suffering. The only option is the truth.

"I am disappointed." And it just causes more laughter from Antonio.

"You're disappointed that the man who loves you is trying to save you." His own disbelief was clear as he spoke.

"I'm disappointed he threw everything away, as you said, to *try* to save me." I put as much emphasis on the word try so he understands I know his plan and it works.

"Ahh, my dear Marco. I think you have misunderstood me. Yes, I am going to make you suffer, but I will not kill you. I'm only hoping that your time runs out before anyone has the chance to find you."

"So, what are you going to do?"

"Well, now that you have confirmed Liam's handwriting, I have everything I want. Now it's time for part two of my plan. Making sure that everyone knows that I am not to be messed with."

"A-and how do you plan to do that?"

"With actions!"

Antonio gets up from the chair, walks over to the tripod, and swipes the cell screen. He moves it one way, then the other, and adjusts the legs of the tripod until he is happy with the angle and then slips a device into his pocket before coming back over to me. When he's standing in front of me, he pulls out a gun and slides the barrel around the side of my cheek. I shudder at the coldness of the metal against my skin.

"Such a waste. Are you sure I can't persuade you to join me?"

Another shudder rolls through me at that thought, which Antonio spots and sighs. "I'll take that as a no. Still a shame."

With that, he stands up straight and starts to walk around me, knowing that this scares me. He knows that every time he walks behind me, I'm waiting for that shot. Waiting for the pain to lance through, and with every circuit he makes around the chair, he knows my fear grows, and he gets more and more enjoyment from it.

Just when I can't take it anymore, he stops. He pauses only a moment before walking over to the tripod, checking everything again, and pulling out the small device he pocketed earlier.

"You know what this is?" he asks, holding the object he pulled from his pocket up to me. It's small and oval shaped, like a stretched-out quarter and probably about the thickness of a finger with a button in the middle. I shake my head at him because I really have no clue what it could be.

"This is a remote, and the moment I press this button, I want you to remain completely silent."

My words have completely dried up, so I can just nod my head in agreement. The question I should've been asking was what the remote was for, but honestly, I don't think I want to know. It might be best if I don't.

Never moving my eyes away from his hand, even as the fingers re-swipe the screen of the cell, I grab hold of the arms and remain perfectly still when he presses the button—but nothing. He places the device back into his pocket and raises his arm holding the gun and brings his other hand over to steady himself. He looks at the screen and shuffles forward. Antonio is still staring at his hands as he flips the safety and aims. He gently pulls the trigger, the sound of the shot vibrating around the room. Then there is pain. I was supposed to stay silent, but I couldn't, and a scream falls from my mouth before the darkness descends over me.

Chapter 28 — Liam

It took me a long time to get over seeing the image of Marco on the cell. By the time I re-entered the room, the paleness of Lorenzo, Wyatt, and even Frank told me they had seen the image, too, and were discussing what we should do next when the phone beeps. All of us jump and stare at the device for at least five minutes before it startles us again by beeping for a second time.

Picking it up, I can see the two text messages waiting. Opening the first, I see a text soon followed by a photo message. I read the first message at least five times before it makes sense to me. Whoever has Marco is demanding I bring all the information to an address plotted with coordinates... and within the next two hours. When I open the picture text, the nausea comes flooding back, and I have to take deep cleansing breaths until the feeling passes. Seeing the picture of Marco tied to the chair had been horrific, but seeing this picture with blood dripping down his chin is so much worse. I must have made a noise because Lorenzo comes rushing over to wrap me in his arms, just holding me.

We all remain silent for a long time. Lorenzo and Wyatt are deathly white after seeing the second picture, but eventually we compose ourselves enough to spend the next thirty minutes discussing the options we have. Then Frank comes up with the idea to make a fake file. If we hand write all the information, it will look like the genuine article.

So that is what we do, and lucky for us, Wyatt has some empty file folders in the apartment. After a questioning look from me, he explains he keeps some at home for when he does work at the apartment. It takes us a lot longer to make the file than we thought, so we're rushing to make the meeting time. The address they sent us turns out to be in Union Square Park, and the weirdest part is the coordinates seem to be pointing to a park bench near the entrance.

After hailing a cab, I am lucky that traffic is on my side and manage to get there with a few minutes to spare, so I sit down, looking around and hoping to spot Marco, but I'm surprised when a bike courier pulls up in front of me.

"Are you Liam Smith?"

"Yeah."

"Cool. I thought this was a joke. 'Deliver a parcel to a Liam Smith who'll be waiting on a park bench and collect one at the same time,' but the guy paid well over the norm, so I thought what the hell." The young man shrugs and hands over an envelope after getting me to sign for it and then just waits, staring at me. "So, you got something for me?"

Shit, he means the file. *Fuck.* This guy is smart, but maybe the courier can tell me where he is going from here. Handing the file to the courier, I watch as he pulls out an envelope from his messenger bag and slips the file inside, then places it back in the bag without attaching any labels. As he turns his bike around to leave, I pull out my police badge and flash it at him.

"Wait," I call out, and thankfully he stops and looks at the badge. "Do you have the address for that?" I ask while pointing to his bag so he knows that I mean the letter.

"It's not an address. Taking it to a PO Box. Normally I wouldn't, but like I said, higher pay."

Fuck, even if this guy gives me the PO Box address, then I am almost one hundred percent certain it would be a fake name.

"Can you at least tell me where the PO Box is?"

The courier is hesitant for a second, but he gives me the address of the post office and leaves the park. Sitting back down on the bench, I look at the envelope, trying to decide if I should open it in the park or back at the apartment. But considering what Antonio has sent me before, I figure it's probably best to open the package when I have Lorenzo and Wyatt around me for support.

Keeping a tight grip on the envelope, I leave the park and can see that traffic had increased and decide to run back to their place, thankful that as I was leaving, Lorenzo gave me a key. When I place the key in the lock, I notice my hand is shaking. I want to put it down to the physical activity of rushing back from the park but know it's more than that. It's the thought of what's in the envelope and hoping it isn't more photos.

The moment I step into the apartment, Lorenzo is rushing up to me.

"Where is he? Why isn't he with you?" he says, and he's looking behind me like I'm hiding Marco from sight.

"He wasn't there," I tell him.

"What the fuck do you mean he wasn't there? Was it the wrong place?"

"Nope, it was the right place," I respond, holding up the envelope to show him. "But instead of Marco, there was a courier who gave me this."

"What is it?" Lorenzo asks.

"Don't know. Wanted to open it with you guys close by."

"Come on then."

We make our way back over to the couch. Wyatt and Frank haven't moved, but it looks like they are looking for Marco behind me with their eyes, too, and so I just shake my head and keep moving to the chair. Once I sit down, I look over to the rest of the party and see them all staring back at me, so this means it's time to open the envelope. Not bothering to put on gloves, I carefully open the flap and pull out a piece of paper that matches all the other letters that I have gotten.

KEEP THE CELL PHONE CLOSE. YOU'RE GONNA WANT TO WATCH IT.

What the fuck is that supposed to mean? Watch it do what? Does he mean that something will be sent... but when? How long do we have to wait? And while we're waiting, what is happening to Marco? *Oh god.*

"What does it say?" Lorenzo asks, and I hand over the piece of paper to him. "Watch what?" He looks up at me, puzzled.

"No idea. Have there been any messages on the phone?" I ask

"None." Lorenzo states.

Originally, the plan was to take the cell with me when I went to the park in case there had been further instructions, but with the rush to leave, I had completely forgotten it. I figured if anything had been sent, Lorenzo or Wyatt would have forwarded it to my own cell.

"In that case, we will have to wait," Wyatt pipes up after he's looked at the piece of paper.

So that is what we do. We wait and wait and wait. None of us are really talking, but we're watching the cell like it's some prized possession. Eventually, after about two hours, the damn thing beeps, the sound echoing in the silence of the room. Picking up the device, I swipe it open.

"Looks like they sent a link to a video," I say.

Lorenzo and Wyatt get up off the couch and walk around so they are standing behind me and can watch over my shoulder.

"You okay?" Wyatt asks, squeezing my shoulder.

"Not really. But we have to watch, right?" I say as I turn my head to look at them.

The subtle nod of his head is the only confirmation Wyatt gives. I turn the cell slightly to make sure we can all see the screen and hit play. At first, all we can see is Marco sitting in the chair, but he looks tense and is just staring at the camera but not actually *looking* at it, but maybe something off to the side. Then, the gun appears. I grab at the armrest as my worst fears are realized, the gun going off and hitting him on the side of his thigh. For a spilt second, a sense of relief fills me. He wasn't killed instantly, but as I keep looking at the screen, I see Marco slump forward, blacking out from the pain. Whoever shot him knew what they were doing. Shooting him where they did misses any major arteries, so the bleed out will be slower, prolonging the death and agony.

Lorenzo screaming Marco's name brings me back to the moment, and my cheeks feel damp. I hadn't even noticed I was crying. Looking around the room, I see that Lorenzo has crumpled to the floor sobbing, and Wyatt is holding him, rocking slightly. Frank is just staring at the three of us, and by the greyish tinge to his skin, he has guessed what's happened.

Looking back down at the cell, the video has ended, and the reply symbol has appeared. Muting the sound before hitting the bottom, this time, I try to take in the surroundings, but my eye still wanders to Marco, and I have to force myself to concentrate. There are no windows that are visible in the area around Marco, but he's sitting in daylight. I can't see any features that would give away the location. The gun appears and doesn't have a silencer. The kidnapper isn't worried about the sound of the shot, so he must be away from the city. Once the video has ended, I open the details, but all the information is blank. The kidnapper has to be using some kind of software to hide the details.

"Wyatt," I call out, and he jumps on hearing his name, being so focused on Lorenzo who has stopped crying and shaking but still looks lost. When Wyatt finally looks up at me, his own face is blank and just as lost as Lorenzo, and he's just staring at the cell in my hand. We need to get moving, and fast, and by the looks of the other three, it will be up to me.

"Wyatt," I say, but more sternly this time. "We need to get this to the station. Get our tech guys to look at the cell. They might be able to see if they can find something."

Finally, my words register, and Wyatt starts to act. He picks Lorenzo off the floor and places him back on the couch, but Lorenzo remains mute. He must have gone into shock, and we really shouldn't leave him, but we have to if there is any hope of finding Marco.

"Frank, can you stay with Lorenzo? We cannot lose any more time," I say, looking over to him.

"Of course. I'm going to make some phone calls. There has to be someone who's willing to talk."

Suddenly there is yet another beep from the cell, and all eyes turn to look at me. Another text message. Opening it, I can see that it's a link.

"He sent a link to a website," I tell them

Wyatt walks over and, just like before, is looking over my shoulder as I press the link. An image of Marco still slumped in the chair appears, but with a deep red stain now showing on his trousers. This image seems different from the video that was sent, grainier. Taking a closer look, I realize this is a live video. The link he sent must be from a live streaming site. The kidnapper wants us to watch Marco. Watch his suffering, and if my instincts are right, he wants us to watch him die.

Wyatt must have realized this at the same time because he's suddenly moving faster, rushing around the apartment to grab his keys and jacket before coming over to me.

"Cell," he demands while holding out his hand.

"I'm coming with you."

"Like hell you are. Captain told you to stay here. Now give me the cell."

"Not fucking happening. I'm coming with you. This changes everything."

Wyatt opens his mouth to argue with me, but I shake my head. This is one argument I'm not going to stand down from.

"Fine, but we'll have to tell the captain everything. He's not going to be happy. You know that he isn't likely to put you back on the case."

"Yeah, I know. But I need to be there."

Wyatt goes over to Lorenzo and quickly hugs him, and I hear him say, "We'll find him," before kissing his forehead. He tells Frank that he'll call the moment anything is found out. The pair of us leave the apartment in silence, and when we are settled in the car and on the way to the station, I check the cell again. Swiping the screen to open it up, Marco hasn't moved since the last time that I checked, but I can now faintly hear what sounds like a groan coming from him.

"He still hasn't moved," I say out loud.

"That's a good thing. If he's unconscious, he isn't going to be feeling any pain."

"I know, but it's hard to see him like this. The stain on the trousers is getting bigger."

"We'll find him. You know that, don't you?"

"I hope so," is all that I can manage as I look back at the screen.

When we arrive at headquarters, I want to go straight to the tech lab, but we have to bring the captain up to date first. Wyatt knows I'm not happy wasting valuable minutes. I even suggest that Wyatt go talk to the captain and I'll go to the lab, but this is again shot down. In the end, I say I'm giving them *two minutes* and that is it.

The moment we get to the office, the captain spots me and is standing in the doorway of his office bellowing, "Detective Smith, you are supposed to be at home." His voice is stern and filled with his displeasure at seeing me standing there.

"Yes, sir, but there has been a development," I explain quickly.

"Better come into my office then."

We both rush over and shut the door behind us, but whereas Wyatt takes a seat, I hover by the door so I don't waste any more time when I need to leave.

"Are you planning to sit down, Smith?"

"No, sir. Time is against us."

"You better explain, and quickly."

"Yes, sir. They took someone. About thirty-six hours ago… Friday night to be exact. We should have come to you then, but I just wasn't thinking straight. He demanded a file containing all the information on the case and me… we"—I motion my hand indicating me and Wyatt—"came up with an idea to give him a fake one, thinking there would be a swap. But we were wrong."

"Who was taken?" I can hear the concern in the captain's voice, but I hesitate for the briefest of seconds. Wyatt opens his mouth and is about to say something, most likely a lie, but this all started because of lies, so I shake my head at him.

"My boyfriend, sir. Marco Romano."

At first, my words don't register with the captain. He just grabs a piece of paper to write on, but the moment they do, his head snaps up to look at me.

"Did you just say boyfriend?"

"Yes, sir." But before he can say anything else, I wake up the cell and pass it over so the captain can see the video of Marco. "We got this link just before leaving Wyatt's and think it's a live stream. I need to get it to the tech lab ASAP. I have to find him."

"Go. Detective Johnson can explain everything else and follow you shortly."

"Thank you, sir"

Snatching the cell from the captain, I race out of the room to the lab. The lab is on the second floor and is just a room with a few tables on either side that have several monitors and some other specialized equipment. Handing over the cell to one of the guys, I quickly explain that the captain has given permission and watch as they plug the cell in some hardware.

"Will this take long?" I ask, pacing the office as an image of Marco tied to the chair appears on one of the desk monitors.

"Hopefully the guy isn't that tech savvy," the technician states and starts tapping the keyboard and then mutters "shit."

"What!" I stop my pacing, a frisson of fear lacing through me.

"This guy is good. Looks like he's managed to route the website signal through quite a few cell towers. This will take longer than I thought. I'm going to have to trace it back one by one, and then I might only be able to give you a rough idea of location."

"It's better than what we have now." I smile gratefully before starting to pace again.

Ten minutes pass, then another ten, and my pacing starts to get quicker. How I manage to keep quiet, I don't know, and somehow I make sure not to try to rush him, either. The entire time, I've kept an eye on Marco and don't think the blood stain has got any bigger, but I've only been paying attention to his chest to make sure it's moving.

"Got something." The words from the tech stop me in my tracks.

Rushing over to him, I watch as he taps a few more buttons on the keyboard and the image of Marco disappears and is replaced with a map and a huge circle.

"He is in the Brooklyn dockyards. Sorry I couldn't pinpoint it more."

"It's a start. Keep working on it, please. Can you text me an image of that map?"

"Sure," are the only words that I hear as I rush out the room and make my way back upstairs, hearing my cell beep as I go. Wyatt is back at his desk as I get there.

"He is in the Brooklyn dockyards." I say and am already turning to leave.

"Wait one second."

I stop and turn around, knowing what he will say and already prepared to tell Wyatt it's not happening, I *am* coming along. Wyatt is striding across the office and knocking on the captain's door, then sticking his head in, but from my position, I can't hear what is being said. I see Wyatt nod his head before closing the door and making his way over to me.

"I managed to persuade the captain to let you come along. Told him you would go there with or without his permission. If you come with me, I can keep you safe. He wasn't happy, but he did say he will get us some backup who will meet us at the old Navy Yard, but Liam?"

"What?" I ask, shocked that both the Captain and Wyatt agreed for me to go.

"Don't do anything stupid. Cap only agreed because I said I would keep an eye on you."

"Of course. Thank you. But what about Lorenzo? We need to update him, anyway."

"I'll call Frank from the car. If they agree to stay behind us, they can meet us there. The knowledge Lorenzo has could be useful."

I hadn't thought of that. He would be able to point out the warehouse he used, ruling it out, so that would mean one less place to search.

Once we're in the car and out in traffic, Wyatt flicks a switch on the dashboard to get the emergency light flashing so we can snake our way through the busy streets quicker. He's then talking to the car's Bluetooth system asking it to call Frank, and after just one ring, his voice fills the car.

"Hello?"

"Frank, he's at the Brooklyn dockyards. Get Lorenzo and meet us at the old Navy Yard."

"Where in the dockyards?" But the question comes from Lorenzo and not Frank.

"No idea."

"Wyatt! Do you have any fucking idea how big the dockyards are?" Lorenzo snaps back.

"Lorenzo, we've been given a rough idea of the area, which is why you're meeting us there," I interrupt before the pair can get into an argument.

"Fine," comes his response before he hangs up the phone.

Wyatt makes a *hmph* noise, obviously pissed at the attitude from Lorenzo, and I feel like laughing and enjoying the distraction from the situation, if only for a couple minutes.

"He's just worried about Marco," I say because Wyatt isn't impressed with Lorenzo's behavior.

"We all are," he retorts.

"I know. Just cut him some slack, okay? You two fighting will not help us get to Marco."

Wyatt goes quiet after this, and thankfully with lights going, we're able to get to the dockyards in about ten minutes. Parking, we look around at the buildings. Back in World War Two, this area was a bustling hive of activity, but today, the buildings are only shells. Getting out of the car and walking to the front, I look around and see that there must be at least twenty buildings, and Marco could be in any one of them. With all the redevelopments going on in the area, I thought I'd hear the noise from traffic or... something, but it's eerily quiet. Pulling out the cell, I bring up the image of the map that was sent to me. Looking at our current position, we're just on the edge of the search area, but as I cross reference the area to the map, I can see there are certain areas that would be too populated with businesses and bars, which means a gunshot would have been easily heard.

"Any ideas?" Wyatt asks, coming up to me.

"Yeah. Have a look at this." I show him the map and voice my theory about the other areas being too busy, and he agrees but then looks at all the buildings behind us.

"But where do we start?" he asks.

"No idea. Lorenzo should be here soon. Let's see if he used any of these places, and then we'll have to split up. We're out in the open, too, so Lorenzo won't be able to stay out of sight."

"Yeah, I just figured that out. He'll have to stay behind me," Wyatt says, but I can tell he isn't confident that will happen.

"Good luck with that." I smirk at him.

Five minutes later, Frank drives into the parking lot, and the car isn't fully stopped before Lorenzo is out and running over to us.

"Do I want to know how fast Frank was going to get you here so quickly?" I ask him.

"Probably not. Where do we stand?"

I go over everything with him that I already have with Wyatt, and he agrees that the buildings behind us will be our best shot.

"Did you use any of these buildings when you, um.... had your chats?" I ask Lorenzo rather sheepishly. It's not something I ever really wanted to talk to him about. His past is between him and Wyatt.

"No, I never came up this far. My dad's company owned a warehouse further south, and I made sure that all my chats happened at night when everything was closed."

"Oh, um, okay. So, any idea on the best place to start looking?"

"It needs to be a place back from the road, not easily seen, and probably surrounded by buildings that will muffle the sound of the shot, too."

As we are finishing up, two squad cars pull into the parking lot and park next to Wyatt's SUV. This must be the backup the captain promised. The officers get out and go straight up to Wyatt.

"We're here to help with the search," one of them says to Wyatt.

"Great," he says as he grabs my cell out of my hand and shows the map to the officers. "Can you take the north end buildings?" he asks as he's pointing to areas on the map. "And we will have a look around here. Contact us if you find anything."

We watch as both men start walking to the north of us, and I turn to Lorenzo. Taking my cell back from Wyatt, I open a search engine and load the maps app and change it to the satellite image.

"Lorenzo, look at this." I show him the image on the cell. "Do any of these buildings look promising?"

Taking my cell, he looks closely, spending a good few minutes studying the image, sliding his fingers on the screen making it bigger and smaller and probably moving the image around.

"Here. Building 128. This place would have a few offices in it, it's out of the way, and surrounded by other buildings. That would help muffle any sounds."

"Great, come on and let's get going. Too much time has passed already," I say, snatching the cell out of Lorenzo's hands.

Rushing towards the building, I can hear Wyatt telling Lorenzo to stay back until they can confirm that the area is safe and then Lorenzo protesting that he can protect himself. Sometimes I think Wyatt forgets who Lorenzo used to be. It takes us a few minutes to get to our target, and if the parking lot was eerie, it is *nothing* compared to this building. Even in daytime's brightness, the place looks dim and lifeless, almost sinister.

We search around the perimeter of the building and see no sign of any movement. When we're happy the outside is clear, we enter a side entrance and find ourselves in a huge, open room that must have been the factory floor. Working our way down the side of the room to a set of stairs, Wyatt, Lorenzo, and I make our way up. At the top there is a small hallway with a few doors along it. We open each door as we go, finding nothing, but all the rooms look wrong. They all have windows facing the outside. We need to find a room that probably has a sky light instead of windows.

We gather back at the top of the stairs, taking advantage of the higher position, and look around the floor trying to see if we have missed anything. Then, right in the far corner, there looks to be a tiny office that the factory foreman probably used, and the windows look higher up so wouldn't be seen on the video and the door faces the factory floor. One way in, one way out.

"Look over there," I whisper to them.

This time we don't take our time getting to the office, instead running full speed across the floor. When we're all standing outside the door, I reach forward, turning the handle to find it doesn't move—fucking locked. And then hope rises. All the other offices were open. Taking a step back, I kick out, connecting my foot to just below the handle, and the door flies open. Both me and Wyatt are drawing our guns as we enter the room, scanning as we walk to make sure we are alone.

Suddenly the next few seconds feel like eternity. I spot the tripod in the dim light and use the direction it's facing to locate Marco, and that's when

I see him, shrouded in shadow and slumped over in the chair. My whole world stops.

"*Marco!*" I don't realize I've screamed his name until I hear it echoing around the room. Not caring about any possible dangers I should be, I holster my gun. All I care about is getting to Marco. I'm vaguely aware of another voice screaming Marco's name but don't register who it is.

Once I'm in front of Marco, I look over my shoulder and shout, "Call 9-1-1," and it's then that I spot Wyatt's arms wrapped around Lorenzo, who seems to be squirming as if he is trying to escape. It must have been his voice I heard. He wanted to get to Marco as badly as me, and I'm confused as to why Wyatt is stopping him.

Looking back at Marco, I check for a pulse, and when I feel the *thump, thump* under my fingers, I almost cry with happiness. I push him gently so he's now leaning against the back of the chair and untie his arms and legs. Placing my hand on his cheek, I run my thumb back and forth.

"Marco, it's Liam. Can you hear me?" I plead, praying that we aren't too late.

His eyes flicker open briefly, and he whispers "Liam" before the darkness takes him again.

"I'm here," I murmur, knowing he probably can't hear me, but I need to say those words to him, anyway. Leaning down, not caring about the other people in the room, I kiss him softly on his lips and then crouch down, holding his hand as I prepare to wait for the medics to arrive. A hand lands on my shoulder, and I look up to see Lorenzo.

"Wyatt wouldn't let me come over." Lorenzo states, a hint of bitterness at being stopped. But as he looks down at Marco, I can see the worry written all over his face.

"I just thought it would be best for Liam to be there first," Wyatt says from across the room. Looking over, I see him standing by the tripod and starting to remove the camera with gloved hands to put in an evidence bag.

"He's gonna be okay," I reassure Lorenzo as I turn back to him.

"I know," Lorenzo replies, and a small smile touches his lips as he glances at mine and Marco's hands. "You really do love him, don't you?"

"Yeah, I do. More than anything," I say and turn back to Marco, never letting go of his hand.

Chapter 29 — Marco

Something is different. The room smells odd with a clean, disinfected kind of scent. I move my arm and find that it's free, but now it feels like there is something stuck in the back of my hand. Slowly opening my eyes to give them a chance to adjust to the brightness, I take in my surroundings. The walls are white, clinical. There's a wooden chair in the corner with a garish orange seat that I'm sure is made from vinyl, and a glass door. Beyond the door, I can see people walking around in blue uniforms—hospital. *I'm in a hospital room.* But I don't remember being moved.

Becoming more aware of my surroundings, a strange beeping sound reaches my ears, and I tilt my head toward the sound and see a machine showing a heart rhythm. Watching that thin line go across while making quick up and down motions in time with the beep is relaxing, and I track the wire to see whose heartbeat it is and discover that it's attached to me. That's when I see a hand clasped with mine... It's one that I recognize... Liam. He's sitting in an identical chair to the empty one but is bent over, his head resting on the bed, sleeping. He looks pale even as he sleeps, and his wavy brown locks are messy and dull as if he's run his fingers through them too many times.

Shifting to my side, a sharp pain shoots up my leg and I now remember that I'd been shot, which also explains the hospital bed. Settling back down, I wait for the pain to pass. Reaching over, I carefully stroke the hair off Liam's face and just watch him. There is a gentle squeezing of my hand followed by a mumble into the bed sheets, but I can't make out what he says. Stroking his hair again, he unconsciously leans into my touch.

I'm so engrossed in watching Liam that I don't hear the door open and only look up when the sound of footsteps on the tile are closer. A man in a white coat with a stethoscope slung around his neck is now standing beside the bed. Raising a finger to my lips in the classic 'shh' sign, I incline my head towards Liam. The doctor just smiles and pulls the chair over next to me.

"Good morning, Mr. Romano," he says in a hushed tone. "How are you feeling?"

"Good, considering I was shot," I reply in a raspy voice.

"I am going to have to check all your vitals now, is that okay?" he asks with a reassuring smile. "Does anything hurt?"

I nod my head when he mentions checking my vitals and confirm that my face feels like it has gone a round with Mike Tyson and my leg is painful. The doctor gets back up from the chair and leans over me after picking up a clipboard from a holder on the side of my bed that I hadn't noticed. I can see his eyes flickering over whatever information is on there and then he then proceeds to take my temperature, pulse, and blood pressure. Just when I think he's finished, he pulls out what I thought was another pen but turns out to be a penlight.

"Just need to shine this in your eyes so I can check your pupils' reaction," he whispers to me, and it makes me smile that he is still being quiet.

Once he has finished all his tests, he writes a note on the clipboard before placing it back in the holder and takes a seat next to me again.

"So far, no sign of infection, and your vitals are good." He then looks over to Liam. "He hasn't left your side since they brought you in. Refused to leave even when it was suggested that he go get some sleep in his own bed. He really must care about you. Now get some more rest. I'll come back in a few hours."

Nodding my head, I close my eyes and soon feel sleep taking me under. I give one last look over to Liam before the darkness wraps me in its embrace completely.

The feeling of a thumb rubbing back and forth on my hand brings me out of my slumber and I turn my head and can see Liam is awake, still holding my hand, but he isn't paying attention to me, so I squeeze his fingers. His head snaps over in my direction, and a smile spreads across his face.

"You're awake." The joy in his voice can't be missed. "Let me go get the doctor."

"He was here earlier..." But before I can finish my sentence, Liam is jumping out of his chair and out the door. Looking around the bed, I find what looks to be a remote but has pictures of a bed on it in different positions and a cord running back behind my head. Pushing one of the buttons, I lift the bed until I'm in a sitting position and wait. Liam returns a few minutes later, the doctor hot on his heels.

"Hello again," the doctor says to me. "You still feeling okay?"

"Yes, doctor." Liam's watching the exchange between us, his brow creasing with confusion. "As I was saying, I woke up earlier," I start, directing my words at Liam, "and the doctor paid me a visit."

"But I've been here the whole time. I don't remember him coming in."

"Because you were sleeping," I interject, "and I didn't want to wake you up."

"You should have woken me," he replies, sounding slightly pissed.

At this point, the doctor speaks up. "You needed to sleep. Ideally, you should have gone home." And the look he gives Liam is a clear don't even think about arguing. "I wasn't in here long, just checking some vitals."

"Wouldn't the nurse normally do that?" Liam fires back, completely ignoring the statement on where he should have been sleeping.

"They do, yes, but us doctors still like to check them every now and then. Confirm readings and the physical reactions with our own eyes." He stops looking at Liam and turns to me. "Now that everyone is awake, we can talk about your care." We both nod in agreement and wait for him to continue.

"When you were admitted yesterday, we took you straight to the OR where the bullet was removed. You were incredibly lucky it missed the bone and major artery. We won't know about any nerve damage until it starts healing."

"Is there anything we can do to help that?" Liam pipes up.

"Apply ice packs to the area every day but try not to get it wet. Also, no showers or baths for a few days. Sponge baths *only*."

I burst out laughing at the look of excitement that has appeared on Liam's face at hearing this, and I guess I know who will be giving me those.

"Will he have to come back to have stitches removed?" Liam asks.

Stitches. It never even occurred to me I might have gotten stitches, but at least Liam seems to be thinking ahead.

"We used dissolvable stitches inside the wound and surgical tape to seal it after the surgery. It's the least invasive. The tape should come away naturally within about seven days, but if it hasn't happened by then and the wound looks closed, you can take them off. But I would also like you to rest the leg for a few days."

"Is there anything else we need to look out for?" Liam is asking again, and when I look over, I'm surprised to see that he has his cell phone open, and he is typing away—he's making notes.

"If his temperature goes up and stays up, then it could be a sign of an infection, and he'll need to come back to the hospital straight away."

"Okay. So when can I go home?" I ask, already itching to get out of this bed.

"We want to keep you in for forty-eight hours to minimize the chance of infection. So as long as your vitals are still good, I can see us letting you out tomorrow."

"That soon? Seems a little quick for a gunshot wound," Liam voices.

"Shut up, Liam! If the doctor says I can go home tomorrow, we listen to him."

The doctor laughs at my reaction. "If the shot had been an inch or more to the left, then the bone would have been broken, not to mention more muscle damage, and he would have been staying here a lot longer, but I think being in his own home will be the best treatment."

Just as the doctor is finishing up, Lorenzo and Wyatt turn up.

"Doctor Winston?" Lorenzo says, surprised.

"Why, Mr. Romano, I was wondering if Marco was related. We don't have many Romano's coming through the door."

"My brother, Doctor."

"Okay, I'm confused. How do you know each other?" I ask into the room.

Lorenzo comes over and sits on the chair that is still beside my bed. "Doctor Winston was the doctor that treated me when I was mugged."

"I was, and if I remember correctly, I think I told you I didn't want to see you here again, but that didn't mean to send your brother in."

Lorenzo laughs. "Sorry, Doctor," is all he says, but he doesn't look sorry at all.

"Hang on." I turn my head to Liam. "Didn't you tell me you came to the hospital with Wyatt? How come you didn't recognize him?"

Liam blushes at this, actually *blushes*, as embarrassment fills his features. "I did but wasn't sure what to say." We all burst out laughing at this, and Liam glares at us all in turn. "Hey, it's not every day that your boyfriend is shot, brought to the same hospital as your partner's fiancé, and then to top it off is treated by the same doctor."

We're all laughing again when one of the words he said registers with me and causes my laugh to cut short.

"Boyfriend?" I say out loud in surprise.

Seeing the shift in the atmosphere of the room, the doctor politely excuses himself with an assurance that he will be back in the morning to check on me. The moment the door is closed, I'm turning on Liam.

"Boyfriend? You just said that word out loud. Everyone heard you."

Liam opens his mouth to respond but is cut off by Lorenzo. "Yeah, Liam told us everything and when you are better, we are having a little chat."

"Hey, he's already been shot once. Seems a little mean to do it again." Liam smirks at them.

The three of them are laughing again, but I have no idea why, and it irritates the fuck out of me.

"That's not bloody funny," I snap at them.

Three heads turn to me, all of them now stifling their laughs.

"Sorry," Lorenzo finally manages to say. "Forgot that you missed that part of the conversation. When I had to do Dad's dirty work, I called it a 'little chat,'" He's using those stupid finger air quotes with the last two words.

Okay, I can see why that might be funny and find myself smiling along with them now, too.

"What did the doc say? How long do you have to stay?" Lorenzo asks.

"Hopefully he can go home tomorrow," Liam answers for me. "But he needs to rest for a few days."

"You know that I am awake here, right?" I say to the pair of them as they continue talking as if I'm not there.

"We know," they both say together as they carry on discussing who will stay with me, Liam voicing that he is sure that the captain will give him some time off.

"Um, Liam, not sure if you remember, and I know you just called me your boyfriend, but we broke up. It's the reason that I went for a drink." Thinking back, I realize I have no idea what day it is. "Wait, what day is it?"

"It's Monday. We got to you yesterday," Liam answers, and I can hear the pain in his voice.

"Shit! School! I need to call the principal," I say as I start to panic, sitting forward in bed and ignoring the twinge in my leg when I make the motion too fast.

"Don't worry, I called the principal this morning and explained everything. Not sure he has ever had a teacher kidnapped before. He said he'll get coverage for your classes and to come back when you're ready, but to keep him updated. I think you'll definitely be the cool teacher when you go back," Liam tells me, gently pushing me back against the pillow.

"Thanks." I respond, resting my head back on the pillows, suddenly feeling tired, so I close my eyes briefly.

"Get some more sleep. I'll be here when you wake up," Liam says, and hearing movement, I open my eyes to see that he's gotten out of the chair and is talking to Lorenzo, not noticing that my eyes are open.

"Can you stay with him? I really want to get a change of clothes and pick up some stuff for him. Shouldn't be more than an hour." Turning to me, he sees me watching them and gives me a sweet smile. "Thought you were sleeping." He comes over to me and kisses me on the forehead but hesitates as he's turning away and looks back at me before leaning down and giving me one of the sweetest kisses on the lips and whispers, "Won't be long," before leaving with Wyatt hot on his heels.

"Right, now that we are alone, can you please explain why the *fuck* you didn't tell me about you and Liam," Lorenzo states with the slight edge to his voice, betraying how annoyed he is with me.

"I was just shot. Can't we do this another time." I'm really not wanting to have this conversation at the moment.

"Nope." And now I know there's no way I will get out of this.

When I lean back further into the pillow and close my eyes, hoping to gather my thoughts so I can explain and make him understand that it was nothing against him, he speaks up. "And no pretending to sleep, either."

Sighing, I open my eyes and look at him to find that he's moved to the seat next to the bed that Liam had been occupying.

"I wasn't sleeping. I was getting my thoughts together. Look, it all started when you were back home with Dad, and I just couldn't say anything. I never thought it would last. I wasn't out at work, and I was scared shitless that the school would fire me. Liam wasn't sure how the guys at the station would react, either. He's only ever talked about girls, so we kinda agreed to keep it quiet."

God, when I say it out loud, it sounds so pathetic. Two grown men too scared of what other people might think to be open, but there is nothing that we can do about it now. We thought we were doing the right thing, even if it looks like it was for nothing.

"You could have told me." And this time there is no mistaking the pain in his voice that I didn't talk to him.

"Yeah, I know, and believe me, I wanted to. But as more time passed, the more I convinced myself that you'd hate me for keeping it a secret. I really wanted your advice."

"I won't lie. I'm disappointed that you didn't come to me. I thought we were closer than that, but I won't ever hate you. But you'd better believe me when I say I won't let either of you forget this."

"We *are* close, Lorenzo. I was scared. Sorry, but it doesn't matter anymore, anyway. We broke up." Saying the words out loud brings back all the pain, matching the one in my leg.

"Um, have I been seeing things? He hasn't left your side, and unless my eyes are deceiving me, that was a kiss goodbye, too."

"Yeah, I don't know what that's all about."

"Look, he's been worried sick about you, and I have no idea what he said to you, but that's something you'll have to talk to him about. I know one thing for certain. Liam loves you. And you still love him, too, don't you?"

"More than I ever thought possible," I tell him honestly.

"Thank fuck. Now, when he gets back, talk to him. Sort this shit out. Until then, get some sleep. It'll help with the healing."

I don't argue with him and instead lean further back into my pillows and think about what Lorenzo said. During the entire time I was tied up, I had hoped that maybe Liam would come and rescue me, which only grew stronger when I had seen the folder on Antonio's lap. He wouldn't have risked his job if there wasn't a shred of feeling there, but hearing it from Lorenzo makes that seed of hope grow even bigger. Now I am excited to talk to Liam, and with that thought in my head, I drift off to sleep.

As promised, the next time I wake up, Liam is sitting next to me looking at something on his phone.

"Hey," I say, and he jumps when he hears my voice. "Sorry." I quickly apologize and give him a sheepish smile.

"It's okay. Just wasn't expecting it." Liam gets up from the chair, and at first I thought he was going to get the doctor, but instead, he leans over and kisses me, lingering there for a second before moving back and smiling at me. "Hey."

"How long have I been asleep?" I ask

"Not long. Only a couple hours."

Really? Only a couple hours. It felt a lot longer.

"Where's Lorenzo?" I should have said we need to talk, but the words couldn't… or maybe *wouldn't* come out.

"They've gone to get some coffee. I asked them to give us some time." Liam sits back down in the chair and takes my hand in his, lifting it to his lips. "I never meant it," he whispers.

"Never meant what?" I ask, confusion filling my mind.

"What I said Friday night. Everything was a lie. I thought by breaking up with you I was going to keep you safe. Please…" There is an edge of pleading and despair in his voice. "Please tell me I haven't lost you."

"You're a very good actor," I reply, the words tumbling from my mouth. It was what I was thinking but didn't mean to say out loud. What I had meant to say was *Of course you haven't lost me.*

Liam squeezes my hand and places it on his cheek, appearing to need that contact with me. "You didn't see my face. That's why I didn't turn around. What I did broke me more than you'll ever know. I love you so much. Marco, please, I can't lose you." He closes his eyes and leans into my hand.

"Liam," I say, but he doesn't open his eyes. "Liam," I repeat, more firmly this time, and I rub my thumb over his cheek. "Look at me." He hesitantly opens his eyes and looks into mine as I say, "You haven't lost me."

The smile that spreads across his face is breath-taking. The shine literally lights up the room and is completely infectious.

"Honestly? But you said that if I walked out the door that it was over."

Chuckling, I say, "Liam, you had just broken my heart. I was going to try anything to get you to stay."

Liam moves so fast that I jump the moment his lips are on mine. This is not the gentle kisses he has been giving me thus far. He's throwing everything into this kiss—his hope, his regret, but most of all his love—and I kiss him back with just as much feeling. His tongue runs along the seam of my lips and they part, wanting to deepen this kiss as much as he does. Our tongues are dueling together as if we have been apart for years, not mere days. He wraps his arms around me pulling me closer, never once breaking the kiss, and it feels so good to be held by him again.

We are so engrossed in the kiss that we don't hear the door to my room open until there is a very loud "hem" coming from the corner, and we break the kiss to see Lorenzo and Wyatt standing there with stupid, gleeful grins on their faces.

"How long have you been there?" I ask, slightly embarrassed that my brother just witnessed that kiss.

"Long enough. That is a kiss a brother should never see. It was pure porn. If either one of you had groaned, I swear."

"Sorry." I'm really not. It's just the automatic thing to say.

"No, you're not," comes his reply, and I just shrug.

Liam settles back down in the chair and holds my hand again, and I lean back into the pillows. Who would've thought kissing would take so much out of you? But that kiss had been so worth it.

"Marco," Wyatt says, "sorry, but I had a call from the captain earlier. Looks like a couple of detectives are coming to see you. I tried to put them off till you were home, but they wouldn't wait."

"It's okay. Better to get it done and over with." It never dawned on me that I'd have to give a statement, but it's best to do it when the memories are still fresh. "I'm not going to be able to tell them much. He didn't really say much."

"Tell them anything you can, but I will ask that if they ask about Lorenzo, please don't mention anything about his past."

"Wyatt, really? I am not that fucking stupid." I can't *believe* Wyatt just asked that of me, and I shake my head at him.

Thirty minutes later there's a tap on the door, and the three of us look around to see two men standing on the other side. Both are wearing dark slacks and pressed, white shirts and are just screaming detectives.

"No shit," Lorenzo whispers.

"What?" I whisper back, trying not to move my lips as I wave them in.

"These were the guys who interviewed me after my attack," he replies while still keeping his voice to a murmur.

Before I have a chance to say anything back, the detectives are by my side and looking at the faces of Liam, Lorenzo, and Wyatt before moving back to Lorenzo, and a look of surprise flashes over their faces.

"Mr. Romano!" One of the detectives states, the confusion clear on his face as he looks back to me and then to Lorenzo, who's biting his lip to stop the smile on his face.

"My brother," Lorenzo finally states.

"Oh," one of the men says, and he shoots a look over to his partner but doesn't say anything more before turning his attention back to me. "Mr. Romano, I'm Detective Dylan Rogers, and this is my partner, Detective Morris Tyler. How are you feeling?"

"Please, call me Marco. My leg hurts like a bitch, but other than that, I'm okay."

Detective Rogers smiles when I comment about my leg. "Yeah, gunshots aren't pleasant." Oh, so that must explain the smile. Looks like he has some experience with a gunshot wound himself. Detective Rogers continues, "Are you up to answering some questions?"

"Yeah, go ahead."

For the next twenty minutes, I answer all the questions as best I can even though what I say doesn't seem that useful. I'm not able to remember the face of the person who took me or the type of vehicle they took me in. The only thing I can confirm is the name of my kidnapper and his plans of becoming the next big wig.

"Thank you, Marco. Just a few more and we should be done. We understand that they targeted you because of your connection to Mr. Smith. Do you mind me asking why you were keeping the relationship a secret?"

"Um, when we got together, I wasn't out to my family or at work and so we decided to keep it quiet and later"—I look over to Liam who just nods his head—"we were too afraid to come out. But can I ask why this would be relevant?"

"Just trying to figure out why you were targeted and if the relationship being out in the open would have made a difference." It's Detective Tyler that is answering this time, but he keeps looking at Lorenzo as if there is something that is bothering him. "Mr. Romano," Detective Tyler directs his attention to Lorenzo. He must have decided to ask about whatever he's been thinking about. "I thought you said that you didn't talk to your family anymore?"

Looking up at Lorenzo, I can see that he is trying to figure out what to say, so I jump in first. "That is down to me. I kinda overreacted. He must have told you about the big family fight when he came out to them. Hence me staying quiet. But when I hadn't heard from him in a week, I went to the police and reported him missing. He found out and got in contact, and we met in secret."

I'm hoping this would be the end of the questions, but I can already see they have more, and so I wait. So far, I haven't lied, but I will make sure that Lorenzo doesn't answer anything. They must know Alfredo died and are probably trying to link everything together.

"Did you know what type of business your dad was in?" Detective Rogers asks this time.

"Well, I thought it was just the flower import business, but Antonio corrected me on that. Would you believe it? He was a *drug* smuggler!" I reply, trying to add a tone of astonishment to the final part. Glancing over quickly, I catch Lorenzo biting his lip but letting it go before either of the detectives' notice, though no one else but me can spot the look of worry in his eyes.

"He died recently, didn't he?" Detective Tyler asks, and even though it looks as though he is asking me at first, he turns his head toward Lorenzo for an answer. Lorenzo somehow manages to remain stone faced, not giving anything away.

"Yeah. It was a heart attack, which was caused by stress, I believe. Considering his line of business, I'm amazed it didn't happen sooner." I reply to the detective, making him look in my direction.

"True…" You can see they have more questions, but so far, I haven't said anything they didn't already know, and just as they open their mouths, a nurse enters the room.

"Marco, ice pack time," she sing-songs before she looks at all the visitors. She furrows her brow before putting her hands on her hips. "There are too many people here. Out of here, all of you."

"Our apologies," the detectives say, obviously not wanting to get on the nurse's bad side. "We were just leaving." Detective Rogers reaches into the pocket of his pants and pulls out a card and hands it to me. "If you think of anything more, give us a call," he says before they both take their leave.

Lorenzo and Wyatt are still hovering, not wanting to go, but the nurse has other ideas. "And you three, out as well," she snaps at them but still doesn't move. "Mr. Romano needs his rest."

"Can Liam stay, please," I plead.

The nurse sees us holding hands, and a smile briefly touches her lips as her eyes soften. "That will be fine. I can show him what to do when you go home. But I'm going to have to ask you both to give Marco some quiet time. I mean it." Wyatt mumbles something about getting coffee and reluctantly leaves with Lorenzo on his heels.

The nurse takes her time, showing Liam how to wrap the ice pack in a towel to stop the dressing from getting wet. She carefully removes the bandage over my wound, and for the first time, I see a small line on my thigh a couple of inches long that is being held together with strips of white tape.

"Hold the ice pack gently on the wound. Try not to apply too much pressure. Here, you try." The nurse is giving instructions to Liam, who hesitantly takes over, trying to copy what she was doing.

"Okay?" he asks me, concerned that he is causing me pain.

"It's damn cold, but you aren't hurting me."

"Keep the ice pack on for ten minutes, daily. If he can't do ten minutes, drop it to five, but then do it twice a day," the nurse instructs.

Ten minutes and I have reached my limit, and I'm glad when the ice pack is taken away. Hopefully, I won't have to do that for too long. I'll have to remember to ask the doctor how many days to ice for. The nurse finishes up, takes away the ice pack, and gives Liam a smile as she leaves.

"I think we'll be doing that only five minutes at a time," I say once she's gone. "Was getting a bit much at the end there."

"Thought so. You started to look uncomfortable. Why didn't you say something?"

"I didn't see the point. It was almost over, anyway," I tell him.

"More like you didn't want to risk not being able to go home if you didn't last the ten minutes." Liam states.

Shooting him a look of disbelief, he just smiles. When the fuck did he get to know me so well? He *knew* I wasn't being totally truthful about why I didn't stop the nurse, and that fills me with this warm, fuzzy feeling. Lying back onto the pillows in complete contentment, I close my eyes. The feeling of something moving causes me to open them, however, and I see Liam's face hovering over me while he pushes the button on the bed remote to lower me back down.

"Get some sleep. Tomorrow, we'll go home." And then Liam kisses my forehead, and I fall asleep with images of a brown-haired, naked man in my arms.

The following afternoon, the doctor returns with my discharge papers, which I sign straight away, wanting to get out of the hospital as soon as possible. He also has some extra bandages, antibiotic cream that needs to be applied every time the dressing is changed, and a walking stick for me to use until I'm fully healed. Liam takes them from him before I have the chance to.

"I'll take those." He gives me a look that tells me don't argue with him, and I hold my hands up in defeat and the doctor just smiles at the pair of us.

Now that everything has been signed and the doctor has explained the symptoms that we need to keep an eye out for and is satisfied we understand his instructions, he leaves, telling us that an orderly will be along shortly.

"Orderly?" I ask, looking over to Liam.

"Yeah, with a wheelchair," Liam states like this is something I should have known.

"I am more than capable of walking out that door just fine by myself. Just get me the walking stick."

"Not gonna to happen," Liam replies, and from the look on his face, I know there is no arguing. "We are going to follow the hospital rules so we can get you home where you belong."

Liam hands me some soft jogging pants, a plain t-shirt, and some slip-on shoes. Carefully, I swing my legs off the bed and shimmy to the edge, gingerly placing my feet on the floor. When I start to rise off the bed, Liam is suddenly by my side, and I place a hand on his outstretched arm so that I can stand up. Letting go of his arm, I take a few small steps. My wounded leg still feels a little strange, and when I step on the foot, there is a slight pain that shoots up my leg into my hip.

Sitting back down on the bed, I start to get dressed, but after a few attempts at trying to get my pants on, Liam must have seen me struggling and comes over again. He helps me into the pants and then crouches down and slips on the shoes. When he then removes the hospital gown, he deliberately runs a hand up my chest before slipping the t-shirt over my head. Finally I'm dressed, and he settles me back down on the bed to wait.

A few minutes later, the orderly arrives, and suddenly being pushed in a wheelchair might not be so bad. The man in front of me, who has to be six foot tall with dirty blond hair, places his hands under my underarms to help lower me into the chair, and I thank him as I lean back.

Liam comes over to me to hand me a clear bag with my belongings, and as he does, whispers in my ear, "Might want to wipe your mouth. You're drooling."

I'm just about to snap at him for thinking I'd have eyes for anyone but him, but when I look up, I can see the humor in his eyes.

"Ready?" I ask Liam as the orderly starts to wheel me to the door.

"Hell, yes, and the first thing we're doing when we get home is having a sponge bath." And with that, he winks at me, and that warm fuzzy feeling is back, and I can't wait to get home.

Chapter 30 — Liam

The sound of groaning wakes me to a room that is shrouded in darkness, and it takes me a minute to figure out the noise is coming from Marco. Leaning over and clicking on the bedside light to illuminate the room, I turn over and then can see the beads of sweat clinging to his brow as he is thrashing his arms about. *Shit.* He's having another nightmare.

We've been home from the hospital for a week now, but the first nightmare happened on the second night, and they've been happening almost every night since. Each time he wakes up, I try to get him to talk about them, but he's refusing, and the nightmares seem to be getting worse with each passing day. At first, he just woke up breathing hard, then he started moving about, but this is the first time he's made any sounds.

Scooting over to him and brushing the damp hair from his face, I kiss his temple. "Marco. I'm here. It's okay," I whisper to him, not wanting to startle him awake.

He starts to thrash his head back and forth. Getting closer to him and pulling him into arms, I try to give him some comfort. As I continue to keep hold of him, thankfully, the thrashing seems to ease, but suddenly he screams my name and wakes up, breathing hard.

"Liam?" he says, and I can hear the worry in his voice.

"It's okay. I'm here, Marco." I pull him tighter to me and feel him relax into me. "They're getting worse, aren't they," I ask him. "Please talk to me. I'm worried about you."

Expecting him to clam up on me like every other time before, I'm surprised when he takes a deep breath and starts to talk.

"He's chasing you, and I'm tied to the chair and can't get to you. Then he pulls a gun and shoots you in front of me, and there isn't anything I can do to stop it. When I start screaming to you, he turns the gun on me."

Holy fuck, I knew they weren't good, but I never thought he was reliving the events surrounding his kidnapping or distorting them to include me, too.

"I'm here, baby. We're both safe." I say and kiss his temple again. "But you really need to talk to someone."

I've been saying this for a few days, but he's been ignoring it, wanting to try and deal with this himself, but I have a plan to help him to understand that it's okay to get help.

"You still up for going out today?" I ask, hoping that the nightmare hasn't put him off, and he nods his head. Turning off the light, I move onto my side and pull him to me, his back against my chest, and hold him tight. "It's too early to get up. Let's get a few more hours sleep," I say, but I don't think he hears me, his breathing evening out as he falls back to sleep after feeling safe in my arms.

A few hours later finds us standing outside my childhood home, getting ready to go inside.

"You ready for this?" I ask, but he looks so nervous.

"Ready to meet the parents? Is anyone *ever* ready to meet the parents?"

"They're going to love you," I reassure him.

When Marco had been in hospital, I called my family and told them everything. They hadn't been happy that I came out to them in a telephone conversation but had been surprisingly supportive, which had made me feel even more guilty that I hadn't had the courage to tell them before. They also made me promise to bring him over to meet them when he had been feeling up to it, so, here we are. But what Marco doesn't know is that I've also invited my brothers and sisters, one of whom I'm hoping will be able to help Marco with his nightmares.

"Come on, we can't stand here all day," I say and grab his hand, pulling him towards the house. I can see his hand tighten around the huge bouquet of flowers he's holding, which is Lorenzo's handiwork.

Knocking on the front door once before opening it, I walk into the house shouting, "Hello," and stopping in the front room to wait for a reply.

"Liam, we're in the kitchen," my mom responds, her voice light.

The kitchen is at the back of the house, and we have to walk through the living area to get there. My brother and sister are sitting on the couch as we pass, and I give them a quick hello before dragging Marco past them as he quickly looks at them before turning back to me with a frightened, deer-in-the-headlights look on his face.

Once in the kitchen, I find my mom is at the stove, stirring a big pot of something, and my dad is chopping vegetables for what I'm guessing will be a salad. Dropping Marco's hand, I walk up to Mom and kiss her on the cheek. Dad stops chopping, gets up, and embraces me in a hug before standing next to Mom, who's stopped stirring and is now looking at Marco.

"Mom, Dad. This is my boyfriend, Marco." I'm not sure that I've ever seen Marco look so shy, "Marco, this is my mom, Jessica, and my dad, Robert."

Finally, his manners kick in and he walks up to my mom. "It's a pleasure to meet you ma'am. These are for you," he says as he passes the flowers to my mom before turning and holding his hand out to my dad. "Pleasure to meet you, too, sir."

"Did you honestly just say ma'am and sir? How the hell did you find someone so polite?" I hear my brother saying as he walks into the kitchen, pulling me into a hug, and I spy my sister following him.

"Ignore him," my sister states, pointing at my brother. "I'm Emily, his much younger, nicer sister, and that thug is Ryan, our apparently older, *wiser* brother." and I watch as Emily pulls Marco into a hug.

"Pleasure to meet you both. It's nice to put a name to the body," Marco says to Emily.

"What?" Emily says, and even I'm confused for a second.

"I saw you once," Marco starts to explain. "Well, the back of you. I thought you were Liam's girlfriend. I felt like an idiot when Liam explained you were his sister."

"Oh, yeah," I say, laughing. "I'd completely forgotten that."

"Girlfriend?" Emily pretends to shiver with revulsion. "What a horrible thought."

"Yeah, I swear we almost died when Mom said Liam was bringing a guy home. None of us saw that coming. But you're a lot nicer than some of the other losers Liam has introduced to us," Ryan says.

Marco seems at a loss as to what to say to this, so he just smiles, and I'm thankful that my mom comes to my rescue.

"Ignore my idiot son, Marco. These are beautiful flowers, thank you. And please call me Jess, and that's Bob," my mom says pointing to my dad.

"I wish I could take the credit, but that's all my brother's handiwork. He owns a shop in the east village," Marco explains

"Wait, as in Romano Flowers?" my mom asks.

"Yep, the same, except he changed the name recently to More than Roses." And there's no mistaking how proud he is of Lorenzo as he speaks.

"Wow," my mom replies, seeming to be seriously impressed.

"The next time you want flowers, just tell him your Liam's mom, and I'm sure he'll give you a deal. You know, family and all."

And just like that, Marco has won my mom over, and by the impressed look on my dad's face, he is pleased, too. I can't help but feel proud that so far, my family has been so welcoming.

"Food is almost ready. Liam, set the table," my mom says, and she unwraps the flowers from the cellophane, placing them in a vase and setting them on the dining room sideboard.

"Can I help?" Marco asks

"Okay, I think now I'm agreeing with Ryan. Where the hell did you find someone so nice?" Emily pipes up before turning to Marco. "Please, take a seat. You're a guest, plus that way, you can tell us how you met."

Marco just smiles at this. "Well, we kinda meet through Wyatt."

"Your partner, Wyatt?" my dad asks me.

"Yeah," Marco answers for me. "Lorenzo is my brother."

"Hang on one minute," Mom says to Marco before turning on me. "Are you telling me that Lorenzo is the owner of my favorite florist, and you never told me?"

"How the hell was I supposed to know that he was your favorite florist? Since you've met him when Wyatt and he came around, I just figured you would have said something about what he does." Honestly, I'm really surprised that Mom never put together who Lorenzo was and where he worked.

"Sorry, Marco. Carry on." But my mom is still giving me the evil eye.

Marco explains about the missing person report, but just like when he was talking to the detectives, he says it was a misunderstanding, and my parents seem happy with his answers. The atmosphere in the room is so friendly that if someone were to walk in, they would never say this was the first time that Marco and my family were all meeting.

"Food's ready," Mom says as she brings over the big pot and places it in the center of the table, followed by the salad that Dad had been, in fact, making. "It's pasta and sauce. I know it won't be as good as your mom's, Marco, but I wanted something quick."

"I'm sure it will be lovely, Jess," Marco replies, and I watch him closely to see if the mention of his mom causes any reaction, but he just stays as calm as he was before.

If I'd been hoping that the topic of parents would end with the discussion on food, I had been very wrong.

"So, Marco. What do your parents do? We'll have to organize a family get together."

Shit. Looking over to Marco, I try to gauge what he's feeling or even what he will say, but he's giving nothing away.

"My dad passed away a few months ago, and unfortunately, my mom is no longer talking to me, but maybe we can arrange something with Lorenzo and Wyatt." His reply is so matter of fact, no hurt or even anger in voice. It's just a statement of reality, but my mom looks completely shocked.

"Oh, Marco, I am *so* sorry to hear about your father, but do you mind me asking why your mom isn't talking to you."

"Of course. I don't mind. My mom comes from a very traditional Italian family and being gay just wasn't acceptable. I was supposed to get married and have children. Keep the family name going."

"But doesn't she understand that you can still get married and have children?" My mom is getting really worked up listening to Marco. She's never understood how a parent could disown a child, but having it told to her first-hand is breaking her heart.

"Not in her eyes. Marriage is between a man and woman only." But Marco seems to pick up on my mom's distress and tries to ease it. "But if my mom cannot accept me for who I am, then she is the one missing out, not me. She won't get to meet Liam and see how outstanding your son is, so I've made my peace with it. Plus, I still have Lorenzo and Wyatt, and that's all the family that I need."

When my mom hears Marco say about his mom missing out on meeting me, I think she melts in front of me, and I have a feeling that Marco will be a very frequent guest at this house.

"Mom, do you think we can change the subject?" I ask, not wanting to stay on this topic.

"Yes, of course, dear. So, Marco, what do you do for a living?" Going back over all the conversations I've had with my parents explaining what had happened, I had forgotten to give them any background on him. All I had told them was that I was seeing a man, but that was about it.

"I teach sophomore English." And as Marco talks about school, his students, and the LGBTQ club that he'll be heading, he completely lights up, and I don't think I realized how much he loves his job until today. Him sitting there talking about wanting to be a role model for kids, making sure they know that there is nothing wrong with being gay, causes my heart to swell with even more love for this man.

We spend the rest of the meal just chatting about general topics, and when all the plates are clean, I suggest that we move to the living room so we can carry on talking in comfort. We all get up from our seats, but Marco surprises me by turning to my mom.

"Jess, do you want any help with the dishes?"

"Oh, Marco, that is so kind of you. But we'll just throw them in the dishwasher later and Emily can help. You go into the sitting room."

I grab Marco's hand before he asks to help them load the dishwasher since I need to get him relaxed so the next part of my plan can happen. When we both settle on the couch, I make sure to sit next to him, keeping hold of his hand. Ryan is already sitting in one of the three armchairs opposite us, and he spots my very public display. I catch the smirk on his face, but he doesn't say anything.

"So, Marco, how are you doing? Liam's told us what happened," Ryan says, and I'm so happy that he decided to broach the subject first.

"I'm doing well, healing well. We're still doing the ice pack twice a day, which isn't fun."

"Yeah, I remember them. So freakin' cold."

Without missing a beat, Marco picks up on that. "Wait, have you been shot?"

"Not shot, but I was in the army and got posted to Afghanistan where I got hit by some shrapnel. I was one of the lucky ones. Some others in my platoon weren't so fortunate."

"Shit," Marco replies, completely shocked. "When did this happen?"

"It was a few years ago. My leg healed pretty quickly, but my mind was another matter."

"Your mind?" Marco asks, sounding confused.

"Yeah, I had nightmares for a while after that. Ended up having to go see someone," Ryan explains.

"Are you still in the army?" Marco asks.

"No. After that, I decided to leave. It wasn't an easy choice, but it turned out to be the best decision. Now I have a private security firm."

"When did your nightmares stop?" Marco asks, leaning forward, and I see that he's paying close attention to what Ryan is saying. It seems my plan is working perfectly.

When Ryan got injured, we'd all been so worried, but then he seemed to heal. We never saw the mental scars until the day that Ryan sat us all down and explained he was leaving the Army and had been seeing a therapist. He'd always been the tough guy and hearing that had been hard, but we'd also been so proud of him for telling us and getting the help he needed, and I am hoping that Marco will see that, too.

"It took a while but talking definitely helped. I can get you the number for my therapist if you'd like. He's a good guy," Ryan offers.

Holding my breath, I wait to see what Marco will say, silently keeping my fingers crossed.

"Yeah, I would like that. Thanks."

Oh, thank god. I want to pull him into my arms and tell him how proud I am of him, but that might be a little too much emotion in front of the family. Ryan writes a number on a piece of paper and hands it over.

I'm certain that my parents and Emily have been listening from the kitchen because the moment Ryan has finished talking, they're all coming into the living room. I move closer to Marco to make room for Emily on the couch while my parents take a seat in the other two single armchairs.

"Is there any news on the case?" my mom asks the pair of us.

"Yeah. The police managed to catch Antonio. Our tech guys were able to use the cell he gave me originally to trace back the messages to his phone. They even managed to use the PO Box. It was registered in an anagram of his name. I have no idea how they were able to get an address, but they did, and I don't think he thought he would be found out because when his home was raided, not only did they find the fake file and his cell, but they also found a lot of information linked to his drug empire. His name had looked familiar when I'd first heard it, and I figured out that I'd seen it on a list of companies who were transporting the fuel into Mexico." I explain.

"Oh, that's good. Will you have to testify?" It's not surprising that my dad is asking this, probably concerned that Marco will have to, but it is also lovely that Marco has made such an impression that my father is already concerned.

"We hope not. But if we do, we'll try to do it by a video link. But we're hoping that with everything that was found, he'll just plead guilty," I answer for him.

"Just stay safe, son." I had thought my dad had been talking to me, but when I look up at him, he's talking to Marco, and I know in that instant that my relationship has been completely accepted.

We spend the next few hours together just chatting. My family is getting to know Marco, and it turns out to be a nice evening, but we are both glad to get back to the apartment.

"Your parents are really nice. You're very lucky," Marco says as we're getting ready for bed.

"They liked you, too. I think you will be seeing a lot more of them."

"Can I ask you something?" he asks, sounding hesitant.

"Of course. You know you can ask me anything." I confirm.

"You never told me your brother and sister would be there. Did you set that up?"

God, I hope he knows that I only wanted to help him. "Originally it was just going to be Mom and Dad, but when you had the second nightmare and weren't talking to me about them, I thought that maybe if you heard Ryan's story, it would help you. So, I spoke to him." I tell him truthfully. "Was that okay?"

"Hearing that someone has been through something similar was good. I don't feel so much of a freak. No, I don't mind at all." Marco gives a small shrug of one shoulder.

"Are you going to call his therapist?"

"Yeah, I'll give them a call first thing in the morning."

"I am so proud of you." I say, drawing him close for an embrace.

Once we're in bed, I pull Marco into my arms, holding him tight, and when I feel him relax into me, I turn off the bedroom light and surround us with darkness.

"Thank you," Marco says into the blackness.

"For what?" I ask, pulling him tighter to me.

"Everything. Looking after me, being here. Just everything," he says back to me.

"I wouldn't be anywhere else," I say to him as we snuggle into each other's bodies and drift off to sleep in each other's arms, knowing that nothing will hold us back now.

Epilogue

One Month Later

"Come on! We're going to be late, and I really don't want to piss off Lorenzo today," I say to Liam, and we both look around for our suits.

"Look, it's not my fault. You just looked too damn good in that suit."

"Yeah, but there is no way I'm going to tell Lorenzo we're late to his wedding because we were having sex."

"That's probably not a good idea," I reply, but he's still smiling.

Looking at my watch, I see just how late we are. "Fuck. Have you seen the time? I didn't think that we'd been that long." Grabbing my tie and jacket, I run out of our bedroom, shouting over my shoulder that I'll see him later.

All I can hear is laughing coming from our room before a shout of, "Say hi to Lorenzo for me," follows me down the hall.

Just as I open the front door of the apartment, I think *fuck it* and turn back, rushing into the bedroom to pull Liam into my arms and kiss him. Before he has a chance to catch his breath, I'm running out the apartment again.

Twenty minutes later, I'm entering Lorenzo's apartment after Frank lets me in to find him pacing in the living room.

"Where the fuck have you been?" Lorenzo snaps, and I know that he isn't angry, just stressed. He comes over to adjust my tie that I barely managed to get on in the cab ride over.

"Sorry, I got side-tracked." And I can feel the heat rising on my cheeks as I speak.

"Oh, for fuck's sack, you were having sex. When I needed you here, you're having sex! I knew I should have got you to stay with me last night."

"If you remember, I offered, but you gave some bullshit excuse about wanting to be on your own, and anyway, we have plenty of time." He still isn't happy and continues to pace, so I cross my arms and ask, "Okay what's the matter?"

Lorenzo looks up at me. "What if he changes his mind and I'm standing at the alter looking like a fucking idiot?"

"Really? That is what you're worried about? I thought something had gone wrong. Wyatt loves you; he isn't going to stand you up, and if he does, I'll set Frank on him."

Lorenzo stops pacing and looks at me. "Set Frank on him?"

"Well, yeah, by the time you teach me to fight or even shoot, years will have gone by. It would just be easier to set Frank on him." I shrug and look over to Frank and give him a wink so he knows I'm joking. "And no offence, but you are *so* much scarier than me."

Lorenzo misses the wink Frank returns to me before saying, "No offence taken. If Wyatt stands you up, he'll be missing by nightfall."

Lorenzo tries hard not to but bursts out laughing, the tension falling from him, and he comes over and gives me a hug. While his back is to Frank, the man mouths, "Thank you."

"I'm guessing that Liam looked hot in his tux then." Lorenzo asks, stepping back.

"So hot. But I'm still not going to tell you what he's wearing." Lorenzo and Wyatt had decided that they would choose their own wedding outfits and leave it as a surprise on the day, but they wanted us to match. So I am wearing the same black three piece with a bright red tie as Lorenzo, and Liam is wearing a dark grey suit with a black tie. All of us have red roses, supplied by Lorenzo, of course, in our lapels; even Frank has one.

"Really? Not even a tiny little hint," Lorenzo whines.

"No!" I reply and check the time. "You only have to wait another forty minutes, but we'd better get going."

The three of us leave the apartment, and when we get onto the street, I spot Lorenzo's Mercedes out front covered in ribbons and Frank holding the door open for him.

"Thought the three of us were going to get a cab?" I say to Frank.

"There's no way I'm going to let Lorenzo travel to his wedding in a cab. I plan on taking Lorenzo and Wyatt to the hotel after the ceremony, too. A friend of mine is going to collect the care from there so I can join the celebration."

"Thank you, Frank," Lorenzo says, and you can hear just how touched he is.

The pair of us get into the back, and we watch as Frank walks to the driver's side, suddenly wearing a hat and looking very much part of the official driver. Once he's in, he starts the car and pulls us out into traffic. Even though it's a beautiful, sunny day, the traffic is flowing at a good pace. Before we know it, we're pulling up to Central Park. Lorenzo and Wyatt spent ages trying to find a place to get married and then they discovered the Cop Cot, and it was perfect. It's a beautiful, round wooden structure on top of a hill within Central Park that gives you great views of the city, but best of all, the ceremony takes place at one end of the structure, so the angled seating means you are surrounded by your friends and family.

By the time Lorenzo and I get to the Cop Cot, it's already full, and I'm surprised to see Bob, Jess, Ryan, and Emily sitting towards the front.

"I didn't know you invited Liam's family," I say to Lorenzo, who just shrugs and continues to look for Frank who went to park the car. When the date for the wedding had finally been set, Lorenzo had come to me and asked if I would mind if he asked Frank to walk him down the aisle. He'd already asked me to be best man, and I'd thought it was a wonderful idea, especially considering how close they'd become. "Looks like I better get to the front."

"Um..." And he looks around frantically. "Can you just wait, just till Frank gets here?"

He's suddenly acting very strange again, probably thinking that he's going to look like an idiot just standing there on his own, so I agree and start looking out for Frank to return. I spot him a few minutes later walking up the path to the Cop.

"Wyatt and Liam are right behind me," Frank tells us both, but then I see him looking around at the guests.

"Are you looking for someone in particular, Frank?" I watch as a blush pinks his cheeks. Holy shit, Frank is blushing. There's a story there, but before I can question it, he's asking the pair of us if we're ready, both of us nodding in answer. Looks like it's time to get to the front.

"See you at the front, big brother," I say before turning to walk to where the officiant is now waiting.

"Walk with us," Lorenzo suddenly bursts out. "You two are the most important people in my life, anyway."

"I think that's a lovely idea," Frank says to Lorenzo, his focus back on us. Lorenzo stands in the middle, crooking his arm out to each of us, and before I can even comprehend what's happening, I'm walking Lorenzo down the aisle, then the three of us are at the front waiting for Wyatt and Liam. Turning, I spot them just as they come to the brow of the hill, both looking stunning. Wyatt's dad has also joined them, and I'm confused when I spot Bob getting up from his seat and walking over to Liam. Looking at Lorenzo, I can see that he's trying to hide his smile.

I watch as the four men walk down the aisle and join us, Bob and Wyatt's dad sitting back down, but Liam doesn't move, and the officiant starts to speak.

"Good afternoon, Ladies and Gentlemen. We are here today to celebrate the marriage of Lorenzo and Wyatt, but first, I believe Liam would like to say something."

Turning to Liam, I'm confused by what's going on, but he just smiles and pulls me forward so I'm standing in front of him. Watching as he takes a deep breath, I now notice how nervous he looks.

"Marco, when I met you, you flipped my life upside down in the best possible way. You made me feel things I'd never felt before, made me dream things I never dreamt before. You quickly became my best friend and lover, but I want you to be more." And with that, he goes down onto one knee. "I want you to be my husband. Will you marry me?" He pulls open a ring box with a beautiful silver ring that seems oddly familiar, and it's perfect.

Gasping, I hold my hand to my mouth. I cannot *believe* he did this, and on Lorenzo's wedding day, but I don't care it might have taken something away from Lorenzo's day because I've never felt so much joy as I do now. I nod my head before managing to get a "yes" out, to the great cheer of the crowd. Helping him up from his knee, I press my lips against his before leaning back and holding out my hand for him to slip the ring on, but he doesn't. Instead, he stands up, goes into his pocket, and hands four rings to the officiant, who places them on a folder in front of him. Three faces are staring at me waiting for me to figure out what is going on, and as I look at the rings, the suits, and Liam's family, the penny drops.

"Are we getting married, too?" I ask, stunned, and the three of them start to move around with huge smiles on their faces. Liam comes to stand by me, and Lorenzo moves to be beside Wyatt, and then, with a nod, the officiant starts.

The End.

Acknowledgments

My editor Beau LeFebvre for encouraging me to keep going and having the patience to make this story the best it can be.
Thank you for everything.

About Author

Kelsey Hodge has always loved reading; it is something she has been doing since she was a child. Loving the escape the imagination can bring. The desire to write stories of my own was a dream, that Kelsey never thought would become a reality, but after encouragement from a wonderful partner, the words started, and they haven't stopped. Writing has become a passion, the characters in her books, her friends and Kelsey cannot wait to bring you along on the adventure ahead.

Also By Kelsey Hodge

For the Love of Flowers
For the Love of the Best Man
Legend of the Easter Dragon
Mistletoe and Dragons
Resurrection of the Easter Dragon
Return of the Christmas Dragon
Christmas Tree Wishes
Racing Hearts
If Only He Knew

Printed in Great Britain
by Amazon